The Ring Pack

Other works by Jordan Wells

LOGGED OFF: MY JOURNEY OF ESCAPING
                THE SOCIAL MEDIA WORLD

MIRRORS AND REFLECTIONS

THE HEALING

A LONELY ROSE

IT'S FUN BEING A HUMAN BEING

MADAM PRESIDENT

The Ring Pack

A Novel

By

Jordan Wells

Scott and Scholars Press
East Orange, New Jersey 07017

Scott and Scholars Press® is a registered trademark of
Jordan Wells Publishing

Copyright © 2021 by Jordan Wells

Publisher's Cataloging-in-Publication data

Names: Wells, Jordan, author.
Title: The ring pack : a novel / Jordan Wells.
Description: East Orange, NJ: Scott and Scholars Press, 2021.

Identifiers: LCCN: 2021912120 | ISBN: 978-1-955975-40-7 (hardcover) |
978-1-955975-11-7 (paperback) | 978-1-955975-00-1 (paperback) | 978-1-955975-04-9
(paperback) | 978-1-955975-05-6 (Kindle)
Subjects: LCSH Marriage--Fiction. | Friendship--Fiction. | Women--Fiction. | New York
(N.Y.)--Fiction. | Erotic fiction. | Love stories. | Romance fiction. | BISAC FICTION /
City Life | FICTION / Erotica / General | FICTION / Family Life / General | FICTION /
Family Life / Marriage & Divorce | FICTION / Romance / General
Classification: LCC PS3623.E4698 R56 2021| DDC 813.6--dc23

First Edition 2021
Jacket design by Jordan Wells
Art illustration Copyright © 2021 by Jordan Wells
For special inquiries, please email us at scottandscholarspress@yahoo.com

Printed in the United States of America
10 9 8 7 6 5 4 3 2 1

CONTENTS

This one is for the gift of life. Let us enjoy every moment of it with appreciation and optimism. You're too alive to sleep on your dreams.

Author's Note

Hello, welcome to the new journey that I have prepared for you. May I ask if you are familiar with my work by now and have supported me since the very beginning of my writing career? I would like to say that you are a fantastic soul. This novel is my fifth book. If you have been an avid reader of my work and read all four of my previous books, let me just say that I love you dearly for your consistent support.

Your support is what motivates me to share my creativity with you and the rest of the world. I would thank you a million times if I could. I thank you for the support in all of my poetry books, as well as my first book, *"Logged Off: My Journey of Escaping the Social Media World."* But with this new book, "*The Ring Pack*," my first novel, I have a real treat for you. If you are brand new to my work, if this is the first book that introduced you to me, I say welcome to you, and thank you very much. I hope you, too, become an avid reader of my work.

So, as I mentioned, this is my first novel. I bet you may be wondering, how does a young man, such as myself, write a book about five women who are married? Well, I felt I wanted to give myself another challenge. I wanted to present you with a story that is not out there as often as you may hear or read about today. In most cases, you may read about a group of *single* women who are ready to mingle. But I wanted to tell a different story. I wanted to let the world know that there are some happily married women out there. Married women who are also mothers. And who are very successful in their professions. But just because they are happily married does not mean their lives are perfect.

But before I go any further, let me give you some back story on how I came about writing this rare story. In my fourth book, "*A Lonely Rose*," I wrote a short story called "*Charli's Chance*." In *Charli's Chance*, I wrote about this forty-year-old woman named Charli, who, at nineteen years old, fell in love with this man named Jason. They only met for one night, and then he left her without a trace. Twenty-plus years later, he reached out to her, they met, and fell back in love. That is all I want to share with you about that particular short story. I do not want to ruin it for you, just if you have not yet read it. But anyway, it was that short story that inspired me to write this book. Writing *"Charli's Chance"* sparked such inspiration and excitement to write about these five women.

As I was finishing up on my fourth book, I began to write ideas for *this* book. Let me tell you, designing the book cover was a real challenge. I had to go back to the drawing board repeatedly because I am a perfectionist at times. But also, *very* minimalistic. I believe that less is more. I did not want the cover to look cluttered with objects that did no justice to the story you are about to read. But I kept drawing, kept discovering, and finally came up with the cover you see in this book.

I must say this; I had a fantastic time writing this novel—many different discoveries, so many thoughts and ideas. And as I got into the groove of it, the story honestly did write itself. It was just an overall great time writing this book. As you read, you will notice that my writing style is not your traditional novel style. There is *a lot* of perorate dialogue between the characters. The first chapter is significant and the most extended branch, as you, the reader, will be introduced to all five of the ladies. Then afterward, you will get to know them on an individual basis.

We are now in this politically correct society. I feel that I must give you a fair warning of the content in this book. First, I will say that *this* book is NOT for anyone under the age of eighteen. I repeat it; this book is NOT for anyone *under* the age of eighteen. I would go even further to say that it is not for anyone under the age of twenty-one. But that may be pushing it. I believe there are some mature readers between the ages of 18-21.

There is strong adult content, strong adult language, and strong sexually explicit content in this book. There are also talks about politics. There are moments in the book that deals with homophobic and transphobic dialogue and situations. There are also acts and discussions of racism. With all of that said, if you find *any* of these subjects offensive to the point where you cannot read it, that is understandable, and I respect that.

However, I would like for you to give it a chance. Even though this novel is entirely fictional, these five women are dealing with real-life situations. Situations that you or I have to deal with every single day. Mind you, these women are from different cultures. But even with their differences, their bond maintains its great strength. Their sisterhood remains solid. And you may disagree with how they handle things. But again, we all have our differences. And that is okay.

Oh, and one more thing. The hands of these women that you see on the book cover. There is no specific reason for why their hands are in those positions. Except for the hand of the character of Zarin, on the bottom right of the cover. Zarin's family still follows the old Indian tradition of wearing the wedding ring on the right hand. I thought it would look better at the bottom right of the cover. I did not place them in that position based on class or superiority. Just in case inquiring minds wanted to know.

Now, with that said, I genuinely hope you enjoy *The Ring Pack.*

Introduction

Welcome to Manhattan! Of course, Manhattan; the city that never sleeps. It is home to millions. But five friends, who all happened to be happily married, are coming together on a cold, February Friday evening. All five of them coming from a hard day's work. Monica Taylor, a thirty-five-year-old attorney; Zarin Khan, a thirty-seven-year-old news broadcast journalist and TV news anchor; Collette "Coco" Fernandez, a forty-year-old realtor, Wendy Date-Collins, a thirty-three-year-old wedding planner, and lastly, Tomi Belacone, who is the oldest of the group at forty-three years of age. Tomi is a world-famous fashion designer who has made history in such a short period with her fabulous clothing line, *Orell Llero* (Or-rell-Ler-ro).

As these successful women pack up for the evening, they all make their way to *Lucille's,* a popular Manhattan restaurant owned by Collette's husband, Martin Fernandez. Monica is usually the one who is always running late, as she is working on a severe attempted murder case. Tomi always arrives at *Lucille's* a little early to avoid the paparazzi and onlookers. She doesn't like to bring such attention to her friends, even though Martin doesn't mind. It's free publicity for the restaurant.

Zarin, who is of Asian descent, Indian background to be specific, is married to her husband, Dr. Neal Khan, specializing in, surprisingly, gynecology. He is one of the very few male doctors in the city who is a gynecologist. Before Zarin makes her way to *Lucille's,* she or Neal always drops off her two daughters, Darsha, who is ten, and Joshna, seven, at her parent's house, where they usually spend the night. Colette always calls in ahead of time at the restaurant. She likes to make sure their reserved table is adequately cleaned and set up to her liking and ready for their traditional Friday rendezvous.

Wendy sometimes runs a little late because she works in Queens, and she always has to beat rush hour traffic. Wendy, who is of Asian descent, Japanese to be specific. She is happily married to her husband Edward Collins, an Artistic Director of many ballet performances. They have a five-year-old son named EJ, which is short for Edward junior.

Collette is of Latina descent. Her family roots come from the Dominican Republic. With Martin, they share two kids: their twenty-year-old son, Emilio, and their fourteen-year-old daughter, Mia.

Monica is African American. Most of her family comes from Chicago, and that is all she knows. Monica is married to her husband, Sammy Taylor. A famous trumpeter. They share two kids as well—their ten-year-old son, Miles. Sammy named him after the late great Miles Davis, who is *still* Sammy's idol. They also have their six-year-old daughter, Briana. As for Tomi, she is of Caucasian or European descent, Italian to be exact. She is the second generation of her family to be born in America, even though she has dual citizenship in America and Italy. Tomi's husband, Thomas (*Toma*), is a well-known, critically acclaimed architect and sculptor. As far as any offspring, they are the only married couple without children, but we'll get into that later.

Some may be thinking, why did I include such information about their ethnicity? Well, the world does not see much diversity brought to the light. With America being such a melting pot, especially living in Manhattan, these five women have made it work. Them coming together as friends, having things in common to share, and being all married women. With them coming from different backgrounds, you will embrace what life is like, walking in their shoes. You will experience how the world and society treat them and how they make it through their everyday lives.

Before I bring you into this story, perhaps I should give you some *back story* of how they all met and became friends. It all started with Monica and Tomi. About eight years ago, Tomi and her husband Thomas had a wonderful evening dinner. Thomas was in the mood for some eloquent, unpredictable sounds of jazz music. So, they both headed over to the world-famous Blue Note on West 3rd street, in Greenwich Village. As they walked into the Blue Note, they were greeted instantly with the smooth sounds of a trumpet. Monica's husband, Sammy, was up on stage, blowing pure magic in the air through his horn. Sammy played a song called "*Spanish Key*" from Miles Davis' album "*Bitches Brew.*" The crowd loved every second of it, especially Thomas and Tomi, as they couldn't get enough. After the final session, Thomas made his way towards Sammy to introduce himself and introduce Tomi. Sammy shook hands with Thomas and called over *his* wife, Monica. As Monica and Thomas shook hands, Thomas then introduced her to Tomi, which then sparked an inseparable bond.

A few months after Monica and Tomi became friends, they went to a ballet production happening at Lincoln Center. It was an adaptation of *The Nutcracker*, directed by Wendy's fiancé at that time, Edward Collins. It just so happened that Wendy was sitting right next to Tomi and Monica in the audience. Tomi asked

Wendy, "Have you ever seen this production before?" Wendy responded, "Oh, of course, actually, my fiancé, Eddie, is the director of this show." Wendy and Edward were not yet married when she first met Tomi and Monica. They were engaged, three months away from their wedding. Of course, after meeting them, Wendy invited both Monica and Tomi to her wedding, as well as their husbands.

A month after Wendy's wedding, now it's the three of them: Tomi, Monica, and Wendy. Tomi just came back from a business trip in Paris, and she heard of the grand opening of a restaurant called "*Lucille's*." As mentioned, *Lucille's* is a restaurant owned by Collette's husband, Martin Fernandez. As the grand opening was a success, Collette walked around to make sure their guest was doing okay with their meals, and that everything was going smoothly for the evening. As Collette made a full round at everyone's table, she came across a table of these three women, laughing the night away. Those three women were Monica, Tomi, and Wendy. All Collette was seeing were these smiling women, laughing, eating, having a fabulous time, and she wanted a piece of that action. Collette made her way over to their table and introduced herself. They all welcomed Collette with open arms as they made a new friend.

The last one to enter the pack was Zarin. Precisely a month after the grand opening of *Lucille's,* business was booming. It gained such notoriety for its sophisticated interior design and the luxurious quality of delicious dishes to choose from on the menu. Being that Zarin is a news journalist, she was able to schedule an interview with Martin. As Zarin completed her interview with Martin, he introduced Zarin to Collette. They exchanged numbers, and the rest was history.

And there you have it, the birth of "The Ring Pack." Five New York women, ready to conquer the big apple. Fate was in complete form when it brought these five together. As we move forward now to the present time, I should say the *future* since this takes place in the year 2023, post-*COVID-19*. So, this is the current time in the book. These five have been solid with their friendship ever since.

It seems as if they have it all, right? Loving husbands, children, careers, and much success. No complaints whatsoever, right? Well, life always kicks us in the butt when we least expect it. And as you go on this journey, you will see how life does *just* that with these five gals.

Be prepared for some laughs, be prepared for some cries, and be prepared for a story that opens your mind to other possibilities of friendship, love, betrayal, forgiveness, and sacrifice. You will see how these women deal with the good times they share and the bad times and the ugly situations to come. But with all of that said, you will also see how they never break their bond, no matter what. They look out for each other as if they are sisters. Well, they are sisters.

I hope you enjoy what I have prepared for you. May you find much entertainment in this story. I present to you, *The Ring Pack*.

Chapter 1

Taxis are hard to find right now during rush hour in Queens. A chilly Friday evening as Wendy is on a hunt for a cab to take her into Manhattan. Her cold hand is raised in the air, trying to get the attention of a vacant taxi. As one approaches her, she keeps her hand raised, as she expects the cab to slow down and stop for her. But the cab did no such thing, as it drove right past her. "Are you fucking kidding me right now?" Wendy shouted out in complete frustration.

Wendy then took a look at her Lyft app. She saw that there was one Lyft driver nearby and booked it immediately. As she waited for her Lyft driver, she sent a group text to the rest of the girls saying, "Hey ladies, as usual, I am running a little late. I'll be there at around 7:45. If you have to order without me, can one of you order me the sushi special with Lobster Bisque?"

Monica responded to Wendy, saying, "Hey, Wendy babe, I'm in the same boat. I might be there a little after 7:45. The court was a drag, but on my way, too." The Lyft driver finally arrived; Wendy peeked in to make sure it was the accurate driver.

"Hi, are you Dereck?" Wendy asked the driver.

"Hello, yes, ma'am. I am," Dereck, the driver responded.

As Wendy was riding in the back of the Lyft, she put on her face covering and sanitized her hands. Even though it has been two years since the *Covid-19* pandemic, she likes to keep herself protected, especially when riding in stranger's cars. As Wendy was riding, she received a response from Tomi, who had already arrived at *Lucille's*. Tomi responded, "You bitches always late, like a period, LOL! No worries, I'm at our booth, sipping on my wine. See you guys soon."

A ton of "LMAO" came flooding into the group chat as they were all hysterical about Tomi's response. Collette was only five minutes away from the restaurant. She was walking with such excitement, as she just closed a big deal with a client. As mentioned, Collette is a realtor. Collette was showing her client a brand-new spacious apartment overlooking Central Park. The client fell utterly in love with it; they couldn't say no. So, Collette came skipping into the restaurant.

"Coco, finally someone is here," said Tomi. "I almost ordered a third glass of wine."

"Hey bitch," Collette spoke. "Oh, I just *love* this new outfit you have on. Is this new from your collection?"

"Why, of course," said Tomi. "Here, let me show you."

Collette gagged at Tomi's outfit. Tomi just had to stand up from the booth and show off her new white *Orell Llero* piece. It fitted Tomi's five-foot, eight-inch frame perfectly. Tomi had such a massive obsession with the eighties. She loved the whole padded shoulders look from back in the day. With her new collection, she included some retrospect of looks from that time.

"Yes bitch, I'll be sure to get a dress from your new collection as soon as it's released," Collette said as she finished admiring Tomi's outfit. As the two of them begin to share a bottle of white wine, Zarin came in to join them. Zarin had on a dress that she wore at her news station, a very formal, rose red dress from Tomi's old collection. Zarin had a beautiful look to her. She had long black hair, great eyelashes, with a beautiful Caramel complexion.

"Look at our best friend coming in here, giving us runway vibes, GO GIRL!" Collette said as Zarin was making her way to their booth.

"Coco, girl, you're a mess. Where's the other two?" Zarin said after she let off a few laughs.

"Oh, they're running late; we'll give them until 8:05, and then we're ordering because I am *starving*," Tomi said as she looked at her 18 kt gold BVLGARI watch.

Lucille's was one of a kind. It has two levels; all the waiters wear these fabulous jet-black suits, while the host gets to look their best in upscale attire of their choice—the restaurant seats at least two hundred people. Martin, Collette's husband, was going to give his restaurant a dress code, but he decided at the last minute not to go through with that decision, as he did not want any discrimination issues taking place. The restaurant was named *Lucille's*, after Martin's mother, the Late Lucille Fernandez. His mother was a legendary cook, a genius even. She would make some of the most irresistible fried Empanadas you would ever have. Her lifelong dream was to open a restaurant. But that dream was tragically cut short, as was her life. About ten years ago, Lucille suffered a massive stroke, which left her paralyzed on the left side of her body. Her health never recovered, and eventually, she passed on, not even a year after her stroke.

However, Lucille left her legacy behind. She had multiple cookbooks filled with some unique recipes. Martin, who was not a bad cook himself, thought it would be a great idea to get into the restaurant business, open his restaurant, and name it in honor of his late mother. And that is what he did; well, him and Collette, as she helped with finding the real estate since she is a realtor. They both brought their finances together and made his mother's dream come true.

Almost at the same time, Wendy and Monica arrived in front of *Lucille's*. Monica came out of a taxi, and of course, Wendy hopped out of her Lyft ride. The time was two minutes past eight, so they made it just in time before the others were going to order. Wendy and Monica spotted each other outside, in front of the restaurant.

"Oh my God, Nica," said Wendy. "I could not get a Goddamn cab tonight. Maybe if I had *tits*, I could've flashed a cab, and *then* they would pull over."

"Well shit, do you want to borrow mines? I think I need a bigger bra," Monica said as she made a minor adjustment to her dress shirt.

"Ah, no, but If I had your *ass*, no one would be able to tell me *nothing*," Wendy humorously said as they both walked into the restaurant.

Monica and Wendy finally made it to join the others for their traditional Friday evening rendezvous. Being that they have known each other for over eight years now, nicknames have taken shape. At least for Monica and Collette, the ladies call Monica

"Nica" (Nee-Ca), and, for Collette, they call her "Coco." The other three prefers to be addressed by their actual names.

As the five of them have a seat in their reserved half oval-shaped booth, they all begin to acknowledge themselves, as they have not seen each other since last Friday. It becomes complicated for all five of them to see each other during mid-week with their careers and families. But they make it very much mandatory to have dinner every Friday night, as well as watching a movie and socializing back at Tomi's penthouse.

"Good evening ladies, you all look fabulous tonight," said Amber, the waitress. "Are you all ready to order, or you still need a few minutes?"

"Amber, my love, we are ready to order. I will have the steak stripped linguine with extra alfredo sauce," Tomi said with hunger in her soul.

The rest of the group was still looking at their menus with hesitation. Wendy then said, "Um, earlier I wanted sushi with Lobster bisque, but now I change my mind. I'll just have your garlic parmesan chicken salad with extra chicken." As Amber was writing down the orders, Collette received a phone call from her daughter, Mia, and excused herself from the table. Before she left the table, she said to Amber, "Oh, Amb Hunny, just give me my usual, the *Lucille's* Pollo Guisado." Martin's mother, Lucille, loved to cook that dish. It is a trendy Dominican recipe, but Lucille added her special sauce to it. Martin used many of his mother's recipes for the restaurant, while some he keeps within his family. As Collette walked away from the table, she answered her phone.

"Hey, mom, look, I know I'm grounded," Mia said. "But can I please, *please* stay over at Sara's? Please?"

"Mia, you are so lucky that you're not staying over in a juvenile center this week. After what they found in your bag? Your father and I were mortified." Collette said to Mia with a pinch of anger.

"I know, and I'm *sorry*," Mia responded. "It won't happen again."

As Collette still had that mother and daughter talk on the phone, the rest of the gals were sitting at the booth, waiting for their delicious entrees to arrive. Zarin and Monica both ordered the spicy empanadas, another special recipe from Martin's mother's cookbook. As they waited, they begin to talk about how their week went.

Zarin sparked the conversation, talking about the things that happened to her during the week. She opened up by saying, "So, this past Monday at the news station, the production hired a new makeup artist and hairstylist. Her choice of colors for my *eyes*? Oh my God, I could tell it was going to be a disaster. When I tell you, I could have *died* when I saw myself in the mirror, like I wanted to *kill* her. And don't even get me *started* with the hairstylist. First, she tried to *cut* my hair, then she wanted to put my hair in these big curls, and I was telling her my hair doesn't do well with curls. This shit was happening to me *all week long*. I just had to bring in my regular hairdresser from my salon." A round of laughter coming from the other three as Zarin tells her verbal summary. Zarin could not help but join in on the laughter herself.

Their meals had arrived, everything looked astonishingly delicious. Collette had made it back to the table after her talk with Mia and joined the rest of them. Collette brought along some hand sanitizer for them to use, but Tomi instead scooped an ice cube from out of her glass of water and rubbed the ice cube in between her hands. "What? I'm not as *boujee* as you guys think I am," Tomi said as the rest of them looked at her with a surprised look on their faces.

As they all were ready to dig in, Tomi raised her glass of white wine to make a toast, "Ladies, this is a night of celebration. Next week, I will be opening the brand-new storefront of my company, right there on the iconic Fifth Avenue. It's been a hell of a journey, but damn it, I made it. Salute!" Tomi said as they brought their glasses together to cheer.

"Congratulations, girl, I am so proud of you. Seven years of hard work has paid off enormously," Monica said to Tomi.

"Yes, and we will *all* be there to support you. I cannot wait to see it," Wendy said, sitting right next to Tomi.

Tomi, so overwhelmed by the love and support of her friends. She looked at all four of their smiling faces while she told them the good news of the launch of her new storefront for *Orell Llero*. This storefront is one of many, as there are many others all over the world. There is one in Paris, Tokyo, Milan, London, and Hawaii, just to name several. There are several storefronts on the west coast, in Beverly Hills, San Francisco, and Las Vegas, but this is the fourth to be opened on the east coast. As of today, Tomi's net worth is close to $11.7 billion.

You may be thinking, why would a billionaire such as Tomi be associated with other women who are doing very well for themselves but are far from billionaires? You may ask why she does not socialize with other wealthy people. The thing about Tomi is she would choose real, genuine friends over associating herself with other billionaires. Tomi hates to talk about money all the time; the other four keep her humble and honest. In her mind, there is nothing more valuable than true friendship, and Tomi would do absolutely anything for her friends.

Enjoying their tasty meals at the booth, Collette began venting about her daughter, Mia, regarding what took place several days ago. Collette said, "I just had to tell you guys about this crazy situation with Mia. Can you believe she brought weed to school? But that's not all she brought. And I'm a little embarrassed to say." "Aww, Coco, we wouldn't judge you, you know that," Monica said as she and the others were eager to hear the rest of the story.

So, Collette then told them the whole truth and said, "Okay, so she brought a black dildo to school, along with the weed. Martin and I grounded her, but she refuses to tell us where she got her hands on those things," Collette said with an embarrassed expression on her face.

All their jaws slowly dropped after hearing what Collette just said. Collette looked at them with instant regret, and she wishes she could rewind about five minutes back and not even mention the situation about her daughter Mia.

"See, I knew you guys couldn't resist judging. Can we just forget I even said anything?" Collette said as she looked away from the table, sipping on her wine.

"Coco, listen, you have no reason to be embarrassed around us. These conversations are what we have been doing every Friday for the last seven years. We talk about *everything* that's going on in our lives," Wendy said as she assured Collette not to feel shame.

Collette then carried on by saying, "I know, I know…I know I can talk to you guys about everything, and I truly appreciate you all for that. But it just bothers me, that's not like Mia at all, to bring something like that to school. I have to talk to her about it tomorrow. And she can't even go back to school; she's suspended for two weeks." As Tomi and the others sunk in Collette's story, Collette said, "Well, Wendy, Nica, what's been going on with you guys this week?"

As Monica skied the last piece of oil and vinegared lettuce off of her porcelain plate with her fork, she said this to Tomi, "Oh, I need a minute to collect my thoughts; Wendy, you go ahead." Monica then took her last bite for the night.

Wendy then wiped her mouth with her napkin and began to elaborate on her day. Wendy said, "*So*, next Saturday is the wedding. But today, I received a call from the mother of the bride. She said to me, "*Oh hi Wendy, so I know the wedding is next Saturday, and this may be concise notice, but we changed our minds with the flower arrangements. Instead of the white roses, we'd like to go with the Sweet Avalanche. Oh, and also, if you can find a place that sells Beluga Caviar, that would be amazing. I want to make a great impression.*" I'm sitting there at my desk saying to myself, "*bitch*, are you fucking kidding me right now?"

The others began to laugh at Wendy's story about the mother of the bride. But Wendy was not finished, as she carried on, saying, "First of all, we ordered those white roses months ago, and there's nothing in the theme that goes with Sweet Avalanche roses. And why the hell does she want Beluga Caviar all of a sudden? The groom's family wants to keep it modest with just baked chicken, steak, and pasta. *That's* why I was running late coming here tonight. I had to cancel the white roses, and they charged us a huge fine for late cancellations. *Then* I had to make multiple phone calls to a florist who carries Sweet Avalanche roses, and because I had to ask for rush delivery, they charged extra for that. And the Beluga Caviar, I could have cried when I heard the price. But that's what they want, and they're paying for it. So, it is what it is. I'm so pissed off with this wedding, though. I'll be glad when it is Sunday morning of next weekend."

The other ladies could not help but acknowledge Wendy's frustration. They could tell that she was under some stress and enormous pressure. "Oh my God, Wendy, I can't even imagine," Zarin said with sympathy. "Yea, I've been under a little stress this week, especially since this wedding is the one that could make me a partner. And me being a partner at thirty-three years old, I would be set for life. It would be a dream come true," Wendy responded as she guzzled her glass of wine.

As Monica was the last to talk about her week, she received a text from her husband, Sammy. The text said, "Hey babe, sorry to bother you, I was just about to put the kids to bed, but I can't find Briana's Barbie pajamas. You know I don't know where that stuff is." Monica replied, "I put the barbie PJs in the third dresser, right next to her socks."

Monica then put her phone away as she began to go on about her week. Monica said to the group, "So, obviously, I can't really talk about my client or the case, but this week we just had the closing argument for the prosecution. So that means I am up next week for the closing argument for the defense. It's been a roller coaster ride, and I am just praying that there will *not* be a "hung" jury. I'm not trying to have a retrial. But I'm fighting for my client."

"What did he do, *exactly*? Did he kill somebody?" Tomi asked Monica.

"Oh, Tomi, shit! Don't ask that," Collette said with a twisted face.

"Oh, right, I'm sorry, *please* ignore me," Tomi said with embarrassment.

"No, it's fine," said Monica. "And no, my client has been charged with attempted murder. But he is innocent until proven guilty."

It was reaching a quarter to ten as their meals turned into empty dinner plates. They continued conversating while Collette was the last to finish up on her dessert, a melted fudge brownie with butter pecan ice cream. As Collette was eating, she began to think in her mind and speculate about where Mia could have got ahold of the cannabis and the black dildo. Collette feared that she received it from a friend of hers or a stranger out on the streets. But Collette's biggest fear is that Mia stole it from Emilio, her son. Collette understands the cannabis, not that she approves of it, but she knows Emilio indulges from time to time. But what gives her anxiety is if the black dildo belongs to Emilio as well. She's scared to death to find out. Even though she has told the ladies about Mia bringing it to school, she wanted to keep her speculations and assumptions to herself.

"Okay, so what are we watching tonight? I hope it is something good," Wendy said to Tomi.

"Oh, I have the perfect movie," said Tomi. "How about "*Some Like It Hot*?"

"That sounds good," Collette spoke. "I need a good laugh tonight."

Collette then called over Amber, the waiter. As Amber placed the bill on the table, Tomi asked Collette how much the check is. But Collette always assures Tomi that she doesn't have to pick up the tab. But Tomi could never accept that. Feeling too guilty being a *billionaire* and not pay for anything. As Tomi stood up from the booth, she said to Collette, "Well, at least let me leave a nice tip Coco, please?" Collette welcomed the tip, and Tomi left quite a generous tip. As Tomi opened her *Orell Llero* handbag, she whipped out a stack of bills and placed them in the bill holder. Amber, the waiter, opened the black leather bill holder; she saw nothing but green Franklin faces as Tomi left a $1,200 tip. That left Amber speechless, with multiple tears falling down her eyes.

As the five were ready to head out, paparazzi were already outside, waiting for Tomi to exit. The other four have been through these situations for years now, yet none have become used to it. The press cannot help themselves; they are too obsessed with Tomi. And Tomi is quite an exotic beauty. Miss Tomi was once a fierce model herself. She always had the looks and the body of a top model. The woman was pre-ordained for success. Even at the age of forty-three, she still has that gift of gab. The other ladies are pretty gorgeous as well, which is a plus for them.

"Oh God, get ready for the Circus," Zarin said as they head out of *Lucille's.*

Tomi walked out, cameras and people flocked to her with their flashing lights and the overwhelming shouts of her name, begging her to look in their direction for the perfect Kodak moment. Tomi and the other four: Monica, Collette, Wendy, and Zarin, were not used to the attention. But they did not ignore it either. They did not mind standing still as they were dressed to kill. Well, at least Tomi. As Collette was the last to exit the restaurant, her husband, Martin, stopped her.

"Hey, babe, what are you doing here?" Collette spoke as she kissed Martin. "I thought you headed home early."

"Yea hun, I know," said Martin. "But not tonight; I'm going to pull an all-nighter tonight. I have to deal with overhead and go over some other expenses. So, don't wait up," Martin said. Martin then said goodnight as he kissed Collette on her plumped, burgundy-colored lips.

As Collette said goodnight to Martin, she exited out of the restaurant, only to be captured by the multiple flashes that the other four had already endured. The others were waiting in the limo for Collette as they were heading to Tomi's penthouse. Awaited them inside the limo were five bottles of *Louis Roederer Cristal 'Gold Medallion,* close to four grand per bottle. Tomi is definitely about that life, and she *shares* this luxurious life with her friends. As Monica was sipping on some Louis Roederer, she received another text from her husband, Sammy, saying, "Hey, thanks, I found them. The kids are now sound asleep. Enjoy the rest of the night with your ladies. Love you." Monica always loves it when Sammy texts her saying he loves her and then sends her a ton of heart emojis. Monica then replied saying, "I love you more. Kiss the babies goodnight for me, Muah!"

Another bottle of the bubbly potion opened as the five ladies were now feeling loose and liberated from their hard day's work—laughter in the air with a bunch of smiles and selfies. Tomi, who is an advocate for cosmetic procedures, became very critical about how her face looked in the selfies. Tomi has grown to be more analytical about her fading features rather than embracing the aging lines underneath her eyes. "Damn, wait, Nica, we have to take another selfie. I need to put a filter on me," Tomi said as she scrolled up and deleted all the pictures she took. "Girl, you look fine. You don't need any filters. You know damn well you are a bad bitch," Monica said, trying to butter up Tomi.

Tomi was appreciative of Monica giving her praise. "Aww, Nica, I love you. But you know I have an image to keep up, and I *cannot* be walking around with all these lines *and* wrinkles staying on my face. Next week, I have a date with the *baddest* bitch on the west coast, Dr. Ginger," Tomi said as she was looking at the screen on her phone.

As the limo arrived in front of the building of Tomi's penthouse, she realized that the driver made an error. Tomi said to the driver, "Benjamin, sweetheart, you're at the wrong penthouse. I said go to the penthouse in Soho." Yes, as mentioned before, Tomi is about that life, the *Good Life*. She owns multiple penthouses and condos across the five boroughs of New York. The cheapest penthouse Tomi owns cost her $14.5 million. Not to mention she owns several art pieces by Jean-Michel Basquiat, Andy Warhol, and Keith Haring. A plethora of investments she has placed for herself. Tomi has given her a status such as "The Queen of New York."

"Damn Tomi, I forgot you have that penthouse in Soho," Collette said as she sipped another glass of Louis Roederer.

"Oh, I know," said Tomi. "I meant to sell one of the penthouses. But then I said, "what the fuck? I'll keep it. Tommy could use the space for his sculpting."

As they arrived at Tomi's Soho penthouse, Benjamin exited out of the driver's seat and made his way over to the right side of the back seat to let them out. As Benjamin opened the door, Wendy was the first to step out of the limo. Wendy, dressed in her green turtleneck sweater, with black pants and red bottom heels, topped with a beige Burberry trench coat. No matter what Wendy wears, there are two accessories you will always see her wearing: her wedding ring and her green Japanese jade link bracelet. Wendy received it from her great-grandmother when she was ten years old when visiting her relatives in Tokyo and Kyoto, Japan. Wendy's great-grandmother lived to be a hundred and five years of age, an incredibly long life lived. When she gave the jade-link bracelet to Wendy, her great-grandmother said in Japanese, "This will bring good luck to your life, Wendy-san."

Collette was the second to exit out of the limo. She had on a thick burgundy turtleneck sweater dress with brown knee-high boots with a gray wool topcoat. Her long, dark-brown curly hair was exquisite; watching it blow in the chilly winds was perceptually breathtaking. Of course, she is sporting her four and a half-carat square-cut wedding ring and a black strapped bracelet with a gold cross.

The next to come out was Zarin, wearing her rose-red dress from Tomi's collection, with a black suede collar-belted coat. Zarin also devotedly wore her wedding ring and her black beaded Rudraksha bracelet with the Om charm. She wears it for her yoga and meditation. Every day, Zarin does a ten-minute meditation before going on live television. Zarin has been a news journalist for over fourteen years now. She already knows that bad news is what she will be presenting to the world, and she wants to be spiritually prepared.

As Monica came out of the limo, professionally dressed in her black dress suit, with a white dress shirt, she asked Tomi if she could hand over her Camel double-face wool coat, as she was burning up in the limo and had to take it off. Tomi handed Monica's coat to her as she was the last to exit out of the limo. Tomi, sporting her cream *Orell Llero* peacoat with crystal-studded buttons. Underneath, she had on her off-white piece from her new collection, as mentioned before. As the others already went in to keep warm, Tomi gave her limo driver, Benjamin, a larger tip than the one she gave Amber at *Lucille's*.

"From one Benjamin to another," Tomi said as she handed Benjamin fourteen of those green Franklin faces.

"Oh shit, thank you so much, Mrs. Belacone! Oh, sorry for cussing. Goodnight," Benjamin said as he stuffed the money in his pocket and closed the back seat door of the limo.

As Tomi then walked into the lobby of her penthouse, she greeted the doorman and security. Tomi had charisma, as those men in the lobby waiting area could not take their eyes off of her. And she did not want them to. As the others were waiting for Tomi at the penthouse elevator, they could not help but look at Tomi themselves. They all smiled at Tomi, knowing she was relishing in the attention the men were giving her in the lobby.

"See bitch, I *told* you, you don't need none of that Botox shit. These men are getting a hard-on right now because of you," Monica said to Tomi with conviction.

"I know, I know I still got it, I guess. But you know me, Nica. I'm a stubborn bitch, with a shit load of money," Tomi responded as she broke into laughter.

As they all entered the golden elevator, Tomi had to insert her unique key to go up to the penthouse. She placed the key in, and the elevator door closed. They all were able to see their reflection through the golden elevator doors. When Collette saw their reflection, she just blurted out and said, "Damn, we are the finest married bitches in Manhattan right now! We *have* to get a picture."

Before the elevator made it to the penthouse, Tomi pulled out her authentic diamond-cased iPhone and lifted her arm high enough to capture a group photo. When it came to photos, these women knew their angles.

If you could call a place of residency paradise, Tomi's Soho penthouse was just that, absolute paradise. She had everything; high-priced artwork hanging on her walls, all-white furniture, very spacious, as well as a second floor with all the bedrooms. The most incredible view you could ever see. It overlooked the Manhattan skyline. This particular property was the penthouse that they come to sporadically, as Tomi's husband, Thomas, uses it for space to do his sculpting. But tonight, Tomi wanted to bring the girls over, as she recently had installed a brand new 8k projector in her theater room.

"Okay, ladies, let's get some cheese, crackers, popcorn, and my new favorite, red licorice," Tomi said as she grabbed snacks from the pantry in the kitchen."

"Tomi, I told you about the licorice. Your blood pressure will go sky high," Zarin said to Tomi.

"*Yes, mom!*" Tomi sarcastically responded to Zarin.

"Okay, since you guys are getting the stuff, I'm going to make a quick phone call to check on EJ," Wendy said as she walked out of the kitchen.

"Oh, yes, Wendy, thanks for reminding me. I have to call my mother and make sure the girls are in bed now," Zarin said as she also made a quick phone call.

As Tomi, Monica, and Collette made their way into the theater room, Wendy made her way into the restroom, as she called her husband, Edward. The phone was ringing, but she received no answer. Wendy found that odd because she knows Edward is at home with EJ. He would always pick up. Wendy then placed her phone on the bathroom sink and began to "handle her business." Wendy was fascinated with this luxurious bathroom; it was not your ordinary bathroom with just a toilet and a sink. The bathroom had a chocolate marble finish—a full walk-in shower, with four separate rain-showers hanging from above. Wendy was in awe of the alabaster white marble sink, which was crafted to look like a giant seashell. As Wendy finished up in the bathroom, she received a call from Edward and answered her phone.

"Hi Eddie, is everything alright?" Wendy asked. "I just wanted to check in and see how EJ was doing?"

"Hey babe, Yea, I'm sorry. I left my phone in the living room while I was putting EJ back to bed. He had another accident, in *our* bed," Edward said to Wendy.

"Oh, God, did he pee on my side again?" Wendy asked Edward.

"Nope, he peed while he was lying on top of me. He got me good too," Edward said with a light chuckle.

"Aww, my poor baby," said Wendy. "And he was doing so much better with that. It's been almost two months since he last wet himself."

"Yea, he was doing better. I guess we just have to be patient with him, you know?"

"Yea, our boy will grow out of it. Well, listen, don't wait up if you don't want to. I'll probably be home at around a quarter to one in the morning, okay?"

"Yeah, okay, I might still be up. So, I'll see you a little later."

Over in the living room, Zarin gave a call to her mother to check on her daughters, Darsha and Joshna, as the two of them are spending the night at their Nani and Nana's house. Even though Zarin's mother can speak English very well, she likes to speak their native language of Hindi. Zarin's mother answered, and they began to conversate for a few minutes. Her mother told Zarin about how she had to take away Darsha's phone, as she was spending an excessive amount of time on it, and she was not focused enough on her schoolwork. Zarin's mother also mentioned how Darsha became upset with her Nani for taking her phone away and didn't bother to eat dinner.

"Mom, I don't like her having the phone either. But you know we have to let Darsha have one so that we know where she is at all times," Zarin said to her mother in their native language.

"Yes, I understand that situation," said her mother. "However, you and Neal will have to set some ground rules for when and how long she can use this phone. You know these phones cause addiction."

"Yes, I know that, mom," Zarin said. "Neal and I have set ground rules for her phone use. She's normally not on it as much when we are home. How was Joshy tonight?"

"Joshy was good. She was her sweet self as always. They're both sleeping now. Their Nana read them a bedtime story."

"Great! Well, okay, mom. I just wanted to see how the girls were doing. Thank you again for watching them, and I will be picking them up in the morning. Have a good night."

"Goodnight, oh, and by the way, what the *hell* was going on with your hair and makeup this week? Your father and I were *livid* that you would go on live television looking like that."

"Mom, don't even mention any of that. Goodnight!"

As Zarin made her way back to the theater room, the movie "*Some Like It Hot*" was already playing for twenty-five minutes. Collette and Tomi were fast asleep as the wine knocked them out cold. Monica was only halfway there to catching some Zees herself. All who were still awake to watch the movie was Wendy and Zarin. But instead, Zarin and Wendy just sat next to each other in the theater room and had a whispering conversation, as they didn't want to disturb the others. "So, how are the girls?" Wendy asked Zarin.

Zarin responded, "Oh, they're good. I just called my mother to check on them. My mother was telling me that Darsha's phone use is getting too much, and that Neal and I should make strict rules on her using the phone. And we do, but we just let her use it over there because we know there's nothing to do over there. The girls get bored. But anyway, how's my godson EJ doing?"

Even though Wendy may feel a little embarrassed about mentioning EJ's bedwetting problem, she thought it was important to practice what she preached earlier when she said to Collette that they don't judge. So, she knows that Zarin wouldn't judge either. Wendy said to Zarin, "EJ was doing okay. But he *did* have an accident, *on* Edward. He hasn't wet himself in months, so we thought we made progress."

Zarin understood Wendy, and she was able to relate to Wendy's situation well. Zarin mentioned to Wendy how her youngest daughter, Joshna, had a bedwetting problem as well. Zarin said to Wendy, "Yea, it's just a phase, though. EJ will grow out of that. Neal and I told Joshna to make sure she uses the bathroom *before* sleeping. And also, we stopped allowing her to drink liquids right before bedtime. So, maybe just some things to think about."

As Wendy listened, she considered Zarin's advice and then called it a night. Monica had already joined Tomi and Collette, as the three of them were counting sheep for the night. Wendy then said good night to Zarin and collected her things. She then put on her red bottoms, her Burberry trench coat and left for the evening.

As Wendy went down the penthouse elevator, she looked at herself in the golden reflection of the elevator doors. She then fixed her long, jet-black hair, as it was a bit tangled from laying on the theater room chair. As the elevator doors opened and she walked into the lobby, she waved and said good night to the security at the desk and walked out front, trying to wave down a taxi. As you know earlier, Wendy does not have much luck with taxis in the city.

As Wendy waited in the cold, an unidentifiable person was walking towards her. At first, Wendy was a little worried because it was dark. Wendy could not see the person's face. But some light began to reflect on the person's face as the person came closer. That person's look was *very* familiar. It was the face of her high school sweetheart.

"Oh my God…Oh my God, Wendy?" The guy said to Wendy.

"Mark? Oh my God, how are you?" Wendy said to her sweetheart as they both went in for a quick hug.

"I've been great! I'm doing well. Jeez, it's been a while. I think the last time we connected was the night before we went our separate ways to college, right? God, you look so incredibly amazing."

"Why, thank you! And yes, I believe that was the last time we saw each other. You went to UCLA, right?"

"Yes, I was there for two years, then I transferred to Stanford University and graduated."

Wendy then asked Mark why he came back to the east coast. His response was, "I'm back on the east coast, on a business trip for several weeks. I just left some friends; we had dinner and drinks. I've been trying to catch a cab back to my hotel for about fifteen minutes. But I'm not having much luck tonight." "Oh, me too; I'm trying to get home myself. But anyway, I don't want to hold you up any longer. It was *great* to see you after so long. I'm glad you are doing well," Wendy said to Mark.

Mark was not willing to just end the engagement with Wendy so briefly. He wanted to stay in contact with her and asked her for her cell number and her social media accounts. Wendy was hesitant to exchange information, being as though she is not on the market. Wendy said to mark, "Um, to be honest with you, Mark, I am a married woman now, happily married, with a child. It was great to see you and catch up briefly, but I don't think it would be appropriate or necessary now. I hope you understand."

Mark gave an impression as if he understood where Wendy was coming from respectfully. In response, he said, "Not to worry, I completely understand. I have my lady back out in LA. But here, at *least* take my card. I'll be in town for another week or so. Give me a call if you have time for a drink." Wendy then reached her hand out and slid his card out of his fingertips.

Wendy looked at the card and then looked at Mark. Through all the talking, she couldn't help but acknowledged how handsome he still is. He looks even better than the last time she's seen him. He wasn't too tall, but not short. Just the right physical shape. A fair complexion with a neatly groomed stubble. And Wendy was an absolute sucker for his blue eyes. Mark was then able to wave down a taxi. As the cab came to a complete stop, Mark opened the back seat door and said to Wendy, "hop in." Wendy, with a smile on her face, said, "Oh, no, thank you. *You* take this one. I'll just wait for the next one." Mark then scoffs as he said, "Oh, don't be ridiculous. There may not be another cab for a half hour. And it's cold out here. Come on, get in."

Wendy thought about it and got into the back seat. Mark then got in after her, unbeknownst to her that they were *sharing* this cab. Wendy then gave Mark a surprising look, as she was unaware that they would be sharing.

"Oh, I hope it's not a problem we're sharing this cab?" Mark spoke. "I told you I was looking for one too."

"Well, we're in here now. I guess it's alright," said Wendy.

"Awesome, driver, there will be two stops. I'll be going to the Dominick Hotel, and *where* are you going?"

"Um, I'll be going to Hell's Kitchen, west 42nd street. Port Authority would be better."

But Wendy gave the cab driver a false address, as she didn't want Mark to know her exact place of residency. For the next seven minutes, there was nothing but quiet and awkward energy in the back seat of that taxi ride. At this moment, Wendy wished she would have just stayed at Tomi's penthouse for the night. As the taxi pulled up to the Dominick Hotel, Mark pulled out some cash to pay his share. When he opened the door and got out, he turned and leaned down and said to Wendy, "You care to come up and have a drink?"

Wendy, now looking at Mark with instant disgust as she shook her head, reached into her coat pocket, took out the business card that he gave her, and then flicked it at him as it landed on the street. "Goodnight, Mr. Homewrecker!" Wendy said as she stared him down.

Mark looked down at his business card on the ground. Then he looked up at Wendy and then looked back down at the card. As Mark picked up his card, he smiled at Wendy as he flicked his card back to her without saying a word. He then closed the cab door and walked away with secured confidence, believing that Wendy will eventually give him a call for that drink, or perhaps something else. Wendy then gave the cab driver her actual home address.

It was a good twenty-minute drive before she would get home. Wendy gathered her thoughts together in her mind. As she was riding in the back seat, she pulled out her phone to make a tweet about her recent encounter with her once high school sweetheart, Mark. In her tweet, she said, "*Life is truly a trip. You just never know who you are going to run into at any given moment. But even sweethearts turn bitter. Don't fold out here, ladies. It's not worth it.*" As Wendy was trying to post her tweet, she had to make a few adjustments as she reached the max on the character limit.

The taxi finally made it to the front entrance of her apartment building. Wendy then reached into her purse to pull out some cash and paid the cab fare. She stepped out of the taxi and closed the door. Wendy walked through the revolving doors of her apartment lobby with much fierceness and a lot on her mind. But there is one detail that has to be shared now. Keep this in mind. Mark's business card was *not* left in the back seat of the cab that night.

Chapter 2

As Wendy turned the key to unlock the door to her apartment, the door was not budging. She kept trying for a decent minute. But that one minute felt like ten minutes as her frustration increased. Until Wendy realized that she was using the wrong key, she had to laugh it off. Perhaps the late-night was getting to her way of thinking. Or her mind was still preoccupied with what had just occurred with Mark. She finally made it into her house. She took off her red bottom shoes, as her feet were red and cold from standing outside waiting for the cab. As part of her Japanese culture, she removes her shoes *before* walking around their apartment. She then removed her coat and placed it in the closet. The living room was clean, as was the kitchen and dining room.

Even though it was five past one in the morning, Wendy was in the mood for some tea. She went into the kitchen to boil up some water. She was going back and forth about what kind of tea she had a taste for at that moment. Finally, Wendy said to herself, "Hmm, do I want Chocolate Chai Tea or Peppermint Chocolate?" Wendy grabbed a quarter from her coin jar and flipped the quarter in the air: heads for Chocolate Chai, tails for Peppermint Chocolate. Even though the quarter landed on tails, Wendy went ahead and chose the Chocolate Chai Tea.

Wendy waited for the water to boil; Wendy began to look at the feedback received from the tweet she posted when she was in the cab. She received two thousand retweets, over thirty-thousand likes, and close to twelve hundred comments. Wendy is a well-known wedding planner who planned several high-end, A-list celebrity weddings. She is quite the popularity queen, with over three hundred thousand followers on Twitter. Wendy is even more popular on Instagram, with eight-hundred and seventy-five thousand followers. And also, she has a blue verified check.

But Wendy found herself stuck on Twitter, looking at all the comments. She kept scrolling and scrolling, almost hypnotizing herself. One comment said, "*I love your work, Wendy. Let's collaborate.*" Another comment said, "You're so beautiful. Can *we* get married, LOL!" Then, of course, that one *negative* comment, that one "*troll*," who has to ruin it for everyone. The negative comment said, "*Just because you plan weddings doesn't mean you know about love.*" And without hesitation, Wendy highlighted that profile and said, "You're blocked!" She then had to close the app and put her phone down, as she remembered what Zarin said earlier about her oldest daughter, Darsha, and how she has a hard time putting down *her* phone.

The water was at a nice boil; Wendy turned the nozzle off on the stove and poured the boiling water into her Nutcracker coffee mug. She then turned off all the lights in the kitchen, and with her tea, she went into EJ's room to check on him. EJ was sleeping in his Disney Pixar's *Cars* bed. Wendy took a minute as she stood there watching her son sleep. They decorated his walls with race cars, race car posters, and even a rotating race car night light. EJ has an enormous love for cars and racing. Nothing makes him happier. As Wendy placed her tea on EJ's dresser, she walked to his bed and leaned over to kiss him on the side of his head. Then, out of curiosity, she checked his mattress and felt on his pajamas, just to make sure he did not have another accident. Wendy was relieved to find everything dry.

As Wendy turned around to walk out of EJ's room, she almost let out a scream, stepping on one of EJ's action figures in the middle of the floor. Even though she held it in like a champ,

Wendy most definitely pantomimed herself, saying, "FUCK!" Wendy then picked up and threw the action figure across the room, which coincidently landed in a pile of EJ's clothes, creating no loud sound. If only you could see the look on her face at that moment. Wendy then took her coffee mug with the tea inside and walked out of EJ's room, now walking with a minor limp.

As Wendy made her way to her bedroom, she realized she left her phone on the kitchen table. She went to grab it and made her way back to the bedroom. All she saw was her husband, Edward, lying in bed asleep with the television remote in his left hand and his phone lying on his chest. The blue light of the television screen was shining on Edward as if the television was now watching him. Edward tried to wait up for Wendy but gave in a little early. Perhaps EJ wore him out. Wendy then put her Nutcracker mug down on her nightstand. After she undressed and put on her nightgown, she then went into the bathroom to remove her makeup, brushed her teeth, and wrapped her hair into a messy bun.

As Wendy looked into the mirror, she began to think about the encounter she had tonight with her high school sweetheart, Mark. She could not get over how unexpected it was to see him after so many years. But Wendy also could not get over how attractive Mark still is after so many years. As Wendy continued to look at herself in the mirror, she looked down at her wedding ring. At that very moment, Wendy realized she did the right thing by staying in the cab. She realized that she is a married woman, happily married with a child, and jeopardizing that would ruin her family.

Wendy then gave herself a pat on the back and a smile in the mirror. She flicked off the light as she walked out of the bathroom and climbed her way into bed. Her tea was just the right temperature to where it was not too hot but deliciously enjoyable. She sipped away as she gently took the remote from Edward's left hand and began to click her way through the channels to see what shows were playing. Wendy then came across a top-rated movie, Nora Ephron's "*Sleepless in Seattle*," starring Tom Hanks and Meg Ryan. One of Wendy's favorite movies, she decided to watch it as she enjoyed her tea. As Wendy was watching the movie, she found herself staring at her husband. She began to reminisce about the night they first met.

They met a little over eleven years ago. Wendy was just finishing up her college degree in business, with a minor concentration in event planning. Upon graduating from New York University, she went to see a ballet performance, an adaptation of "*Swan Lake*." A college friend of hers had an extra ticket, and Wendy tagged along to see the show. Wendy loved the show; she thought the performance was incredible. At the end of the show, Wendy's college friend asked her if she wanted to hang out at the after-party with some of the cast and crew; Wendy said, "of course, I'd love to."

As they went to the after-party, Wendy spotted this good-looking young man standing on the other side of the room. She assumed he was an actor, being that he was so attractive, but he was the assistant director for "*Swan Lake*." So, as Wendy walked over to her college friend, she asked, "Hey Rebecca, do you know that guy over there?"

While Wendy was asking, she pointed her finger at the guy, and he spotted her pointing at him. Wendy tried to play it off as if she wasn't, but it was too late. He made his way towards her and Rebecca. As he made his way towards Wendy, he introduced himself and said, "Hi, I'm Edward, but you can call me Eddie." With Wendy, she didn't believe in love at first sight, but she could not take her eyes off of Edward. She then responded to Edward, saying, "Hi, I'm Wendy. It's nice to meet you, Eddie."

Edward and Wendy were utterly inseparable ever since. She would see him every chance she would get, whether at one of his shows he was directing or when they had free nights to go out on dates. Wendy loved Edward more than anything, and he felt the same vibrations, perhaps even more. Finally, three years after dating, Edward decided to propose to Wendy, and without hesitation, she said yes. Then three years after they married, little EJ was born.

As Wendy took the last sip of her Chocolate Chai Tea, Edward began to awaken by the sounds of the television. Wendy looked at him and said, "Oh, I'm sorry, babe, I didn't mean to wake you." She then turned the volume down.

"It's okay," said Edward as he kissed her right hand. "I tried to wait up, but EJ was a handful tonight. How was your day?"

"It was tiresome earlier," Wendy responded. "I had to work overtime with this wedding coming up. But my ladies always make my Fridays better after work. How was yours?"

Edward then responded, "My day went well. We have two more weeks of rehearsal. The last week is tech week, and then it's showtime. We're finally allowed to have more than three hundred people in the audience. That *Covid-19* shit kicked our theatre asses. I'm so happy things are coming back to normal."

Wendy was glad to hear that the theatre shows are now allowed to have more people in attendance. She hasn't been able to see many shows since Broadway opened back up. But now that Edward is directing his first show since the pandemic, Wendy will not miss it for the world.

"Well, I *cannot* wait to see your adaptations of Shakespeare. I know you have been working so hard on this," Wendy said as they both lay side by side in bed.

"Thanks, babe, you've been such huge support these past couple of years. With the pandemic shutting everything down, you really kept our family together financially. And you were *so* smart to open up a savings account, as well as making those investments. I don't know what I'd do without you," Edward said as he kissed Wendy on her face.

"Thanks, Eddie, I needed to hear that. I love you," Wendy responded as she then laid on top of Edward.

It was almost three in the morning, yet Wendy and Edward were not quite ready to fall asleep. Their kissing session grew into a more fornicating behavior. Edward then removed his white t-shirt as Wendy pulled off her silky nightgown. To close the night's chapter with lovemaking, it was just what the two of them needed.

As the light of the sun shines through their windows on a Saturday morning, Wendy and Edward are fast asleep after a romantic ending of the night. As the two of them were still sleeping, there was a gentle knock on the door. A couple more knocks then came, but still, they didn't budge. Then, a little hand began to turn the doorknob and opened the door. It was EJ; he usually sleeps in on Saturdays, as does Edward and Wendy. But he was up early, hoping to have some cereal. EJ then climbed up on his parents' bed, took the television remote, and turned to his favorite show on YouTube, "*Zerby Derby*." *Zerby Derby* is a Canadian car show for kids, and being that EJ loves his cars, he became obsessed with the show. "*Vroom, vroom!*" EJ said, making car sounds as he watches the show.

As EJ continues to watch *Zerby Derby*, Wendy has awakened by the noise of EJ's voice. Wendy was briefly surprised that EJ was in their room so early, and the fact that she was completely naked under her comforter, as was Edward, she had to tell EJ to step out of their bedroom for a few moments.

"EJ, honey, Good morning," said Wendy. "Could you do mommy a favor and step out in the hall? I just need to get dress, and then you can finish watching your show, okay?"

"Yes, mommy," EJ said as he paused the show and stepped out.

Wendy then woke Edward up and told him to slip on some shorts and a t-shirt while she put on some underwear and her orange silk Kimono robe. After getting dressed, she opened the door to let EJ back in to watch his show. But instead, he wanted some cereal. So, Wendy then grabbed her empty *Nutcracker* coffee mug, walked with EJ to the kitchen, as he was looking forward to a bowl of his favorite cereal, "*Lucky Charms.*"

She rinsed off his little race car bowl and poured him some cereal. But then she stopped and asked EJ, "baby, did you use the bathroom and brush your teeth?" As EJ looked at Wendy, he gave her a horizontal head shake and went straight to the bathroom. As EJ was in the bathroom, Wendy took out a gallon of milk from the refrigerator and placed it on the kitchen table.

Wendy then dumped her used Chocolate Chai tea bag from the coffee mug last night and began to brew some coffee for herself and Edward. As the coffee was brewing, Wendy went back into her bedroom to check her phone. By that time, Edward was already in the bathroom freshening up. When she opened her home screen, she received a few texts, as well as a few friend requests on her Facebook account.

One of those texts came from Zarin saying, "Hey girl, I left Tomi's place about an hour after you left. I just wanted to make sure you got home safely. Have a good night, love." Of course, being that Wendy is the youngest at thirty-three, the rest of the ladies check on Wendy the most. Wendy then responded to Zarin, saying, "Hey, thanks, I got home just fine, but rather under *unusual* circumstances. I'll explain more in detail to you all later. But thanks for checking on me. Have a great day."

It always warms Wendy's heart to know she has real friends who have her back and care about her. So, as she then checked her Facebook page, Wendy took a look at those friend requests. One request was from a stranger she never met, and the other was from; well, can you guess who? It was her high school sweetheart, Mark. As Wendy looked at her phone and saw the friend request from Mark, she then looked at the bathroom door, where Edward was behind, in the bathroom. Then she looked back at her phone. Wendy had a feeling that he would look for her on social media and try to connect. But as hesitant as she was to accept his friend request, she was even more curious about what was on his profile.

So, Wendy began her nosey roam on Mark's Facebook page. She saw many of his photos from different locations worldwide, family photos, and recent photos that Mark posted last night. After Wendy finished snooping around Mark's Facebook page, she had a decision to make; either she accepts his friend request, or she declines it. She was going back and forth in her mind as if the final Jeopardy theme music was playing. Then all of a sudden, the bathroom door opened, and Edward came out. Wendy hastily hit decline on Mark's friend request out of rapid impulse and placed her phone on the bed. Edward looked at Wendy's jittery face and asked her, "You alright, babe?" Wendy responded, "Yea, I'm good. Just getting EJ some breakfast."

Wendy panicked at that moment. She was about sixty-five percent on hitting the accept button and thirty-five percent on declining. But when Edward walked out of the bathroom, Wendy took that as a sign and decided to end her curiosity. She did not want Edward to find out about her run-in with Mark last night.

"I made some coffee," said Wendy. "It should be ready by now."

"Oh great, thanks!" Edward spoke. "Oh, by the way, were you watching *Sleepless in Seattle* last night? I was certain I heard Tom Hanks' voice screaming, "*Jonah, Jonah*!"

Wendy looked at Edward with laughter and said, "I was; I love that movie. I was drinking my tea and enjoying every minute of it. It always puts me into a romantic mood."

Wendy then walked to Edward and hugged him. She looked into Edward's gorgeous grey eyes, smelling the echo of scent from his Listerine breath. Her late-night encounter with Mark quickly began to fade from her memories. Then, as she and Edward gave each other good morning kisses, there was yet *another* knock on their slightly opened door.

"Mommy, daddy, I had an accident," EJ said from outside the room.

"Oh God, not again. I'll take care of it," Wendy said to Edward with a disappointed face.

As Wendy opened her bedroom door and saw EJ's wet pajamas, she said to him, "Baby, how did you wet yourself when I sent you to the bathroom?" But the thing is, EJ *went* to the bathroom and took care of business. But his patience grew thin, waiting for his mother to pour *"milk"* into his cereal. So, EJ took it upon himself to grab the milk on the kitchen table and pour it himself. But unfortunately, that did not work as planned for him.

As Wendy and EJ went into his room, she pulled out some clean, dry underwear, shorts, and a t-shirt from his dresser. She gave EJ a few minutes to get dress and told him to put his wet pajamas into the pile with his other dirty clothes. As Wendy walked back into the kitchen, she was dumbfounded by what her eyes showed her.

Wendy realized that EJ did not wet himself, but he simply spilled some milk on himself that he tried to pour on his cereal. The milk had halfway spilled on the kitchen floor, yet Wendy was not as upset, knowing that EJ had a completely *different* accident than expected. She was somewhat relieved. At that moment, Wendy thought about the saying, "*Don't cry over spilled milk, just look for a paper towel.*" And that is what she did; she cleaned up, took whatever milk was left, and fixed EJ his breakfast.

Chapter 3

Zarin was already getting her day started not too far away from Wendy, as she already got dressed, soon to head out to pick up Darsha and Joshna from her parent's house. Zarin's Husband, Neal, was having a slow morning. Neal had a busy Friday as he had over a dozen patients. And then, after work, he dropped off Darsha and Joshna at Zarin's parent's house and came back home to catch up on some work. Usually, that is their weekend routine. On Friday nights, Neal or Zarin drops the girls off at Zarin's parent's house, and in the morning, he sleeps in while Zarin picks the girls up.

Zarin was finishing up her oatmeal raisin bagel with plant-based butter. Then, she began to take a look at her phone to check her e-mails. Zarin then saw the text that Wendy sent to her this morning. It put a smile on Zarin's face, knowing that her friends appreciate her. After Zarin wiped out about seventy spammed e-mails from her account, she then took a look at a few news articles from the *New York Times* website, as well as *The Wall Street Journal*. Being a news journalist, Zarin is always looking for what is going on globally, gathering as much information as she can.

As Zarin scrolled on her phone, looking at different articles, she came across an article about a fatal house fire that took place in The Bronx, killing a grandmother and her two grandchildren. She read that article, and it hit home for her very closely, as that could have been *her* mother and two daughters. Zarin always hates to be the bearer of bad news every day when she has to go on live television and speak sad stories; with professionalism and a straight face.

While Zarin continued scrolling, she received another text message. This time it was a group text from Tomi, saying, "Hey my loves, sorry I passed out on you ladies last night. The combination of *Louis Roederer* and red wine put me in a fucking coma. LOL! But I just wanted to say enjoy the rest of your weekend with your family, have a wonderful and productive week, and I shall see you next Friday. Kisses and much love."

Zarin hit the "loved" reaction on Tomi's text and replied, "I love you too, babe, thanks for having me over, along with the rest of the ladies. You have a great week, too, and keep being the ambitious boss bitch that you are."

As time was already pushing close to ten 'o'clock in the morning, it was time for Zarin to head over to her parent's house and pick up the girls. When she went to the closet to grab her navy blue peacoat, Neal came downstairs.

"Good morning handsome, you get enough sleep?" Zarin said to Neal.

"Hardly, but I didn't want to be in bed all day long. You're going to pick up the girls now?" Neal said as he kissed Zarin.

"Yea, I'm heading over to my parent's house now. Did you need anything while I'm out?"

"Um, No, I think I'm okay, thanks!"

As Zarin made her way outside, she locked the doors to their brownstone and made her way down the stairs. Both Neal and Zarin share a black Range Rover with a beige interior. As she headed to the Range Rover, Neal's voice stopped her.

"Hey, I think you'll be needing these," Neal said as he was twirling the keys to the Range Rover with his index finger.

"I *do* need those. Thanks, baby," Zarin laughed.

Zarin has a good twenty-five-minute drive before she arrives at her parents' house in Queens. At that moment, she began to think about what kind of gift she would give Neal for their sixteenth anniversary.

While Zarin was driving, a thought came to her mind about the first time they met in college. Zarin studied journalism at New York University, while Neal attended the New York University Grossman School of Medicine. They crossed paths with each other in an elevator in the admissions building.

Neal was this tall, well-built, knowledgeable, handsome young man with a great sense of humor. Not as if he was a comedian, but he had just the right jokes at the right time. Zarin was leaning up against the wall in the elevator as Neal was standing near the control panel. Zarin looked at him with instant attraction, and she was hoping a conversation would spark during that eleven-second elevator ride. But then, Zarin had a very flirtatious impulse as the elevator reached the admissions level. Before the elevator doors opened, Zarin grabbed Neal's arm and said, "are you seeing anyone right now?" Neal looked at her with a grin and said, "Yea, I'm seeing *you* right now." They both broke out in laughter as she got a taste of his humor. As they had a brief moment of conversation, right there in the elevator, the doors closed, and they began to go back down to the first floor.

After they finally took care of their business in the admissions building, they had lunch together. Neal asked Zarin about her family and where her roots came from in the world. Zarin told him that her father's side of the family came from Jabalpur and that her mother's side came from New Delhi. Zarin mentioned how both her parents met in America as exchange students, and they have been together ever since. Zarin also said how she is the oldest sibling out of her and her younger brother.

Neal then mentioned how his father's family is from Bangladesh, and his mother's side is from Rajasthan, which was not far from New Delhi. He also said how his mother's family came from a poor background, and his father was from a wealthier family. So, his parents being together was not acceptable to his father's side of the family. But they decided to be together still, no matter what, because they were so in love with each other. So, Neal's parents fled to America and started over. They first had Neal's older brother, Mukul, and then they had Neal and his twin sister. But unfortunately, Neal's parents' love for each other did not last, and they divorced. After the divorce, Neal stayed in America with his mother, while his twin sister and Mukul moved back to India with their father. That arrangement left Neal a bit heartbroken ever since.

The chemistry between Zarin and Neal grew solid as the glare in their eyes became magical. As they were finishing up with their lunch date, Zarin talked about how she was studying journalism and how it was her dream to be a news broadcaster. When Zarin was a little girl, she would always practice in front of a mirror with a hairbrush as her microphone, telling stories. As for Neal, he told her how he is studying to be a doctor. To her surprise, Zarin could not prepare for what medical field Neal was studying. When Neal said that he was studying to be a Gynecologist, she looked at him with instant judgment. She thought it was rather odd for a man to be interested in being a male Gynecologist. Neal said to her, "I already know what you're thinking, and no, I'm *not* a pervert. I am just so pro-life, and I want to help women fulfill their dreams of being mothers. Even though it is God's plan, but I would like to help in the process." When Neal explained to Zarin why he is studying to be a Gynecologist, she then understood that his logic comes from a moral and generous purpose.

As both of them exchanged numbers, they said their goodbyes and went their separate ways. But the separation was not for too long. Neal called Zarin that very same night, asking her if she could come over to his apartment for the evening. Zarin, without hesitation, said, "fuck yeah, but give me an hour." She then washed up, put on some makeup, took her eyelash brush, and gave it a few strokes upon her beautifully long, natural eyelashes. It brought out the color of her brown eyes. Zarin then combed her long black hair, got dressed, and headed out the door.

As Zarin ran over to Neal's apartment, she realized that she did not bring any protection with her. Zarin always liked to have condoms in her purse, even if she didn't need them. But *that* night, she had every intention to use one. So, she went over there, hoping Neal had plenty. About ten minutes after she left her place, she made it to Neal's apartment. She then pushed the buzzer to his apartment. He answered, saying, "Yea, is that you, Zarin?" She responded, "Yea, it's me."

Neal then buzzed her in. Zarin had to walk up several flights of stairs, as he lived on the third floor. As Zarin made it to his apartment, Neal was already waiting for her at his door. He couldn't get over how beautiful she was, and she was beginning to have a firm grip on his heart. When Zarin walked inside of Neal's apartment, it was relatively clean, very clean actually. One would say that Neal is a neat freak but in a good way.

Since this was back in the early 2000s, the year 2007 to be exact. Neal had all the new technology up to date. Steve Jobs just released the first-ever iPhone. Neal recently purchased an iPhone, and he showed Zarin how it worked. Zarin was amazed at how advanced the iPhone was, as she still had her razor phone. They talked for most of the night as they chowed down on some Chinese take-out and a few Heinekens. Zarin began to get a little more comfortable as the night was winding down. She then removed her button-up shirt, leaving on only her sports bra and her jeans. Neal was beginning to acknowledge that the rest of the night was going to be very rip-roaring. He wanted her just as bad as she wanted him. He then took off his *Prince* t-shirt, showing off his very physique upper body. Both of them were just looking at each other, ready for their first romantic encounter. Neal began with a kiss, a soft, gentle kiss on Zarin's fully plumped lips. Kiss after kiss as they were dismissing their clothes from their bodies. Then their fornication went from the couch to the bedroom.

As they both landed on the bed, Neal went on a kissing adventure all over Zarin's nude body. His gentle touch set Zarin's soul on fire. She never felt such stimulation before. Mind you; this was not Zarin's first time. Neal made his way back up to her face, kissing her cheeks, forehead, lips, and then all over her neck. She was in absolute paradise. But right in the middle of all that pleasure, Zarin briefly snapped out of her sexual hypnosis and said to Neal, "Wait, do you have protection?" Neal then responded, "Yes, of course, I do."

The fornication continued; Neal then proceeded to make his way down to Zarin's breast, to her belly button, and finally to her most *sacred* treasure. As he was down there, he then looked up to Zarin, looking straight into her eyes as he asked her, "Are you ready?" Zarin responded with a bit of confusion, "Yea, I guess I'm ready?" Unbeknownst to her, Neal was about to give her the most prolific oral stimulation of her life. Being that Neal is studying to be a Gynecologist, he knows *all* there is to know about a woman's vagina, especially her "*G-spot.*" And Neal most definitely found Zarin's G-spot *that* night. Let's just say that Zarin's vocals were going off as if she was on *American Idol* or *The Voice. That* night, Zarin had no control over herself. And she loved every second of it.

But let's spare any further graphic details about the rest of their pleasurable evening. Both Zarin and Neal were completely satisfied after that night. As they woke up the following morning, they said good morning to each other, went at it a few more times, and then had brunch. After that night, there was no separating the two of them. And that is how Zarin and her *now-husband*, Neal, came to be.

As Zarin made her way to her parent's house in Queens, she came up with the perfect gift for Neal. A gold Rolex Presidential with a diamond bezel. But then she decided that an original gold Rolex presidential *without* the diamonds would be more his style. So, after Zarin picks up Darsha and Joshna, she will take a look at a jewelry store not too far from where she lives. Zarin finally arrived in front of her parents' house. She then made her way up the stairs and rang the doorbell. Darsha, who is Zarin's oldest daughter, opened the front door and then the screen door.

"Momma!" Darsha said as she hugged Zarin.

"Hi, my baby, how are you today?" Zarin responded as she kissed Darsha.

As Zarin came inside, her mother was in the kitchen, washing dishes and silverware. Zarin then said, "Hey mom, where's dad?" Zarin's mother responded, "He went to grab some fresh veggies and fruits from the market." Joshna then came down the stairs with her book bag and her favorite teddy bear. It was a lavender teddy bear that her father, Neal, won for her at a carnival game two years ago. She fell in love with it ever since, taking it with her everywhere she went. The bear had a pink, plastic, heart-shaped stud on its chest, and it had a smile on its face. Joshna named the bear "*Dula*," which is short for Lavandula, commonly known as lavender, as the bear had a lavender shade of color.

"Hi Joshy, how are you, baby girl?" Zarin said as she hugged and kissed Joshna.

"Hi, mommy, I'm good, still tired," Joshna said to Zarin.

As Zarin was getting the girls' stuff together, heading out of the door, her mother said, "Oh, and make sure you talk to Darsha about that phone, no more phone time here." Zarin responded with slight irritation, "Yes, mom, *I will*. Please give dad my love, thank you again, and I will talk to you later." The girls headed out the door first as Zarin locked both doors with her keys, as she has keys of her own to the house, just in case of emergencies. Zarin then took her car key and pressed the unlock button to let the girls get in.

Zarin then got in the car and began to drive back into Manhattan. As they were on the road, Zarin brought up the phone situation to Darsha. She said, "Baby, your father and I gave you that phone for emergency purposes *only*. Not to be playing games all day. Nani said that you were playing around with it too much, and we don't want you on the phone for more than twenty minutes a day. So, your father and I will both be checking the screen time on your phone every week to make sure. Do you understand?" Darsha agreed with a gentle "yes," and a head nod.

Zarin also brought up how Darsha did not eat dinner at her grandparent's house and asked Darsha why she did not eat. But Darsha pleaded her case by saying, "Momma, Nani puts so much of that curry stuff on the food. It's so strong, and I don't like it." In Zarin's mind, she had no other choice but to find that humorous. She understood Darsha completely, as *she* grew up with her mother's cooking, and agrees that her mother is very generous with the curry powder.

"Well, baby, this time, I'll give you a pass. But you have to eat your dinner, okay?" Zarin said to Darsha.

"Okay, I ate some of it, but just not much," Darsha responded.

A little later that Saturday, as the evening was approaching, Zarin began to plan dinner for everyone. Being that Neal lives on a plant-based diet, she cooks according to his regime. Zarin, however, loves cheese, eggs, and yogurt way too much to compromise. So, the meals are neutrally appetizing. She allows Darsha and Joshna to have meat while they stay with their grandparents, but for the most part, it is strictly veggies and plant-based entrees.

As the girls were in the living room, coloring in their coloring books and watching *SpongeBob SquarePants* on Television, Neal came in the house. As he went into the living room, he said, "Girls! Come here, give me hugs. I need my hugs." Darsha and Joshna came running to their father and gave him the biggest hug a father could ever receive from his daughters. Neal then made his way over to Zarin and gave her the most incredible kiss a husband could ever give his wife. Every year their love has grown stronger, as well as their bond. "How was the rest of your day, babe?" Neal asked Zarin. As Zarin was cooking, she responded, "It was good; I just went to get the girls. My mother was telling me about Darsha and her using the phone excessively. So, maybe you want to give her a little talking to? Please? I don't want her on it too much either."

Neal agreed and said he'll bring it up when he puts them down for bed and reads them a bedtime story. As Zarin was stirring this homemade sauce she had prepared for dinner, she took a spoonful of the sauce for Neal to taste. Neal gave it a few smooth blows to cool it down before he tasted the sauce. Zarin knew the sauce was on point by looking at his aflame face, and he could not wait to dig into the meal.

After Zarin finished preparing the meal, she received a text message. Her phone was in the living room on the grey marble coffee table. As she walked into the living room, she told Darsha and Joshna to wash their hands and get ready for dinner. When Zarin picked up her phone to see who text her, it was a group text from Tomi. In the text, Tomi said, "Hey ladies, I have to go out of town this week. I'm flying out to L.A. tomorrow morning for a business trip. So I may or may not be at *Lucille's* next Friday evening. But I will let you know by Thursday. Love you all."

Monica responded, saying, "Okay, sounds good. Let us know when you get there and that you are safe. Love you too." Collette jumped in with her text saying, "Love you, Tomi, be safe over there. Can't wait till you come back." Wendy responded with a handful of heart emojis and a text saying, "I love you more, have a safe trip." Being the last to respond, Zarin text, "Thanks for the heads up, have a safe trip."

Zarin then put her phone back down on the marble coffee table. As soon as she turned around to walk back to the kitchen, she received another text message. As Zarin picked up her phone, it was another text from Tomi saying, "BITCH, you better tell me that you love me!" Zarin was hysterical after she read Tomi's text. The other ladies began to text a chain of "LOL" and "LMAO." Zarin then responded with, "HAHA, I'm sorry, babe, of course, I love you. Hurry back, okay?"

As you can see, the bond these five women have with each other is solid as a diamond, absolutely unbreakable. The love they have for one another is unique. Here it is, five women from different ethnic backgrounds, different career paths, different lives to live. Yet, they make it work somehow. Their friendship is for real. It is honest and filled with happiness. Not to say that it is perfect, they have their ups and downs, just like any other friendship. But there is nothing or no one that comes between them. However, there is an unsolicited challenge that awaits them.

After Zarin finished group chatting with the others, she left her phone on the coffee table in the living room and made her way back to the kitchen. She prepared a very colorful salad with tomatoes, cucumbers, olives, and a minimal amount of onions, as Joshna *hates* onions with a passion. Still, she wants Joshna to eat more vegetables. Zarin grabbed the salad dressing from the refrigerator and made her way to the dining room table.

"Where's your father?" Zarin asked the girls.

"He went upstairs to change his clothes and wash his hands," Darsha said to Zarin.

Zarin decided to wait for Neal to come downstairs before they began to eat. On the dining room table, Zarin noticed something that she did not want to see. Darsha had her phone on the table, lying face up. As Zarin saw the phone, she said to Darsha, "Sweetie, you know what mommy said about having that phone at the dining room table while we have dinner. It's our family time, and it's not every day that we get to sit as a family and have dinner together. You know your father sometimes has late nights." Darsha then looked at her mother with a face of guilt and sorrow. She said to her mother, "Sorry, momma, can I put my phone in my room?" Zarin then said, "Actually, give it to me; *I'll* put it in your room. You guys go ahead and eat. I don't want it to get cold. And I'll go see why your father is taking so long."

Zarin took Darsha's phone and made her way up the stairs. As she reached the top, to her left is the bathroom; next to the restroom, is Darsha and Joshna's bedroom, and then down the hall is Zarin and Neal's bedroom. Zarin went into the girl's bedroom and placed the phone on Darsha's little nightstand. A cute little Princess Jasmine-themed nightstand from the Disney movie *Aladdin*. As Zarin walked out of the girl's bedroom, she heard Neal talking on the phone with someone. The tone of his voice was rather aggressive, somewhat out of his character. So, Zarin wanted to know what was going on. But she did not want to eavesdrop on his phone conversation.

So, in her Chanel sliders, Zarin gently crept her way down the hallway to their bedroom. The closer she came to the bedroom door, the more disturbing the conversation sound. Zarin got as close to the crack of the bedroom door as she could without being noticed. She saw Neal sitting on the far side of the bed, with his back turned to the door. For a good minute, Zarin stood there and overheard what Neal was saying on the phone. As Zarin listened, Neal said, "You *have* to have this baby. This moment right here will be your greatest achievement in your life. No, it's okay; it will all be okay. I will be there for you and the baby. I will take care of you both. Yes, I *promise* this will stay between you and me. No one else will know. No, Zarin doesn't know about this situation."

After Zarin heard what Neal just said, her equilibrium became disorderedly shot. She began to hyperventilate as she walked down the hallway. Upstairs in the hallway, through her mind, it looked as if the hallway was stretching. As if Zarin was walking down the hall from the movie "*Poltergeist.*" She ran as quickly as she could to the bathroom. She turned on the cold-water faucet and splashed handfuls of cold water on her face; over and over again. Her whole body was shaking, and she had no control over herself at that moment. She did not know what to do. She did not want to cry and have Darsha and Joshna see her emotionally. Her mind was in a thousand different places. As Zarin looked in the mirror, her face dripping wet, she began to think about who Neal was talking to on the phone. Who is that woman on the other line? Is he having an affair? Or worse, is *he* the father to that baby he mentioned? And why, *why* would he withhold that information from Zarin?

Zarin had to get herself together. So, she dried off her face, took some deep breaths, and went back downstairs to check on the girls. The girls were already halfway done with their meals, and at the moment, Zarin could not take one bite of her food. Neal was still up in the bedroom; he did not come down yet. Joshna noticed that Zarin was not eating her dinner, so she asked her mother, "Mommy, you're not hungry?" Zarin looked at Joshna's sweet little face and said, "No Joshy, Mommy's lost her appetite."

Zarin is giving her absolute best to perform, being assertive and not trying to think about what she just witnessed upstairs. Neal finally made his way down the stairs. Even after all of that, he did not even change his clothes as he said he would. As Neal came to the dining room table, he said, "Oh, I'm glad everyone started without me." Zarin could not bear to even look at him. At that very moment, she wanted to rip his head off. But she had to hold it in for the sake of the girls.

As Neal began to eat, he started a cute conversation with the girls. A conversation about princesses and castles and how the girls saw themselves as princesses, like Princess Jasmine from *Aladdin*. The girls loved Princess Jasmine because she looked like them. Zarin just sat there, not saying a word. But to not draw any attention to herself, she began to take a few bites from her dinner plate to blend in with the moment.

"Hun, this is delicious. I needed this meal tonight," Neal said to Zarin as he stuffed his face.

"Glad you like it," Zarin responded as she still has not made eye contact with him.

As Neal just about finished his plate, Zarin was refilling her glass with white wine. While she was taking her little sips, she began to look at her wedding ring. Then Zarin looked over to *Neal's* hand, only to find the absence of *his* wedding ring. For Zarin, that was a spark of evidence she had, signaling that Neal may be stepping out on her. Neal never went without wearing his wedding ring, never. Zarin could not hold it in anymore. Anxiety began to grow in her core and work its way straight up to her mind. Finally, she stood up from the dining room table and said with a broken voice, "I'm going to take a shower. Leave everything on the table, and I'll clean it up afterward."

Zarin then quickly made her way up the stairs. She walked into their bedroom and began to undress. Zarin then went into their master bathroom and turned on the showerhead. She felt the throbbing knob lodged down her throat. It was getting hard for her to breathe again. Zarin hurried into the shower, slid the drape across, and just broke down and cried. Tears were falling from Zarin's face, racing the water drops from the showerhead down to the finish line of the drain. Zarin cried, and cried, and cried. She was letting it all out while she had a chance to do so, privately. After all these years, all the beautiful moments, the memories, Zarin cannot believe he would possibly be cheating on her. And to think, earlier she was planning to buy him a Rolex watch for their sixteenth anniversary. Zarin continued to cry in the shower until she had no tears left to contribute to her heartbreak.

After a good thirty minutes in the shower, Zarin was able to calm herself down and gather her thoughts. She was not ready to confront Neal about the situation she overheard. Perhaps she did not want to approach him and be lied to right in her face. As she shut the water off, she grabbed her bathrobe from her bedroom closet, as well as her fluffy white slippers. She then walked out into the hallway to grab another towel from the hallway closet to wrap around her hair.

The sound of laughter was beginning to grow from the living room. Zarin headed down the stairs to see the girls sitting on the couch with Neal as they watched *Aladdin* on Television. Zarin stood there from a distance, looking at Neal as he laughed along with the girls. Then, she began to think and asked herself, "How could this son of a bitch be sitting there, with *my* daughters, laughing as if he's not on the verge of destroying our family?" As Zarin continued, standing there next to the staircase, she began to zone out and daydream.

"Honey? Zarin, Zarin, ZARIN, HONEY!" Neal shouted, trying to get Zarin's attention.

"Huh, yes, I heard you. What?" Zarin responded.

"You sure? I just called your name several times," said Neal. "Are you alright? I mean, you barely touched your plate, and you just up and left the table to take a shower. You feeling okay, babe?"

"I'm fine; I was just feeling a little sweaty from all the cooking, that's all."

Zarin then made her way to the dining room table to clean up. But to her surprise, the dishes were already cleaned and placed in the cabinets. Neal projected to Zarin from the living room, saying, "Oh, the girls and I already did the dishes, babe, so don't worry. You can relax." Even though he did the dishes, Zarin was not pleased, as she needed something to do to keep herself occupied. At that moment, there was only one thing she wanted to do. So, Zarin got in contact with her four ladies and chatted with them.

As Neal and the girls continued to watch *Aladdin,* Zarin grabbed her phone from the living room coffee table and headed up the stairs. As Zarin was halfway up the stairs, Darsha said, "Momma, can I have my phone now?" Zarin immediately rejected Darsha by saying, "No baby, no phone tonight. Besides, it's almost you two's bedtime, so just enjoy the rest of the movie, okay?"

When Zarin got back up the stairs, she began to type away in the group chat with the rest of the ladies. In Zarin's text, it said, "Hey ladies, I'm so sorry to reach out to you at this hour. But I'm going through some rough shit right now. I may be dealing with an "*Oink* Situation." Now, you may be wondering, what the hell is an "*Oink* Situation?"

So, an "*Oink* Situation" is something that Tomi came up with as their girl code. So, *if* or *when* one of their husbands ever were to be caught flirting, creeping around, or having an affair with another woman, they would reach out to each other and say, "I have an "*Oink* Situation." And of course, by *Oink,* they refer to their husband as a pig; get it?

Anyways, in no time, Zarin received text messages from both Wendy and Collette. Wendy responded, "Are you fucking kidding me? And right before you guy's anniversary? Do you need us to come and get you and the girls?" Collette responded to Zarin, saying, "That piece of SHIT! Who's the *puta*? We'll go fuck her up." Then came along Monica, who text, "Aww baby, I'm so sorry to hear that. And don't ever apologize to us. We are always here for you, no matter what. But are you sure he's messing around?" Being that Monica is an attorney, she goes by the rules that he's innocent until proven guilty. Tomi was the last to respond as she text, "Oh my God, Zarin, I could cancel my trip if you need me right now; really, I could."

Zarin then said this, responding to everyone, "Thank you guys for getting back to me. I'm just in a very shitty situation right now. And Nica, I'm not sure if he is *exactly*. I just heard him talking to a woman on the phone about having a baby and how he's *not* going to tell me about it. And Tomi, please, you don't have to cancel your trip. I could be just a little paranoid or jumping to conclusions. I just wanted to let you all know. I'm not very happy right now."

They all continued with the group chat for another twenty minutes. Wendy then told Zarin that she would meet up with her the following evening. Zarin then said to the others not to worry and that she will be okay.

As Zarin laid on her bed, she heard little soft footsteps coming up the stairs, as it was Darsha and Joshna making their way to bed. Neal was following behind them, as he promised he would read them a bedtime story. As Neal was in the girls' bedroom, Zarin grew more curious to find out exactly who he was talking to on his phone. His phone was five feet away from Zarin, right there on his nightstand. Zarin wanted to check his phone, but she did not want to be caught by Neal. So, she got out of her bed and tip-toed her way to Darsha and Joshna's room, just to make sure Neal was still reading to them. But Zarin knew she had very little time, as she saw the girls' eyes growing heavy, ready to fall asleep.

Zarin quickly tip-toed back to her bedroom, crawled over to Neal's side of the bed, and tried to unlock his phone. Being that Neal had an iPhone, it required a passcode. For Zarin's first attempt, she put the numbers of his birthday; *access denied*. Her second attempt was Darsha's birthday, but no luck. The third attempt was *Joshna's* birthday. Unfortunately, the passcode had rejected her entry again. Zarin had two more attempts left before the iPhone would be disabled. So, she had to make them count. She had to think quickly and sharp;

what other event could be the numbers to Neal's passcode? Then she thought, "Oh my God, our anniversary." As she put the numbers of the date of their anniversary, Neal's iPhone unlocked.

Zarin made a quick jester of celebration as she figured out Neal's passcode to his iPhone. She was in, and she did not know where to begin. First, Zarin looked at his text messages. She did not see anyone suspicious—some of his colleagues from his office. And some of their mutual friends from events and parties. But nothing explicit such as nude photos from women or nude pictures of himself. But as Zarin took a look at his recent call history, she noticed an unknown number with an unfamiliar name. The obscure name was "Meli." She never heard of a Meli before. However, when she looked at that particular phone call, it went for as long as forty minutes, so Neal had quite a conversation with this "Meli" woman.

Zarin was hesitant now, hesitant to push that call button and talk to "Meli." She urged to hear her voice, but still, she hesitated. Zarin was going back and forth about calling this woman. Then suddenly, Zarin received a phone call from *her* phone, and it was her mother. Zarin then put down *Neal's* phone to answer her phone.

"Mom, yes, what's going on?" Zarin said as she wants to make this as quick of a phone call as possible.

"Zarin, did you talk to Darsha about the phone?" Zarin's mother asked with a rigorous tone of voice.

"Oh my God, mom! Yes! Neal and I both talked to her! Now please, go to bed! Good night!" Zarin said as she took some of her reserved frustration out on her mother.

As Zarin then hung up *her* phone, she noticed a voice, a woman's voice coming from Neal's phone, and it was *not* Siri. As she looked, Zarin realized that she accidentally pressed the call button on that unknown number, and "Meli" picked up.

"Hello, Neal, is that you?" Hello, Neal?" "Meli" shouted through the phone.

Zarin quickly hung up the phone. After that, she then did something that she thought would be best for her family. Zarin blocked the number. She deleted the call history and blocked the number to keep "Meli" from calling Neal. At that moment, it gave Zarin a small fragment of closure, as she thought in her mind that she was just protecting her family. But the reality is, Zarin is terrified to face the unknown truth that will soon reveal itself.

Zarin then placed Neal's iPhone back on his nightstand as Neal made his way back into the bedroom. Neal headed into the bathroom to freshen up while Zarin put on a burnt orange nightgown and hopped back into bed. Even though she blocked the number, she realized that there were still some unanswered questions burning inside her. Perhaps blocking the number was a disservice to her. Now she cannot prove anything. Her swift impulse could have been an impulsive mistake.

Neal finally came out of the bathroom and got undress, all the way down to his Tommy Hilfiger boxer briefs. He then slid underneath the covers, leaned over to Zarin, kissed her, and said, "Goodnight, baby." Zarin hesitated briefly and finally responded, saying, "Goodnight."

Not the best way for Zarin to end the night, that's for sure. However, the one thing that will stick in her mind for quite some time is that woman's voice. Zarin knows that even though she blocked that number from Neal's phone, this will not be the last time "Meli" reaches the surface. She understands that it is far from over, and the fact that Neal is hiding this from her applies the unwanted pressure she is receiving. After sixteen years, Zarin hopes that she is not lying side-by-side with a self-serving, adulterous pig that broke her heart.

Chapter 4

A n early Sunday morning flight awaits miss Tomi Belacone. But Tomi is not flying alone as she is bringing aboard her entourage. Her hair and makeup artist, Nicole, her publicist, Cassandra, and her two bodyguards, Omar and Harrison. Last but not least, her protégé, her lovely assistant, Carmelo. Carmelo is Tomi's pride and joy; she adores every little bit of him. Carmelo is what you would call a flamboyant, charismatic ball of fire. A six-foot-tall, incredibly handsome young man, hair and makeup always on point, olive skin tone, and neatly groomed stubble facial hair. A multi-cultural background: Carmelo just looks like something out of a dream. I bet you're wondering what his sexual orientation is, right? Well, that would be his business, yea? Let's just say he is a balanced lover, although his love life has been off-balance, leaning more on the men's side.

As they are making their way to the airport in Tomi's stretch limousine, her assistant, Carmelo, is going over the schedule for the next four days. As Carmelo goes over the list, he says, "Okay, Ms. Bellas, so, later on, this afternoon, you will have lunch with some new potential buyers. You also are planning to take a look at a few houses in Beverly Hills and Calabasas. And you said you wanted to take a look at the *Orell Llero* storefront at the Beverly Hills location, correct?"

As Tomi was finishing up some emails on her phone, she responded, "Oh, yes, yes, that all sounds *wonderful*. Fabulous, I love it. And did you schedule my consultation with Dr. Ginger for Monday?" Carmelo responded, "I did, and she cannot wait to see you." As they are still riding, closely approaching the airport, Carmelo said to Tomi, "You know Ms. Bellas, I still cannot believe you get Botox done by this *one* and *only* doctor, who lives three-thousand miles away from you. You don't trust anyone else?" Tomi responded, "Oh fuck no! Melo, my love, Dr. Ginger is a *bad bitch*. She takes care of me, she knows my face, my bone structure, and she *never* disappoints me. I don't care if she's on the *moon*; I'll *Apollo 11* my ass right to her before I let anyone else touch my face." A round of laughter comes from her entourage.

For the last nine years, Tomi and Carmelo's bond has been robust and sustainable. She met him at a fashion show as she was looking to scout new models for her men's collection for *Orell Llero*. As soon as Carmelo hit the runway, Tomi was livid. She completely drooled and gaged over him. As he then walked the catwalk, Tomi could not take her eyes off of him. She knew that he had to be the face of the men's brand for her line. After the fashion show came to an end, Tomi went backstage and asked to speak with Carmelo. As he walked towards Tomi, he had on nicely fitted black jeans and a crispy white tank top, absolutely no wrinkles. Tomi introduced herself and shook Carmelo's hand.

"Hi babe, I'm Tomi Belacone. You did such an excellent job tonight," Tomi said to Carmelo.

"Oh, thank you so much! That means so much to me. I'm Carmelo McDaniel," Carmelo spoke. "Um, is it okay if I call you "*Ms. Bellas*?"

"Hmm…Well, since I *adore* you, I'll allow you, and *only* you, to address me as "*Ms. Bella*," Tomi said with a sense of humor.

"Oh no, Ms. *Bellas*, with an "*s*."

"Okay, my dear, Ms. *Bellas*, with an "*s*" it is."

Tomi became infatuated, instantly fell in love with him. Though he was doing well with his modeling career, Tomi did not like the choices he was making off of the runway. She did not like the company Carmelo was keeping around him. He was being young and reckless, showing up late to go-sees with hangovers. So, Tomi got in contact with him. She sat him down one day and said, "Melo, baby, I have seen it all. I have seen young, gorgeous men like yourself hit rock bottom in this industry. I even had to bury some of these young men because their families could not afford funeral services. *Please* do not be another statistic; please do not put me through that heartache once again."

Carmelo was so touched that Tomi even cared so much. He found a mother figure in Tomi, as his real family kicked him to the curve because of his unapologetic sexual identity. Tomi loved him as if he was her son, and she wanted nothing but the best for him. So, she brought him under her wing, kept a close eye on him, and ended up making him her assistant. And for the last eight years, he has been Tomi's knight and shining armor.

As they made it to the airport, Tomi gathered her things together, carrying her $150,000 handbag from her brand's 2023 collection. This bag is so luxurious that armed security *delivers* the bag to the buyer's house. A buyer cannot buy it right out of one of the stores because the security risk is too high.

Exiting out of the limo, Tomi thanked her limo driver, Benjamin, with a $2,500 tip. As Tomi and her entourage made their way up the stairs of her private jet, the flight attendants greet her with fruit and champagne, as well as *Rice Crispy Treats*, which is Tomi's favorite. Tomi even had a name for her private jet; she called it "Robin." She named her jet plane "Robin" from the song *"Fly Robin Fly."* A song by the German disco group, *Silver Convention*. Tomi's mother played that song constantly when she was a little girl.

As Tomi and her entourage settled on the plane, she sent a group text to the other ladies, letting them know that she is about to take flight. In her text, she said, "Good morning, my beautiful loves. I'm about to go *California Dreamin'* and just wanted to say I love you all, and I'll let you know when I have landed."

"I love you too," and heart emojis were the responses from the other ladies. The captain was ready to close the plane door and hit the runway. Right before the plane takes off, Tomi always likes to do a brief prayer right there in her seat. It is her ritual for every flight she takes, praying for a safe flight. The plane takes off, making its way up in the cloudy winter sky. At first, a little turbulence, but smooth sailing for the rest of the trip as Tomi takes her last sip of champagne and sleeps through the whole flight.

About five and a half hours later, *Robin* safely lands in Los Angeles. The entourage begins to clap their hands, celebrating the safe landing. The sound of clapping hands woke Tomi up as she realized that they have landed, and she too began to clap her hands. As the jet plane was making its way down the runway to a complete stop, Tomi then texts the ladies to let them know that she landed safely. The ladies were happy to know she arrived safely and gave her well wishes. Tomi then sent a text to her husband, Thomas. In that text, she said, "Hey my love, I have arrived safely in your hometown. The weather is crystal clear, with the sun shining down on the city of Angels. I'm going to close some deals, possibly buy a new house for us, and I will hurry back to you. Love you much."

Tomi and Thomas have been together since they were teenage kids. They met each other in a rather funny but embarrassing way. Tomi was a model when she was eighteen years old, and Thomas was a model as well. One night during a fashion show, Tomi walked the runway while Thomas was already out on the runway. Not even 6 feet out, the heel on Tomi's shoe broke off, which sent her face-first to the floor. She laid there on the runway in front of hundreds of onlookers, absolutely embarrassed. Until this very handsome young model made his way back down the runway and did something relatively humane; he lent Tomi a helping hand and helped her up. Before he headed backstage, he said to her, "make it count." Tomi then got herself back in character, took off the broken shoe, as well as the other, and continued her catwalk down the runway barefooted. As she looked at some of the onlookers from her side vision, she could see the smirked faces as they had their chuckles. As Tomi made it backstage, she saw Thomas get crucified by the creative director.

"*Never* drop out of fucking character. If someone takes a fall, walk over the bitch!" The creative director viciously said to Thomas. Not only did Tomi feel embarrassed about taking that fall, but she also felt responsible for getting Thomas in trouble with the creative director. But Thomas is a Leo, and he did not sit quietly after the creative director snapped at him. Thomas let him have a taste of his own medicine. "What the fuck is your problem, asshole? She fell and hurt herself. Have some damn compassion," Thomas said with vexed emotion.

The creative director fired Thomas on the spot. He told Thomas that he will never work in this business ever again. But Thomas could care less. He had other goals and dreams already set for his life. After that night, Tomi and Thomas stayed connected. They loved how they share the same name, even though the spelling is different.

Thomas, a Los Angeles native, coming from hippie parents who were very proactive in the sixties, had much knowledge of the world and was very interested in being an artist. When Thomas was a child, he would love to play with blocks. Thomas would make little buildings with blocks, even skyscraper type of buildings. One day, when Thomas was nine, he built a skyscraper, and the blocks came tumbling down unexpectedly, hitting him on the right side of his face. Surprisingly, it left an open wound. His father rushed him to the emergency room because he needed stitches. After the injury healed, it left a long scar on Thomas' right cheek. Growing up, kids teased him about it. Kids would call him "Scarface" or "Tommy Montana." But Thomas was always a strong person. He would always laugh with people instead of taking it personally.

But the scar left on Thomas's face was a mark for his destiny. After he retired from modeling, he went on to college to pursue his dream as an architect. When it comes to designs, Thomas is a creative genius. He was the architect who designed Tomi's new *Orell Llero* storefront in Manhattan, which is soon to be open for the public. Thomas's work became well known in a brief period. He has developments all over the world now.

Not only that, but Thomas has also done very well as a sculptor. He loves sculpting images of people. But the brilliant thing is that he puts a scar on their faces when he sculpts those people. I guess you could say that placing a scar on the faces of the figures he sculpts has become his signature brand. Thomas' message with that is *"everyone comes with a story."* Some stories are worth writing about, and some are worth sculpting and carving. It is his way of saying to the world; no one is perfect.

As Tomi and her entourage hit the LA rush hour traffic on the highway, Thomas replied to Tomi's text. He said, "Hey baby, I'm so glad you made it there safely. I am so proud of you and your success and with potentially closing this deal with the buyers. I am honored to be your husband." Thomas sure knows how to draw out a few tears from Tomi. She thanked him with a dozen heart emojis and a selfie of her beautiful smile that could melt your heart into a red puddle.

The traffic was beginning to open up, Tomi and her crew were on their way to the Beverly Hills Hotel. Tomi loves staying in such a luxurious atmosphere. It inspires her to keep focused and motivated to be successful. She was driving around Beverly Hills, looking at all the palm trees, all the storefronts on Rodeo Drive, including seeing *her* storefront. Los Angeles is her home away from home. But the one thing Tomi loves to do every time she is in LA, she loves to drive by the famous nightclub, "Whisky a Go-Go" on the Sunset Strip. It is the nightclub that featured her all-time favorite band, The Doors. When I say Tomi is *obsessed* with Jim Morrison, she is *smitten*. She learned about The Doors from her mother.

Interestingly enough, Thomas talked about how his mother went to a concert back in the sixties, premiering The Doors. His mother was able to snap many pictures of the band members; John Densmore, Robby Krieger, Ray Manzarek, and Jim. Thomas also mentioned to Tomi how his mother even snuck a kiss on Jim

Morrison's cheek. After she did that, Jim shouted, "Alright, Alright, ALRIGHT!"

The entourage finally arrived at the Beverly Hills Hotel. As Tomi exited out of the limo with her costly handbag, she noticed a woman with two small children walking out of the hotel lobby. Tomi saw the three of them, surrounded by this aura of happiness. One of the children, a little girl, said, "I love you, mommy." The mother responded, "and I love you too, baby. I love both of you. You both make me such a happy mother." When Tomi saw that, she could not help but feel a sudden pinch of sadness, as *she* is not a mother.

Tomi then checked into her luxurious suite, close to five grand a night, and that is just pennies for her. Tomi gave separate rooms for her two bodyguards, Omar and Harrison. Nicole, her makeup and hairstylist, Cassandra, and Carmelo all stayed in the same suite. As they all get settled in, Tomi sends a personal text to Zarin to make sure she is doing okay after knowing about Zarin's "*oink* situation." Tomi texts Zarin saying, "Zarin, my love, just reaching out to you again to see how you're doing today? I will be a bit busy for the next several days, but just know I am thinking of you girl. And when I get back to the city, we will get to the bottom of this together. I love you."

In no time, Zarin replied by saying, "I don't know what I would do without you or the others. You have no idea how much I love and appreciate you. And yes, I'm still hurt and upset. I blocked the other woman's number from his phone. I don't know if that will help. But I'm just not ready to face the reality of this. I'm so scared, Tomi."

A sudden pain, a sudden sense of sorrow began to overwhelm Tomi after reading Zarin's text. She feels an enormous amount of grief for her friend right now. Tomi responded to Zarin, saying, "I know you're scared, baby. But deep down, I have a feeling that this is all a huge misunderstanding. But we will get to the bottom of this. Just play it cool, and don't let Neal know what you now know." Tomi then begins to text, one by one, the other ladies, telling them to look after Zarin and that she will be back as soon as possible.

A group of quick knocks came tapping on the master bedroom door. Carmelo was outside the door, letting Tomi know that they are ready to head out to the meeting with the buyers. Tomi confirmed and asked that they give her a few more minutes. A lot on her mind for the day. About her business moves, about her friends, and herself. But now is not the time. Tomi leaves those thoughts of doubt in the hotel room and gets ready to be *Tomi Belacone*, Fashion designer extraordinaire.

Chapter 5

B ack in Manhattan, some three-thousand miles away from Los Angeles. As well as being three hours ahead of the pacific time zone, Monica is up and making a late breakfast for her family on a Sunday morning. The coffee is dripping in the glass pot; the eggs scrambled, toast, and jam on the table. Monica loves to cook when she has the time and when her husband, Sammy, is in town. She likes to enjoy the moments when they are together as a family and enjoy a homecooked meal.

Sammy is a well-known, world-famous trumpeter; most of the time, he is out of town on a gig or recording sessions at the studio. Yet Monica and Sammy manage to do very well as coparents, as well as being happily married. As Monica just finished cooking the last few strips of turkey bacon, her son Miles makes his way down the stairs into the kitchen.

"Good morning baby, where's my sugar?" Monica said to Miles as she opened her arms for an affectionate embrace.

"Good morning, mommy; look, I lost another tooth," Miles said as he pointed at the open space of his smile.

"Aww, baby, where's the tooth?" Monica asked.

"It fell down the sink while I was brushing my teeth," Miles laughed.

Monica then kissed Miles on his forehead and told him to get his sister and bring her down for breakfast. Sammy was still upstairs; before Monica came down to cook, he was already in the shower. As Monica turned the stove off and had all the food ready, she went into the living room to grab her phone. She saw the text messages from the group chat. Her concerns for Zarin were growing by the hour. She felt that she wanted to help but did not know what she could do for her friend.

Monica then sent a private text to Zarin to reach out to her and see how she is doing. In the text, Monica said, "Hey my sistah, I know you are hurting right now. If you need anything, let me know. You do not have to deal with this alone. We have your back." As Monica sent that text to Zarin, her husband Sammy made his way down to the kitchen table. Monica then made her way back to the kitchen, giving Sammy four consecutive good morning kisses.

Sammy; a six-foot three-inch handsome man. Well-built and two years shy from hitting the big "four-zero." Desirable features but could not grow a full beard to save his life. So, for the most part, he keeps his face clean-shaven.

"Good morning, wifey; I see you still have on your hair bonnet cap. You know I was disappointed last night when you put it on and got in bed," Sammy sarcastically said to Monica. "Look, you can't be hittin' it every single night now. Momma needs a break. Besides, I have so much on my plate right now," Monica said to Sammy as she poured him a cup of coffee. Sammy laughed and responded, saying, "Alright, I'll give you a *little* a break," Sammy said as he gave Monica a quick tap on her voluptuous bottom. "Mmmm…You just took me back to when we first met. You were *so* goddamn drunk that night," Monica said as she strolls down memory lane.

Back when Monica was in her final year of law school at Rutgers University, she had to do some community service for a particular scholarship she received while she attended the school. So, Monica was a volunteer at a ticket booth for a jazz performance. It was only for two nights; Monica did not mind collecting tickets for the jazz performances. Monica would always have these uniquely colored nails with such abstract designs. As she ripped the tickets and handed them back to the guest, the guest would always compliment her on her nails.

On the first night of the performance, a tall, handsome, brown-skinned man made his way towards Monica. The moment she laid her eyes on him, she felt his instant charisma. It was as if he had gravitational pull with her, pulling her into his world, simply with his eyes. As he came closer to her in the ticket booth, he said to Monica, "Excuse me, I am one of the musicians performing tonight. Can you point me in the direction of the green room?" As Monica observed this handsome man, she responded, "Not until you tell me your name."

He smiled at her with a growing spark of chemistry. He said, "My name is Sammy, Taylor. Sammy Taylor. And you are?" For a brief second, in her mind, Monica pictured how her name would sound if her last name were "Taylor." Yes, she was already thinking of having this man's last name. "Excuse me; I asked what your name is," Sammy said. "Oh, sorry; my name is Monica James. And the green room is rather complicated to direct you. So, I'll just walk you to it," Monica said as she exited out of the ticket booth to escort Sammy.

For the three-minute walk that it took for them to reach the green room, both Monica and Sammy had a swift exchange of words, enough that created an interesting conversation. A conversation that they wanted to continue after the performance.

They both agreed to meet up after the concert and have drinks. And since Monica was a volunteer, she was able to watch the jazz performance for free.

The show began; Monica took a seat at the very back of the auditorium. Monica did nothing except kept her eyes on Sammy. She did not know what exact instrument he played until he took it out of his bag. It was a shiny blue trumpet. And when Sammy put that trumpet to his lips, the music he played; there was just nothing like it. It was hypnotic, thrilling, mysterious, and unpredictable. Sammy had this ritual; he would place a poster of Miles Davis on stage with him for every performance. Miles Davis is his idol, his spiritual mentor, and Miles Davis's poster on stage was like Sammy having his mentor observing his performance. Sammy spent years trying to sound like Miles. Until one day, Sammy found *his* way, *his* craft. Now, he is on the verge of being one of the greatest of his generation.

Monica kept staring, and she kept listening. As she heard his music, she thought in her mind, "I don't *ever* want to let go of this genius." Monica did not move from her seat in that auditorium for the remaining forty-five minutes of the show. She stayed until the show was over. Sammy played "Round About Midnight" and "Nature Boy" during his session, which was all Monica needed to hear to fall in love with him. But the night was far from over.

After the show, Sammy and Monica went out for those drinks. But little did Monica know; Sammy liked the bottle a little more than he should. Even though Monica was twenty-one and of age to drink, she was not much of a drinker. Just give her *a* Corona Light or a Heineken, and she was good to go. But Sammy, Sammy loved the *dark* liquor, which then brought out the dark side of him.

About five shots of vodka, Sammy was loose, Sammy was wild. Monica's interest in him was still there, but his aggressive behavior put her interest on the decline. After a while, Monica was becoming uncomfortable with Sammy and was ready to call it a night. But before she headed out, she told him that she had to use the ladies' room. As she got up from out of her seat, Sammy did something to her that was the ultimate red flag. He gave her a heavy-handed smack on her butt.

Monica was livid; she turned around with a look of absolute shock and humiliation. Sammy saw the look in her eyes. He knew at that moment, he upset her and screwed up. Monica then sat back down and had an adult conversation with Sammy.

Monica, with an angry tone, said, "My brother, I don't know who the fuck you have me confused with, but don't you *EVER* put your Goddamn hands on me in such a degrading, vulgar, and shameful way. How fucking dare you?" Sammy sobered up quite a bit after Monica let him have it, as she should have. And being that Monica was a law student, she knew all her rights and knew she could have him thrown in jail.

Sammy felt a colossal amount of guilt and sorrow. As Monica sat there with a stern look on her face, staring him down with the heavy expectation of an apology. Looking at the half-empty shot glass on the table, Sammy realized that he outdid himself this time. He then looked at Monica and said, "Monica, I am so sorry for inappropriately placing my hands on you and embarrassing you. I'm very drunk and just out of my character right now. Please forgive me; I'm so sorry."

Monica is not one to just microwave forgiveness. It takes her some time to accept apologies and to forgive people. Still a little disgusted with Sammy, she collected her things and left the bar. But before Monica left, Sammy quickly said, "Wait, if I could just ask you, do you have a favorite song?" Monica turned her head to look at him, confused at the question, but just gave him a random song as she said, *"Everything"* by Mary J. Blige. Then Monica speed-walked out of the bar that night.

It was the following night, which was the last night of the two-night jazz performance. Sammy and Monica meet again. Well, they crossed paths in the lobby, neither exchange one word with each other—a few glances at each other, but no dialogue. Then came the show, Monica took the same seat she had the previous night, and she let her ears go on to a musical paradise. When it was time for Sammy to do his piece, he played a very familiar tone, a tone that Monica instantly recognized. Sammy was playing, with his trumpet, the song *"Everything"* by Mary J. Blige.

The audience enjoyed it, but not half as much as Monica did. From ear to ear, she smiled as Sammy played the song. Even though Monica was still a little upset with him for his improper behavior, there was a better side of him that she could not ignore. A sweet, brilliant, and romantic side that she wants to discover. They still had much to learn about each other, but what sold her is when after Sammy finished playing, he walked over to the microphone and said, "Thank you very much. I would like to dedicate that song and playing for you all this evening to my future wife. Even though we met yesterday, even though I almost blew it so soon, but I know one day, she's going to be "Mrs. Taylor."

Monica was surprised at such a statement made by Sammy but could not help to shed joyous tears. She then stood up from her seat and began to clap her hands, which encouraged the rest of the audience to give Sammy another standing ovation. Thus, Monica reached the finish line of forgiveness from that night on, and she eventually became "Mrs. Taylor."

Back at the kitchen table, Monica and Sammy talked about how their first night became their worst night. Then Miles and Briana made their way down the stairs to the kitchen table to have breakfast. Briana, who turned six last September, was still a little tired and was not fully awake. In addition, she had some missing barrettes from her braids, as well as a lost earring.

"Bri, where's your earring?" Monica said to Briana.

"Um…It might still be on my pillow, mommy," Briana responded with an unsure face.

"I told you, you toss and turn too much in your sleep for you to be sleeping with them in your ears. So many of your barrettes are lost," Monica said as she pours the kids some Orange Juice.

As everyone was sitting, chowing away on their breakfast, Monica's phone received a notification. She did not want to take a look at her phone during family time and assumed that Zarin responded to the text she sent earlier that morning. So, Monica decided to wait. Sammy was the first to finish his meal, but he wanted some more coffee. So, as he was about to get up with his coffee mug, Monica said, "Oh, baby, please, have a seat. I'll pour you some more coffee."

Monica, without question, adored being a courteous wife to her husband and a mother to her children. Nothing made her happy to feel wanted, needed by her family. And she loved nothing more than to take care of them. So, as Monica poured the coffee, Sammy kissed her on her hand and said, "Thanks, babe, I appreciate you."

"That's weird, daddy; who kisses on a hand?" Briana said as she was sipping on her Orange Juice.

"It's not that bad, better than kissing ass," Miles said bluntly.

"Hey! Boy, where did you hear that from?" Sammy said as he pinched Miles' shoulder.

"From grandma's house, on T.V.," Miles said, looking back and forth at Sammy and Monica.

Even though Miles said it was from the television, Sammy knew precisely where that language came from instantly. It came from *his* parents. Sammy's parents babysit both Miles and Briana. Whenever Monica is having a busy day at the law firm or when Sammy is out of town at a gig, his parents are the ones who step up to watch them. Sammy's parents have been married for thirty-seven years, and they have been fighting, verbally like cats and dogs since day one, cussing up a storm.

Sammy knew that what Miles just said came directly from the mouth of either his mother or his father, and Miles just mimicked it. Monica then said to Miles, "Baby, that kind of talking is not for you or your sister to repeat, okay? At ten years old, mommy doesn't want you speaking like that, even *if* you hear it from your grandparents. And that goes for you too, Bri." As Monica turned to look at Sammy, he looked as if he already knows that he has to talk with his parents about their language around the kids. "I know, I know, I know. In fact, I'll call them later on this afternoon, and we'll have a chat," Sammy said to Monica.

Monica did not say a word. Instead, she rolled her eyes and put all the dishes in the sink, rinsing and scrubbing them clean. After that, she told Briana to head up the stairs to find her other earring. Miles made his way into the living room to watch his cartoons.

"Uh, Miles, did you finish your homework?" Monica asked as she walked into the living room.

"Um…Most of it, I think?" Miles said with a guilty look.

Monica took the remote out of Miles' hand and clicked the television off. She then waved her hand, giving him a "bye-bye" gesture. Miles then went upstairs to his room to finish his homework. Monica then picked up her phone. She assumed that the text notification she received was from Zarin, but it was actually from her assistant at the law firm. Her assistant wanted her to know about some discovered documents, which could be helpful for her current case. But being that Monica's case is already at the stage of "closing arguments," those documents are too little, too late.

"Oh, goddamn it! Just what I fucking need," Monica shouted with anger and frustration.

"Uh, yea, talking about *my* parents' language, you're doing very well yourself," Sammy said as he laughs and sips his coffee in the kitchen.

Monica ignored Sammy's sarcasm as she reached in her briefcase to look over her written statement for her closing argument. As she received an email about the new documents, she felt that her case would be solid even without it, and her confidence within herself would leave her victorious. But even with all that confidence, Monica loves having Sammy around for that support system. So, as she sat down back at the kitchen table with her paperwork, Sammy took her by the hand and said, "You got this, babe, don't stress it all. You've been kicking ass for *months* on this case, and there's no way you're going to lose. So, keep the faith, babe, keep the faith."

A gentle kiss on Monica's hand, as he did before when she poured him coffee. She could not help but give him that same smile that he fell in love with when they first met. The support system between these two is as solid as they come. When Sammy is hard at work or has a gig in the local area, she always makes sure she is there. Even if she is pulling an all-nighter at the firm, she would pack it up and still make her way to see her husband play a midnight session.

His appreciation for her is what she treasures. He loves how knowledgeable she is, her wisdom, her conversations, and then, of course, the fire and drive in her. Monica most definitely has a big day ahead of her this week. This case is one of her most important ones. If she pulls this off, this will exclusively put her and the law firm on the map. But for now, it is time for her to practice.

Chapter 6

A cross town, over on the east side of Manhattan, Collette and her husband Martin are having a *steamy* afternoon delight. They have been going at it for about forty-five minutes, and they do not plan on stopping anytime soon. But then, there came a knock on their bedroom door. At first, Collette and Martin ignored it and kept going, but the second knock came harder and heavier as if the police were knocking the door down.

Being that Martin was on top, missionary, his favorite position, he got off of Collette so she could get the door. Collette then got out of bed, grabbed her robe to cover her naked self, and opened the bedroom door. She had a look on her face that read, "What the fuck do you want?" It was Mia at their bedroom door, giving off a smirky grin, as she already knew what her parents were doing on the inside. "I'm sorry to disturb you two porn stars, but can I have some money for Starbucks?" Mia asked with a sense of sarcasm.

Collette closed the door, grabbed a crispy green bill with Ulysses S. Grant's face on it, and said to Mia, "Take this and come back in an hour and a half." Mia took the money and went on her way. Collette then disrobed herself and jumped on top of Martin, now in *her* favorite position, the cowgirl position. She began to ride him like an equestrian. Collette was giving Isabell Werth a run for her money.

About three positions later, their afternoon delight reached its orgasmic destination. They laid there in their damped sheets, completely satisfied. Even though Martin is not super fit, he can please his wife in the bedroom; make no mistake about it.

As she laid there in bed, Collette began to think about whether or not her sex drive with Martin is somehow the trigger for Mia's recent odd behavior. As mentioned earlier, Mia, suspended from school for bringing a sex toy and cannabis. One of her classmates snitched her out, and she then had to go to the office.

The school called Collette immediately and informed her of Mia's situation. Surprised at what she heard, Collette went straight to the school and confronted Mia about this bizarre situation. Mia, however, decided not to tell her mother the truth about where and how she came about obtaining a dildo and a dime bag of cannabis.

Lying in bed next to Martin, Collette said, "Babe, do you think us doing what we do is the reason why Mia brought the dildo and weed to school? I mean, we make love on the regular, and she's not stupid; she knows what we do in our bedroom. But I'm a little nervous now that our sexual behavior may be triggering something in her or perhaps motivating her to grow up too fast." Martin looked at Collette with reassurance and responded, saying, "Honey, that is nonsense. She made a mistake. Teenagers make mistakes *all* the time, and they get into trouble. I believe she has learned a valuable lesson. When she is ready to sit down with us and talk, she'll tell us the whole truth. We're her parents, and I know she trusts us. I just don't want *you* to worry about it."

Martin then gave Collette a double kiss as he then got out of bed, walking in the nude towards the bathroom. He asked Collette if she wanted to join him in the shower. She respectfully declined the offer and said she would wait until he finishes. Collette decided to wait for Mia to come back home. She wanted to have that girl talk, a little one-on-one conversation with her daughter.

Collette then stepped out of bed, put on some underwear and robe, and made her way to the kitchen to brew some decaffeinated coffee. She stopped drinking regular caffeinated coffee after she suffered an anxiety attack one early morning during an appointment with one of her clients. Collette felt that her anxiety was due to the caffeinated coffee and made a switch to drink only decaf.

As the coffee began to ripple into the pot, smelling the French Roast aroma in the air, Mia finally made her way back home, just in time for her and Collette to have their sit down and talk about what happened at school.

"Mia, baby, come here. I want to talk to you," Collette said as Mia was on her way to her room.

"Ma, can this wait, *please*?" Mia said as she tries to plead her way out of talking.

"NO, come here, have a seat."

Mia then took off her jacket and Ugg boots, placed them in the hallway closet, and made her way to the kitchen table. Collette began to pour the freshly brewed coffee into her favorite coffee mug that says, *"There's Nothing Realer Than a*

REALTOR." Her realtor company had those made, and she loved them.

Collette then poured her half and half cream into her coffee, stirring the cream in with a spoon, and took a seat at the kitchen table across from Mia. Collette wanted nothing but the truth from Mia. She wanted to know what precisely motivated Mia to number one, bring a sex toy and weed to school, and number *two*, is she indulging in drug use and using the dildo on herself? Collette did not want the conversation to come off like an interrogation. She made the conversation more settled with Mia. "So, are you up to date with all your assignments? Because you're going to be out of school for another week," Collette asked Mia. "Yes, I'm keeping up with everything. I miss being in school, though, with my friends," Mia responded while she took a bite out of the cinnamon roll from Starbucks.

Collette then gave a few blows to her steaming hot coffee and then took a sip. As she was sipping, Collette wanted to discuss not *why* Mia brought a sex toy and weed to school but where or *who* she got them from initially. Sitting there in the kitchen with Mia, Collette said, "So, you've received your punishment from the school, you've received punishment from your father and me, so, it is what it is. But what *I* want to know is who gave you those things? Did one of your friends give it to you? Did you take it from someone? I want nothing but the truth from you, Mia."

Mia looked at her mother with a face of exposure and defeat. Mia knew she could not lie out of this situation. Only the truth could be helpful to her at this time. But still, she was hesitant to say. "Mia, this is *mommy* you're talking with, not the police. I need you to tell me who gave you those things. Even if you're exposing someone else that you don't want us to know. I want to know the truth, baby," Collette said with a concerned look in her eyes.

"I found them," Mia said as she began to shed a few tears.

"Where, baby? Where did you find them?" Collette asked.

As Mia was fixing to say where she found the dildo and weed, a key made its way into the lock, the front door opened, and incomes Emilio. Emilio, Collette's oldest, moved out into his apartment several months ago while taking courses at New York University.

Collette was delighted to see Emilio, so much that she cut the conversation with Mia short, got up from the kitchen table, and went over to hug Emilio. As Collette hugged and kissed Emilio, she said, "Papi, I'm so happy you came to visit. How's the apartment going?" Emilio went on to tell Collette about how his life is going. They both made their way into the living room to have a conversation.

Five minutes go by, Collette and Emilio were having a *wonderful* mother-and-son conversation while Collette completely neglected the mother-and-daughter conversation she was having with Mia. Mia did not take that lightly; she took it to heart. "Great conversation, mom! Yea, let's do that again sometime!" Mia sarcastically said as she stormed off to her room and slammed the door. "Is everything alright? What's wrong with her? She didn't even *speak* to me," Emilio said to Collette.

"Oh, she's been having a rough week. She was suspended from school. I don't even want to *say* what for. I don't want to embarrass her," Collette responded. "I see; well, I just came by because I left some things in my old room that I wanted to get for my apartment. Is dad around?" Emilio said as he got up from the living room couch, heading to his old room. "Yea, your father's in the shower, you know how he likes to take those one-hour showers. I'm going to take a shower myself. Maybe while I freshen up, you can talk to her?" Collette asked Emilio. "Sure, yeah, I'll have a *big brother* talk with her," Emilio responded.

Collette headed back into her bedroom. Martin was still in the shower, singing "*Qué Lío*" by Hector Lavoe and Willie Colón. Collette then made her way towards the bathroom as she stripped down in complete nude. Collette began to sing in duet with Martin, as this is their favorite song. Collette opened the glass shower door and said to Martin, "Did you save some warm water for me? Martin then responded as he looked at Collette from top to bottom, "As hot as you are, babe, you'll keep us both warm in here." In the shower, Collette told Martin that Emilio stopped by and that he's going to talk with Mia.

As they both soaked in the water, they also soaked in the romantic moment. The two were passionately kissing each other all over. Martin, firmly gripping Collette's right breast with her back pressed against his chest. Her head turned as she kisses him, shower drops cruising down their naked anatomy.

Their love for each other is very amorous, as you can tell. It has been that way since the very first time they met. It was love at first sight for both of them. However, the timing could not have been worse.

Twenty-one years ago, when Collette and Martin met for the first time. Collette was nineteen at that time, and Martin was twenty-four years of age. They met at an engagement party, *Martin's* engagement party to be exact. Collette was working as a manager for the venue that the engagement party was held. Collette's father owned the venue.

When Martin walked into the venue and saw Collette for the first time, he grew such a colossal infatuation for her. Collette was flawless, with long dark brown hair with highlights, the natural curves of a true Latina, and a face of beauty, as close to perfection as it could reach. Martin had a hard time focusing on his fiancée that night.

Not to mention, Collette also kept *her* eyes on Martin. Martin had such great individual style, nicely dressed, handsome features. Collette loved how he was clean-shaven with a thin mustache and black slicked-back hair. Martin reminded her of the Gomez Addams character, and she wanted to be his Morticia. It was something about Collette that pulled Martin in instantly.

That same night, after Martin raised his glass and made a toast, he excused himself from the engagement party to use the restroom. He ran into Collette in the hallway and introduced himself. They began to exchange some words, and then they exchanged numbers. A few days later, they met up and *exchanged* what you would call "bodily fluids" during their sexual intercourse. Collette, who was very aggressive about having Martin, was not willing to settle for being his mistress on the side. She refused to be a woman living in his doubled life.

On the night of Martin and his fiancée's rehearsal dinner, Collette came to the dinner with some essential news to share with Martin. Have you ever heard of something being both good news and bad news? Well, that is what Collette had for Martin. When she saw Martin at the rehearsal dinner, Martin was furious as he told her that this is *not* where she should be.

But that good news/bad news, Collette shares it with him. She tells Martin that she is now pregnant with his child. Martin was in complete disbelief. Collette looked at him and said to him that she is having *their* child, and he has to do what has to be done. Collette was *very* aggressive about this situation and was not taking any rejection from him.

Collette told Martin that he has to call off the wedding. But him being a man, Martin was not going to allow Collette to order him around. So, he ignored Collette and went on to marry his fiancée, Lily Lopez.

The months went by quickly, and Collette was not willing to go away so quietly. She was able to have a quiet, low-key relationship with Martin. It was sneaky, but it was what it was. They had a child now, and Martin was in love with Collette. But the situation he put himself in was a terrible one. He was now married, with a woman on the side—Collette, and *their* infant son, Emilio.

Martin's doubled life ran smoothly with Collette until one afternoon; he was caught red-handed by his then-wife, Lily. She saw Martin walking down Lexington Avenue, holding Emilio in his right arm and holding hands with Collette. If only you could see the shock of devastation, the disappointment, and heartbreak in Lily's eyes. Martin knew at that moment; he could not explain himself out of that situation. And that he was a liar, a deliberate cheater, and he betrayed his wife, Lily. At that moment, Martin handed Emilio over to Collette and tried to make his way towards his wife, Lily. But she walked out to the curb, hailed down a cab, got in, and drove off.

Martin then told Collette to go home and that he will see her later. But as he went to the apartment he was sharing with Lily, she destroyed everything in sight. Lily cut up Martin's clothes. She ruined all of his personal belongings. Lily even took her lipstick and wrote *"Adulterous pig"* all over the walls and "Liar, cheater, bastard" on the bathroom mirror.

Martin's guilt was at an all-time high, but as mentioned before, Collette was aggressive about what she wanted, and *all* she wanted was Martin and to have *their* family. That night, Martin went to Collette's place and told her that this would be a very shitty and bumping road to come. Weeks later, Martin signed divorce papers, moved in with Collette in a new apartment, and they have been together ever since. They never saw his ex-wife, Lily Lopez, ever again.

Back in the shower, Collette and Martin finished their wet and wild session. Collette dried off, wrapped a towel around her head to dry her hair, and then began to get dressed. Martin did the same, minus putting a towel over his head.

When Collette came out of her bedroom, Mia was in the living room, on the couch, crying. Collette went over to Mia, put her hand on Mia's shoulder, and asked, "Baby, what's wrong?" Mia, a little hesitant to respond, but says, "I can't say, I can't tell you." But Collette, using her aggressive tendencies, said again, "TELL ME, *por favor*!"

Mia then looked at her mother and said, "The dildo and the weed that I brought to school, I found them in Emilio's room.

They belonged to him." It was exactly what Collette thought. And Collette did not know what to say at that moment. Her mind went utterly empty, not a word or thought envisioned. Collette could not process what Mia had just said to her. Collette, still in a bit of a shock, cannot hear or process Martin's voice as he is calling her name. Martin then walked over to Collette to snap her out of the shocking discovery.

"Hey, what the hell is going on? Where's Emilio?" Martin said to Collette.

"Um...I guess he, he went back to his apartment," Collette said to Martin.

Martin took a look at Mia and asked her if she was okay. Collette assured Martin that everything was fine and for him to finish getting dressed. As Collette had some thoughts recovered in her mind, she began to think about Emilio. In her mind, she was asking a question about her son; in her mind, Collette was asking, "Is Emilio *gay*?"

Collette told Mia to go to her room and wait as she will join her in a few minutes. Collette then went into the kitchen and fixed herself a drink, straight vodka. As she took a hard swallow of the third shot, she went to Mia's room, shut the door behind her, and got to the bottom of this bizarre situation.

"Okay, Mia, baby, explain to me again. You found the dildo and little bag of weed in Emilio's room, correct?" Collette asked. "Yes, mommy, it was in one of his dressers. It was *green shirt day* at school that day, but I didn't have a green shirt. I thought Emilio would have one in his room. So, I looked in his dresser and found the dildo and bag of weed hidden in his sock drawer," Mia said as she sat on her bed and confessed everything.

When Collette went to shower with Martin, Emilio went into his room to obtain the dildo and bag of weed. That was his reason for coming home. But when he found that it was missing, he grew worried that someone had found out about him. As he left his room, he went into Mia's room and asked her a question that she was afraid to answer. When she did not answer his question, Emilio just walked away without saying a word, and he left.

So, Collette finally received the answers that she was looking for from Mia. But the answers came with a powerful shock, and now Collette will have to have *another* one-on-one conversation with her son, Emilio. The thing is, Collette has already been dealing with a situation such as this before with another family member.

Before Collette left Mia's room, she made Mia promise not to share this with her father and to keep this between the two of them. Mia could not agree more as she put her thumb and index finger together and rubbed it across her lips, giving the gesture of her keeping her lips sealed.

As Collette left Mia's room, she went back into *her* bedroom, where Martin was getting dressed. He asked again if everything was alright. Collette told him that everything was fine. She then grabbed her phone and began to text Emilio. In the text, Collette said, "Hey Papi, listen, I talked with Mia; she told me where she found the dildo and weed. You know I am not the kind of mother who would judge her own son. I don't want to assume anything. So, how about you and I sit down over dinner one of these nights, and we'll just have a talk. No pressure, just you and me; how does that sound to you?"

After Collette pressed the send button, she then sent a group text to the other ladies, hoping that their day was going better than hers. It seems like all five of them cannot wait until Friday comes to meet up again.

About five minutes later, Emilio responded to Collette. In his response, he said, "I will meet with you. I'm free Wednesday night. Does dad know?" Collette told Emilio that his father does not know the dildo and bag of weed belonged to him and that she will see him on Wednesday evening.

Being a wife is one thing. But being a mother to two kids is another task that comes with hardly *any* breaks and no paychecks: just pure unconditional love. But Collette is somewhat scared of what Emilio has to say. Even though she is not one to judge, she does not know how Martin would feel about this. His one and only son, who is a gay man? How will he respond to that? Will he accept his son as such if that is the case?

Collette will just have to see when she meets with Emilio on that Wednesday evening.

Chapter 7

Later that evening, Wendy met up with Zarin, as she promised, at a very low-key bar and lounge. As Wendy spotted Zarin at the far-end booth, she made her way towards her. Zarin got up, and they gave each other the biggest hug, lingering in the emotional support.

As Zarin and Wendy sat down at the booth, Zarin began to share her appreciation for Wendy coming to see her this evening. "Thanks for coming babe, I didn't want to make a huge fuss with you girls. I know everyone has their own life going on.

But this has been driving me *crazy*. I couldn't sleep last night at all," said Zarin. Wendy saw the intractable pain in Zarin's eyes. Wendy did not know what to say, what to think about her friend's situation, but tried to stir up some words of encouragement.

Wendy then said to Zarin, "I can't even imagine what you're feeling right now, Zarin. But you have to stay strong for your girls and yourself until you figure out this whole situation. But just take me back; what exactly did you hear Neal say?"

Before Zarin began to tell the story, a waitress approaches them at their booth. The waitress asked them if she could offer them a drink. Zarin asked for a Vodka tonic with lime, and Wendy asked for an apple martini. As the waitress went off to grab their drinks, Zarin begins to tell the story. Zarin said, "The other night, while we were having dinner, I went up the stairs to put Darsha's phone in their room. As I put her phone in the room, I heard Neal talking on the phone in our bedroom. I sort of crept my way up to our bedroom door to listen in closely. Then I heard him talking to this woman named "*Meli*." I never heard of a Meli before. But as he talked to her, he said something like, "*You have to have this baby, nobody knows about it, and Zarin doesn't know*." When I heard that, my heart just dropped, Wendy, and when I had the chance, I looked through his phone. I somehow called the girl, Meli, by accident. She answered, but I just hung up and blocked the number. I'm so scared, Wendy. I'm scared to know the truth about my husband, my love, my soulmate, is cheating on me and got another woman pregnant."

As the drinks made their way to the table, Wendy asked the waitress to pour another apple martini, as she will need several for the evening. Wendy felt for Zarin, but she did not entirely agree with Zarin blocking the number. Wendy felt that perhaps if Zarin could have just talked to the woman, Meli, she could have this whole situation figured out.

Wendy said to Zarin, "You know Zarin, I kind of feel that by you blocking that women's number, you may have made things worse. Well, first off, there's social media. Chances are, she'll still be able to get in touch with Neal through the internet. *And* she'll tell him that her number was blocked, and *then* he'll know that you were on his phone. You see?"

Zarin did not see it from that perspective. After what Wendy said, she realized that she could have gotten to the bottom of the situation. But Zarin panicked; she thought that what she was doing was for the best, for her family.

Wendy then gave Zarin some advice about how she should deal with the situation. She told Zarin that she should confront Neal and let him know that she overheard his conversation with "Meli," find out who this woman is and if he is having an affair. Zarin agreed, and she told Wendy that she would talk to him about it when the time was right.

About two Vodka tonics and three apple martinis later, Zarin and Wendy called it a night. Before they headed out, Zarin and Wendy both took a trip to the ladies' room. They grabbed their purses as they walked inside. They both went into their separate stalls and took care of business; Wendy came out first, but Zarin took a little longer than expected. As Wendy finished washing and drying her hands, she heard her name called; softly.

"Wendy? Can you come here real quick?" Zarin said from inside the stall.

"Yea, are you okay?" Wendy responded as she does not know what she's about to see.

The stall door opened just a few inches; as Wendy saw Zarin, still in a squatting position, Zarin said to Wendy, "*So*, I just got my period, and I wasn't expecting to have it for another couple of days, and I don't have any tampons. *Please* tell me you have one?" It was Zarin's lucky night, as Wendy pulled out her only tampon from her purse and gave it to Zarin.

"I'll wait for you outside, okay?" Wendy said as she gave off a light chuckle and walked out of the restroom. Afterward, Wendy and Zarin then headed out of the bar on a cold winter city night. Frost coming out of both of their mouths, and there was not a taxi in sight. But being that Zarin drove, and Wendy took a cab, Zarin told Wendy that she would drive her home. But Wendy lived in a different direction from where Zarin lived and did not want to make Zarin go out of her way. But Zarin did not care. She would take Wendy to Pennsylvania if she had to. These two are close nit.

"Oh my God, Zarin Khan, right? I watch you on the news every day. I'm such a fan. Do you mind if I have a picture? If it's not too much trouble?" Said a stranger, walking on the sidewalk. "Oh, sure thing, honey," Zarin said as she put on her best smile for the selfie.

Even though Zarin is not world-famous such as Tomi, she is well known in New York City as a news journalist/TV news anchor. Zarin has done countless interviews with celebrities, politicians, and just regular everyday people. The public loves her for her body of work.

After Zarin's encounter with the fan, she and Wendy headed in the Range Rover and then took off. As they were driving, Wendy received a phone call from her mother. Wendy's mother, Suzi, is a second-generation born in America, and she still likes to speak with Wendy in Japanese. So, for the next seven minutes, Wendy and her mother had a conversation.

As Zarin made her way to the front of Wendy's apartment building, she was able to find a parking space. Wendy then got off of the phone with her mother and told Zarin a little about the conversation. Wendy said, "I'm sorry, my mother was going on and on. She and my father are planning a trip to Tokyo soon, and they want me and EJ to come with them. But I'm just *too* busy with work. So, they asked if EJ can go with them, but I don't know about that. I think he's a little too young for such a long trip. God forbid something goes wrong, and he's thousands of miles away. *That* won't sit well with me. I know you understand."

Zarin agreed as she responded, "Oh, hell no, that's way too young for EJ to travel without you or Eddie." So, after that, Wendy hugged Zarin and said goodnight. Wendy reminded Zarin to have that conversation with Neal and get to the bottom of what is going on.

Alone in the Range Rover, Zarin was driving back home. She began to think about what she and Wendy previously discussed in the bar. However, Zarin is a little different than her friends. She does not like confrontation or approaching bad situations. She likes to let things flow; her family is everything to her, and she does not want anything to ruin that.

As Zarin stopped at the light, she received a text from Neal. As she read the text, she caught a whiff of anxiety. In the text, Neal typed, "We have to talk about something, something important. So, hurry back home." Zarin did not like how that text made her feel. She was thinking that Neal found out about her blocking "Meli's" number on his phone. A little shocked at the moment, Zarin could not move. The light turned green ten seconds ago, but she did not move. Funnily enough, there was no traffic behind her at the moment. Then the light turned red again; then, finally, she snapped out of it.

Fifteen minutes later, Zarin arrived at her brownstone on the upper west side. She looked at the stairs from inside the Range Rover, as she was a little afraid of what is about to go down with Neal. Her anxiety and paranoia are tag-teaming her right now. But before Zarin went inside, she held onto her black beaded Rudraksha bracelet with the *Om* charm and began to meditate. She stayed inside the car for another ten minutes to relax her nerves, calm herself, and got her breathing under control.

Zarin then got out of the car and walked her way up the stairs. As she opened the front door, she was expecting Neal to be there waiting for her, but he was not. Zarin took off her brown suede boots and jacket and then took a look at her phone. She noticed the time; twelve-thirty-seven in the morning. Zarin had to be up by six o'clock to get herself ready for work and the girls ready for school.

So, Zarin then shut off the hallway light, headed upstairs, took a peek into the girls' room, as they both were sound asleep. She then walked down the hall to *her* bedroom, and there Neal was, lying in bed, fast asleep. He had Zarin all worked up for nothing. It ticked her off, but she was too tired to make a fuss about it. She then got undress and put on her nightgown. As she finished brushing her teeth, she heard Neal's phone sound off.

He then woke up, turned around to his nightstand, and checked his phone. Zarin came from out of the bathroom and looked at Neal. As Neal was looking at his phone, he then looked up at Zarin.

At that moment, Zarin wanted some answers. She decided to take Wendy's advice after all and talk with Neal about what she discovered. As she looked at Neal from the master bathroom, she said, "who's calling and texting you at such a late hour? Is it Meli?" Neal, looking directly at Zarin, was hesitant to respond.

Right in the middle of this tension, Joshna was able to cut right through it as she walked into the bedroom. Walking in the bedroom with her favorite teddy bear, *Dula*, Joshna said, "Mommy, daddy, can I sleep in here with you tonight? I had a bad dream." Neal immediately said yes, as he was trying to circumvent his way around the situation and avoid answering Zarin's question about "Meli."

Zarin now knows that something scandalous is happening. Neal's hiding something from her. As she then picks Joshna up and puts her in the bed, in comes Darsha.

"Is Joshy sleeping in here? Can I sleep in here too?" Darsha asked as she climbed up on the bed.

"I tell you what," said Neal. "You girls can *all* sleep here, and I'm going to sleep on the couch for the night."

Neal then kissed both Darsha and Joshna good night.

As Neal began walking out of the bedroom, Zarin kept her eyes on him every step of the way. The fear and anxiety Zarin possessed from this situation was transforming into anger and hatred towards Neal. Not only is he protecting a secret, but he is now keeping his distance from Zarin.

Why? What is going on? Who is Meli? What is Neal keeping from Zarin that he does not want her to know? As the girls fell asleep on the bed, Zarin laid on *her* side of the bed as tears began to fall horizontally down her face. As Neal's wife, Zarin feels that he should *never* hide something from her. And the fact that he *is*, Zarin believes more than ever now, that heartbreak is soon to come in their love life and their marriage.

Chapter 8

A few days go by, on a Wednesday morning, to be exact. Monica is on her way to the courthouse, where her client is on trial for an attempted murder charge. It is her turn to make her closing argument, and she is in for quite a challenge as the jury has been very unidentifiable and unpredictable.

In twenty-seven minutes, the court will be in session. But Monica is less than thirty-five minutes away from the courthouse, as she just dropped off Miles and Briana at school. Her husband Sammy had to go out of town on a gig Tuesday morning, leaving

Monica to handle things independently. But this was one of many, as she has been doing this for years. Monica finally made her way to the courthouse. She found a great parking space, really close to the building, where she did not have to walk very far. Monica did not bother to wear any jewelry or wore a belt; that way, she could go through the metal detectors as quickly as possible and head into the courtroom. In she goes as she opens the doors, dressed in her olive-green business suit, briefcase in one hand, and the other hand, her notepad that she reviewed over, and over, and over, as she was practicing her closing argument during her drive.

"Ms. Taylor, very glad you can join us. Whenever you are ready," The judge said as she looked at her watch.

"My apologies, your honor. I'll begin in one minute," Monica said as she placed her briefcase on the floor and took off her jacket.

As Monica looked at her client, she said good morning to him, only to see that it was not a good morning for him at all. He had on a navy-blue suit, white button-up shirt, red tie, and black shoes. But that was not Monica's focus. All she saw was the bruised black eye and cheekbone on her client's face as if he was in a scuffle in the correctional facility. Monica then leaned over and asked her client, "What happened to your face, Mr. Jamestown?" He looked at her but did not say a word. The judge's patience began to drown in frustration as she projected, "Ms. Taylor, if you please, we must start; thank you."

Monica grew worried about her client's bruised face, as that could trigger or perhaps influence the jury to assume that her client, Amir Jamestown, *is* a violent man and find him guilty on the attempted murder charge.

But Monica remained calm; she stayed focused and prepared herself to give her closing argument. Then, Monica, being the brilliant and intellectually gifted attorney she is, presented her closing argument to the court.

About halfway into Monica's inventive closing argument, she said, "My client's innocence speaks for itself. The evidence presented by the prosecution was deemed inadmissible. The prosecution has *failed* to prove that *my client*, Amir Jamestown, attempted to *murder* Reginald Walker. They showed you a gun; however, there were no fingerprints on that gun that belonged to my client. The prosecution showed you surveillance videos from *three different angles*, and yet *none* of those videos shows my client chasing down Reginald Walker, trying to kill him. As the eyewitness, Roger Nelson, had stated. My client, Amir Jamestown, is a *great* human being. He is a good man that was placed in a bad situation. A situation that left him to defend himself. A situation that compelled him to *act* in *self-defense*, where my client himself felt that *his* life was, for a fact, in danger. Amir Jamestown has every right to protect his life, his *only* life.

Put yourself in his shoes, and *ask* yourselves, "what would you do?" What I ask of you, the jury, all I ask for is simply *justice*. Justice is what I want for my client, Amir Jamestown. Justice is the ticket that will take my client to the destination of freedom, and he will pay for that ticket with his innocence. Justice is all I ask of you. Thank you."

As Monica went back to the desk to sit next to her client, the judge then had the bailiff escort the jury to the jury room as they prepare for deliberations. Monica then looked at her client more closely, observing the fresh bruises on his face. She followed her client to the holding cell, where he must wait until his transportation arrives to take him back to the correctional facility. Monica is standing on the other side of the cell, disgusted with her client at the moment. She said, "Mr. Jamestown, I do not know who, what, when, where, or why you have those bruises on your face. Of *all* days, why did you have to cause trouble for yourself?"

As Amir Jamestown looked at Monica, he said, "The cousin of Reginald Walker, the guy I had an altercation with, he's in the same facility that I'm in. He found out that I was the one, and then he attacked me." For a few minutes, Monica went back and forth with Amir. Monica then said, "Well, listen, I'm not going to tell you *not* to defend yourself in there. But this jury has been a wall of no emotion or expression for the duration of this trial. And for you to have those bruises on your face? It's like you gave them new evidence that could prove their assumptions correctly of you being a violent and conflicting man. And right before deliberations?" Amir did not like how Monica's elaboration of his situation seems as if he has now jeopardized his chances of being acquitted.

"With all due respect Ms. Taylor, isn't that *your* job? To keep me looking as innocent as possible to that jury? Isn't that *your* job to keep me out of trouble?" Amir said to Monica. Monica then swiftly turned her head, staring at her client with a very offended look on her face. Monica responded, saying, "NO! Mr. Jamestown, it is not *my* job to keep you out of *trouble*. *My* job is to keep you out of *prison*. Just so we are crystal clear on that."

After their brief discussion, Amir just sat there without saying a word, still waiting for the transportation. Monica then looked at her watch as it was still early, and she was getting her belongings together. Right before she headed out, Amir exchanged a few words with Monica.

"Ms. Taylor...Thank you. I apologize for what I said and for potentially hurting my chances out there. You've worked very hard for me these last several months, and I couldn't ask for a better attorney. Thank you for everything," Amir said as his transportation just pulled up. "Mr. Jamestown, it was my pleasure. It's not over just yet; we still have to wait for the jury to reach a verdict. It wouldn't hurt to pray. But I know when all the smoke clears, you'll be a free man," Monica said as she exits out of the holding area.

As Monica walks out of the courthouse, she received a text message. Monica broke into laughter as she looked at her phone and saw that it was a text from Tomi, who sent Monica a picture of her Botox face with a text saying, "I'm going to be a *bad bitch* once it all heals." Monica responded saying, "LOL! Tomi, you've always been a bad bitch. You don't need all that shit in your face, babe. But you know I love you regardless. Just bring your ass home so we can help our girl, Zarin. She needs all of our support right now."

Tomi then sent Monica half a dozen heart emojis and told her that she is flying back to the city late tomorrow evening. Of course, Monica was happy to know that. But as of right now, she is very concerned about this particular case. This case is crucial to her. It will put her on the map, as well as the law firm she works for in the city.

It was always Monica's dream to be a lawyer, ever since she was a little girl. When Monica was nine years old, her uncle was unjustly sent to prison for twenty-five years for a murder he did not commit. Monica remembers that day very clearly. Her mother screamed at the top of her lungs in the courtroom when the judge gave the sentence. Monica was only able to see her uncle four times throughout the years.

The injustice of Monica's uncle was her spark of drive to become who she is today—a very successful lawyer. Once Monica passed the bar exam and officially became a lawyer, the first case Monica was blessed with was her uncle's case. It took some time, but with her intelligence, witty persona, and determination to win, her uncle was found innocent. His case was dismissed, and he was acquitted. But tragically, he passed away from complications from diabetes shortly after his release from prison. But Monica made sure she filed a lawsuit, her family *won* the case, and they won big. $5.8 million, to be exact, which was helpful for Monica since she could pay off the $125,000 she had in student loan debt. And Monica's mother was well off financially.

The case Monica is working on now is like déjà vu. Only this time, she has the power to fight for justice for her client and prevent him from spending *years* in prison. Monica has been an attorney for over eight years now. She has won every case, but this one, this is the case of her redemption. Monica never did have a chance to have a relationship with her uncle. But she refuses to let that happen with someone else's life. Not on her watch.

Chapter 9

That afternoon, Collette took off from work as she had a meaningful event to tend to at the local hospital. It was not an appointment for *her*, but an appointment for her sister, Lisa. Collette picked Lisa up yesterday morning and took her to the hospital, as Lisa was undergoing an extraordinary and monumental surgery. What surgery, you may be thinking? It was the most crucial procedure in Lisa's life, a process that will now change her life forever. Lisa underwent transfeminine bottom surgery. Lisa is a woman of trans-experience.

Collette is the only one in Lisa's family who supports her; she has supported Lisa ever since they were teenagers. Collette has been trying to make it up to Lisa for something that happened during their childhood, which Collette profoundly regrets. When Collette was thirteen, Lisa did not yet emerge; Lisa was *"Liam,"* Collette's younger brother, five years younger than Collette.

One evening, Collette was in her room listening to music. Their mother was cooking dinner, and their father stepped out to grab some dessert. Collette then stepped out of her room to use the bathroom. When she turned the doorknob and opened the bathroom door, Collette saw something that she found deeply confusing, or in her mind, disturbing. She saw her brother, Liam, wearing their mother's high heel shoes. Collette looked down at the shoes and then looked up at Liam's eyes. Liam had a look in his eyes as if there would be trouble and punishment coming directly his way.

Collette ran straight to the kitchen and told their mother what she just witnessed in the bathroom. Their mother went on a cussing fit. And this was not the first time Liam had been caught. Their mother caught Liam several months before then, and she gave him hell. Their mother told Liam to start acting like a boy; Liam was only eight years old at the time. Their mother made Liam promise not to wear her clothes again.

After Collette told their mother, she went straight to the bathroom where Liam was and gave him the beating of a lifetime. Liam cried and cried and cried until he could barely stand up. But unfortunately, it was not over. Their father came back from the store, and their mother made Collette tell him *precisely* what she saw in the bathroom. But Collette was terrified to tell him what she saw Liam doing in the bathroom because she did not want their father to beat on him. Especially after seeing what their mother did. But their mother said, "Either you tell your father what Liam did, or you'll get worse than he got."

Collette told him that Liam was in the bathroom wearing their mother's shoes, and their father completely lost it. Their father went after Liam and did the unthinkable. Their father did something to Liam that no kid could ever possibly forgive their father for doing. Their father grabbed Liam by the neck and brought him downstairs into the middle of the street in the Bronx. On a hot summer's night, where everyone was outside.

Collette went after them, and she saw her father beat Liam out in the middle of the street. He was cursing at Liam, calling him names that no parent should *ever* say to their child. As their father was beating Liam out in the middle of the street, he shouted this out, "Yo everyone, listen to this, my son here likes to dress in his momma's clothes! Yea, you heard me right; my *son* wants to dress in high heels; he wants to be a *woman*! You don't want to be a man, huh, Liam? HUH?" As their father kept beating on Liam, other kids and even grown adults were laughing at that horrifying altercation. They were *laughing*. Collette never cried so many tears. Tears of complete guilt, as she felt solely responsible for Liam being beaten and humiliated at home and out on the street. Even though Collette did not understand Liam at that time, she still begged and begged for forgiveness. It put a wedge between her and Lisa. Collette and their parents just did not understand or realize who Liam truly was on the inside.

Being that Collette did not understand Liam, she could not support him. At least until a few years later, when she walked in on Liam, holding their father's gun to his temple, as he was contemplating suicide. Collette was devastated by that imagery of her sibling, who she *loves*, who the neighborhood kids were constantly bullying after their father humiliated him. Liam felt stuck with his true identity, *trapped* in a body that is not aligned with his true spirit. The spirit of Lisa.

Collette walked to Liam in his bedroom, collapsed to her knees as tears collapsed from her eyes. She begged Liam to put the gun down. Liam cried tears as well, saying, "I can't do this anymore, Coco. I can't be in a world where nobody loves me. How can I love myself in a body that doesn't belong to me? The *real* me?" Collette gently moved her hand towards the gun as she slowly and gently removed it from Liam's temple. Then, she said to Liam, "Let go of the gun, let go of it, please?"

Liam finally let go of the gun and just lost it. Crying so many tears, as was Collette. She hugged him so tight for so long. From that moment on, Collette said to herself that she would rather have a living sibling than a dead one. And Collette has been supportive of her *sister*, *Lisa*, ever since.

Back at the hospital, Collette made her way to the room where Lisa was beginning her post-op recovery. When Collette walked inside the room, she saw Lisa's eyes, filled with tears of joy, excitement, happiness, and the satisfaction that at least one of her family members cared enough about her permanent decision.

"CoCo, you have no idea what this means to me. I love you; I love you, I love you," Lisa said. "You're my sister, and I was *not* going to let you go through this alone. I love you more, baby. It has been a long time coming," Collette said as she kissed Lisa on her forehead.

Lisa, who grew out her long curly hair, with her facial features and how she carries herself, you would not even know. On her best day, Lisa looks like a movie star. But as of right now, she looks like a hospital patient. Collette stayed with Lisa for a bit; they talked about some things, especially about Mia and what she found in Emilio's bedroom. As Collette spoke, she said this to Lisa, "It was just déjà vu all over again. I don't think I would have handled this situation the way I did, had I not seen what happened to you. That was the worst decision I could have made by telling Mamí and Papí about you wearing those heels. I wish I could take that back." Lisa then took Collette's hand, comforting her as she tells the story. Lisa said, "CoCo, just let me have a few days of recovery, and I'll talk to Emilio. Don't worry about it."

Collette appreciated Lisa's help, but she told Lisa that she wants to talk with Emilio first. Sitting next to Lisa, Collette said, "I'm going to sit with Emilio, and we're going to have a mother-and-son conversation. If he's gay, then I'll just have to accept that. But I know Martin will not, and *that* is what scares the hell out of me."

A family is a group of people who comes with much conflict and complications. Collette has had her unfair share of that throughout her life. After what happened to Lisa, she had no place in her heart for judgment. Collette knew that no matter what, she was going to love her son, and she would never abandon him. However, Martin was never a supporter or ally of the LGBTQIA+ community.

"My nephew is going to be fine, CoCo. He knows who he is and what he likes. There's no blame in that or no shame," Lisa said to Collette.

"We'll have our talk, but I'm a little concerned about Mia and how this will affect her," Collette responded.

As Collette was getting ready to call it a day, she received a text. It was a text from Tomi, sending the same picture that she sent to Monica, a selfie after she received Botox with a text saying, "*Bad bitch coming soon! HAHA.*" Collette looked at the picture and then showed Lisa; they both broke out in laughter. Tomi *loves* Lisa and Lisa loves Tomi. Tomi hired Lisa to walk in several of her fashion shows. As a result, Lisa was the first Trans-woman to walk for the *Orell Llero* women's fashion line.

Amid this discussion about Emilio, Collette asked Lisa how it feels now that her body is anatomically aligned with her mind as a woman. Lisa just looked at Collette with the biggest smile. Lisa made a life-changing decision for herself. Perhaps some would say *life-saving*. Even though society is not all on board, and maybe never will be. Lisa is just very grateful to Collette for loving her and supporting her transition. As mentioned before, Collette will do anything to make peace with Lisa.

Collette then kissed Lisa on her cheek as she is getting ready to head out for the evening. Lisa thanked Collette for coming and told her how much she loves and appreciates her. Before Collette left, Lisa asked her for one favor. "Can you tell Mamí and Papí that I love them no matter what, and I hope one day they could be proud of me?" Lisa asked Collette. "I'll tell them you said that. Hopefully, they *are* proud of you," Collette responded as she blew a kiss at Lisa and left the hospital room.

As Collette headed towards the elevators, she knew for a fact that her parents would *not* be proud of Lisa for making her transition. Their parents disowned Lisa when she was sixteen years old. Collette was twenty-one at that time, who just had Emilio with her now-husband, Martin. Collette refused to allow Lisa to be homeless. So, she brought Lisa into her home, and Lisa went on to finish high school. Lisa then went off to college, graduated, and earned a degree in human rights. However, even with all the accomplishments, their parents could not accept Lisa for who she is. And Collette could not change their mind.

As Collette got into her car, she called Emilio and asked him if they could meet tomorrow evening at *Lucille's*. He confirmed with her that he would be there. Collette does not know how to explain this to Martin, Mia, *or* her parents about Lisa and Emilio. Collette feels that when all the smoke clears, *she* will be the one who has to keep *this* family together. Collette needed to clear her mind. So instead of driving home, she began to make her way to *Lucille's.*

As Collette arrived at *Lucille's*, she went up to the office, with its own private bar. She made herself a drink and began to reflect on what is going on in her life. Her sister, Lisa, just completed a life-changing procedure. In addition, her son Emilio will possibly be coming out to her, and she has no idea how her parents *or* Martin will respond to all of this. As Collette sits in the office, she sips, sips, and sips on her third drink at the bar. Collette then makes her way to the couch with her glass and plops down.

While she lays on the couch, Martin walked into the office. Surprised at Collette's presence, as he was not expecting her to be in the office, laying on the couch. "Hey babe, what the hell are you doing up here?" Martin said as he walked over to Collette. "Oh, babe, I just had a lot on my mind. I needed to wind down and have some drinks. And I didn't want to run into anyone. So, I came up here," Collette responded to Martin.

Martin then grabbed a blanket from the closet and draped it over Collette. He then said to her, "Well, take a rest then. You had too many drinks for you to drive. So don't you move, I'll take you home in an hour, and we'll talk about what's on your mind when we get home."

Collette was then beginning to fall asleep on the couch. One could only imagine the pressure and stress she is having from this swirling in her mind. Usually, Collette can always count on her ladies for their advice, help, love, and support during times like this. Right before she fell asleep, Collette sent a group text saying, "I can't wait to see you all on Friday night. I need my girls." Five minutes after she pressed the send button, she passed out. And that drunk sleep never felt so good.

Chapter 10

Thursday morning came with gentle snowflakes as Wendy was on her way to work in Queens. She rode in a taxi, sporting her cream, faux-fur collar winter coat with the waist strap and gold-plated buttons. Her hands grew cold and red as she forgot her gloves on the way out of her home. Edward told Wendy that he would take EJ to school, as it was *her* day to take him, but she was running late. Wendy and Edward have this pattern for EJ. During the week, Edward would take EJ to school the first three days of the week, and then Wendy would bring him the remaining two. The following week, *Wendy* would take EJ to school for three days, and then Edward would take him for the remaining two. And that is the cycle they went by. It may not work for some people, but it does for them.

As Wendy makes it to her office building, she handed the cab driver a fifty-dollar bill. Her fare was only twenty-seven dollars, but she told the cab driver to keep the change, as she did not want to be late. Also, Wendy hates using her credit cards in taxi cabs. Wendy speed-walked into the office. She loves to be punctual and make a good impression on her colleagues. After all, she *is* on the verge of becoming a partner at her wedding event company; at the very young age of thirty-three.

As Wendy walks into her office, she is greeted by her boss, Vicky Shultz, with who Wendy could potentially start a partnership. Vicky Shultz, a fifty-three-year-old Jewish woman with a pleasant demeanor and positive attitude. Those reasons alone are why Wendy would love to be partners with Mrs. Shultz. However, Mrs. Shultz is not so quickly welcoming to putting someone else on top right beside her. Mrs. Shultz's wedding company, "*Schultz Weddings and Events,*" is her baby. She built it from scratch. If Mrs. Shultz is willing to offer someone a partnership in the company *she* created, she has to trust that person. And Wendy has been busting her ass as Mrs. Shultz's protégé for ten years now. Wendy wants this promotion.

As Wendy and Mrs. Shultz began to conversate in Wendy's office, Mrs. Shultz said, "Wendy, my love, I'm so glad that you did this wedding that will take place this Saturday. I know the mother of the bride is a piece of work. But the way you have been handling everything is quite remarkable. I appreciate your hard work and dedication. *Unfortunately*, I'm afraid that my proposal of making you a partner has been revoked. I'm so sorry, my dear."

Wendy could not believe what her ears just let in. She thought she was having audiology issues and asked Mrs. Shultz if she could repeat herself. Mrs. Shultz then repeated herself and told Wendy that she would *not* be promoted to partnership at her wedding company.

Wendy's hands were no longer cold. She turned red from anger and fury as she was incredibly perturbed. Wendy looked at her boss Mrs. Shultz, who knew Wendy was not happy about what she just told her, and Wendy demanded a *thorough* explanation of why Mrs. Shultz had a sudden change of heart. "Mrs. Shultz, I can't believe this. *Why* are you lowballing me like this? You know I've worked my *ass* off for this opportunity," Wendy said to Mrs. Shultz.

Mrs. Shultz then responded with reassurance, "Oh honeybun, don't get me wrong; *you are a genius*. I *love* your vision; *your* vision and creativity have changed the wedding planning game. The way you add your touch of Japanese culture in your themes, you leave me speechless all the time. But I still feel that you are very young and maybe even a little wet behind the ears on some things. I want you to *grow* in this business. There is no need to rush your destiny. In time, you will possibly have *your* wedding and events planning company."

Wendy knew that was a possibility. To be an owner of a Wedding and events company one day. But that was not what she was after. The truth of the matter is; Wendy *idolizes* Mrs. Shultz. She has been working with Mrs. Shultz since she was twenty-three years old. She showed Wendy the game, taught her so much. Wendy was such a visual planner; Mrs. Shultz kept her close for all those years. Grooming her to be the wedding planner that she is today. It was Wendy's dream to be working side by side with her idol, Mrs. Shultz, as her partner.

"Excuse me," Wendy said as she walked out of her office. Wendy's eyes were beginning to glare up and form a trail of tears as she quickly walked her way over to the women's restroom. As Wendy went into the bathroom, she went into one of the stalls, locked the door, and began to weep her eyes out. She stayed in that stall for ten minutes, crying and crying her hopes and dreams away. Wendy could not get over how unfair this situation is for her. But her mother always told her that this world was never built on fairness.

A few moments later, another woman walks into the restroom. Wendy still shedding tears, making heavy sniffles. The woman overheard Wendy's weeping emotions.

"Honey, are you okay in there?" The woman asked Wendy.

"Yes…Yea, I'll be okay. Thank you," Wendy responded as she was wiping her nose.

The woman then headed out of the restroom. As Wendy then finally came out of the stall. Her tears practically ruined her makeup. As she looked in the mirror, her face looked so defeated and drained. She had her jet-black hair up in a bun. Mind you, she did not even take her coat off yet. Wendy could not go back out there with her face looking like she just had a mental meltdown. So, she texted her co-worker and asked her if she could meet her in the ladies' room with her makeup kit.

About five minutes go by, her co-worker, Jessica, a tall Taylor Swift look-alike, came walking into the bathroom. She looked at Wendy's face and wanted to know what happened.

"Wendy, what's wrong, babe? Did you get fired or something?" Jessica said as she hugged Wendy.

"No, it's not that…Mrs. Shultz decided not to promote me as her partner. And I'm just feeling a little devastation about it," Wendy responded to Jessica.

Jessica felt much sorrow for Wendy. But unfortunately, she did not have any words of encouragement, as Jessica has only been working there for seven months. Jessica did, however, bring her makeup kit with her. She gave Wendy a few touch-ups on her face with some red lipstick. Wendy tanked Jessica and hugged her on her way out of the restroom.

Wendy made her way out of the restroom and into her office. She untied her waist strap from her coat, took it off, and wrapped it around her black leather chair. Wendy then placed her phone on her office table and began to look out her window. She had a beautiful view of the Manhattan skyline. Even though it was a snowy and foggy day, only seeing the bottom half of One World Trade Center.

Wendy then sat down at her desk and began to reflect on what just happened. As she sat there, her boss, Mrs. Shultz, came back to her office. Mrs. Shultz could see that her decision *not* to promote Wendy up to partnership has upset her. But Mrs. Shultz did not want any bad blood between them. She loves Wendy, and she wants her to still work for her.

"I know you were not expecting this, Wendy. But *believe* me, it is for the best. You'll thank me for this one day. By the way, is everything settled for Anderson's Wedding this Saturday?" Mrs. Shultz said to Wendy. "Yes, Mrs. Shultz, I took care of everything. It is going to be one of the most prodigious weddings this company has ever produced," Wendy said with a face of disgust.

Mrs. Shultz thanked Wendy again for all her hard work. Before she left Wendy's office, she asked Wendy to give EJ a kiss from her "Aunt Vicky." As Mrs. Shultz turned to walk away, Wendy said, "I just want you to know that after this Anderson wedding is through, I'm taking my off days and going on a *much-needed* vacation. I'll use them starting today. I'll see you at the wedding on Saturday."

Wendy gathered her things together, put on her coat, and walked out of her office. Heading outside in the cold, she hailed down the first taxi she laid eyes on in the street. As she got in the cab, she told the taxi driver to head towards Manhattan, as she would pick up EJ early from school.

Not the best way for Wendy to start Thursday morning. Wendy had high hopes that Mrs. Shultz would make her a partner and give her the opportunity she felt she deserved. During her ten-year career working for Mrs. Shultz, Wendy has planned over a hundred weddings. It may not seem like a lot, but Wendy needs to have excellent chemistry with her clients. So, less was more. But the visual quality of Wendy's wedding ceremonies has always been brilliant and remarkable.

Wendy cried her tears for the day. Riding in the back of the Taxi, she dialed Edward's number as she wanted to let him know that she was leaving work early. But Edward did not respond. Again, that's not like him not to respond. Usually, he would answer rather quickly, but Wendy assumed that he was in the middle of rehearsal.

As Wendy was heading into Manhattan, she thought about taking her mother up on the idea of going to Tokyo and taking EJ with them. She thought that would be the perfect way to spend her much-needed vacation after this wedding. She then called her mother to let her know that she and EJ *will* be coming along for that trip. And that put a smile on that beautiful face of hers.

Chapter 11

Later in the afternoon, Zarin was with her news crew on a burning apartment building scene. Even though it was freezing outside, the cold air was doing nothing but helping the roaring flames. Zarin stood in front of the camera, with her maroon peacoat and the matching hat and gloves. The cameraman made a countdown as to when they would go live. "In three, two, one...Go! Go! Goooo!" The cameraman quietly said as Zarin was in a daze.

Zarin quickly snapped out of it and began her live coverage of the burning apartment building. As she finished her coverage, her cameraman looked at her and began shaking his head. "Hey Zarin, what the hell is going on? This energy isn't like you at all. Maybe you should take some days off," The cameraman said to Zarin. But Zarin was in *no* mood for criticism. "How about you mind your own *fucking* business, Jerry. Don't give me no Goddamn advice on what I should do," Zarin said with much cruelty. Jerry, the cameraman, was in complete shock. As this too was not Zarin's character. She was not the type of person to use much profanity, nor is she the confrontational type.

They then drove off back to the news station. Zarin apologized to Jerry for her outburst. She has been taking things with her husband, Neal, in a tormenting way. Zarin still has been holding back on confronting him about this "Meli" woman he talked to several days ago. For the whole week, she could not take her mind off of this woman. Even though Zarin blocked Meli's number, she knows that Neal has still contacted Meli. And he is still hiding something from Zarin. But for the sake of their daughters, Zarin has been keeping things low-key.

Back at the news station, Zarin was sitting in her dressing room. She called her mother to ask if she could take the girls and have a three-day weekend with them. Since the girls did not have school on Friday, her mother told her that would not be a problem. Zarin needed to clear her head and have a one-on-one conversation with Neal without the girls around. Zarin then received a call from Wendy, as she too was having a bad day.

"Hey honey, how is your day going?" Zarin said to Wendy over the phone.

"Hey...I'm, I'm kind of having a really shitty day. To be honest," Wendy responded as she became emotional.

"Aww, Wendy, what's wrong, honey?" Zarin responded.

Zarin and Wendy began to have a conversation on the phone. Wendy told Zarin about how her boss, Mrs. Shultz, is no longer giving her the promotion of partnership. Zarin expressed her sympathy. She did not know what to tell Wendy at that moment. But Zarin allowed Wendy to speak. The previous night, she and Wendy went to the bar, and Zarin talked about *her* situation with her husband, Neal. This moment was the time for Zarin to lend *her* shoulder for Wendy to cry on a little.

Wendy told Zarin that after the wedding is over, she and EJ *will* go on that trip to Tokyo with her parents. Zarin thought that would be great for her. To relieve herself of all the stress her job is causing her.

"Oh, Wendy, I have to go now. But we can talk more about this tonight or even tomorrow night when we get together at *Lucille's?*" Zarin said as she was called on the news set.

"Okay, yeah, we'll talk tomorrow night. Thanks for listening. Love you, Zarin," said Wendy.

"I love you too," said Zarin. "And give EJ a kiss for me."

As Zarin headed out onto the news set, she was given the breaking news of how a car crash injured two little kids and a father on FDR Drive. Ironically not too far from the Rockefeller University Hospital. This sad news drove Zarin's anxiety through the roof. It is news such as this that Zarin deals with at her job, every single day. Tragic, devastating, heartbreaking news that she has to cover with a straight face on camera. Whether it is a fire, car accident, kidnapping, murder, or some disease passed around. Zarin tries her best not to let such breaking news break her down. But with everything going on at home and hearing about two kids and their father suffering injuries in a car accident, Zarin had a minor anxiety attack. That story hit too close to home for her. She imagined that being *her* two daughters and Neal in that car.

As soon as Zarin finished on the news set, she quickly went into her dressing room, locked the door behind her, and removed her boots. "Hey Siri, play ten-minute meditation," Zarin said as she begins her meditation. Zarin then crossed her legs in a yoga position. Next, she closed her eyes as the meditation music began to take its course.

For ten straight minutes, Zarin did nothing but breathe. She cleared her head of everything she possibly could that was the cause of her stress and heartache: no news, no fears, and *no* Meli. Zarin would do this every day at work, and it works like magic. She clears her mind, breathing in the positives vibes and exhaling the negative energy.

As Zarin's ten minutes were up, she looked at herself in the mirror and began to smile. Sometimes for her to get through the devastation of the news reports, she would think and say in her mind, "It is just my job, and I *don't* have to take this home with me." When Zarin says *that*, she gets through the news reports without her anxiety getting the best of her.

Right before Zarin headed out for the day, her boss asked to have a few words with her. Her boss, Mr. Zenberg, was a tall, heavyset man with hair on the side and some balding in the middle. A Jesse Ventura, looking kind of guy. He may be a large guy, but Mr. Zenberg is a teddy bear. A *wise* teddy bear who gets things done. "Hi Zarin, I talked with our cameraman, Jerry. He told me you both were having some difficulties earlier this morning. Is everything okay?" Mr. Zenberg asked with a concerned look. "Yes, Mr. Zenberg, sorry that you had to hear of my behavior this morning. It won't happen again. And I apologized to Jerry as well," Zarin responded to Mr. Zenberg.

As mentioned, Zarin does not like confrontation, and Mr. Zenberg was sort of an easy-going guy. So, that conversation was short-lived. After Zarin talked with Mr. Zenberg, she gathered her belongings and left for the day. It was a quarter to four in the afternoon. Zarin's father had already picked up Darsha and

Joshna from school, as the girls will be spending the weekend at their Nana and Nani's house in Queens.

As for Zarin, she and Neal will have the house to themselves. This moment would be the opportunity for them to get to the bottom of this very confusing and mysterious situation that could jeopardize their family.

Chapter 12

A glance at her phone; it was ten past nine. Collette is now on her third glass of wine as she is waiting for Emilio to arrive at *Lucille's*. She is sitting in the reserved booth, where she always sits when she and the rest of the ladies come every Friday night for dinner. Collette is a bit nervous about what she will find out about her son, Emilio. After going through everything she went through with her sister Lisa,

Collette is afraid that she might not be prepared for her son coming out to her as a gay man.

Eleven minutes later, Emilio comes walking in the front entrance. Collette waves him down to grab his attention. He sees her and makes his way towards the reserved booth. Collette sometimes has to stop and observe how handsome Emilio is, as he likes to change his look every so often. Emilio came dressed in a very formal outfit. His burgundy turtleneck sweater looked great with his navy-blue winter coat.

"Hey, sorry I'm late, had to take a Lyft," Emilio said as he kissed Collette on her left cheek.

"It's okay, babe; I didn't order any meals yet. I wanted to wait until we talked first," Collette responded.

As Emilio sat there, he began to feel a bit awkward about this moment. Collette was just sitting there, not saying a word to him, now sipping on her *fourth* glass of wine. Emilio, who only had a glass of water to sip on, felt he needed to spark the conversation. As he and Collette sat there, Emilio said, "*So*, I guess we are here to discuss what Mia found in my room. Well, first and foremost, let me just apologize to you guys for bringing weed into your home. That was very disrespectful. And I'm sorry that *Mia* had to be the one who found it as well. As for the dildo? I, I, there's something that you must know."

After Collette heard that, she knew what Emilio was fixing to say to her. She knew that her son, Emilio, would have his "come out" moment with her. But before he could get another word out, Collette said to him, "Look, baby, I know this is probably one of the most difficult things you have ever come to tell me about in your life. But it takes *a lot* of bravery and courage for you to come to sit down with me and tell me the truth, *your* truth. I'm going to let you say it. Say who you are and say it *proudly*, Papì."

Emilio looked at his mother with tears growing in his eyes. He was expecting a completely different outcome than this. As he wiped the tears from his light-brown eyes, he looked up and said, "I am hungry." Collette was in immediate shock. If only you could see the look on her face as she was confused as hell. But then she quickly turned around and understood why Emilio said what he said. Martin, her husband, Emilio's father, walked over to Collette and Emilio sitting in the booth. She understood that Emilio did not want his father to overhear him speaking about his sexuality.

"Son, what the hell are you doing here? You don't usually come to the restaurant," Martin said as he shook Emilio's hand.

"We're having a mother and son date. Just shooting the shit. Oh, can you take this wine bottle, baby?" Collette said to Martin as she handed him the empty wine bottle.

Martin took the empty wine bottle and left the table. As awkward as it seems, Emilio thought it would be safer to simply text his mother what he wanted to say to her. That way, no one else could hear anything. When he did, Collette looked at the text, but she did not like that at all. She wanted him to be *proud* of who he is and not ashamed.

"No, Emilio, Papì, I need to hear you *say* it. Don't be afraid, mi Amor," Collette said as she held his hand.

"Okay, Mami, your son is a proud gay man," Emilio proudly said to his mother as tears slid down his face.

He was not the only one shedding tears. Collette quickly joined him as the night became an unexpected celebration. But there was one thing Emilio begged of his mother; he made Collette promise *not* to tell Martin. He knows about his father and how he disapproves of same-sex behavior. Collette told Emilio not to worry about his father, as she was already ahead of the curve.

Ten minutes later, they decided just to have some desserts instead of dinner. Ice cream with hot brownies draped in caramel sauce. Emilio was having a grand ole time with his mother. He began to tell Collette how his junior year in college is going. He is looking to go straight into the fashion industry after he graduates. To Collette, that was not a bad idea for him. She told him how his aunt Tomi would be thrilled to have him work for her, for her clothing line.

Collette also mentioned to Emilio that his *other* aunt, Lisa, would like to have a conversation. Emilio confirmed that he would reach out to Lisa after she recovers from her surgery. Even though Collette received the answer from Emilio himself, she still wanted to know more about the subject. As Collette took the last spoon full of her ice cream, she went on to ask questions. "Papi, when was the very first time you felt that you would like, *men*?" Collette said to Emilio.

Emilio took a brief moment to think about that question. He looked down at the scrapped caramel stains inside his empty bowl. Emilio then looked at Collette and said, "Would you believe me if I said I knew who I was, ever since I was two years old?"

Collette responded with a straight face and said, "Yes, hun, I would believe you. Is that when you felt it?" Emilio slowly went up and down with his head, confirming. Collette could believe it, as her experience with Lisa taught her that many people know at a very young age. But what upsets her is the fact that she did *not* know before this moment. And Collette did not like that at all.

Emilio then looked at his Apple watch and told his mother that he has to head back to his apartment. He has an early morning of back-to-back classes, and he does not want to be late. Collette got up from the booth and gave him such a firm and affectionate hug. She then kissed him on his cheek and said, "I love you so much, and so does Mia, and so does your father. When the time is right, *we* will tell him together. If you want?" Emilio then looked at Collette and said to her, "You know that is not going to happen so easily, right? You and I both know dad. Goodnight, Ma, and I love you too."

Collette sat back down at the booth. She had one last sip left to her glass of wine. Collette quickly swigged it up and left a tip for the waiter. She then gathered her things together, ready to head out. But Martin made his way back to the booth.

"Where's Emilio? I wanted to talk to him for a little while," Martin said as he looked around.

"Oh, he left, babe," said Collette. "He said he had to get up early for classes."

Martin was very curious to know about the conversation she was having with Emilio. But being that Collette made a promise to Emilio, she quickly tried to change the subject by creating a little *seduction* and flirtation. Collette wrapped her arms around Martin, looking up to him as she gives him multiple kisses, one after the other.

"Mmmm…You taste like caramel and chocolate," Martin says as he licks his lips.

"Yea, but I have something else for you to *lick* and taste, Papi," Collette said with a fornicating tone of voice.

That was all Martin needed to hear from her. He took Collette by the hand and brought her up to his office. As soon as they walked into his office, they went at it. Taking each other's clothes off; his tie, her sweater, her jeans down to her ankles, and as Martin gets down on his knees, he prepares for a vaginal feast.

"Wait, wait…Make sure you locked the door," Collette said as she was half-naked, sitting on Martin's desk.

Martin quickly went over to lock the door. He then swiftly made it back over to Collette as he began to give her a night of unforgettable pleasure. Up and down, *thrusting* with his tongue. Collette grabs a handful of Martin's hair as his head is between her legs. Her moans grow louder and louder, but no one can hear downstairs. Privacy is in their favor. Martin is getting closer and closer to her g-spot. And she is getting louder and louder as she prepares to reach orgasm.

"AY PAPI, OH PAPI! OH, DON'T STOP! OH SHIT, DON'T STOP!!" Collette shouted and moaned as Martin continues to pleasure her.

"Shhh…Not so loud, baby," said Martin. "Mmmm….This is *my* dessert."

"Oh, *shut* the fuck up and just keep licking," Collette projected.

Next thing you know, his face is drenched in her, well, you know. Collette *did* have a lot of wine, after all. But Martin did not seem to mind; he loves pleasuring his wife. And she *loves* when he pleases her. Collette's legs were shaking and trembling, heavy breathing as she climaxed. It was just what she needed after dealing with Mia's suspension, Lisa's operation, and Emilio coming out to her. "Oh baby, I needed that so bad. You always knew how to please a woman. That's why I said yes," Collette said as she laid flat on the desk. "Anything for my wife. I have to stay and take care of some business. Don't wait up unless you want more?" Martin said as he kissed Collette. Being that Martin's shirt was heavily stained, he grabbed a new shirt from his closet and changed into it.

"Oh, babe, do you mind?" Martin said as he handed Collette the shirt.

"Sure, baby," said Collette. "I'll take it home and wash it."

What a night indeed. Collette was not expecting to end her night in such a random, seductive, passionate state of affairs. She was walking on cloud nine, all the way out the door of *Lucille's*. As Collette made her way into her car, she sent a group text to the rest of the ladies. Collette said in her text, "*Girls, I think I just had the best orgasm of my life! Martin just fucking ate me out like I was apple pie! Like his life depended on it. I'm sorry if this is TMI. But I had to share it with somebody. LOL!*"

In come the responses from the others. Wendy was the first to respond, saying, "Bitch, I'm eating apple pie right now. Now I can't eat anymore. Thanks a lot! Lmao." Then came Monica's text as she replied, "Really? OMG, I'm going to ask Sammy if he could do the same. He just came back home. LOL!"

Tomi was the third to text back. She responded by saying, "Yes, Coco, there's nothing like having an orgasm with the man you love. I can't wait to see you crazy bitches tomorrow night. Oh, and I didn't forget about the "*oink* situation."

All the ladies responded, except for one. Zarin saw the group text, as well as everyone's responses. But she was not as upbeat to say something in return. She is still going through this weird situation with her husband, Neal. So, Zarin simply "loved" Collette's text and left it at that. However, Collette gave Zarin an idea of how to break the ice between her and Neal. Zarin thought about the fact that she and Neal have not had sex in over two months. Work has been hectic for both of them, and Darsha and Joshna are a handful. But both of the girls are spending the night at their grandparents for a three-day weekend. So, Neal and Zarin will have the house to themselves.

But as soon as Zarin had the idea to have sex with Neal, she immediately disappointed herself and canceled that idea. Unfortunately, she is *still* on her period. However, Zarin thought to herself *again* and said, "Well, that's just *one* hole that is out of order. But there's one more still open for business."

Zarin sits on her living room couch, dressed in her cozy brown sweater and black leggings. As she waits for Neal to come home, Zarin realizes that this relaxed look is not as appealing and went upstairs to put on something much more exotic. She feels that this right here will remind him who truly loves him. She wants him to know that she is the *only* woman in his life who loves him and would do *anything* for him. Sometimes that is truly necessary for marriage. You need that sudden reminder from your significant other. And tonight, that is what Zarin is going to do.

Chapter 13

A half-hour past ten. Neal finally walks into the house, exhausted after a hard day's work at his office. Zarin came down the stairs, dressed a little different than the brown sweater and black leggings she was wearing. Neal looked at her with swift suspense as she came down in her very *sexy* rose-red lingerie—the whole nine yards: knee-high stockings, bra and panties, and opened-toe high heel sandals. As Neal stood there, he thought he walked into a strip club. His eyes went directly to Zarin in a dead stare.

Neal could not move, frozen in place. He was at a loss for words. Zarin then made her way to Neal as she began to take off his coat and scarf. As she takes off his jacket, she begins to talk with him. "Hey hubby, so I *know* this may come as a surprise for you. But I just thought, "Hey, the girls are at my parents' house, and we have the house to ourselves." You've been working *so* hard. I just want to make you feel better. I want to give you what you want, what you desire," Zarin said, seducing Neal.

Neal is still a little shell shocked but begins to snap out of it as he said, "Baby, it's been a while since I've seen you all, *exotic*. What's the special occasion?" Zarin then puts her index finger in front of Neal's lips, as she does not want him to say another word. She pulls him by his midnight purple tie and sits him on the living room couch. Then she gets on top of his lap in a cowgirl position, beginning her borage of kisses on his lips. Kiss after kiss, her red lipstick is being printed all over his white button-up shirt as she starts kissing on his chest.

Neal is no longer tired. He is ready to get all the way busy. He reaches behind Zarin's back to unhook her bra. After a good minute, Zarin then helps him as he was unsuccessful. The bra comes off. Neal then plants his face right into the cleavage of her breast. His firm grip on her breast gets Zarin to arise. Her head tilted up, looking at the ceiling. Neal keeps going, licking each of her nipples, then slowly making his way down her belly button.

Now he reaches for her panties. As Neal tries to remove them, Zarin stops him and says, "No, no…I can't."

"Babe, I'm as *hard* as a fucking *Bar exam* right now. Hard as a *diamond*. You did all of this just to say you *can't*? What the fuck?" Neal frustratingly said as he sits on the couch.

"No, no…I'm on my period. *But,* there's another alternative. If you know what I mean?" Zarin said as she gets on her knees and unzips Neal's pants.

Neal's frown has now turned upside down. He knows what he's about to receive. He then sits back and relaxes as Zarin gently performs fellatio. Neal's moans began to grow louder as Zarin keeps going. He gently caresses her head as her seductive suction takes Neal to the destination of climax. Zarin is in full form. She keeps *going* and *going*. And without warning or hesitation, Neal reached climax. Deep breathes and a clammy forehead as Neal sits on the couch. Zarin then makes her way up and Kisses Neal multiple times on his face.

"Wait, wait. Did you, did you *swallow*?" Neal asked with a curious expression on his face.

"Yes, honey, I did," Zarin said as she lays on his lap.

Five minutes later, after Neal recovered from his moment of pleasure from Zarin, he headed upstairs to the bedroom. He wanted to change out of his work clothes and into his pajamas.

As Neal went up to change, Zarin remained on the couch. She feels good that she was able to please her husband. Zarin felt like she made a statement saying, "this is *my* man, *my* husband, and no other woman is taking him away from his family."

Until there was a sudden buzzing coming from his coat pocket. Zarin, knowing what she knows, grows suspicious and decided to check Neal's phone. She gently walks towards the stairs and looks up, just to make sure that Neal was not coming down. Zarin went to dig in Neal's coat pocket as the coast was clear and pulled out his phone. Neal didn't change his code, so Zarin had easy access. And what Zarin saw on the screen of his phone is what she predicted. It was Meli, the woman whose number she blocked several days ago.

Zarin's heart was racing as if it was being chased by daggers, looking to stab her heart to the point of no return. But what Zarin found more devastating is the *message* that Meli sent to Neal's phone. The text said, "Neal, my love, I am now flying out a few hours early. I booked an earlier flight for Sunday. I hope it doesn't complicate things for you. You may arrive at the airport a little late. But that's okay. The flight information says I shall arrive at JFK airport this Sunday morning by 8:35 a.m. So, I'll be waiting for you. I can't wait to see you. And I love you. Meli."

Zarin stood there in absolute shock. Neal's phone fell from her fingertips onto the floor. After giving her husband a night of absolute pleasure, Zarin felt the way she felt, back on the night when she first heard him on the phone with Meli. Just when Zarin thought she was taking four steps forward, she now had to take eight steps back.

Neal then came down in his German chocolate pajamas. He then walked over to Zarin and kissed her on her now drained face. He looked at her face and asked her if she was alright. Zarin put on a pretend smile and said, "Oh, yea, I'm fine. It's just my jaw is a little hurt, you know? I forgot how big you are." That comment right there made Neal's Night. After Zarin said that, Neal could *not* stop smiling. But Zarin did not want Neal to know that *she* now knows Meli is flying into town. So, Zarin played it off with a compliment. Again, confrontation was not her specialty. But Zarin does not know what to do. In three days, this woman is coming to see her husband. She does not know what to expect. Is Neal having an affair? Is he the father of Meli's unborn child? What is this secret that he is keeping from her? Zarin is so scared that this will end up being the end of her marriage.

As Neal was in the kitchen, making himself a sandwich, Zarin made her way up the stairs. Slow steps, slow movements; her smile has now turned into a frown. Zarin went into her bedroom to undress out of her rose-red lingerie, which *blossomed* but has now deteriorated. Standing in the nude, she walks into the bathroom, turning the shower nozzle to a lukewarm temperature.

Zarin cried more tears than ever before. Her anxiety has defeated her tonight. While she leaned up against the wall of the shower, all she could think of was Darsha and Joshna. She thought about how this could affect the two of them. But this is a situation that she does not want to face alone. Come tomorrow night; Zarin will sit with her ladies as she plans to settle this thing once and for all.

Chapter 14

It is Friday morning. Monica's husband, Sammy, has taken the kids off to school, and a verdict has been reached for her case. Today, Monica had to be on time, no exceptions. As Monica arrived at the courthouse, she saw a very familiar face. It was the face of one of her former clients. She represented this particular client when he was charged with armed robbery. But with Monica's genius quality and wit, she pulled off a miracle by getting him off. But unfortunately, he is right back in the system. He is on trial for not only armed robbery but also murder. Monica just stared at him, and he stared right back. She did not say a word to him. She gently shook her head and went on with her business.

As Monica walked into the courtroom, her client, Amir Jamestown, had not yet arrived. But there was time, as the court will not be in session for another twenty minutes. So, she had to wait. All Monica could think of was seeing her former client out there, right back where he started, in trouble once again with the law.

Ten minutes later, Monica's client finally arrives. He was dressed in the same navy-blue suit, with a white shirt and red tie. The bruises on his face had somewhat healed since the last time she saw him in court. Amir then took a look at his family, who were all sitting in the court as the audience. Now, the defense and the prosecution wait for the judge.

"Good morning Mr. Jamestown," said Monica. "How are you feeling today?"

"I'm scared shitless," Amir said as he was shaking his right leg.

"Everything's going to be alright," said Monica.

"All rise for the judge!" The bailiff said as the judge entered the courtroom. The judge was a tall and beautiful woman. Desirable features; had a face for film and television. She could easily be a movie star. Judge Westervelt told the court they could be seated. As judge Westervelt got situated, she was ready to hear the verdict. The entire court stood again as the jury entered. As the jury took their seats, one of the jury members handed the bailiff the envelope with the ruling. Monica kept her eyes focused on that envelope with the verdict. Her heart was racing, probably just as much as her client, Amir Jamestown. Monica has never lost a case before, and she does not want *this* case to be her first.

Judge Westervelt opened the envelope and said, "*We, the jury in an above-entitled manner as to second-degree attempted murder, find the defendant, Amir Jamestown, not guilty. As verdict agreed to this tenth day of February 2023, at 10:25 a.m.*" Even though Monica had to keep her composure, she jumped for joy and did cartwheels in her mind. However, her client, Amir Jamestown, just *had* to show his emotions as he shed tears of happiness and relief.

Another win under Monica's undefeated career. As her client's family approaches her, they thanked her with a bunch of hugs and kisses. All Monica could think of saying at that moment was this, "You're very welcome, this was a long journey, and I am just grateful for this verdict. I would love to celebrate with you all, but I have so many other things to take care of today. It's been an honor." Monica then collected her things and stuffed them in her briefcase. Then, finally, she was ready to head out of that courtroom and take that heavy load off of her shoulders. But before she left, her now *acquitted* client had something to say to her. "I cannot thank you enough, Ms. Taylor. You've saved my life," Amir said as he reached out his hand. As Monica shook Amir's hand, she said this to him, "You're welcome, but the real way to thank me is by changing your life. I may have saved your life. But you must now *change* your life. Stay out of the streets and out of trouble."

Monica then walked down the aisle of the courtroom. To the left of her was the family of Reginald Walker, the man involved in the altercation with Amir Jamestown. She saw the look of disgust and disappointment on their faces. They were infuriated that there was no justice for Reginald Walker. Monica simply ignored their expressions and walked out of the courtroom. Unapologetically, with confidence in her victory.

As Monica began walking down the cold street of lower Manhattan, she made a phone call to her husband, Sammy. She wanted to let him know that her client was acquitted, and she won her case. Sammy was so proud of her for winning this case. She was fighting hard for several months. Sammy then told Monica that they would celebrate this weekend as a family.

Usually, when Monica wins a case, she likes to take a walk down Battery Park. Specifically on the Hudson River Greenway. Even though it was cold out, the sun was shining enough to give a balance of warmth. So, she grabbed a cup of pumpkin spice coffee from Starbucks, located in Brookfield Place, right next to the Hudson River Greenway.

In one hand was her cup of coffee. In the other was her briefcase. She found a bench to sit on and began to enjoy her pumpkin spice delight. Sip after sip, Monica starts to reflect and think about her life. Unfortunately, she often does not have a chance to think about things while dealing with her kids, career, and Sammy. As a result, Monica rarely has time to think about herself. Since the Amir Jamestown case is over, Monica can put that in her past and focus on the present.

Monica sits and sips, looking at the waves of the Hudson River, looking over at the skyline of Jersey City. As Monica continues to reflect, she had thoughts that she could not get out of her head. She asked herself, "Is there something *missing* in my life right now?" Her life has been pretty straightforward. She was born in Chicago but grew up in New Jersey. She was raised by her parents, who have a *great* relationship and are still happily married. Monica then went to Rutgers to study law. Nothing too traumatizing happened during her childhood. Still sitting on that bench, Monica thought more and said to herself, "I have everything a woman could ever *dream* of having. I have a successful career. I have a loving husband, two *beautiful* kids, and four friends who I love as my sisters. I have a great life. Not to mention, I am an African American woman. Do I have it *too* good? Is there such thing as being *too* blessed? Is there something missing in my life, or do I simply have no worries?"

As Monica takes her last sip of coffee, she begins to question her happiness. For so long, Monica relied on her success as an attorney for her happiness. But now, her *happiness* is becoming very unclear. All of a sudden, she gets a vibration from her phone. It was a group text from Tomi, telling everyone that she safely landed, and she is back in the Big Apple. That put a smile on Monica's face. Monica responded, saying, "Yes bitch, I can't wait for us to get together tonight." Monica then got up from the bench and made her way home. Sammy said he would pick the kids up from school. So, Monica went home to take a well-needed nap before heading out to *Lucille's* for the evening.

After walking a few blocks away from Battery Park, Monica was able to hail down a taxicab. As she was riding, she began to look at the tiny television in the backseat of the cab. It was showing the news, and by sheer coincidence, Monica saw Zarin as one of the news anchors. She laughed and pulled out her phone to take a picture. Monica then sent it to Zarin with a text saying, "I see you, you sexy bitch. LOL!" A few minutes later, Zarin got back to her and replied, "LMAO! Love you, babe! See ya tonight."

As the commercials came on, there came a brief ad on the side of the television. It was an ad for this therapist by the name of Dr. Melissa McAdams. When Monica saw the ad, she gave it some thought. She thought to herself, "*Would that help? Should*

I look into seeing a therapist? Perhaps a therapy session would give me some clarity?"

There was a barcode that takes you to Dr. Melissa McAdams' website. Monica scanned it with her phone and began to take a look. As Monica looked, she read some of the testimonials that Dr. McAdams' patients left. Though Monica found Dr. McAdams' credentials impressive, she still was unsure if she would be willing to share her personal business with a stranger.

About twenty-three minutes and thirty-two dollars later, Monica arrives at her home. She got to the front door of her brownstone and grabbed the mail from the mailbox. "Nothing but bills, bills, bills," Monica said, looking through the envelopes. As Monica came inside, she went to the hallway closet, dropped her briefcase on the floor, and took off her Ivory peacoat. She then took off her heels and made her way into the kitchen. On the refrigerator door, Monica saw a note with a rose taped beside it. On the note, it said,

"Take off all your clothes and meet me in the bathroom.
Hurry before the water gets cold."

At first, Monica was confused. She was not expecting Sammy to be home. But Monica played along and walked over to the stairs. As she listened, she heard the sound of music. The lovely, poetic voice of Jill Scott was playing upstairs. Monica then took off her suit jacket, then her shirt, and then her pants. As she reached the top of the stairs, she made her way to the master bathroom. She opened the bathroom door to find her husband, Sammy, soaking in a bubble-filled bathtub. Monica could not help but smile and sigh.

Sammy filled the bathroom with lit candles; rose peddles on the floor and in the bathtub. The first thing that came out of Monica's mouth was, "*How romantic....*" Sammy then put his hands together and began to give her a gently round of applause. "What's the special occasion?" Monica said as she stood there in awe.

Sammy looked at her from in the tub and said, "I said we would celebrate together as a family. But I wanted to start *our* celebration early. So, I called your mom; she's picking the kids up from school, and they'll stay with your parents for the weekend. I just wanted to have you to myself. And to tell you that I am *so* proud of you. You work so hard, saving people's lives, defending your clients, and helping them achieve justice. You're smart, beautiful, and you're an excellent mother to our kids— such a supporter of my career. I could not be happier to call you my wife. I love you, baby. Now, *get* your *sexy ass* in this tub with me."

Monica just stood there, wiping away her tears of appreciation. Even though Valentine's Day was only a few days away, she was getting special treatment early. She then slowly took off her bra and then her panties. She got into the lukewarm bath, took a deep breath, and exhaled. Sammy was on one end of the tub. In contrast, Monica was on the other. As Monica lays there, she began to close her eyes and smile, while Sammy starts to rub and wash her right foot. He even gave her foot a few kisses. Nor Monica or Sammy said much during this special occasion. Nor was anything needed to be said. They were in the moment.

Monica then changed her position in the tub. Instead of laying across from Sammy in the tub, she laid on top of him, with her back pressed against his chest. Sammy then took his hands and began to massage her neck and shoulders. The sounds of Monica's moans, creating a romantic cadence. Without question, she needed this. She needed this feeling of appreciation and love. To be loved and appreciated is what Monica felt was missing, perhaps? After experiencing this, she realized that her husband is still in love with her. He acknowledges her hard work, as an attorney, as a mother, and as a supportive wife.

Monica now knows how blessed she is. Even though she still has that therapist in the back of her mind. But right now, at this very moment, all she needs is her husband. So, as Monica opened her eyes, she looked at Sammy, kissed him, and said, "I love you more, hubby, and thank you so much." Perhaps sometimes, the healthiest thing to do in a marriage is to show your *love* and *appreciation* for each other. Otherwise, what is the purpose of being married?

Chapter 15

The boss has entered the building. Tomi has arrived at her high-rise office in Mid-town Manhattan. As the gold elevator doors opened, she is greeted by many of her staff and few assistants. Everyone around her saying, "Good afternoon Ms. Belacone." Tomi came in with her stylish midnight blue jacket, white turtleneck, white pants, and white heels. Not to mention sporting her brand new $5,500 ivory marble shades from her *Orell Llero* 2023 collection.

Walking into her office, Tomi had a sudden taste for a B.L.T. As she took off her jacket, she reached over to the left drawer of her desk and pulled out a menu.

"Carmelo, my love," said Tomi. "Can you get me some of the best coffee and a B.L.T. sandwich from that diner down the street? Oh, and please do not forget the avocado."

"Yes, Ms. Bellas," Carmelo spoke. "I'll tell them to toast it, and would you like home fries?"

"No, just the coffee and sandwich, please. Thank you, baby."

Tomi then handed Carmelo a fifty-dollar bill to pay for the sandwich. Tomi's office was a majestic environment. She had a white suede couch, three softly cushioned sitting chairs, and her all-black marble desk. Her office gave off a *Cruella de Vil* vibe once you stepped inside. She kept a mini bar on the side with her favorite wine, champagne, and vodka for an emergency drink. She also had the perfect view of Manhattan. Even though Tomi fears heights, she got used to her office being on the top floor. On her wall were three life-size pictures. One was of Audrey Hepburn, who is her absolute favorite actress. The second picture was of Jim Morrison. And last but not least, a photo of her grandfather, the late Orell Llero.

Let's go back to the history of how *Orell Llero* became Tomi's empire. Tomi's grandfather, Orell Llero, was born in Florence, Italy, in 1921. By the year 1925, Orell came to America with his mother and father. They came through Ellis Island, as did many immigrants. And like many other immigrants during that time,

Orell and his parents started with very little money. To find work, Orell's father became a tailor, and his mother was a designer. As Orell got older, he began to learn how to design and tailor clothes as well. He had a gift, impeccable vision, and Orell had his eyes set on the prize.

In the year 1939, Orell met the love of his life, Marie Piazza. They met when Marie came into his father's tailor shop to get some pants hem. When Orell saw Marie, it was love at first sight. Their first date was to the movie theater, watching one of the most anticipated movies of that year, "*The Wizard of Oz.*" After watching the movie, seeing all those colorful outfits worn by the munchkins. The film hit Orell with such inspiration for designing clothes that would be innovative and revolutionary.

Orell went on to design these overly utopian outfits. He created *hundreds* of different sketches and saved them in his drawing books. He even saw himself collaborating with Walt Disney one day.

Orell wasted no time marrying Marie and getting her pregnant. Their first child, a son they named Orell Jr., was born on August 21, 1940, and their second and last child, Arianna, who is Tomi's mother, was born on February 27th, 1942. Of course, during these times, World War II was in full effect. The attack on Pearl Harbor happened, and many American men were drafted from the west coast to the east coast. One of those men was Orell.

Orell was devastated to fight in this war. He was leaving behind his children, his wife Marie, and his dreams of becoming one of the world's most fabulous designers to ever lived. And unfortunately, *his* dreams would never come true. On November 13th, 1942, Orell's wife, Marie, received a telegram from the army. Marie did not even get to the second sentence. All she saw was, *"We regret to inform you."* The love of her life was gone, leaving behind her and their two children.

Several decades later, the Vietnam War violently emerged. Orell Jr. enlisted, even after his mother, Marie, told him not to. Orell Jr. survived the war physically. But mentally, he was never the same again. As for Arianna, she lived her life throughout the years, met men, partied, became involved in the sixties' political era, and started making babies. Her first child, Pauly, was born on April 4th, 1968, her second child, Frankie, was born on September 11th,1974, and her last child, Tomi, was born on February 24th, 1979, which is unique because she and Tomi's birthday are three days apart. Tomi is the special one. Not just because she is Arianna's one and only daughter, it is because Arianna was not planning to have Tomi. She planned on having an abortion. Arianna did not want to have any more children. Not to mention, she did not even know who the father could be. So, the day before her appointment, Arianna took a look at her father's sketchbooks of his designs. Arianna thought and asked herself, *"What if I have a girl? She could be the one to carry on my father's legacy."*

That appointment never took place. And Arianna had a beautiful baby girl. Arianna put her father's sketchbooks in Tomi's hands at the very young age of five years old. She told Tomi that the choice is hers with how she will choose to live her life. But what Arianna hoped was for Tomi to carry on her grandfather's legacy. And *that* is what Tomi did, proudly and successfully. Tomi did the work; she modeled, went to design school, found some investors to form her own company, and almost two decades later, she's on top of the fashion world. In honor of her grandfather, Tomi named her brand after him. After all, she used many of his sketches for her collections, which were remarkable in every way.

As Tomi sits in her office, waiting for Carmelo to come back with her coffee and B.L.T. sandwich, she took a long stare at the picture of her grandfather, Orell Llero. She thought about what it would have been like to meet him. To have been able to sit on his lap while he reads her a story. Or to even sketch and design clothes with him. Tomi never had that chance, that life experience. Then came a knock on her office door.

"Hi Ms. Belacone, do you have a minute to look over our upcoming spring collection?" Said her design team supervisor.

"Yes, Sarah, now's perfect; come in," Tomi responded.

As Sarah placed the booklet on the desk, Tomi put on her glasses and closely analyzed each piece. Tomi had the magic eye for details and patterns. She used some of her grandfather's sketches and collaborated on ideas of her own. But her team is the masterminds of bringing it all together as the *tangible*, finished product. But after looking at the forty new pieces for their spring collection, Tomi was not entirely impressed or satisfied. Tomi got up from her chair and said this to Sarah, "We are *not* pushing the envelope enough with these pieces. We have to take some fucking risk. We must break away from the clichés. Tell the team that I will be down in the draping room as soon as I finish my lunch. We have work to do."

Sarah then took the binder of the spring collection and left Tomi's office. Tomi may be a little pussycat towards her friends. But when it comes to *fashion*, she could easily be the devil who wears Prada. Well, in her case, the devil who wears *Orell Llero*. About ten minutes later, Carmelo came back with Tomi's lunch, but he had a very distraught look on his face. He said, "Ms. Bellas, I'm so sorry for the delay. But I am *livid* by their piss poor service at that diner. The waiter was a *bitch*, with a capital "*ITCH*," so I canceled that shit, and I seriously doubt they have the coffee right. But I had a backup plan and got your favorite, fried calamari with garlic parmesan dip."

Tomi was a little disappointed that she was not going to be having a B.L.T. for lunch. But she would be okay with her fried calamari. She thanked Carmelo and told him to meet her in the draping room in forty-five minutes. One by one, Tomi enjoyed every piece of fried calamari. With two more pieces to go, Tomi had to stop immediately. Her stomach was growing rather upset as the fried calamari and coffee were *not* the best food and drink collaboration. Tomi's stomach was not happy at all. Tomi then grabbed her phone and began to speed walk her way out of her office and into the ladies' room. She made it just in time to take care of her business—that *poor* toilet.

As Tomi sits in the stall, someone else came into the ladies' room. Tomi hears a familiar voice talking on the phone. It was the voice of her design team supervisor, Sarah. As Tomi listened, she was utterly appalled at what Sarah was saying. Sarah went on and on about Tomi. About how she cannot stand the sight of her or work for such an evil and unappreciative bitch. But Tomi is *no* bitch to be played with at all. And she knew just what to do. Tomi then took her phone and opened it to her voice recording app. Tomi then pressed record and documented the rest of Sarah's rant. Unbeknownst to Sarah, she was not alone. And what was worse, Tomi, her boss, was inside there with her.

Finally, after five minutes of recording, Tomi saved the file and hung up her phone. She then waited for Sarah to walk out of the restroom. If only you could see the look on Tomi's face.

She could not be any more prepared to hand Sarah that pink slip and give her the boot. So, Tomi then came out of the stall with a somewhat calm and confident facial expression. She looked at herself in the mirror and said, "Let me go out here and fire this fucking cunt."

As Tomi made her way back to her office, she walked over to one of her assistants. "I need Sarah in my office *right now*," Tomi projected. Tomi then waited for five minutes, wearing a very smooth smirk on her face. And in came Sarah.

"Hey, Ms. Belacone, you wanted to see me?" Sarah said with the biggest smile on her face.

"Yes, I wanted to see you. Please close the door," Tomi said to Sarah.

Sarah took one look at Tomi and knew this could not be good. She then attempted to take a seat, and Tomi, *so* infuriated, said, "Don't you *dare* sit your fucking two-faced ass in my chair." Sarah then stood there with a very fearful look on her face.

"Do you have something that you would like to say to me, Sarah? To my *face*?" Tomi said to Sarah.

"Umm…Uh, no, Ms. Belacone," said Sarah. "I was just waiting for you down in the drapi—"

"*Draping* room? Right. You certainly had a *lot* to say in that bathroom, didn't you?"

"I don't know what you're talking abo—"

"Keep quiet and listen."

Tomi was not a woman to waste any time. She held her phone in her hand and began waving it side to side. Tomi told Sarah that she overheard her phone conversation in the bathroom. And not only did she *hear* Sarah, but she recorded what Sarah said. Tomi then placed her phone down on her desk and pressed play. In the recording, Sarah said this, "I am so *fucking* done with this wannabe Anna Wintour, Coco Chanel, plastic fake bitch, and her sorry ass clothing line. She had the nerve to tell *me* that we are not pushing the envelope enough and have to do more. How fucking dare her? *Right*, how dare she say that to me? I was standing there in her office thinking to myself, "Are you *fucking* serious?" *Maybe* if she wasn't traveling three-thousand miles to get Botox done on her wrinkled ass face, she could be more productive here. But to be honest, she's not even that *talented* as the world thinks she is. She just used her grandfather's sketches and got famous off of *him*. She is *not* the genius that everyone believes her to be. And I would tell her that to her *face* if I had the chance!" Tomi then stopped the recording right there.

"And now here's your chance, Sarah," said Tomi. "You have your chance right now to say *whatever* you have to say; *to my face*."

"Ms. Belacone, I am so, so, sorr—"

"You're *Fired*! Get the *fuck* out of my office!" Tomi said as she fixed herself a drink.

Sarah did not know what to say at all. All she could do was cry as she opened the door and walked out of Tomi's office. Employees began to look at Sarah as she made her way to the elevator with a sobbing face. Then everyone started to look at Tomi. But Tomi was in no mood. She looked at everyone and shouted, "DON'T LOOK AT ME! GET BACK TO WORK, OR YOU'LL END UP LIKE HER!" Tomi then slammed her door and fixed herself another drink.

With her back turned, Tomi did not see her husband, Thomas, at her office door. He knocked on the door. As Tomi's back was still turned, she said, "Please, this is not the time. I'm not ready to speak to anyone."

"Tomi, it's me," Thomas said as he opened the door.

"Oh, I'm sorry, honey," Tomi responded. "I thought you were one of the staff."

Tomi walked over, kissed Thomas, and told him about what just happened. She even played the recording of Sarah's rant for Thomas to hear. After hearing the whole recording, Thomas was ready to curse Sarah out himself. He is very protective of his wife, as he should be. But Tomi told him that she already fired Sarah. However, even though Tomi fired Sarah, her feelings on the inside are still damaged. After hearing what Sarah said, Tomi's confidence in herself was pulled from beneath her. She began to feel that her talent was not as exceptional as she believes it to be. That all of her success is solely and *only* because of her grandfather's designs.

It bothered Tomi so much that she had to ask Thomas if she is good enough. He hugged her, then looked at her and said, "Tomi, I've watched you go through *hell* to get this company off the ground running. I saw you bust your ass for *years*. Taking odd jobs, saving money, building a team of people, and *you* created an empire of your own. *You* are my biggest inspiration. Not only do I love who you are, but I admire you. I truly do, honey. Your grandfather had the sketches, but *you* have the heart and soul, the *wit* and willpower. It was *your* destiny to carry on his legacy. And he would be so proud of you, Tomi. All of your success was no accident. It's pure fate. Don't *ever* forget that, okay? I love you."

That put such a great smile on Tomi's face. She needed to hear that from Thomas. As she wiped her eyes, she decided to get her things together and leave the office with Thomas. Carmelo made his way towards the office as Tomi was just walking *out* of her office.

"Ms. Bellas, where are you dipping off to now? I thought we were going to meet Sarah in the draping room?" Carmelo said to Tomi.

"Listen, Melo man," said Tomi. "I had to *fire* that backstabbing bitch. I'm going to Airdrop you the recording of what she said about me. Then you'll understand why."

"Oh, another one bites the dust, huh?" said Carmelo.

"The bitch should've bitten her fucking tongue."

A half-hour past five. Tomi had to make a quick stop home to shower and get ready to reunite with the other four ladies at *Lucille's*. As they arrived home, Thomas asked if he could join Tomi in the shower. "Nothing is stopping you," said Tomi. For a woman in her forties, Tomi still has a body to die for. Years of swimming, yoga, and exercise have paid off for her indefinitely. Thomas himself had a decent body type.

Even though they were both in the nude, showering together, *sex* was not invited. Tomi just wanted his company. She wanted his comfort in the lukewarm drops falling from the four showerheads above them. Tomi looked at him with her piercing brown eyes, staring at her man with the look of love. She appreciated her hubby and what he said to her back at her office. He reminded her of her ambition and dedication, to not only keep her grandfather's legacy alive but to acknowledge *herself* within it.

As she got out of the shower and dried herself off, it was already a quarter to seven o'clock. Tomi already knew that she would be a little late arriving after getting dressed and putting on her makeup. So, she called her limo driver, Benjamin, ahead of time and told him to be downstairs by 7:45 p.m.

As Tomi was putting on her makeup, she received a Facetime call from Carmelo. As they began talking, Carmelo said, "Oh my *God*, Ms. Bellas, I cannot *believe* that *salty bitch*. You should've come from out of that stall and stuck her head in that damn toilet. Not only am I glad that you caught that ho, but I'm glad that you *fired* that ho. Karma's a *bad bitch*, and Sarah got what she deserved." Tomi had no choice but to laugh at Carmelo. That is her baby.

Even though it has been a long day for Tomi, it was not over just yet. Tonight, she is *back* in the Big Apple. Ready to have some *drinks*, have a great time with her friends, her sisters, and also get to the bottom of this "*oink* situation." As Tomi headed to the elevator that takes her from her penthouse to the lobby, she began to think about how lucky she is. Not just about her career, but about her husband and her friends. To be able to go out and be surrounded by people who love and care for her. For Tomi, that is priceless. Something she *truly* appreciates. Something she would *never* trade for the world.

Chapter 16

What a busy night here at *Lucille's*; waiters are being called from left to right, table to table. All the ladies have arrived, except for Tomi. Monica and Wendy were too hungry to wait. So, they ordered some appetizers. Collette and Zarin were okay for now with sipping on their wine.

"God, where is she?" Said Wendy. "Can someone call her?"

"I sent her a text saying that we are waiting for her. But she didn't respond," Collette said to Wendy.

A few minutes later, Tomi shows up. "There's our fabulous girl! Looking all sexy and brand new," said Monica. "Whattaya *hear*, Whattaya *say*? I'm sorry, I had to. I watched

"*Angels with Dirty Faces*" on the plane coming back," Tomi said. Tomi then did a round of hugs and kisses to each of the ladies. As Tomi sat down with the others, she said, "Please forgive my tardiness. I had such a shitty afternoon. And I was in such a rush to get home and get ready to see you gals. I missed you crazy bitches so much. But anyway, you all know how I don't waste any time. Zarin, baby, about this "*oink* situation." I need you to break it *all* the way down for me."

The meals began to arrive on the table of their reserved booth. Zarin went over all the details about her "*oink* situation." She also told the others about how this "Meli" character will be flying in this Sunday. After Zarin finished her elaboration, Collette said, "Who does that bitch think she is? Does she know that Neal is a married man? These fucking homewreckers out here, I swear." "Now wait a minute, Zarin. I mentioned before that this *might* be a complete misunderstanding. Are you sure that Neal is having an affair?" Tomi asked Zarin. "I'm not sure *what* to believe. I just have a terrible feeling about all of this. And this woman is coming on Sunday. What am I supposed to do?" Said Zarin.

About forty-five seconds go by, dead silence at the booth. The ladies began to put on their thinking caps and brainstorm about how they could help Zarin get to the bottom of this profound, mysterious dilemma. Until Collette snapped her fingers and said, "Come this Sunday, we're going to *stalk* that bastard." They all looked at Collette as if she lost her damn mind. Monica said, "Coco, have you lost your goddamn mind? We are *not* about to *stalk* her husband to see if he's cheating. That is an all-time low for us. And Zarin, don't even *entertain* that idea."

"Well fuck it, let's do it. I don't have shit else to do on Sunday," Tomi said as she guzzled down her half-full glass of wine.

"Yea, I don't know about that. I'm with Monica on this one. This all sounds crazy," Wendy said to the group.

Zarin was not at all disagreeable about what Collette had proposed they do. She was even opened to help orchestrate a plan to set up this rather mission impossible idea. But Monica was still against it. Monica was trying to convince Zarin not to pay this thought of stalking her husband any attention. But the idea was already sparked in Zarin's mind. The candle has been lit. And like a melted candle, it was going down.

"I want to do this. I want the truth to come out," Zarin said.

"Okay, this is fucking ridiculous. Count me out," said Wendy.

Tomi insisted that the *five* of them come together and solve this issue for Zarin. But Monica and Wendy were not on board. Monica then brought up a good point by saying, "Wait a minute, ladies, instead of trying to do all of this mission impossible shit, let's just be adults about this. Zarin, what is so hard with just sitting down with Neal and asking him if he's having an affair? *Or* if he got another woman pregnant?" Wendy agreed with Monica and added to that by saying, "Yea, all of this other shit we are talking about could be avoided. Just *ask* him, Zarin."

In Zarin's mind, she felt that having a sit-down conversation with Neal had already gone past her. "I think I have already missed that train. I thought by ignoring it that it would just go away, that *she* would go away. I'm just not used to something like this, and I don't want to face it. I don't want to face it alone. I would appreciate it if all of you ladies could help me. And to think I even gave him fellatio last night," said Zarin.

The rest of the women were hit with sudden confusion. After Zarin told them that she performed oral sex on her husband, they began to lean on the reality that maybe Neal is *not* having an affair. "Uh, Zarin, babe, if you're going down on your husband, I don't think you should be worried about if he's having an affair," Wendy said. "Yea, I'm still not sure if he's cheating, honey. But for you, I'll help," Monica said.

A friendly smile began to grow on Zarin's face. So far, Tomi, Collette, and Monica were on board. But Wendy held on to her hesitant state of mind. After thinking it over, Wendy said to the group, "I'm sorry, I just have a lot on my plate. My boss is not making me a partner. I was looking forward to this for *months*. But Mrs. Shultz telling me no, it just put me in a shitty mood. And I have the wedding tomorrow. Then right after the wedding, I have to finish packing because I'm taking EJ to Tokyo with my parents. I need the vacation. So, this whole stalking situation is just bad timing for me right now."

Zarin understood Wendy's situation and told her that she did not have to be involved if she doesn't want to be. But Tomi chimed in to try to convince Wendy that she is needed. Tomi said to Wendy, "Wendy, my love, if it were you, we would *all* be there for you, baby. Zarin is our sister, and we have to be there for each other, no matter what. I know you may disagree with the stalking part. But she needs you, Wendy."

Wendy took her hands and placed them on her forehead. She then rubbed her forehead and grazed her fingers through her hair as she sighed. "This better be worth it. That's all I'm going to say. What the fuck are we planning to do anyway?" Said Wendy. Collette then waved down their waiter and said, "Excuse me, baby, we're going to need a few more bottles of wine."

As the time was close to the stroke of midnight, the ladies called it a night. *Lucille's* had already closed the kitchen at eleven o'clock, but Collette has the power to keep them in their reserved booth a little longer. As they gathered their coats and purses, they made their way out of the door. Collette had to make a quick stop upstairs at Martin's office. Wendy decided to take an Uber home as she has an early morning and was too tired to wait. Monica and Zarin chose to stay and catch a ride home in Tomi's limo.

A few paparazzi waited out in the cold to snap a few dozen photos of Tomi as the grand opening of her upcoming *Orell Llero* storefront is approaching. Flashes upon flashes, but they do not phase her one bit. Tomi just puts on her shades and goes about her business.

"Tomi! Tomi! Look this way! Right here!" Said one of the cameramen.

"Just take the pictures sweetheart, you'll make money off of any of them," Tomi said as she walked to her awaited limo.

Collette finally made her way out of *Lucille*'s and into the limo with Monica, Zarin, and Tomi already inside. Zarin was the first to be dropped off. Before Zarin got out, she said, "Don't forget Tomi, we're setting up at my house. Be there as early as possible on Sunday. I don't know when Neal's going to leave." Tomi, Monica, and Collette all confirmed their positions for Sunday.

Twenty minutes later, Tomi's limo dropped off Monica, leaving Collette and Tomi in the back of the limo together. Collette asked Tomi if they could drive around and talk for a bit before she went home. "Oh, of course, Coco. I was planning on doing my midnight run anyway," said Tomi. A "midnight run," as Tomi is referring to, is what she does whenever she feels restless and wants to go for a ride. At midnight, she would call her limo driver, Benjamin, and ask him if he is available for a midnight run. He would pick her up and simply drive around the city at the wee hours of the night. Tomi would be in the back seat listening to music, drinking wine, and sight-seeing the city nightlife. Or basically, just to clear her thoughts. Tomi would go all over Manhattan, Queens, Brooklyn, or even Yonkers to gamble at *Empire Casino*. It is very soothing and relaxing for her. And it is *never* a problem for Benjamin because she pays him $10,000 for the night.

They make their way uptown on the east side of Manhattan. Collette and Tomi are having a conversation. Collette began to tell Tomi about what is going on in her family. "So, remember when I told you guys about Mia and how she was suspended for bringing that sex toy and weed to school?" Collette said. Tomi shook her head and said, "Yes, of course, I do." Collette continued and said, "Well, those belonged to Emilio. Mia found them in his dresser at home. And last night, I talked with Emilio. It took him a minute, but he *came out* and told me his truth."

"Oh, wow. Well, *that's* news," Tomi said. Tomi was in a bit of shock. To hear that Collette's son has come out as a gay man. Tomi was curious to know how Collette's husband, Martin, felt about all of this. Collette gave Tomi a side-eye and said, "Girl, he doesn't know *anything*. Martin is not exactly a supporter of other sexualities. And I don't know *when* the right time will be to tell him."

As Tomi took a sip of her wine, she encouraged Collette to tell Martin the truth. "Coco, even though Martin is against that, he needs to know the truth. But then again, I am not a parent. I don't have the answers to, you know, *parenting shit*," said Tomi. Collette laughed and said, "That's okay; when the time comes for Martin to know, he will know."

Another twenty minutes go by, and Collette was ready to call it a night. Her eyelids were growing heavy, and she told Tomi she wanted to go home. Tomi told Benjamin to drop Collette off. As they arrived in front of Collette's apartment building, they said good night to each other. "Okay, my love, it was great to see you all tonight. Have a goodnight, well, good morning," Tomi said as she hugged and kissed Collette. "Yea, it's already twenty past one in the morning. It was great to see you too. And I guess I'll see you on Sunday?" Collette said as she got out of the limo.

As Tomi continued riding around for a half-hour, she began to yawn as she grew tired. She made a call to Benjamin and said, "Ben, my love, I think I'm going to end the midnight run a little early. Can you take me to my penthouse in midtown?"

Tomi then poured herself one more glass of red wine, as she has another fifteen minutes to get there. Suddenly, the limo hit a big pothole. "FUCK! BENJAMIN!" Tomi shouted. The limo hitting the pothole caused Tomi to spill her red wine all over her white pants. As they pulled up in front of the building of Tomi's penthouse, Benjamin got out of the car and rushed over to the back door, where Tomi was seated. Tomi then rolled down her window.

"Ah *man*, Ms. Belacone, I'm *so* sorry," Benjamin said as he saw the mess.

"Ben, honey, *look* at this shit!" Tomi yelled. "I look like I got my *fucking* period. And the *goddamn* paparazzi is out there, *what the fuck!*"

In an instant, Benjamin suggested that Tomi wraps her coat around her waist to cover up the wine stain on her pants. But Tomi, being a genius, thought of a *brilliant* way to market and promote her brand new *Orell Llero* winter coat. She told Benjamin to get back in the front seat and wait for her to call him back out to open the door. At first, Benjamin did not understand what Tomi was doing, but he played along. As he closed the door, Tomi began to undress. She quickly took off her red wine-stained pants. Then she removed her sweater. The flashing lights from the paparazzi's cameras were flashing all through the tinted windows. At that very moment, Tomi did the unthinkable. She took off her bra and then draped her coat over her nude body. Wearing *only* her new coat, panties, and red bottom heels, Tomi was ready to make an *exclusive* appearance. As mentioned before, Tomi has a great body, and she is not afraid to flaunt it. She then called for Benjamin to open the back door.

As Benjamin opened the door and Tomi stepped out, the paparazzi went into an absolute frenzy. Their cameras were flashing a hundred times a minute. Tomi looked incredibly stunning. Her 2023 *Orell Llero* winter coat covered her body, showing just enough cleavage, but she did not present herself in a trashy way. Tomi relished in the moment. She even did a little catwalk for the crowd. She walked back and forth on the red carpet of the building's front entrance. Before heading into the building, she said *this* to the paparazzi, "I hope you enjoyed the show, gentlemen! This is the newest piece from my 2023 Winter collection. You all have a fabulous night."

As Tomi made her way to her special elevator, the concierge looked in shock. "Um, uh, good…Good *evening* Mrs. Belacone," said the concierge. Tomi blew him a kiss and told him to have a good night as well. As soon as the elevator doors closed, Tomi immediately put her hands together in the shape of a ball, blowing air into her hands to make them warm. "*Fuck*, it was cold out there!" Tomi said in the elevator. Even though it made her freeze, she was confident that her sexy stunt would pay off.

As the elevator doors opened, she stepped into her luxurious penthouse. The song "*Windmills of Your Mind*," sung by Sting, was playing in the background. You see an enormous picture of Audrey Hepburn in the living room, two of Thomas' sculptures; one of a half-naked man and a wolf. The fireplace was burning, which meant that someone was home. Thomas came walking into the living room. As he saw Tomi standing there half-naked under her coat, he had to look twice to make sure he was not hallucinating. "*Woah*! Um, is it my birthday or something?" Thomas said as he observed Tomi.

But Tomi did not tell him precisely what happened with the red wine incident. So, she simply played it off and said, "Well, I figured I'd give you an early Valentine's Day gift." Tomi then took her coat off and seductively launched it at Thomas. As he grabbed it, looking at her sexy figure, he smiled and began to walk towards her.

"*God*, you're so fucking sexy. How did I get so lucky to be with a woman like you?" Thomas said as he began kissing all over Tomi.

"Tommy, take me to bed," Tomi said.

Thomas said nothing more and did what Tomi ask of him. He picked her up and carried her into their master bedroom. Earlier, in the shower, sex was not invited. But when he took her into their bedroom, not only was sex invited, *sex* had V.I.P. status.

There is nothing like lovemaking with the help of *Sade's* music playing in the background. The caressing, kissing, the gentle touching, Tomi was in paradise. The damped bedsheets, the romantic aroma in the air. Thomas knew how to please his hard-working wife—kissing her all over her body—stimulating her mind. And then, the climax was reached.

They breathe in heavy harmony. In each other's arms, in an amorous comfort. Thomas runs his fingers through Tomi's mid-length brown hair. As Tomi caresses his chest, she begins to look at her wedding ring. She thought about how fortunate she is to be married to this man. This man is the love of her life. She is in his arms right now. And nothing could be better than that.

As the clock reached six a.m., both Thomas and Tomi were sound asleep. But then suddenly, Tomi's eyes opened, and she could not go back to sleep. So, Tomi slowly slid her naked body out of bed so that she did not wake Thomas. She loved being in the nude as she walked around the house. It made her feel free. As she walked, bare feet, she went over to the living room window. Looking at one of the most beautiful views any human being could lay eyes on as the sun had begun to rise. The picture-perfect image of the sky always takes her breath away. At first, Tomi was going to grab her phone to take a picture. But then she thought about it and said no. Tomi felt that this work of God is only meant to be captured with her own two eyes. It was for her eyes to enjoy and not the eye of a camera.

As Tomi stared at the sunrise, Thomas quietly made his way towards her with her silk robe. He kissed her on her shoulder and said, "Good morning, lover. Last night was, it was, it was magic. *Pure magic.*" Tomi then kissed him, put on her robe, and walked away without saying a word. Tomi believes in magic but does not believe that she was gifted with the magic of conceiving a child. That is the magic that Tomi has been missing for her entire adult life. It was the magic that she would sacrifice her empire for, just to bring life through her into the world. But that train, unfortunately, never stopped for her.

Chapter 17

Wedding bells are ringing on this beautiful Saturday morning. She did it again; Wendy has created yet another masterpiece. This wedding is taken place at the Presbyterian Church on Fifth Avenue. Wendy was able to acquire the Sweet Avalanche roses, as well as the Beluga Caviar. The mother of the bride, Mrs. Appleton, was very much indeed happy with Wendy's swift arrangements.

"Oh Wendy, this wedding looks fabulous! And you got everything done perfectly," Mrs. Appleton said to Wendy.

"Well, thank you, Mrs. Appleton. And Hayley looks exquisitely beautiful in her wedding dress," Wendy said to the mother of the bride.

As the wedding begins, Wendy double-checks the lineup. Making sure everyone is set up in the order they rehearsed. The groomsman and bridesmaids were all present, but Wendy was missing two small elements: the flower girl and the ringbearer. In a church with a capacity of close to two thousand people but hundreds of guests, and the wedding starting in five minutes, Wendy was close to hitting the panic button.

Wendy looked all over the church for the two of them. She looked upstairs in the balcony, in the closet space, everywhere except for outside, which was where they were. Little Bobby and Tiffany were outside throwing little snowballs at each other, which were the remains of a winter storm from a few weeks ago. Wendy could not believe the both of them were outside without any adult supervision. As Wendy went down the stairs, she said, "Oh, Bobby, Tiffany, the wedding is about to start, my loves. I need you to wipe your hands and go back inside with the others, okay?" Wendy said, relieved that she found them.

The wedding has now begun. My God, if only you could see the decorations of this wedding. The vision that Wendy saw through with this wedding was majestic. The Sweet Avalanche roses were beautifully set on each row of seating. The white fabrics draped above people's heads: the white doves, the fairy tale dream she made come true. Wendy stood up on the balcony as she watched the wedding ceremony. While she watched, she took notes. Wendy has been doing this method since she first started planning weddings. She would take notes on certain things, such as the timing of the bridesmaids and groomsman, how long apart they should be coming in after each other. As well as not being repetitive with her decorations. Wendy was very much her *own* critic, as well as a perfectionist.

As Wendy continued to watch the ceremony, she began to feel a buzz on her Apple watch. It was a phone call from her husband, Edward. She stepped away from the balcony and went into a secluded area of the church. As Wendy answered, she said, "Hey, now's not a good time. I'm right in the middle of the wedding." Edward called to let Wendy know that he would not be able to pick up EJ from her parents' house.

With frustration, Wendy responded, "Eddie, I *told* you that I was not going to have time to pick up *EJ*. I told you my parents have to get their paperwork and passport taken care of for our trip to Tokyo. And I'm at this wedding, I cannot just up and leave. Babe, you *have* to help me out here." But help from Edward was not going to happen. He was directing the final day of rehearsals for his show.

Wendy had to make a decision, and she had to make it fast. Does she stay at the wedding until the ceremony is done? Or does she go to pick up EJ? Or *perhaps* she could call on EJ's godmother, Zarin, and ask for a favor? *Wendy* made that call.

Even though Wendy feels somewhat guilty for being hesitant to help Zarin with this stalking plan, she needs Zarin's help right now. Wendy then went downstairs and made that call to Zarin. The phone rang, and rang, and rang. But no answer. Wendy began to grow worried. The ceremony was almost done, and she needed to make a decision quickly.

Wendy's phone then began to buzz, but it was not Zarin calling. It was her mother. Wendy answered, and her mother said, "Wendy-san, when is Edward coming? We have to leave soon." Wendy told her mother that Edward got tied up with rehearsal and could not pick up EJ. At that very exact moment, in comes a call from Zarin. Wendy then put her mother on hold and answered Zarin's call.

"Hey babe, sorry I missed your call. What's up?" Zarin said to Wendy.

"Hey, so, uh…I have a favor to ask of you," Wendy said with a guilty tone in her voice.

Wendy told Zarin about her situation with EJ. She asked Zarin if she could pick up EJ from her parent's house and if EJ can stay with her for a few hours. Zarin felt a little steamed about Wendy needing her. After how Wendy was so hesitant last night about helping with this mission impossible plan on Sunday. But Zarin is not the type of person to hold back and not be there for Wendy, especially since EJ is her godson.

"Sure, babe, I can go pick up EJ right now. Just text me your mother's address and let her know I'm on my way," Zarin said to Wendy.

"Oh God, Zarin, you are an angel. Thank you so much, babe. I'll be there as soon as I can. I love you," Wendy said as she hung up and smiled with relief.

"You're welcome," said Zarin. "I love you too."

"Bye…Yes, mom? *Hello?*" Wendy spoke. "Hello? Mom, you there?"

Wendy's mother couldn't hold on long enough. Wendy then called her mother back and told her that Zarin will be picking EJ up and that she's on her way. "Wendy-san, Edward should be more responsible. Why do they rehearse on Saturday anyway?" Wendy's mother said. Wendy thought about it, as that was a valid point. But being that Wendy was in a hurry, the thought slipped her mind. "Listen, momma; I don't know. But Zarin is coming, okay? Just make sure EJ is ready, please?" Said Wendy.

The wedding ceremony was a success with two newlyweds. Now everyone is eating, laughing, and having a wonderful time at the reception hall. People are up on the dance floor, *too* drunk to dance. As Wendy walks around, she is greeted by none other than her boss, Mrs. Shultz. Mrs. Shultz began to congratulate Wendy on a job well done. She loved the decorations, the choice of colors, the flowers, *and* the dishes. Mrs. Shultz was by far impressed by Wendy's brilliance. But being that Wendy still has a chip on her shoulder about not getting the partnership, she thanked Mrs. Shultz and kept it moving.

But Mrs. Shultz wanted to say something else to Wendy. She took Wendy by the wrist and pulled her to the side. After she took a sip of her champagne, Mrs. Shultz said, "I cannot tell you how much I appreciate you. I truly do, Wendy. I think you have such great potential to be a partner; in *time*. You will grow to be wiser and even *more* gifted. Anyways, you did great, and you make my company look *so* good." Wendy had little to no words for Mrs. Shultz. All she could say was, "You're welcome. Enjoy the rest of the reception."

The wedding finally came to an end. Wendy grew exhausted from all the questions and the hundreds of selfies she took with drunk wedding guests. Wendy also grew disgusted at the sight of the broken dishes and wasted, untouched Beluga Caviar, sitting in the trays next to other *hors d'oeuvres*. Mrs. Shultz had left the reception hours ago. But being that Wendy is the wedding planner, *she* stayed until the very end. She was taking care of the clean-up, returning deposits, and handing out wedding favors with origamis. As the guests began to exit, Wendy is approached by the bride's mother, Mrs. Appleton. Mrs. Appleton indeed had *way* too much to drink herself. On her way out, Mrs. Appleton said to Wendy, "Wendy, you kicked *ass* on this wedding. I'm sorry about the Beluga Caviar; I thought that would be a good touch. Oh, perhaps you should start your *own* wedding event company, yea? You don't need to be someone else's sidekick. Just a thought."

Wendy felt offended at Mrs. Appleton's comment for a split second, calling her a "sidekick." But she did spark something in Wendy's mind. Wendy did not think it would be a bad idea to start her own wedding event company possibly. But after being rejected for a promotion, her confidence took a heavy fall.

As it was close to nine o'clock, Wendy has collected her belongings and was ready to leave. She said her goodbyes to the bride and groom, wishing them a happy and healthy marriage. She did not have to wait long for a cab, as one just stopped at the red light. As Wendy entered the cab, she texted Zarin and told her that she was on her way. While Wendy was riding, she began to think about *her* wedding. Their wedding was a meager budget but *very* creative. After all, Wendy planned her own wedding. Wendy remembered something about her wedding. She remembered how her mother looked at her in her wedding dress. Her mother spoke to her in Japanese and said, "Nothing more beautiful than you came out of me." Even though it was something simple, the way Wendy's mother said it, with compassion and conviction, it was straight from her mother's heart.

As the taxi came to a stop in front of Zarin's brownstone, Wendy paid the cab driver and text Zarin to say she was outside. As Wendy made her way up the stairs, Zarin opened the door with greetings. When they came inside, Wendy noticed that EJ was asleep on the living room couch. She asked Zarin where the girls were. Zarin told her that the girls were in Queens with their grandparents. Wendy then asked if Neal was around, and Zarin said he wasn't home neither. It was a great opportunity, now more than ever, for Wendy to apologize to Zarin.

"I owe you an apology for being such a stubborn bitch last night. I should have just gone along with the plan. No questions asked," Wendy said to Zarin.

"Oh, no, Wendy, it's okay. I'm just glad you're going to help," Zarin responded with ease.

Being that EJ was fast asleep, Zarin asked Wendy if she wanted a glass of wine. Wendy could not say yes fast enough. They walked into the kitchen, and Zarin poured the both of them a glass of wine. They began to have a conversation about their marriages. Zarin was more into her feelings, as tomorrow, she will figure out once and for all who this "Meli" woman is.

"Is this "*Meli*" woman one of his patients?" Wendy asked Zarin.

"You know," Zarin responded. "I've never stopped to think about that. She damn well *could* be one of his patients."

"Well, I guess we'll find out tomorrow."

"Yea…Would you like another glass, babe?"

"I certainly would."

As Zarin poured another glass of wine, she began to tell Wendy more of what was on her mind. She said to Wendy, "I would never have thought something like this would happen. I don't want to *believe* that Neal is cheating on me. Or that he impregnated another woman. I don't want to believe any of that. But what if he did Wendy? What if he *did*? What am I going to tell my daughters? My *parents*, for that matter? I've never been more scared in my life. I love my husband so much. And it would *kill* me if he's having an affair."

Wendy just sat there with Zarin as she held her hand. Her sympathy grew for her friend, her sister. After listening to Zarin, Wendy said to her, "I don't want to believe any of this either. I have high hopes that he's not having an affair. I still very well believe that he is deeply in love with you, Zarin. After tomorrow, when it's all set and done, I'm sure this *Meli* character is all just a misunderstanding."

As the both of them finished their second glass of wine, they heard a sweet little voice. It was EJ calling out for his mommy. Wendy then walked over to the living room. As she saw EJ standing there, she had a look of disappointment, as he had another accident. As Wendy looked and saw that EJ wet himself, yet again, she was worried that EJ had wet himself while he was sleeping on the couch. She hurried over to check the sofa to see if that was wet too. But luckily, it was not.

"Zarin, I'm *so* sorry, but EJ had an accident. Do you possibly have some pajamas or something of the girls that he could borrow?" Wendy asked.

"Oh, yes, I think we have some plain ones. I'll be right back," Zarin said as she went up the stairs.

Wendy looked at EJ, upset that he is having a hard time with his bedroom problem. Since he is only five years old, she is hopeful that he will grow out of this sooner or later. Zarin then came down the stairs with a pair of popular pajamas. It was a pair of princess Elsa pajamas.

"Mommy, I can't wear those," said EJ. "That's for girls."

"I know they are, baby," Wendy responded. "But I can't let you wear these wet clothes outside in the cold. You'll only have to wear them until we get home, okay?"

As Wendy took EJ into the bathroom to help him change his clothes, Zarin grabbed her coat and purse, as she is going to drop Wendy and EJ off at home. A few minutes went by. Zarin knocked on the bathroom door and told Wendy she would wait for them outside so that she can warm the car up. "Okay, we'll be right out," Wendy projected from inside the bathroom. As Zarin went outside to warm the car, she received a text message from Neal. When she opened the text message, her adrenalin began to rise. The text message said, "Hey babe, I'm going to be out with my colleagues a little late tonight. And then, early tomorrow, I'll be doing some running around. I know you have to go to Queens to pick up the girls from your parents' house. So, I'll see you all tomorrow evening. I love you."

Zarin's anxiety also began to creep up on her. But she did not want to make a scene in front of Wendy and EJ. So, Zarin meditated right there in her Range Rover. Zarin was breathing in and breathing out. She even had a meditation track on the playlist of her phone.

Wendy and EJ finally came out of the house. Wendy gave the front door a little shake to make sure the door was locked. Wendy then went down the stairs and opened the back door of the Range Rover to let EJ in. It took Wendy a minute to get EJ situated as the seatbelt was jammed. Finally, after five tries, it clicked. As Wendy made her way into the passenger seat, she said, "What's that you're listening to?" Zarin did not realize that her meditation track was still playing, so she turned it off.

It was not Zarin's lucky night when it came to the traffic lights. She was hitting every red light, one after the other. Finally, they arrived at Wendy's apartment. EJ fell asleep again in the back seat. As Wendy leaned over to hug Zarin, she said, "Thank you so much for picking EJ up and taking care of him. You're the best godmother I could have for him. Oh, and I'll return the pajamas to you." In response, Zarin said, "Oh, you're welcome, girl. I would say keep the pajamas, but then again, EJ probably won't wear them after tonight. So maybe I'll take them later. Good night, Wendy."

Wendy got EJ out of the car, holding him in her arms; she waved goodbye to Zarin. Zarin waited for them to get inside the apartment building safely, and then she drove off. "Oh my gosh, EJ. You're getting so *heavy*," Wendy said in the elevator.

Wendy was drained entirely and dead-tired. She could barely stand in the elevator holding EJ. At that moment, to Wendy, EJ felt like he weighed over a hundred pounds. As they got to the apartment door, Wendy rang the doorbell. She rang once more, waiting for Edward to come to the door. She knew he was not rehearsing this late, but there was no answer. So, she had to put EJ down, look through her purse and take out her keys. As soon as Wendy puts her key in the door, Edward opens it. He was rubbing his eyes as he was already sleeping. Edward said, "Oh, I'm sorry, honey. I had fallen asleep. Here, I'll take EJ." Wendy was too tired to respond. She did not say a word as she locked the door behind her. She took off her flats, removed her jacket, and tossed EJ's wet clothes in the laundry closet. She then went straight to her bedroom and prostrated onto the bed.

As Edward came into the bedroom, he said to Wendy, "Hey, where did EJ get those pajamas from?" Wendy just grunted and said, "Long story, don't worry about it." Edward then gently crawled on top of Wendy. He began to kiss Wendy, taking off her clothes as he is trying to seduce her. But Wendy was *far* from fornication. "Eddie, you have *got* to be kidding me. I have *no* energy to make love right now," said Wendy. As Edward continued to kiss Wendy, he said to her, "I know, I just want to make it up to you. For leaving you hanging today with EJ. I was irresponsible with my scheduling." Wendy vertically shook her head as she could not agree more with Edward. But Wendy gave it a second thought. In her mind, she thought, "Hmm…Maybe I *should* have sex tonight before I go on vacation. It'll probably suck because I'm fucking beat. But it'll be something."

Wendy then turned around, now facing Edward. They both gazed at each other, staring into each other's eyes, even though Wendy struggled to keep *her* eyes open. "Eddie, baby, I can keep my legs open, but my eyes are damn near closing. Either we get this over with, or you'll be making love to yourself, real soon," Wendy said. Edward could not help but chuckle. But they got to it.

Two minutes later, Edward swiftly received his orgasm, and the lovemaking concluded. Neither one of them said a word. They both slept with their backs facing each other and fell right to sleep.

Chapter 18

B reak of dawn; A chilly Sunday morning. The early alarm awakens Zarin. By surprise, Neal was not in bed. Zarin immediately gave him a call. As she called, she walked back and forth in her bedroom at a hasty pace. Neal finally picked up. He answered as if he was sleeping.

"He—Hello?" Neal spoke.

"Hey, um, where the hell are you?" Zarin said.

"Uh, I'm downstairs. I fell asleep on the couch."

Zarin felt a slight sense of idiocy. She then put on her robe and slippers and made her way downstairs. There Neal was, laying on the couch with his clothes still on. This was Zarin's moment to get some last-minute details about his so-called "errands" today. Zarin used her head and outsmarted him. What she did was she went back upstairs, called his phone again, and waited for him to answer it. At first, Neal did not respond. So, Zarin called again. This time he answered but was confused as to why Zarin was calling him from upstairs. Neal then asked Zarin to come down.

As Zarin came back downstairs, Neal said to her, "Why are you calling me from upstairs?" Zarin quickly responded, "I'm sorry, babe, I've been having some trouble with my facetime. Could you open your iPhone and see if I could facetime you?" Neal did not understand the logic, but he cooperated. He opened his phone, and Zarin facetimed with him. It was an awkward moment. The two of them were sitting there in the living room, looking at each other through the screen. Then suddenly, Zarin got into her acting mode.

As Zarin looked at Neal's phone, she said, "Wow, baby can I see your phone? Is this the new iPhone you were telling me about before? The screen is so clear. You know what, I've been meaning to take some pictures of our bathroom. My mother wanted to see the finished look. I'll be right back."

"Wait, so you're just going to walk away with my phone? Really?" Neal spoke.

"I'll be right back," said Zarin. "I just want to take some pictures."

"Then take them with your own phone," Neal projected.

"I'll take some nude shots for you," Zarin responded as she went up the stairs.

"*FULL* nude?" Neal asked.

Zarin now had Neal's *unlocked* iPhone in her possession. As she made her way into their bathroom, she closed and locked the door. Zarin and Neal had their master bathroom renovated a few weeks ago. It had a *beautiful* forest brown marble finish with a glass shower door. Neal did not even stop to think about Zarin's slick scheme.

Zarin then began snooping around on Neal's phone. Looking for anything that has to do with "Meli." She looked at his messages. She scrolled, and scrolled, and scrolled. Until finally, she gave up. She found no trace of Meli on his phone. Not on his call history or even on his social media accounts. But there was *one* place Zarin did not yet look, Neal's emails.

As soon as she opened his Gmail account, she found two emails connected with Meli. The first email had a brief message that said, "Neal, I can't thank you enough for your support for me during my pregnancy. Being that you're already a father, I know you will be able to help me." Zarin's hands could not stop shaking. But that was not it. Neal's response made it clear for her that something was going on between these two. In Neal's response, he said, "I know this was unplanned. But I will support you regardless. And the family does not know. This is *our* secret."

Knots being to tighten in the pit of Zarin's stomach. She was convinced now, more than ever, that Neal was having a baby with another woman. The second email was the flight information for Meli's arrival.

Even though Zarin was on the verge of having an anxiety attack, she kept her composure and stayed focus. She took a screenshot of both emails and texted them to her phone. *Then,* Zarin quickly deleted those screenshots from Neal's photos app. She then closed each app that she opened and took some pictures of the bathroom. Only to make Neal *think* she did what she said she would.

As Zarin came back downstairs, she almost forgot to delete the screenshots of the emails that she texted to herself from *Neal's* phone. So, she quickly went onto the text message thread that she shared with Neal and deleted them both. *That* way, Neal would not figure out what she did. When Zarin came back into the living room, Neal extended his hand and said, "Uh, can I have my phone back, please?" As Zarin gave Neal back his phone, she grabbed *her* phone and went up the stairs. She successfully received the two screenshots that she sent to herself using Neal's phone.

"Woah, hold up, *wait a minute,*" Neal spoke. "Where the nudes?"

"I'm still on my period," Zarin lied.

"*REALLY?*"

"I'm *sorry*!"

Zarin then went into their bedroom. As she reviewed both emails, she sent them to the other four ladies. As she sent them, she also sent a text saying, "Now, I am completely convinced." The rest of the ladies responded in rage, and they are entirely on board with this mission impossible plan to stalk Neal and catch him red-handed. Zarin then sent another text, telling them to get ready and go to their designated places.

In the plan, Monica heads to JFK airport. Zarin told Monica to look for Neal at Terminal 4, the international terminal, since "Meli" is flying in from London. Tomi will be waiting in her limo, in front of Zarin and Neal's house. Tomi will then follow *behind* Neal as he drives to the airport to pick up Meli. As for Collette, Collette will just be waiting at an abandoned location; with weapons. Wendy, however, will be making a *special call* to Neal as soon as she receives her queue call from Monica.

It was 7:05 a.m. Zarin was getting herself dressed and ready, as she will be meeting Collette at the secluded location. Since Collette is a realtor, she found an abandoned site near JFK airport on the real estate market. Collette thought that would be the perfect place to lure Neal in, along with his alleged mistress.

As Zarin was now ready, she headed downstairs to talk to Neal. She told him that she would be staying at her parents' house, in Queens, with the girls for the day. Being that *Neal* knows that he is going to the JFK airport, which is *also* in Queens. He asked Zarin if she wanted him to drop her off at her parents' house. But since *she* knows where he is going, she declined the offer. She told Neal that she is not going there just yet and she will take an Uber over. And *then* her father would drop them off back home.

Neal thought about it, slowly nodded his head, and said, "*Okay*, well, I will be doing some things today. So, I'll probably be home a little late." Zarin smiled at him and said, "Okay, I love you, babe." Neal walked to Zarin, kissed her, and responded, "I love you more, baby. Have a good day." And she *will,* once she sees the look on his face after he is busted. Zarin then grabbed her purse and keys as she headed out the door. As Zarin stood on top of her stoop, Tomi had just arrived in her limo. Zarin called Tomi on her phone and said, "Hey, okay, so he's still inside getting ready. So, I'm going to meet Coco at the location. I want you to follow *every* move he makes. *Every* stop he makes, don't lose him." "Copy that!" Tomi responded. Tomi was so pumped for this mission impossible plan. She was ready to get this show on the road, literally.

Zarin then hailed down a taxi and made her way to the location. Tomi just sat in her limo, sipping on her coffee as she waits for Neal to come out of the house. Ten minutes go by but still no sign of Neal just yet. Tomi has a few swigs of coffee left in her cup. And Neal has yet to come out. Tomi then calls Zarin.

"Zarin, what the *fuck* is taking him so long? He still hasn't come out of the house," Tomi said with frustration.

"He still hasn't come out?" Zarin asked. "Okay, I have an idea. Go by our car and try to open the door. It'll set the alarm, and he'll come out to turn it off. It's the black Range Rover right in front."

Tomi then stepped out of her limo and made her way to the Range Rover. She looked around at her surroundings to make sure no one was looking. As Tomi stood near the Range Rover, she began to pull on the car door handle. But nothing happened. She tried putting her body weight up against the car. But unfortunately, no car alarm went off, nothing. Tomi grew frustrated and angry. Until she thought about it and said, "Duh, let me ring the fucking doorbell." So, Tomi did a ding-dong ditch. She went up to the door and rang the buzzer, and hurried back to her limo. As she got in, Benjamin said to her, "Ms. Belacone, I'm not trying to be nosey. But what the hell are we doing here?" Tomi responded, "Benjamin, sweetheart, the less you know, the better it is for you. Oh, wait, there he is."

Neal finally came out of the house. As he put on his jacket, he looked around to see who rang the doorbell—shaking his head in confusion as no one was there. Neal then looked at his watch, closed and locked the front door. He headed down the stairs, got in the Range Rover, and drove off. As Tomi looked through the crack of her open tinted window, she said, "Benjamin, follow that pig son of a bitch."

Zarin made it to the abandoned location. It was an old warehouse that had been abandon for decades. The natural light from the sun was keeping it from looking haunted. Collette was already there, ready to go to war. She opened the trunk to her car and showed Zarin what she brought with her. Collette had a baseball bat, a hammer, rope, tape, and even a Balisong knife. Zarin looked with complete shock. She said to Collette, "Coco, I was just looking forward to catching Neal red-handed. Not *killing* him in cold blood." Collette shook her head and responded, "Oh, no, no, no, *no*. He's going to *pay* for cheating on *you*. And getting another bitch *pregnant*?" Collette then took the Balisong knife and said, "He wants to creep around and be a pig, then we'll fucking *gut* him like a pig." Zarin could not believe Collette's behavior at this moment. She has never seen Collette like this before with such seriousness, aggression, and conviction. However, Zarin felt that she could use some of that energy for herself.

A phone began to ring. It was Zarin's phone ringing as Tomi was calling. When Zarin answered, she put it on speaker so that Collette could hear as well. "He stopped at a florist shop and bought this bitch some roses. He *stopped* at a *florist* shop and bought this bitch *roses*! That *fucking* piece of shit! We're going to kill him," Tomi shouted.

Collette responded with quickness, "Oh, you fucking got *that* right. We're *going* to kill him. And that bitch better be *glad* she's pregnant." But Zarin asked for the ladies to calm down. Zarin told Tomi to stay on the line and not hang up.

As Tomi stayed on the line, she told Zarin and Collette that she is still behind Neal. Driving down Interstate 678, the Van Wyck Expressway, heading towards JFK airport. As they listened to Tomi, she blurted out, "Oh, FUCK!" Zarin and Collette looked at each other with twisted faces.

"Oh *fuck*?" Collette said. "That doesn't sound good, Tomi. What's the "Oh fuck" all about?"

"The goddamn cops pulled us over. We lost Neal. Tell Monica to get ready and be on the lookout," said Tomi.

"Damn it!" Zarin yelled. "Okay, fine, just meet us here at the warehouse when you can."

Zarin then hung up and reached out to Monica to see where she is. As Monica answered, she said, "Hey, I'm here. I just arrived at the baggage claim area in terminal 4. I can't go any further than this. I'm a non-ticketed person." Zarin forgot that Monica could not wait near the actual gate because that is prohibited. In response, Zarin said to Monica, "Just do your best, Nica. Be on the lookout for Neal. He's coming."

Tomi is still in the back of her limo as she has been pulled over by "the law." Then, suddenly, she gets a knock on her tinted window. Tomi rolls down the window; it is the police officer who pulled them over.

"Hi, hello, officer. Good morning, is there a problem?" Tomi said with her golden smile.

"Hello, Ms. Belacone," said the officer. "No problem at all. Your limo driver told me who was in the back seat. I just thought I'd introduce myself."

The officer began to tell Tomi how much his wife *loves* her clothing line. He also told Tomi how expensive it is for him to buy his wife something from the *Orell Llero* collection. Then, to cut things short, Tomi "*made him an offer he couldn't refuse.*" Tomi said, "I tell you what; how about I send your wife an *extravagant* gift. I will give her three outfits, a handbag, perfume, hats, gloves, *and* shoes. *All* from my 2023 winter collection. If you could just *please* let us go?"

"Are you offering me a *bribe*?" The officer said with a side-eye.

"No, maybe, sort of, I *guess*?" Tomi admitted.

"Oh, what the hell, of course!"

"Oh, *thank you*, officer," said Tomi. "You're a lifesaver."

The officer was ecstatic that Tomi would do that for his wife. "You just made my day. What until I tell her about this," said the happy officer. Tomi immediately said to him, "No! Don't tell her just yet. Surprise her with this. Just give me your information, and we'll go from there. The officer then wrote down everything Tomi needed, said thank you and goodbye. As the officer went back to his vehicle, Tomi said, "Benjamin, let's go!"

Back at the airport, Monica was keeping a close eye on the baggage claim area. In search of Neal and who he is coming to pick up. The terminal was flooded with people—limousine services with signs of people's names. Families were meeting up, hugging each other. And some people are still wearing a facemask in the terminal. Monica knows what *Neal* looks like, but she has no idea who this "Meli" woman is or what she looks like exactly. So, Monica called Zarin and gave her an update.

"Hey Zarin, I'm still in baggage claim, but I don't see Neal. As far as "Meli," she could be right here, and I wouldn't even know," Monica said.

"Nica, look for a pregnant woman. She's pregnant," said Zarin.

Collette thought about it and asked Zarin, "Wait, does this "Meli" have a Facebook or Twitter or something?" But Zarin told Collette she already looked her up and found nothing. Zarin spent over an hour on social media, looking at Neal's followers and friends. But no such "Meli" has reached the surface.

As Monica stayed on the phone with Zarin, she spotted a familiar face. It was Neal, holding a dozen roses that he picked up from the florist shop. He was neatly groomed and dressed for this *special* occasion. Monica told Zarin that she spotted Neal at the baggage claim. Zarin told Monica to keep her eyes on him. As Neal began to walk, Monica began to follow from a safe distance. They walked around for several minutes as Neal waits for "Meli." And Monica stayed on the line with Zarin.

"Is she there? Did she come yet? What does she look like? HELLO?" Zarin screamed.

"Shut up! No!" Monica irritably shouted. "She's not here yet, Zarin. I'm still looking at Neal."

As the crowded baggage claim began to clear up, a woman began to make her way towards Neal. The closer Monica came to Neal, the better she was able to describe this woman. Monica said to Zarin, "I think I see her now. I think this is Meli." Zarin wanted *all* the details: her height, her hair length, the clothes she had on, everything." Monica had to get closer to get the full description.

Then, as the woman came closer to Neal, Monica knew for sure that she was "Meli" since the woman was pregnant. Neal gently hugged Meli; they held on to each other for what seemed to be like forever. The frequent jerks of their bodies as they began to cry. Monica still kept her distance and watched everything that they did. Meli had long black hair down to her back. A brown sweater with a brown jacket, black leggings, and some Ugg boots. Monica could not see her face fully because they were still hugged up.

Zarin was growing angry as Monica was not saying a word about what was happening. Zarin shouted, "Nica, PLEASE! Tell me what's going on?" Monica then gave her all the details she could. Then Neal and Meli finally released each other. As they did, Monica discovered something shocking. But she did not say anything to Zarin.

"What does she look like, Nica? What does her face look like?" Zarin said.

"She's, She's *beautiful*. And she has an *interesting* face." Monica said with a relieved tone of voice.

Monica knew something now that the other ladies did not. But she did not want to say anything just yet, as she does not want to ruin the mission impossible plan. Since everyone went through so much trouble, Monica decided to let it play its course. As Monica continued to watch, she told Zarin that Neal and Meli are on their way out of the terminal. Monica said she would take a cab and meet them at the abandoned warehouse. After she hung up, Monica called Wendy and said, "Wendy, now is the time."

As Wendy made the call to Neal, the phone began to ring. But being that Neal did not recognize the phone number, he did not bother to answer. Wendy called again and again. Finally, Neal answered and said, "Yes, hello, who is this?" Wendy gave a little performance herself. She responded, "Hi, Neal, this is Wendy. Listen, Zarin's with the girls, but they are stranded at an abandoned location. Her father wasn't home, so they had to take an Uber. But something happened with the Uber driver, and he just left them in the middle of nowhere." At first, Neal was in denial about the situation. He did not understand why *Wendy* would call him and not Zarin. Neal asked Wendy, "Wait, so why are *you* calling me then? It's not like Zarin *not* to call me when something happens."

Wendy had to think quickly about what to say next. She then responded saying, "Well, her phone battery had died." But Neal was not a fool. He came back with quickness and said, "*So* if her phone died, how the hell did *you* find out about them being stranded before *I* did? Couldn't Zarin have told *me first*? Not to mention, my daughter has a phone too. You're not going to tell me that *both* of their phones died?"

Wendy could not take it anymore. She dropped the act and just let Neal have it. "Look, you no good cheating, adulterous, slimeball piece of fucking pig shit. Take your ass and your pregnant slut to the abandoned location *right now* and be a *man* about your bullshit. Tell your wife the truth, scumbag." "WHAT?

What the *hell* is going on here?" Said Neal. He could not believe what Wendy just said to him. Meli was in the Range Rover with a startled look on her face.

"Is there something wrong?" Meli said. "Who *is* that?"

"I'm so sorry. I have to see what this is all about," Neal responded.

Wendy then gave Neal the address of the abandoned building. He put it in his GPS and went straight there. The location of the abandoned building was fifteen minutes away from JFK airport. Monica had just arrived at the site. She had a very humorous look on her face. Collette asked her, "What is so funny? Why are you smiling?" Monica responded, "I just can't wait for them to get here, that's all." Five minutes later, Tomi pulled up in her limo. "Now, all we have to do is wait," said Zarin.

And they waited for another ten minutes before Neal pulled up inside the warehouse. The four of them: Zarin, Tomi, Monica, and Collette, all stood there like the four musketeers. As Neal turned off his car, he sat inside with Meli for a good minute. He put his hand above his eyebrow and began to shake his head. He could not believe what his eyes were witnessing. "Get out of the *fucking* car Neal," Tomi screamed. "Yes, get out of the car and tell your sidepiece to get out too," said Collette.

Neal looked as disgusted and mortified as he did when he had patients suffering from genital warts and had to remove retained tampons. But Neal finally got out of the Range Rover. Before he shut the door, he said to Meli, "Don't get out of the car." He walked over to the four of them. As he looked at them, he was expecting some answers, *demanding* answers even.

"You're caught, Neal! You might as well come clean with everything now," Tomi said.

"Yea, bring out that bitch in the car too. Confess!" Said Collette.

"Woah, first of all, don't call her a bitch," said Neal. "*Second*, what the *fuck* is going on here? Why are we here? And *third*, why is your friend Wendy calling me about this cheating bullshit?"

Zarin then began to explain to Neal how this all started. She said, "Neal, sometime last week, I overheard you in the bedroom talking to *Meli*. You were keeping her from me, keeping this a secret. I tried to bring it up to you. But I just couldn't confront you about it. And I wanted to get to the bottom of this. So, all of us came together to lure you here with this woman you've impregnated. I'm *so* disappointed in you. I'm so disappointed in you breaking my heart like this. And getting another woman pregnant? What am I going to tell our daughters? Who is this woman?"

As Neal stood there, he could not believe what he was hearing. He shook his head in disbelief. "My God, this is a *major* misunderstanding here," Neal spoke. He then walked over to the car's passenger seat, opened the door, and helped Meli out of the vehicle. As Meli was revealed to the other three, Monica then looked at each expression on their faces. They could not believe how identical Meli and Neal looked. Neal then said to them, "Ladies, meet my twin sister, Meli."

Zarin's jaw dropped, as did Collette's and Tomi's. Monica knew right away that they were brother and sister when she saw her at the airport. And she knew the rest of the ladies would respond the same way as soon as they saw Meli's face. Neal was not cheating on Zarin after all.

"Wait, your sister, *Chameli*? The one I've never met?" Zarin asked.

"Yes, babe," Neal confirmed.

As they all stood there, Neal broke it down for them and said, "Meli's actual name is *Chameli*. She's the same person. Meli and I were separated when we were babies. When our parents split, our mother took *me*, and our father took *her*. We've only seen each other in person, five times in our entire lives. We've recently been connected, and I wanted to help her while she's pregnant. She met an American guy in London, got pregnant, and she came here to see him. Our mother does not believe in being pregnant out of wedlock. Nor does she support it. So, I told Meli that I wouldn't tell *anyone* until she got here. I know I should have said something to you earlier, Zarin. I didn't think it through properly. But I *never* would have expected you to go *this low* and plan something like this. Listen, we'll talk about all of this later. I have to go drop Meli off at her hotel. She needs her rest right now. I'll pick up the girls from your parents' house. That way, they could meet their aunt. Right now, I, I just have to leave. This is insanity."

As Neal and Meli got in the Range Rover and drove off, Zarin and the others were at a complete loss for words. None of them could put the words together to explain what just happened. So, what else was left to do but blame each other.

"I knew it! I knew it, I knew it, I *knew it*! I *told* you all that this was a misunderstanding," Tomi shouted.

"Oh, okay, let's not do this. Let's not point the finger at anyone. We *all* participated, and we were *all* wrong," said Monica.

Collette was disappointed and frustrated, not so much of the misunderstanding but because she could not use any of her weapons to kick Neal's ass. As Collette walked to her car, she said, "I'm going to have a few drinks at *Lucille's*. And *pretend* this bullshit *never* took place today. Since Monica and Zarin took an Uber to the site, they decided to take a ride in Tomi's limo.

Not much was said the entire limo ride back to Manhattan. The three of them had this deplorable look of grief on their faces. Then Zarin's phone began to ring. It was Wendy calling. Zarin did not want to talk or give Wendy the news of it being a false alarm. Zarin handed her phone to Monica, then Monica handed the phone to Tomi. Tomi did not know what to say either. "Answer it, just answer it," Zarin said. Tomi sighed, answered the phone, and put it on speaker.

"Hello! Zarin? What happened? Who is that bitch?" Wendy shouted.

"Wendy, darling. Just meet us at *Lucille's*," Tomi said and hung up.

The five-hundred-pound gorilla was in that limo with them. Not to mention, it was not even noon yet. The ladies caused such a mess for themselves. Zarin, more than any of them, felt a heavy, colossal sense of guilt and remorse for wasting everyone's time. But she could not put the words together to say what was needed. So, Zarin decided to wait until all five of them were together at *Lucille's*. Zarin owes plenty of apologies. She owes them to her friends, her husband Neal, and Neal's twin sister, Meli.

For the rest of the ride, Zarin stared out through the window. Looking out at the Manhattan skyline as they made their way down the Long Island expressway. The weather was cold, but the sun was shining. Zarin began to think about Neal some more. She thought about how this could affect their relationship and their trust within themselves. This situation may have changed things between them. But what Zarin fears is that there are other hidden secrets, other skeletons locked away in the closet.

As the three of them are riding down the highway, a rapid group of loud popping sounds came from the direction of Tomi. As Monica and Zarin looked at her, all Tomi could say was, "*Excuse* me, ladies." They all broke out into much-needed laughter. "Damn bitch, you call *that* an icebreaker?" Monica said as Tomi "broke the wind." A good thirty seconds of laughter continued inside the limo. Zarin then said, "Monica, *please* roll the damn window down." Laughter was all they cared about at that moment. It was all that was needed to recover their bond and perhaps strengthen it.

Chapter 19

Back at *Lucille's*, it was a quarter to eleven in the morning. The ladies were sitting at the bar, having coffee and tea, as it was too early for any alcohol. And the restaurant does not open until noon on Sundays. Some of the employees were still setting up for the day. Wendy came in ten minutes ago, as she met up with others. After they told Wendy what happened, she was relieved that Neal was not cheating. However, Wendy surely rubbed it in all of their faces, as far as her being right about how ridiculous the plan was. Tomi was just as miffed as Wendy was.

"We are the dumbest bitches on the face of planet fucking earth," Tomi said to the others.

"I *told* you guys," said Wendy. "I told you all. *That's* why I didn't want to do it. I *knew* this was all a misunderstanding."

"I know, *I know*," said Zarin. "And I apologize to all of you for getting you involved in this mess. I should have just been an adult about it, as you guys said."

The whole ensemble sat around at the bar in deep disappointment. Zarin felt terrible about the entire situation. Especially about Neal and his twin sister, Meli. As Tomi took a sip of her tea, she said, "Well, the *good* thing is Neal was *not* cheating on you, Zarin. No affairs *and* he didn't get another woman pregnant. Those are good results. Now, *you* just have to ask him for forgiveness."

But Collette, however, had to chime in. She felt that Neal was no angel about this either. "Now hold on, let's not put this all on Zarin. If *he* would have just been an adult about this situation and told Zarin the *truth*, none of this would have happened. Neal is just as much responsible for this as Zarin. Babe, *don't* kill yourself with guilt over this bullshit," Collette said. Zarin secretly agreed with Collette's statement, and she appreciated it. But Zarin won't be at peace with it until she has a conversation with Neal.

Wendy then brought up Tomi's little "fashion show" the previous night when she modeled her new coat in the nude. "Um, to change the subject, can we just talk about this crazy bitch cat-walking without any clothes on? I *saw* the photos all over social media. You are nuts, Tomi," said Wendy. Tomi just laughed it off. Since Tomi does not have any *personal* social media accounts, she asked Wendy to pull up the picture on her phone. As Tomi and the others saw the picture, they gaged.

"Oh my God, is that not the most *pulchritudinous* bitch you've ever seen?" Monica said.

"Pulchra-WHAT? There you go, Nica, *again* with your lawyer vocabulary," Collette said as she rolled her eyes.

"It means physically beautiful, Coco," said Wendy.

"Look, *whatever*," said Collette. "Just call her a bad bitch."

Pictures of Tomi were flooding the internet. Articles, memes, women were even doing what was called the "Tomi Belacone Challenge." They were posing in the nude with their coats draped around their bodies. Even though Tomi *loved* the attention, and sales went through the roof, she did not stop to think about the young ladies, teenage girls, looking at her and being influenced to behave the same way.

As *Lucille's* was beginning to open, Wendy told the other ladies that she had to get home to finish packing for her trip to Tokyo. "Aww, Wendy, the grand opening for my *Orell Llero* storefront is this Wednesday. You're going to miss out, babe," said Tomi. Wendy responded with sorrow, saying, "Oh, shit. I *completely* forgot that was this week. I'm sorry, Tomi. You *know* I would love to be there." Tomi understood that Wendy needs this vacation. She was okay with Wendy missing out on the grand opening, as long as Wendy will be present for her birthday celebration on the 24th of this month. Wendy then gave each of them a hug and kiss and told them that she loves them. Before she left, she said, "Oh, and don't worry. I will get something special for all of you."

As for the other four, they began to go their separate ways for the day. Tomi decided to stay a little longer and went into the restroom. Zarin knew where she had to go. Straight home to set things right with Neal. Monica had to head home, get her car, and pick up Miles and Briana from her parents' house in New Jersey. As for Collette, she is going to stick around the restaurant and help out with Martin.

Zarin and Monica hugged and kissed Collette as they were about head out. "Ah, *excuse me*, ladies? I know you were not about to *waltz* up out of here and not say goodbye to me?" Tomi said with her arms open for a hug. After Monica and Zarin left, it was just Collette and Tomi. As they were sitting at the bar, Tomi received a text message. A brief moment of silence as she stared at her phone, not saying a word. As Collette looked over at Tomi, she grew concerned with her silence.

"Hey, is everything alright?" Collette asked.

"Huh? Oh, yes, of course," Tomi spoke. "Just received a text from someone."

"Oh, bad news?"

"Just an update on something. It's no big deal."

Tomi and Collette had a pretty long conversation that afternoon. After they got over talking and laughing about the mission impossible plan, they began to speak about Collette's sister, Lisa. "So, is Lisa going to be available to walk the runway? For my climate change fashion show this Friday?" Tomi asked Collette. Collette told Tomi that Lisa is going through some things, and she has to take it easy. But truthfully, Lisa is still recovering from her surgery. And Collette did not want to disclose Lisa's business with Tomi. Tomi then asked about Emilio. But there was nothing else to talk about on Collette's behalf.

"Oh, there's Martin," said Collette. "I'll be right back. I have to talk to him and get something from the office."

"Okay, babe, take your time," Tomi responded.

As Tomi sat at the bar, she began to look around at other people in the restaurant. "People seeing," as they call it. Sitting down at one of the tables were three women. Another woman, who was pregnant, just arrived to join them. Each woman stood up with excitement. As if they have not seen this pregnant woman in so long. They gave her a hug and kiss, as well as a gentle rub on her womb. For some reason, Tomi could not take her eyes off of the pregnant woman. She just kept staring at her. Then one of the women looked over and saw Tomi staring at them. Tomi smiled and then turned away. As her back was turned to the four women, Tomi could hear one of the women saying, "Jesus, why was she staring at us like that? Creepy." Another woman said, "Holy shit, don't you bitches know who that *is*? That's Tomi Belacone. Ms. *Orell Llero*? Everyone's talking about her nude photo on social media." Now, *they* are the ones who are doing the staring. The pregnant woman said, "It sure as hell *is* Tomi Belacone. Wait, I want to introduce myself to her."

As Tomi overheard everything, she prepared herself, as the pregnant woman made her way towards her. "Um, excuse me? Hi, sorry to bother you. But I just *love* your work and your brand. Would it be too much trouble to ask you for a picture? Please?" Said the pregnant woman. Tomi looked down at her womb and smiled. "Oh, absolutely honey, let's do it," said Tomi. The pregnant woman was happy to have a picture with a world-famous fashion designer. As the pregnant woman's friend took the picture, Tomi then held the woman's womb and said, "Wait, take a picture of this too. Of me holding her womb." Of course, as the pregnant woman took a picture with Tomi, the rest of the women asked for a photo as well. After their little photo shoot, the three women went back to their table. Tomi kept the pregnant woman behind and asked her some questions.

"What's your name, beautiful?" Tomi asked.

"My name is Jami, Jami De Mornay," said the pregnant woman.

"It's nice to meet you, Jami," said Tomi. "When's your due date?"

"February 24th. I'm having a boy."

"Aww, that's *my* birthday."

"Oh wow, I didn't know that."

"Yea, that is wonderful, sweetie. Congratulations."

"Oh, thank you so much, Ms. Belacone. And it was a pleasure to meet you."

"You too, my love. Take care. And Jami?"

"Yes, Ms. Belacone?"

"You're very blessed to be a mother. Never take it for granted."

"Thank you so much. And I won't."

Jami then went back to her table to join her friends. At that very moment, Tomi felt this hidden pain beginning to grow inside of her. A pain that she has been dealing with for the past two decades. The pain of not having children of her own. Throughout her life, Tomi had suffered three miscarriages. The first one was at the age of twenty-four, the second was at twenty-nine, and the third was at thirty-four. After her third miscarriage, Tomi could not handle it anymore. She ultimately gave up on motherhood. Tomi accepted the harsh reality that her body could not conceive a child. It devastated Tomi for *years*. That is why when she saw that mother laughing and holding her kids' hands at the Beverly Hills Hotel last week, Tomi had this low, saddened energy for the rest of that day.

It comes, and it goes for Tomi when she sees pregnant women walking up and down the streets—mothers with their kids in the park. As a woman, as a businesswoman, Tomi feels that life has significantly treated her *very* well. God has truly blessed her with success. As for motherhood, Tomi thinks that God has *cursed* her by not allowing her to give birth. That one gift, the magic that she did not possess. Even today, when Tomi saw Neal's twin sister, Meli, who is pregnant. She grew envious of her.

Tomi *loves* her friends to death. She would do *anything* for them, obviously, after what happened today. And she never thought about if her friends were ever jealous of her lifestyle. The glitz and glamour, the financial freedom and fame. But there is one thing that Tomi has always possessed, *deep* inside herself. And that is her envy towards women who can conceive.

Collette made her way back to the bar. Tomi was still sitting there, now drinking a glass of Vodka. Tomi grew so quiet; it began to give Collette some concern. "Okay, Tomi, *what* is going on? You've been acting pretty awkward. What's on your mind, babe?" Collette said. Tomi looked at Collette with watery eyes. Collette saw the pain on Tomi's face and said, "Oh no, we can't do this out here in public. Let's go up in the office, okay?" Collette took Tomi by the wrist and led the way up the stairs into Martin's office.

As soon as Collette shut the door, Tomi completely broke down and began to cry uncontrollably. Collette was not expecting such emotions from Tomi. But she knew that her friend needed to be held for one solid minute. Collette began to rub on Tomi's back to make her feel better and comfort her, even though Collette did not know why her friend was unhappy.

"My God, Tomi, what's wrong, Mamí? What is it?" Collette asked.

"I'm sorry, I just need a minute," Tomi said as she still held on to Collette.

Collette then walked Tomi over to the couch as they both took a seat. Collette told Tomi to calm her nerves and breathe for a few minutes before she spoke. As Tomi got herself together, she said this, "You know what the one thing is in this world that makes a woman feel *so* accomplished? *So* superior? Giving *life*; to give *birth* to a newborn baby. To *hold* another being in your arms that you've carried for nine months. *That* is *so magical*, Coco. But I don't have that magic; I never did. I tried so hard to have a baby. And then when I realized that I couldn't, I just worked even harder in the fashion world to ignore the suffering— trying to bury the pain with my career. *That* is why I am *so* antiabortion. Those ungrateful bitches have *no idea* how lucky they are to bring *life* into this world. It's just not fair. Why me?"

Tomi's vulnerability began to bring tears into Collette's eyes. Collette had no idea that her friend was suffering in this way. With all the money and success, Collette never noticed the pain that lurked in Tomi's heart. As Collette held her hand, she said this to Tomi, "I had no idea this was causing you such grief, Tomi. I can understand where you're coming from with this. My children are the greatest thing that ever happened to me. They are my greatest accomplishment. You're right. But it's not your fault, honey. You shouldn't put yourself through such agony. You have such a great life. I mean, you've traveled all around the *world*. And you've made *billions* of dollars—much success and wealth. Not to mention, you have a loving husband; who's been there with you since day one. Tomi, you are *very* blessed, babe."

Tomi looked Collette straight in her eyes and said this to her, "Coco, I would trade *all* of this wealth and success, *just* to give birth and be a mother. I know that sounds fucking *insane*. But you have *no idea*. There will always be this feeling in the back of my mind. A feeling of not being a complete woman, with a whole purpose."

At that very moment, Collette thought about her sister, Lisa. Lisa said the very same thing to her. Lisa told Collette that even after her transition, she would never feel like a complete woman because she could *never* conceive a child of her own.

Collette gave it some thought and mentioned adoption to Tomi. Tomi immediately rejected that idea. As she wiped her teary eyes, Tomi said, "You don't think I've already thought about *adoption*? I would have adopted a child years ago. But to me, personally, I wouldn't be satisfied with that. I wanted the full, natural experience of motherhood. I wanted it all: the vomiting, the morning sickness, the trimesters, the ultrasounds, and my womb growing and growing. My water breaking and going into labor. The pain and breathing routines, finally giving birth, with Tommy and I watching our child come into this world. *That* is what I wanted, Coco. *That* was my real dream. But, we can't have it all, can we?"

Collette realized something at that moment. She learned that no matter *what* her kids put her through, being a mother is not something to take for granted. It is a gift to be a mother. Regardless if Mia gets out of line at school, or Emilio coming out to her, those are *still* her kids. Those are her babies who she gave birth to, and she must love them unconditionally. And when the world gets rough, or when they are not being loved out there in the world, both Emilio and Mia will know that their mother loves them. No matter what.

Chapter 20

A tranquil and awkward lunch is taking place back at Zarin and Neal's house. Both of them, as well as Darsha and Joshna, are sitting down having take-out. Not much is being said at the dining room table. Only the noisy clanking and scraping by their forks as they eat. Zarin, sitting on one side, looking at Neal. Her heart filled with sorrow. Neal has yet to make eye contact with her. He just eats and drinks. Zarin then looks at Darsha and realized something different about her. She sees that Darsha is not on her phone. Her phone is not even on the dining room table.

"Darsha, where's your phone?" Zarin asked.

"Upstairs in my bag," Darsha responded.

The way Darsha responded had triggered something within Zarin. She felt that something was wrong. Darsha is always on her phone. Rarely would she *not* bring her phone to the dining room table. Zarin usually has to yank the phone out of Darsha's hands. But Zarin then put that to the side. And then Joshna said, "momma, can I be excused? I have to use the bathroom." "Sure, baby, go ahead," Zarin responded. Right after that, Darsha asked if she could be excused as well. Zarin said yes to Darsha as well, being that this would be the perfect time to have a private conversation with Neal.

As Joshna and Darsha went up the stairs, Neal continued to eat and drink without saying a word. As Zarin was about to speak, the doorbell rang. Neal then looked up from his plate. He and Zarin then looked at each other, as neither of them was expecting any guest. Zarin then got up from the dining room table and opened the front door. It was her mother. Zarin was surprised to see her mother, who came from Queens.

"Mom, what the hell are you doing over here?" Said Zarin.

"Your father wanted to take me to buy a gift for Valentine's Day. And the girls left some stuff at our house. Here's Darsha's phone," Zarin's mother said.

A confusing look began to shape Zarin's face. Zarin said to her mother, "Wait, *you* had her phone? She told me that her phone was in her bag upstairs." Zarin's mother responded, "Oh no, she left it over our house. Actually, your father found it in his little trash can. I guess she doesn't want it anymore. Whatever you said to her must have worked. She didn't use her phone all weekend. But listen, I have to get going. Tell Neal I said hello."

Zarin stood there for a brief moment. Looking at the phone, she began to wonder why Darsha lied about her phone being upstairs in her bag. As Zarin closed the front door, she placed the phone on the living room table and Joshna's book bag in the hallway. Zarin then took her mother's request of, *"Tell Neal I said hello,"* and used *that* as an ice breaker to spark a conversation.

"My mother says hello," Zarin said to Neal.

"Oh, did she leave already?" Neal responded.

"Yea, she had to run."

"Oh, I would've said hello."

Zarin took a seat back at the dining room table. This time, she sat closer to Neal. At first, Zarin did not know what to say to him. Or how to even go about apologizing to him for what took place earlier that morning. But Zarin gathered her words together and said to him, "Neal, what happened today was a despicable fluke. I don't know what came over me with orchestrating such foolishness. That night when I heard you talking to Meli, I heard you talk about a baby and how you weren't going to tell me anything about it. I, I thought you were having an affair and that you got another woman pregnant. I was just so scared of losing you. I was scared of losing my family. I got a hold of your phone that night and blocked her number. Then this morning, when I took your phone in the bathroom, I was actually looking *through* your phone to find out who she is. I then found a couple of emails with her flight information, and *that's* how it happened. The other ladies and I came together to catch you red-handed. But I was dead wrong. And I am so sorry."

Neal looked at Zarin with a relaxed look on his face. He then extended his hand to Zarin on the table. And Zarin placed *her* hand on top of his. Neal then responded and said, "Zarin, if there's *anyone* who deserves an apology, it's you, babe. I should've been a man about it and not kept this a secret from you. You're my *wife*; we shouldn't be keeping secrets from each other. I thought I was doing what was best for my sister. Meli did not want anyone to know about her situation. It is a tough situation. She barely knows the father of her unborn child. And our mother, she will *not* approve of this. And that night, when you mentioned her name, I froze. I had the opportunity to tell you the truth, and then I bitched out on you. But I *never* intended to hurt or upset you. And for that, *I* am sincerely sorry, Zarin. I'm sorry if this gave you any heartbreak. Do you forgive me, baby?"

A genuine smile began to form on Zarin's tear-stained face. She kissed her husband, again, and again, and again. As she hugged him, she said in his ear, "Of course I forgive you. No more secrets, okay?" As they let go of each other, Neal said, "Well, there's one more secret I must share with you." Zarin's heart immediately foundered to the ground. Her face dropped, but Neal quickly reassured Zarin that it was nothing terrible. "Oh no, babe, It's nothing crazy. I'm not having an affair or anything. Just wait right here and close your eyes," Neal said.

As Zarin is relieved that Neal's secret has nothing to do with another woman, she cooperated and closed her eyes. Neal walked into the living room. He took out an object from the drawer of the coffee table. Neal then tip-toed his way back to the dining room table and told Zarin to hold her hand out. As she did, he sighed and said, "No babe, I didn't say *raise* your hand. I meant, "hold your hand *out,*" as if I'm going to place something in the *palm* of your hand." "Oh, okay, sorry," Zarin laughed.

As Neal placed the object in Zarin's hand, he said, "Open your eyes." Zarin opened her eyes, had a few blinks, and looked down at her hand. A brief gag as she saw a burgundy leathered ring box. Neal then took the ring box and opened it to reveal a new, six-karat, square-cut diamond ring. "Happy anniversary, my love," said Neal. As mentioned before, Zarin planned to give Neal a gold Rolex for their sixteenth anniversary. But with the drama of Meli, she completely forgot about their anniversary. Neal, however, did not.

As Zarin sat there in suspense, she was speechless, as if words were never born. Neal got on one knee and said this to her, "Baby, since the first day I met you, back when we met on the elevator in college. I felt the magic. The magic of being in love.

The way the wind blew through your hair. The way you looked at me with your big, beautiful brown eyes. I couldn't see my life being any more perfect when I was with you. You simply brought out the very best in me. And for these past sixteen years, my love for you has only grown stronger. There's nothing you can say or do to ever change that for me. You are the love of my life. You are my soul. And I look forward to spending the rest of my life with you. And I hope I said enough because my knee is fucking killing me right now."

"Oh my God," Zarin laughed. *"Yes, you've said plenty, now get up."* A romantic mixture of laughs and tears as Zarin was so moved by Neal's words. Zarin hugged and kissed him with enriched passion. Neal then took the diamond ring out of the ring box and placed it on Zarin's left ring finger. But then Zarin stopped Neal and said, "No, no. Babe, I wear my wedding ring on my *right* hand, remember? It's my mom's old Indian family tradition." Neal quickly removed the ring and placed it on the ring finger on Zarin's *right* hand. My *God*, did it sparkle. It lit up Zarin's whole hand as if she was wearing one of Michael Jackson's Crystal-studded gloves.

"It's so beautiful; Oh my God, I can't stop looking at it. Thank you, baby. I love you so much," Zarin said as she went in for another kiss. Zarin then reached for her phone, snapped a picture of her new ring, and sent a group text to the other ladies. They responded with heart emojis and kissy faces. "Oh my God, well, I guess you guys are all kissed and made up now, huh? LOL!" Collette replied in her text. "That is so amazing! I'm so happy you guys have straightened it out now," Monica text. Wendy, feeling horrible about what she said to Neal, replied saying, "Love it! And Zarin, can you please give Neal my sincerest apologies for the way I talked to him earlier today? I was a real bitch to him. Sorry." Then Tomi came in with a response only *she* would say. She replied saying, "That is a big, beautiful piece of rock. Did you ask him how much it cost? I know *I* would."

Zarin laughed at Tomi's response. But Zarin had to admit; she was curious to know what the ring is worth as well. So, listening to Tomi, Zarin asked Neal, "*So*, babe, I'm not trying to sound like a nosey, trifling bitch. But how much did it cost?" Neal almost choked on his orange juice when Zarin asked him that. "Oh, I'm sorry, I'm sorry. I was just curious. I mean, *six-karats*, you know?" Neal shook his head with a few chuckles. He then put down his glass of orange juice and said, "I can tell one of your friends put you up to that. But hey, no more secrets, right? I paid about $275,000 for that ring you're wearing on your finger right now. I saved up some coins for the past two years." Zarin was in complete shock. All she could say was, "I'm wearing a fucking Lamborghini on my finger?" Zarin looked at her ring and gaged some more. "And you're worth *every* penny of it, more even. In fact, you're priceless," said Neal.

As Neal took another sip of his orange juice, Zarin took the glass out of his hand and placed it on the kitchen table. She then began to rub his shoulders, caressing him. Neal looked at Zarin's right hand and began to kiss it.

"Tonight is your lucky night, my love," said Zarin. "I'm no longer "out of order," as you like to call it. Tonight, I can show you my appreciation."

"Hmm…Well, the girls should be taking a nap right now. Why wait until tonight?" Neal said as he began to unbutton his shirt.

The two of them made their way upstairs. Zarin took a little peek in the girls' room. Sure enough, they were fast asleep. Zarin then tip-toed inside their room, placed Darsha's phone on the dresser, and put Joshna's book bag in the closet. As Zarin came out of the girls' room, she quietly closed the door and made her way into her and Neal's bedroom. Neal, however, was already fully nude.

"Well, *damn*, Tarzan. You're not wasting any time, are you?" Zarin said with her right hand on her hip.

"Well, I do have to help Meli tonight with some things. That's why I'm kind of glad to do this now," Neal said as he crawled into bed.

"Well, you've *ruined* foreplay."

"Just get your sexy ass in bed with me."

About an hour and a half later, Zarin and Neal were lying in bed. Fast asleep after their romantic afternoon session of lovemaking. As Zarin began to toss and turn her body, she woke up to a quiet and dark bedroom. It was the evening now, and Zarin wanted to get up to make dinner. But being that she did not feel like cooking both Neal's vegan meals *and* cooking a regular meal, Zarin decided she would order take-out again. Neal was still counting sheep as Zarin got out of bed. She got dressed in some house clothes and made her way to the girl's room. The bathroom light was turned on, which meant that one of the girls woke up already to use the bathroom. As Zarin walked into their room, Joshna was awake on the bottom mattress of their bunk bed, and Darsha was still asleep on the top.

"Joshy, did you use the bathroom, baby?" Zarin asked.

"No, mommy," Joshna responded. "That was Darsha. I just woke up."

Zarin then told Joshna to go downstairs with her homework so that she can check it. Joshna then got out of bed, grabbed her book bag, and walked down the stairs. As Zarin looked down, she saw something in the girl's trash can, something rather expensive. Zarin picked it out of the trash can, *shocked* that it was Darsha's iPhone. This action was the second time that Darsha put her phone in the trash. What could this possibly mean? Zarin began to wonder why Darsha, who was practically addicted to her phone, wants nothing more to do with it now?

Zarin began to wake Darsha up, as she wanted to get to the bottom of this. It took Zarin a few seconds to wake Darsha up, as Darsha could be a deep sleeper. Zarin then asked her, "Hey baby, why are you trying to throw your phone away in the trash? What is this all about?" Darsha just turned her back to Zarin and responded, "Because I hate it now. I don't ever want to be on it again." Zarin did not like that answer. It was one thing when Zarin had difficulty confronting Neal about the Meli situation. But when it comes to her *kids*, Zarin is *very* confrontational and protective. She then asked Darsha, "Why, baby? Why do you hate your phone? Did something happen? You saw something you didn't like? Did something happen at school?" Come on, tell mommy what happened."

Darsha then turned around, facing her mother with teary eyes and some soft sniffles. Zarin knew this was something serious, something terrible. As Darsha came down from the top bunk, she sat on the floor and began to tell Zarin what happened on Thursday at school. Darsha told Zarin that some of her classmates were sending videos to other kids' phones in the cafeteria. As Darsha's classmates made their way to her, they told her to open her phone so they could "airdrop" a video to her. Darsha has an iPhone, so she received it immediately. And when Darsha opened it, it was a hardcore, pornographic video.

Once again, Zarin had gaged. This time, for all the wrong reasons. Zarin's anxiety went through the roof. She immediately went to Darsha's photos app and looked through the video section. And sure enough, there was the pornographic video. Zarin was livid, furious. "Baby, I am *so* sorry you experienced this. Mommy and daddy will take care of this; *first thing* tomorrow morning. I'll be right back; I'm going to talk with daddy, okay? I'll take your phone for now," Zarin said as she power-walked back to her bedroom.

Zarin woke Neal up and told him the disturbing news. She explained to Neal what happened to Darsha and showed him the video. "I will sue the *fuck* out of that school. Do they have *any idea* how traumatizing this is for a ten-year-old? We're going there, first thing tomorrow morning. They shouldn't even *allow* kids to have those goddamn phones in school," Neal said as he paced back and forth in the bedroom. Zarin responded, "I *agree*, but baby, that's the world we live in now, with these phones. And our kids are just not *safe* out there anymore. We have to know where they are at all times. But I get what you're saying. I'm just going to take a day off tomorrow." Neal then left the bedroom, as he told Zarin that he would sit and talk with Darsha. Zarin asked Neal to check on Joshna as well.

If it is not one thing, it is the other. Zarin has not been able to catch a break this past week. First, it was the Meli situation, which was a disaster. And now, her daughter's innocence, potentially being destroyed. At that very moment, Zarin did what was necessary for herself. She sat on her bedroom floor, legs in yoga position, placed on her mediation music, and prepared to meditate. As the next ten minutes swiftly went by, she opened her eyes. The only thing she was able to say at that moment was, "Anxiety, I love to hate you."

Chapter 21

It was close to midnight on a Sunday evening. Briana and Miles are fast asleep. Monica is in the kitchen, as she just finished putting all the dishes in the dishwasher. Her husband, Sammy, is having a virtual meeting with his band members. They are going over the music for their gig at the Blue Note Jazz Club on Tuesday night. Which so happens to be Valentine's Day. Monica, unfortunately, is swamped with work and will be too busy to attend. She's already working on a new case.

Sammy's disappointment has caused some tension between the two of them this weekend. They have not been as social with each other. As Sammy wrapped up his virtual meeting, he got up from the living room and fixed himself a citrus crush drink. Monica went back to work in the dining room, looking over papers and documents that have to deal with her new case. Sammy then came into the dining room, sat down at the table with his citrus crush, and conversed with Monica.

"That's a lot of paperwork for one case," Sammy said as he took a sip of his drink.

"Yea, well, it's a massive case. I have to team up with other attorneys on this one," said Monica.

Page after page, Monica was reading. She became glued to the documents. Sammy felt that Monica was putting herself through overdrive. Sammy was beginning to feel a bit irritated that she was not giving him any attention. Finally, as he finished his drink, he said to Monica, "You know, sweetheart, I think you're putting *too* much on your plate. You just won your last case, and I'm proud of you. But I think it's time that you take a little break. You've been working nonstop for years now. How about you, myself, and the kids take a nice, *long* vacation together? I think it is well deserved for all of us." Monica did not say a word. She did not even lift her head from the documents. Sammy, feeling ignored, got up from the dining room table to fix himself another drink.

"Okay, it's whatever. Ignore me; that's fine," Sammy said as he opened the refrigerator.

"I'm not ignoring you, Sammy," Monica responded. "I heard you loud and clear. But a vacation is out of the question. For now."

Sammy looked at Monica from the kitchen. Not liking her answer, he slammed the refrigerator door and began to pour another citrus crush. Monica then lifted her head from the papers with a very distraught look on her face. She got up from the dining room table and stormed her way into the kitchen. "First of all, don't you be slamming the fucking refrigerator door. *Second*, that's one too many drinks; slow your ass down. And *third*, I am an *attorney*, Sammy. I can't just take a goddamn vacation whenever I feel like it. When it comes to these cases, someone's life is on the line. And I have to be *fully* invested. No vacations, no breaks, no excuses," Monica said with conviction.

But Sammy was not trying to hear that. His frustrations with her absence from him were causing him great concern. He responded and said, "Listen, I know you want to put on your cape and play Superwoman and save these criminal's lives. But you *have* to remember that you have a life too. I'm your husband, and I love you. We have two beautiful kids who love you and who need you. You are their *mother*. I *know* you do your best, but they need their mother in their lives. You need to be a better mother to our kids and a better wife to me. I need you to be more supportive of *my* work as well. You used to come to all of my gigs in the city. What happened with that, Monica? Come to my gigs, take the kids to the park or *something*. Just be more active in *our* lives. You seem to always be there for your girlfriends. So just be there for us now."

Monica stared at Sammy with a twisted-up face as she could not *believe* his hypocrisy. Especially after the other day when he gave her all that praise in the bathtub. At first, Monica turned around and walked out of the kitchen to get back to work. She was not even tempting to respond to him. But something inside Monica told her to get back in the kitchen and give Sammy a piece of her mind.

Monica then stormed her way back into the kitchen and let Sammy have it. "You know, I *rarely* say this word because you *know* how much I hate it. But in your case, I'm willing to make a *fucking* exception. NIGGA, PLEASE! How fucking dare you stand there, with a straight face, and tell me that *I* need to be a better mother to our kids and a more *"supportive"* wife to you and *your* work? How fucking dare you, Sammy?" Monica argued.

"Will you keep your damn voice down?" Sammy interjected. "No, *fuck* that, you wanted my attention, and now you have it. Did you forget when I was just finishing up law school, when I was working full time, paying *both* of our bills? Back when you had *no* gigs, you were flat broke, not a goddamn penny to your name. But I stood by your side, Sammy. *I* stuck it *all* the way out with you, through thick and thin. I supported your broke ass *and* your dreams for *years* before you became what you are today. I even forgave you, for when you slept with my best friend and her *sister*. You thought I forgot that? I lost my *best friend* because of you. I've sacrificed so much to be where I'm at today. To be a successful attorney, to be a *great* mother to *our* kids, *and* to be as supportive of a wife as I can be. And *this* is how you feel about me? *This* is how you treat me? After *everything*?" Monica said as the tears fell from her eyes.

Sammy had no words for Monica. Absolute silence as he looked at her. At that moment, she did not want to hear anything else from him. Monica then gathered her papers together and placed them in her briefcase. However, she was not entirely done with Sammy. She had something else to say. "I've loved you ever since that night I was a volunteer at your gig—that night when you played the Mary J. Blige song and dedicated it to me. You told the audience that I was your future wife. That was one of the best nights of my life. I'm not saying that I'm a perfect person. I'm far from that. But I need *you* to be a more supportive husband to *me* now. I've been feeling the need to seek therapy. For reasons that I can't explain right now. And I need your *support* with that and not your judgment," said Monica.

Sammy was not expecting her comment about seeking a therapist, as that came from left field. As Sammy walked to Monica, he rubbed on her shoulders and said, "A therapist? What do you need a therapist for Monica?" But Monica slowly shook her head and just shrugged her shoulders. "I just need someone different to talk to, Sammy. Someone brand new, that's all," said Monica.

Monica then walked away as tears came down her face. Sammy just stood there, watching her go up the stairs. "Monica, baby, wait; come here," Sammy begged. But she ignored him. As Monica wiped her teary face, she noticed her daughter, Briana, was standing in the crack of her bedroom door.

"Mommy, did you and daddy fight?" Briana asked.

"Oh baby, you don't have to worry about it," said Monica. "It's okay now. Come on; I'll tuck you back into bed."

After putting Briana back to bed, Monica made her way back into *her* bedroom. Monica was even more upset now because her and Sammy's argument woke up Briana. Monica then undressed, put on her nightgown and hair bonnet. And under the covers she went.

Sammy stood at the bottom of the stairs and looked up to the top. He walked up two of the stairs, but then he back-peddled down and just stood there. Sammy wanted to go up there and comfort Monica with sorrow and love. But he knew he upset her. Hurting her by his choice of words and lack of understanding of where *she* was coming from. That night, Sammy made a bed out of the living room couch. And Monica's pillow began to soak as she cried herself to sleep.

Chapter 22

It is Monday morning, and the late bell has rung. Zarin and Neal are waiting in the main office of Darsha and Joshna's school. They both arranged a meeting with the assistant principal and school counselor about Darsha's traumatic experience last Thursday. They have been waiting for a solid twenty minutes. Zarin's patience was beginning to disappear, and she became vocal about it.

"Excuse me, we have been waiting here for almost half an hour now. When are they going to be available?" Zarin said to the secretary.

"I'm so sorry for the delay," said the secretary. "Usually, it's a hassle getting the kids all settled in during the first period. But they should be with you momentarily."

As Zarin stood at the front desk of the office, another secretary asked her for a picture. Since Zarin is a journalist and a TV news anchor, she is recognized in public from time to time. But Zarin was in no mood for photographs. So, she rejected all pictures. "They have us waiting here for almost a half-hour, and they want a *goddamn* picture. Our baby girl is traumatized right now," Zarin softly said to Neal.

Finally, the assistant principal came out of his office. The school counselor was already sitting inside. "Good morning, Mr. and Mrs. Khan. Please come in," said the assistant principal. Neal took a seat, but Zarin was too anxious to sit. The assistant principal, Mr. Ross, introduced them to Ms. Velez, the school counselor. After the greetings, Zarin did not waste any time as to why she and Neal were there.

As Zarin stood there in the office, she said, "Mr. Ross, Ms. Velez, my daughter, Darsha, *our* daughter, excuse me. Darsha was in the school cafeteria this past Thursday. While she was eating her lunch, one of her classmates sent her a disturbing, *very* disturbing video through the "Airdrop" of her iPhone. It was a pornographic video. As of right now, our daughter is distraught and traumatized. Darsha wants nothing more to do with her phone anymore. As parents, we *expect* our children to be safe and protected on the school grounds at all times. But we are not getting that from this school. Now, what's done is done. I want to know what *you're* going to do to prevent something like this from happening to *another* child?"

The assistant principal, Mr. Ross, was very apologetic about this situation, as was Ms. Velez. Mr. Ross responded, saying, "Mr. and Mrs. Khan, first, we would like to offer our sincerest apologies for what happened to Darsha. I'm terribly sorry about that. And these phones nowadays are just so dangerous when it comes to children. But this is the world we live in now, where these kids *have* to have a phone. Just so you, as parents, *know* where they are at all times. But at the same *time*, the kids have access to all the worst things on the internet. With social media and everything, that student could have possibly saved the video on *their* phone and *then* "airdrop" it to Darsha's phone. But that's no excuse. We will create some better policies for these phones. And we will also look into more site-blocking software, if necessary. But for now, we can find out who that student was who sent Darsha that video. We'll have the student's parents come in, and Ms. Velez will talk with them. And if Darsha wants to talk with someone here, we have Dr. Ford, the school's psychiatrist. How does that sound?"

Zarin, without hesitation, irritably said, "Oh, so you think *our* daughter needs a psychiatrist now? *She* is the victim here. The little bastard who *sent* her the video needs a goddamn psychiatrist." Neal took Zarin's hand and told her to calm down. Neal then interjected and said, "Look, we just want to know that when we send our daughter to this school, that she will *not* experience this, *ever* again." Ms. Velez reassured Zarin and Neal that this would *not* happen again. *And* they will further investigate this incident.

    As Zarin said her piece, she collected her jacket and purse and headed out of Mr. Ross's office. Right before leaving, Zarin said, "We're keeping Darsha and Joshna out of school for the rest of the week until this is resolved. If both of you are parents, I'm *sure* you would understand." Both Zarin and Neal then headed out of the school. Darsha and Joshna were back at home, as Neal's twin sister, Meli, volunteered to watch them.

On the ride back home, Zarin and Neal had a brief conversation. "Un-fucking-believable. They didn't know *what* to say to us. But that's okay because if this happens again, *lawsuit*," Neal said to Zarin as he drives. Zarin said to Neal that she and Darsha would have to talk about this experience when they get home. "I have to talk to Darsha about sex. I was hoping that I could've waited until she was at *least* thirteen or fourteen. But now, I have to sit her down and explain to her that what she saw in that video is *not* appropriate," Zarin spoke. Neal could not agree more with Zarin.

Before heading home, Neal stopped in front of a Starbucks to fulfill his craving for caffeine.

"I'm going to grab some coffee and pastries from Starbucks. You want anything?" Neal said to Zarin.

"Yea, a Blonde Vanilla Latte. Thanks, baby," said Zarin.

As Zarin waited in the car, she leaned her head back on the headrest and closed her eyes. All she heard were the sounds of car horns, police sirens, and cab drivers cursing up a storm as they almost run over pedestrians. Zarin was breathing in and out to calm her anxiety. As she opened her eyes, she had a sudden epiphany. As Zarin looked out her window, all she saw were people, young and old, walking with their heads down, on their phones. She realized how much technology has shaped and changed the world: hundreds, thousands of people walking down these streets, hypnotized by their phones.

Zarin began to reminisce about when she was a kid. Way before these smartphones and social media was even a thought in anyone's mind. She remembers her childhood being more adventurous and imaginative. But now, she understands the world has lost a great deal of its innocence. Zarin grew concerned for her daughters. To be living in a world like this, where the human connection is broken, nonexistent even. Zarin shook her head as she is now aware of *her* addiction to her phone. As she opened and looked at the home screen of her phone, Zarin did something rather remarkable. She pressed and held on to the social media apps, pressed delete, and cold turkey quit social media. Almost immediately after making such a bold decision, Zarin began to smile as she felt a sense of relief. Now, her phone usage will decrease by eighty percent. Neal then made his way back to the car with the Starbucks goodies.

"Here we are; oh, I got a free cookie. *So*, I gave those *geniuses* my name, right? And *they* spelled my name "N-E-*E*-L." *That's* one point lost. But let's see if they got the coffee right," Neal said as he tastes his coffee. "Yes! It's a win for me," Neal celebrated. As Neal put his coffee in the cup holder, he noticed Zarin staring him down like a cat. "What? Why are you looking at me like that? Neal asked.

Zarin, still smiling, told Neal what she just did. She said with enthusiasm, "Baby, take a look around us. What do you see? Fucking Zombies, right? We are surrounded by walking zombies, *hypnotized* by their phones. That's what you see. Well, I'm not participating in *that* bullshit anymore. I just deleted my social media accounts. I've realized how paranoid it was making me. *You* saw how I was snooping around on your profile, looking to see if you were having an affair. No *wonder* my anxiety has been so high. It's because I was feeding into this *bullshit*: the likes, the comments, and all the attention. I don't need that in my life, nor do I want it. I don't need to see what random strangers are doing in *their* lives every day. I have my *real* friends already. I have you, I have the girls, and I now have a sister-in-law that I want to get to know. I will never know those people on social media."

Neal looked at Zarin as if she lost her mind. He did not know how to respond to her decision to quit social media. Neal simply said, "*Okay*, congratulations? I guess?" Neal then took another sip of his coffee and then drove back home.

As they arrived home, Zarin sent a group text to the other ladies. In the text, she said, "Hey ladies, just wanted to let you know that I've decided to quit and delete *all* my social media accounts, cold turkey. So don't send me a message on there. I won't see it. My reason for doing so? Well, something inside me just said to escape. Get off of it, and that's what I did."

Neal and Zarin made their way inside the house. Meli was spending quality time with Joshna in the living room. Joshna had her hand on Meli's womb as she felt the baby kicking. Zarin asked Joshna where Darsha is. Meli told Zarin that she was upstairs in her room. Zarin thought to herself and said this would be the perfect time to have a one-on-one conversation with Darsha. A conversation about sex and what she saw in that video. As Zarin went up the stairs, she walked into the girls' bedroom. Darsha was lying on the top bunk, playing with her doll.

"Hey baby, why don't you come down from there? I want to talk to you about something," Zarin said to Darsha.

"Is this about the video stuff?" Darsha asked.

"Yes, it's about what you saw those people doing in the video."

As Darsha came down the ladder of her bunk bed, she sat on Joshna's bed, and Zarin sat on the floor, in her comfortable yoga position. Zarin just wanted Darsha to listen as she explained to her what sex is, the meaning of it. Zarin said, "So, baby, what you saw in that video. That was *not* an appropriate expression of intimacy. That was an enhanced sexual performance—meant to create an intense climax. Videos like that are made for adult entertainment. It's *not* meant for a child's eyes. It was not meant for you to see that. But you did, baby, and mommy's sorry you were exposed to that video. But when it comes to sex. I still think you're a little too young to understand properly. But it is *my* job, as your mother, to explain to you the "*birds and the bees*," which is an old expression we used to use to describe sex."

As Darsha continued to listen, she cut off Zarin and asked, "Wait, do you and daddy have sex?" Zarin then responded, "That's what I'm getting to, baby. And yes, daddy and I have sex. So, *sex* is something that two grown-ups do. It's when a man and a woman come together; well, in *some* cases, sex involves two *men* or two *women* coming together. But that is a whole *other* conversation, for another time. But for this sake, let's focus on a man and a woman. They become intimate with each other. When your father and I become intimate with each other, we, *we* call it love-making. That's what sex is to your father and me. We make *love* to each other. And it's actually a *beautiful* thing.

"*So*, that video was not lovemaking?" Darsha asked Zarin. Zarin responded, "No, baby, it's not. That video you saw was fake. That was *not* lovemaking, that was *not* intimacy, that was complete and utter taboo. And when you get older, you may meet someone who you will be attracted to. Just how your father and I are attracted to each other. And you are going to want to be intimate with that person. But *only* when you give that person your consent. Only when you know *you're* ready. And hopefully, that person will be respectful to you. Otherwise, mommy will kick their butts."

More than anything, Zarin was hoping and praying that this was getting through to Darsha. And to Zarin's surprise, it *was*. But Darsha had more questions. "Is sex how babies are made, mommy?" Darsha asked. "Yes, honey, that's how babies are made, *naturally*. But, *again*, that's a whole other conversation," Zarin responded.

Darsha then gave it some thought and began to process what Zarin said. "I think I understand a little bit, mommy. The video was not something special between two adults. And that when I'm older, and I'm ready, I will be intimate with someone, only if I give them my *consent*? Is that right, mommy?" Darsha said. Zarin joyfully responded, "*Exactly*! Yes, high-five, baby! That's my girl! *See*? That's all I want for you and Joshy. I want you both to use your head, *think,* and be the smart girls that your father and I are raising you two to be. Great thinking, baby. I'm so proud of you."

As Zarin was ready to wrap up the conversation, Darsha had *one more* question to ask Zarin. With no filter, Darsha asked, "Mommy, is fellatio an ice cream flavor? I heard one of my classmates say it is." After hearing that, Zarin placed her hand across her forehead and began to shake her head. Zarin then sighed and responded, saying, "No baby, that is *not* an ice cream flavor. And I think I'm going to have to switch you and Joshy out of that school and into a private school. You don't need to be around those crazy kids."

Several hours go by, Meli was busy in the kitchen. Neal told the Zarin and the girls that Meli learned how to cook in culinary school back home in London. Meli insisted that she cook to show her appreciation for being welcomed to their home. Being that Neal lives on a plant-based diet, Meli prepared a vegan vegetable curry Casserole and vegan Malai Kofta with pita bread. When they all took their first bites, they were in vegan heaven. There was no talking, just eating. They never tasted something so good.

Halfway through their meal, Neal began an open conversation. "So, how do you girls like the curry Casserole?" Neal asked. Joshna responded, "I like it a lot. *I'm* just glad aunt

Meli didn't dump a bunch of curry in it as Nani does." An ensemble of laughter came among the table. The way Joshna said that with her soft, innocent voice gave it such humor and conviction.

Zarin thought it was appropriate to raise her glass to the occasion as they were just finished with their meal. As everyone held their cups, Zarin said, "So, everyone, I just wanted to make a toast to Meli. And Meli, I know I gave you a bizarre and despicable introduction. But I'm glad that's all over with, and I hope you can forgive me for that *huge* misunderstanding. I'm happy to have you here with us. And Neal and I will do whatever we can to help you with your situation. To Meli, Salute!"

Meli was very grateful to Zarin for welcoming her into their home. At that very moment, another epiphany came to Zarin's mind. She realized that since she deleted her social media accounts earlier, she has not once looked at her phone. Zarin could not believe it. For the first time in years, she has never been away from her phone for longer than twenty minutes. For Zarin, as a journalist and a news anchor, that is a miracle. Zarin did not realize how much those platforms were such an addiction to her.

But then Zarin remembered that she sent a group text to the other ladies. She grabbed her phone from her coat pocket and saw the responses the other four gave her. "That is great, girl! Good for you! I think we can all use a break from that shit. I know I do. But I'm nosey as fuck. LMFAO!" Collette replied.

Wendy responded, saying, "Bravo! You'll be my inspiration to quit. Oh, btw, I'm finally in Tokyo." Tomi replied, "Bitch, you'll be back on that shit next week, looking for mistress #2…JK HAHA! Love ya, girl! That's great!" And finally, Monica chimed in last and replied, "I call that a rebirth, a spiritual cleansing even. You're rising from the ashes like a phoenix, babe. I'm proud of you. Actually, I'm going to do some spiritual cleansing myself. I made an appointment to see a therapist."

That hit Zarin by surprise. To hear that Monica is seeking therapy. But Zarin is not going to judge her. She could understand, knowing Monica deals with clients every week. Zarin then hit the "laugh" reaction to Tomi, Wendy, and Collette's text messages. But for Monica's text, Zarin hit the "loved" reaction. Zarin even replied to Monica on a personal text that said, "Nica, I think that is great that you are seeking therapy. I am proud of you for seeking help and being open about it. That may be my next step as I try to cope with my anxiety. Please let me know how it goes. I love you, babe. XOXO."

Monica quickly hit the "loved" reaction on Zarin's text and responded, "I love you too, honey. Thank you for supporting my decision. And I will definitely let you know how it goes. Thank you for always being in my corner."

That response put such a smile on Zarin's face. She loved that message and replied, "Always," with heart emojis. It's not every day that a group of friends shares such an unbreakable bond. For years, they have had each other's back. Even though their "mission impossible" plan was a bust. What it did was bring them closer together. And for Zarin, to have her family and her friends. This was all she could ask for in her life. Quitting social media today was the answer to her prayers. It cleared out all of the clutter of unnecessary commotion. And that gave Zarin not only healing but also salvation.

Chapter 23

The following morning, Collette is hard at work in her office. "*Fernandez Realty,* LLC," is her baby. She founded her real estate brokerage firm twelve years ago. She's been a member of the *National Association of Realtors* for over thirteen years now. And business for Collette has been booming ever since. Collette is a mastermind when it comes to getting things done. She is exquisite and sharp as a tack with her real estate law, contracts, and ethics knowledge. Her reputation in the game is well known, and Collette always comes highly recommended. But, of course, she had her ups and downs throughout the years. But *nothing* was like the entire real estate market shutting down when the Covid-19 pandemic hit. It completely wiped out Manhattan's livelihood. So many people had moved out of the city. Housing prices dropped tremendously, and properties stood on the market, basically collecting dust. But now, in 2023, the real estate market is beginning to recover, and Collette's business is picking up, slowly but surely.

Standing in her office, Collette cannot help but stare at herself in the mirror on the wall. She is checking out her new haircut. Before cutting it, her brown hair reached down to her back. But she wanted something new, something different to look at in the mirror. So, Collette went to her hairdresser and had a few inches of her hair snipped off. Now, she is sporting a medium, wavy hairstyle with light brown highlights.

Her husband, Martin, loved it very much when she came home last night. And he showed her just how *much* he loved it, *all* night long. So, Collette was definitely in a good mood this morning until one of her real estate agents, Gina, came into her office and gave her some bad news about one of the properties.

"Good morning, Mrs. Fernandez; I, unfortunately, have some bad news about that property in Harlem," said Gina.

"Gina, we've talked about this baby. You don't have to call me *"Mrs. Fernandez,'* just Coco or even Ms. Coco. And what's the bad news?" Collette responded.

Gina explained to Collette how she was going over the contract with the potential buyers interested in a brownstone in

East Harlem. But the buyers stopped taking her calls and just completely ignored her. Collette asked Gina how often she contacted the potential buyers. Gina then broke it down to Collette and said, "So, I was reaching out to them several times a day."

Collette stopped her right there. "*Gina*, sweetie, *that* was the problem. You *must* take a breather and let the potential buyers breathe as well, Mamí. It's not a good look to be clingy in this line of work. Keep in mind that buying a property is a *long-term* decision. Buyers must take their time and go through the process. *Your* job is to *guide* them *through* the process, you know? You *have* to be patient with potential buyers. Buying property is *not* an easy decision for them, okay?" Said Collette.

With an apologetic look on her face, Gina responded, "Yes, Mrs. Fernandez, *oh*, I'm sorry, Coco. I understand. Sorry about that." "It's okay, Gina. I'll cut you some slack on this one. You're still new and a little wet behind the ears. So, moving *forward*, have patience, *don't* be clingy, and oh, this is *very* important. Don't *ever* put your personal agenda over the potential buyers' wishes. This includes you being patient with them. No matter what you have going on in your personal life, it has *nothing* to do with their interest in a property," Collette said to Gina. Collette then informed Gina that there would be another team meeting on Friday. It will be covering some fundamentals on dealing with potential buyers and sellers.

"Okay, thank you, Coco, and I'll definitely be attending that meeting on Friday," said Gina.

"Oh, of course, you'll be at the meeting, babe. It's mandatory," Collette responded as she waved goodbye.

As Collette gathered her coat and purse, she gave her mother a call. "Hey, Mamí, you're home, right? Okay, I'll be there in a half-hour. *No*, I'm coming straight from the office. Alright, bye," said Collette. Before Collette headed out of her office, she told her assistant that she's out for the day and to keep her informed via email if anything comes up.

As Collette went down the elevator, she saw her reflection on the elevator mirror walls. She could not help but play around with her new hairstyle. "Yes bitch, *yes*," Collette softly said to herself as she was embracing her looks. As the elevator doors opened, Collette said goodbye to the security guard of the building and walked outside in the fifty-five-degree weather. However, it was a beautiful sunny sky, not a snowflake in sight.

As Collette made her way to the parking lot, a homeless man made his way towards her. He said, "Good morning, miss, could you please spare a dollar or some change?" But Collette walked right past him without saying a word; she did not even look at his presence. Collette then walked to her brand new 2023 all-black Mercedes Benz. As she unlocked the door, she got in and started the car. Of course, because the weather is so cold, Collette had to wait a few minutes to warm up the car. As she sat there in her car, Collette saw something disturbing. She saw the same homeless man digging out of a trash can, looking for scraps of food. At that moment, Collette shook her head and felt an instant load of shame on herself.

Collette began to think back on her life and realized that she *never* had to dig out of a trash can to look for food. She is *not* suffering, homeless, or in poverty. Right there in her car, Collette acknowledged her blessings: a successful career, a loving husband who takes care of his family, and two loving kids. And what made matters worse, Collette had over five hundred dollars, cash, in her purse. The homeless man then began to walk away from the parking lot. Collette then turned off the car, grabbed her bag, and got out to catch the homeless man. She had to speed walk to catch up to him.

"Excuse me, sir, hey!" Collette said to the homeless man.

"Yes, ma'am?" Said the homeless man.

Collette went into her purse and pulled out three hundred from the five-hundred dollars she had on her. As Collette had it in her hand, she said, "I am so sorry that I just walked past you like that. That was very rude of me. Here, take it." Collette then handed the homeless man the cash. He just stood there as if he was frozen. Not frozen from the cold chills of the air, but frozen to Collette's kind generosity. It brought tears to his hazel eyes.

"Thank you so much, ma'am. I can now have a nice hot meal. Thank you," said the homeless man.

"You're welcome, sir. What is your name?" Collette asked.

"Jimmy, Jimmy Ferguson."

"It's nice to meet you, Jimmy; I'm Collette Fernandez."

Collette then said goodbye to Jimmy, and they went their separate ways. As Collette got back into her car, she cried softly. She could not imagine how so many homeless people ended up in their situations. No home to go to, no friends or family, no love at all. As Collette started her car, she had to wait again for it to warm up. As she waited, Collette put her hands together in a praying position and said a prayer. "Dear father, thank you for all the blessings you have bestowed onto me. Thank you for my family, my husband, my kids, and my ladies. Thank you for bringing my four sisters into my life, as well as Lisa. You are so forgiving, so merciful. And thank you for putting Jimmy Ferguson in my life for that split second. He showed me how fortunate I truly am. I am truly a grateful woman, father. Amen."

Collette needed a moment in her car. She then wiped her face, took a deep breath, and began to drive out of the parking lot. As Collette was on her way to see her parents, she could not stop thinking about the homeless man, Jimmy Ferguson. She wondered how he ended up homeless—thinking of if he has a family or where he stays in the city. In her mind, Collette said another prayer, "Father, if it's meant to be that I see Jimmy Ferguson again, give me a message as to how I could help him."

About thirty-five minutes later, Collette finally pulled up in front of her parents' house in Queens. Her parents moved from the Bronx to Queens right before Collette graduated from high school. And they have been there ever since. As Collette rang the doorbell, she waited there for almost a minute. Her mother finally opened the door.

"Oh, Coco, where's your key?" Collette's mother said.

"I left it at home, Mamí. It's nice to see you too," said Collette.

Collette's mother, Gloria, was busy with the tea. It was already boiling, which caused Gloria to delay answering the door. Gloria wanted Collette to stay to have some tea with her. But Collette was in a bit of a hurry and tried to make it fast. Also, Collette is more of a coffee and wine person. So, tea was out of the question.

"So, Mamí," said Collette. "I just came over to tell you about Lis—"

"NO! Collette, I *don't* want to hear it. I already told you, keep that shit out of *this* house," Gloria said indignantly.

Collette knew that this was not going to be an easy task when it came to her parents. Collette wanted her mother to accept Lisa for who she is, a woman. But Gloria's growing stubbornness was at an all-time high. As Gloria sat down with her tea, with anger, she said, "Listen, Coco, so that we are *very* clear. Your *brother*, *Liam*, is mentally *fucked* in the head. He's been that way since he was a little boy, and he is *still* a boy. Just so we're clear on that. Putting on a dress, putting on makeup, or even cutting his *fucking* dick off, does *not* make *him* a woman. He can dress up all he wants, but he will *never* be you or me, a *woman.*"

Collette's breathing began to grow a little heavy. Her task became harder than she could ever imagine. But she would not give up. "Mamí, I understand that *you* don't understand any of it. But this is not a choice; *Lisa* did not choose this life. She did not choose to be a trans woman. And after what *Papi* did to her out in the middle of the street? For *years* I tried to make peace with her and ask her for forgiveness. Lisa is not asking you for *anything* except for your love and support. That is *still* your child, Mamí."

Gloria said nothing at all. She shook her head, then went ahead and sipped on her tea. But that was not all that Collette had to say to her mother. She was hesitant to mention Emilio coming out as a gay man. But she worked up the courage and told her mother. "Mamí, there's something else. It's about Emilio," said Collette. Gloria looked at Collette and said, "What about Emilio?" Collette told her mother that she and Emilio had a conversation, and Emilio told her about his *true* sexuality. Gloria then stood up from the kitchen table and walked away with a look of disgust on her face. As Gloria walked away, she said, "Ay Dios Mio, WHAT KIND OF *FUCKING* FAMILY DID I RAISE?

Collette had just about enough of her mother. *Now*, Gloria was disrespecting her own grandson. And Collette had *zero* tolerance for that. As Collette stood up from the kitchen table, she said, "Mamí, what you're *not* going to do is talk bad about *my* son. He's your grandson, yes, but *I* raised him, okay? You may not understand Lisa or Emilio, but you *will* show them respect."

But Gloria's stubbornness was as solid as a diamond. Extremely unbreakable, raw, and uncut. Through all the commotion, Collette's father, Raúl, came down the stairs from his afternoon nap. Raúl was happy to see Collette; he rarely has time to see her with his busy schedule. Collette, however, was not as thrilled to see him.

"Hey, Coco, my one and *only* daughter," said Raúl. "*Qué pasa*? You don't come to see your old man *enough* these days."

"You're one and *only* daughter?" Collette said in an irritated tone.

"What? What I say wrong?"

"*Really*, Papí? What's *with* you two, huh?"

Gloria's disrespect went up a notch as she said to Collette's father, "You know our grandson is a homosexual? Ay Dios Mio! *First*, it was my brother, *then* it was Liam, and *now* it's Emilio. I guess it runs in our family." Raúl then looked over to Collette and said, "Coco, is this *true*? I hope *Martin* doesn't know."

"You know what, let me get my shit together and leave before I say or do something that I *won't* regret. You two have some serious issues, and you ought to be ashamed of yourselves. And Papì, don't think I forgot about what you did to Lisa in the middle of the street when we were kids. Because she surely didn't," Collette said. Before Collette walked out, Gloria said, "Oh Coco, you tell *Liam* to stop calling this house. If *he* wants to talk to me, then he better come to me, *dressed* like a respectable *man* and not as some flamboyant drag show."

Collette shook her head in disbelief. She looked at her mother with a solid face and said this one last thing to her. "I love my sister to death. And I am *so* proud of her for living her truth. She is my hero. It takes a lot of courage to live in a world that tells you; you are not enough. That *tells* you who you are *supposed* to be. As if they know what's best for every fucking body. But *Lisa*, only she knows what is best for her. I didn't, you and Papí didn't, only she knows. You and Papí may not accept her. But she'll be okay because she has *me*, Mamí. And I'll *always* have her back. And by the way, you keep this up, and you won't be seeing *me* around here anymore either. *Then* we'll see how you two old farts handle being alone and childless."

Gloria then pointed her finger out towards the door, demanding Collette to leave the house. "Get out! Get the *fuck* out of my house, Collette. And that's *fine*; we don't need you around here. And tell that *freak* never to call here again."

Collette stormed down the stairs as Gloria slammed the door behind her. Collette then opened her car door, slammed it shut, and screamed as she had another episode of tears and sobbing. She just had to let it all out of her system. So much was built up inside of Collette, all those years of seeing Lisa abused, suffering, and Lisa almost taking her own life. Collette just wanted her parents to welcome Lisa into their hearts. But unfortunately, the key to their hearts is so lost.

After Collette calmed down, she looked through her purse and took out her phone. She made a call to Lisa. About four rings later, Lisa picks up. As Collette had some sniffles left, Lisa asked what was wrong. Collette said, "I failed you, sis. I talked with Mamí and Papì. I tried to tell them about you, about Emilio, and they want nothing to do with their own family. And I'm so sorry. I'm so, so sorry. I'm sorry for telling them about you wearing Mamí's shoes when we were kids. I'm sorry for what Papì did to you. I just wanted them to accept you for who you truly are. But they won't budge, baby. But I want you to know that *I* love you with all my heart. You are my hero, and I don't want you *ever* to feel that you don't have a family or a home filled with love. Because you do, Lisa, you do with me."

Now, there were tears and sniffles on both ends of the line. Lisa was not surprised at their parents' reaction. She told Collette to let it go and that nothing else could be done now. Collette agreed, she told Lisa how she did her absolute best, but there was no use. Right before hanging up, Lisa said, "I never took the time to tell you this. But now is a better time than any. I *forgive* you, Coco; I have forgiven you for quite some time now. Through all the abuse that Mamí and Papí put me through, I survived and became the woman that I was *truly* born to be. And I love you more, my sister."

Collette closed her eyes as tears fell and held on to the phone with both hands. That is what she has been waiting to hear from Lisa for so long. Waiting to hear Lisa say, "I forgive you." Collette can finally put the past to rest, and she and Lisa can strengthen their bond that was broken for so many years.

As she drove off, back to Manhattan, Collette decided to stop at *Lucille's* to have a few drinks. She then called Monica to see if she could join her. But Monica was swamped with work and had to *remind* Collette that it was Valentine's Day. Collette could not believe she forgot that *today* was Valentine's Day. She then called her husband, Martin, and put him on speaker.

"Hey, baby," said Collette. "I forgot today's Valentine's Day."

"Oh, you *did*, huh?" Martin responded.

"Yea, are you busy right now?"

"I'm always busy, baby. But no, I'm actually at home, waiting for Emilio."

"*Oh*? Why?"

"What do you mean *why*? I can't see my son?"

"Oh, no, no…It's not *that*. Um, you two made plans?"

"No, he just wanted to tell me something."

"Tell you *what*?"

"Hey, *hey*. What is it with all these goddamn questions?"

"Nothing, never mind. Forget it."

"Listen, why don't you have dinner with Mia tonight?"

"That doesn't sound like a bad idea. I want to talk with her."

"Yea, because she won't talk to me. Maybe *she* could be your Valentine."

"Oh, now you're going to be a smart ass?"

"Okay, you're acting *very* salty today, babe. What's on your mind?"

"You know what, you're right, Martin. I'm sorry, babe. I argued with my parents about Emilio and Lis—"

"Wait, about Emilio? About what?"

"Oh, nothing, don't wor—"

"No, no, *tell me*. Why were you arguing about Emilio?"

"*Nothing* baby, really, it was jus—"

"No, what are you hiding from me, Coco?"

"I'm not hiding *anything* from you. Look, forget I said it. I have to go."

"Coco, don't hang up the pho—"

"*SHIT*! *Fuck* me!"

Collette couldn't push the end button on her phone fast enough. She felt the pressure of Martin closing in on her. After that, Collette immediately called Emilio. She wanted to make sure that Emilio doesn't reveal anything to his father just yet. But as the phone rang, there was no answer. So, Collette left a voice message, saying, "Hey baby, it's Mamí. Listen, I just talked with your father. He told me that you're meeting up with him to talk. But if this is about you coming out, about your sexuality, I think you should hold off on that baby. He's a little steamed right now, okay? But anyway, just call me back when you can. Alright, I love you."

After Collette finished that message, she hung up and made *another* call, this time to Mia. Collette felt she needed a little one-on-one quality time with Mia, who Collette feels she has been neglecting lately. As Collette talked to Mia over the phone, she told her to get ready because they were going out for a Broadway show and dinner afterwards. Mia seemed excited to go out on a nice little dinner date with her mother for a change, especially since Mia was still grounded.

But today was quite a day for Collette. It was a day that she found gratitude, received forgiveness from Lisa, and realized that *some* people in this world would *never* change. But the most important thing to know is "never change who *you* are." *Never* change to appease everyone else's comfort and fantasies of who *they* think you are supposed to be.

Chapter 24

The Blue Note is on fire tonight! Sammy Taylor and his quintet are *jamming* the night away. The saxophone player just finished his solo. Sammy is standing there, looking sharp in his Jade green Italian suit. As Sammy holds his trumpet, he watches his other bandmates give their solo performances.

As Sammy's quintet is already into their second session for the night, Monica walked into the Blue Note. She was able to catch some of the second act. Monica had to say, "excuse me," about seven times before she reached her reserved seating. As Sammy looked, he saw Monica taking her seat. It put such a smile of gratitude on his face. Monica made it after a hard day's work in the courtroom. But by the looks of her, Sammy could tell that Monica was a little drained. But her effort for just showing up was all he needed from her.

And of course, the same poster of Miles Davis from *years* ago was up on stage as part of Sammy's ritual. As the pianist wrapped up his solo, Sammy raised his hand as he wanted to make a special announcement to the audience. As the room became silent, Sammy said, "Happy Valentine's Day, first and foremost. I'm glad everyone made it here safely. And I hope afterward, you all make it *home* safely. I wanted to share something with you all. My *beautiful* wife is here tonight, Monica Taylor." As Sammy gestured to Monica, the crowd began to applaud her.

Monica smiled as the crowd gave her a round of applause. Sammy then continued as he said, "This woman right here, she is, without a shadow of a doubt, the *love* of my life. Since the very first day I met her, I knew she was the one. And years later, we are still together, and we have two of the most *beautiful* kids. And baby, you were right. You've been by my side through it all. Thank you for being the strong woman that you are. This one is for you, my love."

The look on Monica's face was priceless. She appreciated Sammy's words. As Sammy came down from the platform, he made his way towards Monica with his trumpet. Sammy stood there in front of Monica, smiling down at her. As Sammy put his trumpet to his mouth, he began to play one of Monica's favorite songs, "*My Funny Valentine.*"

You could hear a cotton ball drop. That's how quiet it was in the Blue Note—the sounds of Sammy's horn, the freshness, the smoothness, and some piano playing in the background. Monica could not take her eyes off of Sammy. She *loved* seeing his neatly manicured fingers, quickly pressing down on the valves of the trumpet. Monica then closed her eyes as Sammy played and let the music *flow* through her body like melodic blood. It was that moment when Monica was reminded of why she loved him so dearly—his *genius* ability behind that trumpet.

And when Sammy hit that final note, tears were streaming down Monica's face. It was like her love for him was reborn. It was pure magic. As Sammy finished playing, Monica stood up from her chair and gave her man the kiss of the night. The whole crowd began to applaud again. Not only because of the music, but because of their love for each other. After the kiss, Monica whispered something special in Sammy's ear. She gently said, "The magic of our love was *always* in your music, baby. Thank you, and I love you so much."

What a beautiful, angelic way to close the night for this married couple. At first, Monica was not going to attend Sammy's gig. She was still a bit upset with him after the other night. But something told her to go, to bury the hatchet between them. And after hearing Sammy play, it was well worth it.

Chapter 25

A mother and daughter date for Collette and Mia at *Lucille's* this evening. They just took their seats at Collette's reserved booth that she shares with her ladies on Friday nights. But on this Tuesday evening, she is sharing it with her daughter, Mia. They came from watching the new Disney Broadway musical, *"Cruella."* Mia loved it, but Collette was getting a migraine from all of the singing. As the waiter came by to take their order, Mia went first.

"I want a strawberry daiquiri with an extra strawberry, please?" Mia said to the waiter.

"That will be a *virgin* strawberry daiquiri. Without the alcohol," Collette said to avoid confusion.

As they both began to look at the menu, Mia grew curious about why her mother wanted to take her to dinner. "So, ma, I'm still suspended from school, and you and Papì grounded me. Why did you allow me to come out tonight? What's the special occasion?" Mia said to Collette.

Collette thought about it and began to reflect. After what happened earlier with her mother, Collette felt that it was important that she maintains a strong, healthy, and positive relationship with Mia. Collette does not know how her relationship with *her* mother will be now, which is why she will try her best to keep her and Mia as close as possible.

As Collette took a sip of her wine, she said, "I brought you out tonight because I wanted to have some quality time with you. Just the two of us. I feel that you and I are not spending as much time together as we should be. Your father and I have been busy with work, and I haven't always been around. But the *real* reason is, your grandmother and I had a fallout today. And I don't know when we will be speaking to each other again. We're just not on the same page with things right now. Mia, I don't want *our* mother and daughter relationship to be like that, baby. I want to make sure that you and I are *always* good. And that *you* know that I love you, and you can talk to me about *anything*."

Mia did not expect Collette to say that so openly. But she was glad that she did. Mia needed to hear that from her mother. "I love you too, Mamí. I'm happy that you feel we needed to spend more time together. Maybe we can have spa days from time to time?" Mia said to Collette. Collette loved the idea of having spa days. Collette even talked about flying to Miami or the Dominican Republic to see their family roots. Mia was down to go anywhere.

"Mamí?" Mia spoke.

"Yes, baby?" Collette responded.

"I think you should still talk to *Abuela*. Life's too short, you know?"

"You're right, baby. You're absolutely right."

As Mia swirled her straw around the glass, slurping up the remains of her delicious *virgin* strawberry daiquiri, Collette received a call. It was Emilio. "Holá baby, Qué Pasa?" Collette said to Emilio. As Collette listened, all she could hear were the cries and *screams* of her son, Emilio. It startled Collette instantly. Mia became frightened as well as she looked over at Collette's chilling face. Collette kept asking Emilio what happened. And what he told Collette took her breath away.

Emilio told Collette that he came by the apartment to talk to his father about his sexuality. But it didn't quite work as planned. Martin found out about Emilio before *Emilio* could get a word out, and Martin's reaction was rather malicious. Martin cursed Emilio out excessively, slapped him around the apartment, and continuously kicked him on the ground, as he said the most derogative vocabulary he could think of.

As Collette heard all of this over the phone, her face was in utter shock. She held her hand across her mouth as she tried to hold back the tears. She then told Emilio that she is on her way home and hung up her phone.

"Mamí, what's wrong? What happened to Emilio?" Mia asked with deep emotion.

"We have to go to him now, baby. Come on!" Collette said.

As the waiter came out with their meals, Collette told her that she had a family emergency and had to leave. She and Mia then headed out to her car to start and warm it up. Collette began to cry uncontrollably. She barely had the mental stability to drive. But since Mia is underage and could not be the driver, she had to pull herself together and drive. "Jesus, take the wheel," Collette said. But Collette couldn't wait anymore. She pulled off not even thirty seconds after starting the car. She then gave her phone to Mia and told her to call her brother and keep him on the line. As Mia called, the phone went straight to voicemail.

"It went to voicemail, Mamí. What do I do?" Mia said as she cried.

"Keep trying! Keep calling him!" Collette projected.

Fifteen minutes later, after honking her horn over a hundred times, almost crashing into an Uber driver's rear bumper, Collette and Mia made it home in one piece. Collette's body shook the entire time, not knowing what to expect when she got into the apartment.

As the elevator doors opened, Collette and Mia rushed to their apartment. Apartment number *921* is their place of residence. As they both came to their front door, it was wide opened. Collette paused in her tracks. She became hesitant, stepping into the apartment. But Mia went straight in. "Emilio? Emilio? Where are you?" Mia shouted as she walked around the apartment.

Collette then slowly walked into the apartment. As she looked around, she saw drops of blood on the floor of the hallway. She knew it was Emilio's blood. The blood drops on the floor were then met with teardrops from Collette's eyes. She could not believe Martin would do something like this to their own son.

"Mamí, he's not here! I looked everywhere," Mia said.

"Oh my God. Okay, okay, call security, baby. I'm going to ask one of the neighbors," Collette said as she walked out of the apartment.

One by one, Collette knocked on doors and rang bells. But there were no answers. Collette thought about it and realized that everyone was probably still out celebrating Valentine's Day. Then one neighbor at the very end of the hall opened their apartment door to see what was going on. Collette ran down the hall and told her neighbor that something terrible happened to her son and that she did not know where he is. The neighbor told Collette that he did not know anything about it because he just came home, *literally* five minutes ago. At that moment, Collette did not know what to do. She quickly thought about it and made her way back to the elevator. She wanted to see if the security at the front desk had seen Emilio walk out on the security camera.

As Collette went to the elevators, there was a delay on both of them. She kept tapping on the buttons, but her patience was thinner than a sheet of toilet paper. Collette then decided to use the stairs. As she made her way to the staircase, she rushed down flight after flight. She was skipping stairs as she jumped over the last two steps on each staircase. Then all of a sudden, there was Emilio.

Emilio was sitting on the fourth-level staircase: blood-stained hands, a bloody nose, busted lip, and his shirt ripped, leaving visible the bruised ribs. Collette was devastated by the image of her son. She went down some steps as she kneeled, looking up to Emilio. Collette's heavy sniffles began to echo throughout the stairwell. Emilio's face was bruised and bloody, as if he was beaten with a hammer.

When Collette tried to touch his arm, Emilio jumped and twitched as if he was in shock. The trauma of his father attacking him has already begun to sink in. As Emilio lifted his head, he said, "Oh, Mamí, I'm in so much pain." "Shhh…I'm here, baby. I'm going to take care of you. I can't believe this. Your father did this to you?" Collette cried.

As Emilio got his words together to talk with Collette, he said, "Yes, Papí did this. When I came inside the apartment, I thought he wasn't home yet. So, I sat down and checked my phone. I saw your voice message, and I played it on the speaker. He heard you, Mamí; he overheard your voice message, talking about my sexuality. Then all of a sudden, Papí came from behind me, screaming as he threw me up against the wall. Then he slapped me, punched me, and threw me on the ground. He called me a homo, a faggot, *everything*. I fucking *hate* him, Mamí; I hate his guts. I should've never come here. I'm sorry, Mamí. I should've listened to you."

Collette's emotions went from sad to angry. She was Infuriated that Emilio believed he owed her an apology when he did nothing wrong. "Oh, baby, you don't owe me an apology. *I'm* sorry, I should've *never* left that voice message. But right now, baby, please, I just want to get you to a hospital, okay?" Collette said.

Collette then helped Emilio up from the stairs. But she had to be careful of his bruised ribs. Emilio was barely able to walk, as he was beginning to get a little dizzy. All that was going through Collette's mind was the fact that this was déjà vu. As mentioned, the same thing happened to Collette's sister, Lisa, years ago, in the middle of a street. When their father, Raúl, beat Lisa down for who she is. And years later, *Emilio's* father beats him down for who *he* is. But only this time, Collette is not a kid anymore. She is a grown woman *and* a mother. She is not going to let this go, especially since this is *her* son. And *this* time, Collette wants revenge. That very moment, Collette thought about something and felt it was necessary to do it. But before she did it, she said to Emilio, "Baby, I need to do something right now. But I need you to trust me, okay. Just trust me." Collette took her phone from out of her pocket and began to snap some shots of Emilio's bruised and bloody face, as well as his bruised ribs.

"Why are you taking pictures of me, Mamí?" Emilio asked.

"Because someone close to us has to see what hatred towards others can do to people," said Collette.

Collette took eight pictures of Emilio. She then sent all eight of them to her mother via text message. After Collette sent the pictures, she sent this text afterward.

"*This* is what homophobic and transphobic behavior does to people. My husband, *his* father, did this to him. This is *your* grandson. *Now* do you see what this hatred does to people? Even in your own family? *Papí* knows." Collette text.

A few minutes went by; Collette looked at her phone and saw the three dots emerge in the text message thread. Collette's mother, Gloria, was starting to type a response. Collette waited, but after a minute went by, those three dots just disappeared, with no response at all.

As both Collette and Emilio made it back to the apartment, security was waiting for them in the living room. The two security guards helped Emilio on the living room couch. At that moment, Collette did not know what to do. She did not know whether she should go straight to the hospital with Emilio or find Martin.

But the more Collette looked at Emilio's defeated body, the more enraged she became with her husband. She then began to take matters into her own hands. Collette called the number to *Lucille's* to see if Martin was there. As one of the managers answered, Collette asked if Martin was around. The manager said that Martin just walked upstairs into his office. Collette did not say anything else. She ended the call, grabbed her bag, and took off. "Mamí, where are you going?" Mia said to Collette. But Collette did not say a word as she walked out and went straight to the elevator. Finally, the elevators were running smoothly now.

As Collette made it down to the front entrance where her car was parked, she popped open the trunk. Remember all the things Collette brought with her to the abandoned warehouse? Well, they never left her trunk. *Especially* the Balisong knife. Collette took the knife and put it in her purse. *Lucille's* is a twenty-minute drive from the apartment. That was enough time for Collette to come to her senses and prevent herself from doing something that she may regret. A situation like this is when Collette would call one of the ladies and ask for help. But Collette was way past that. And this was more personal. As mentioned, Collette wanted revenge.

About twenty-five minutes later, Collette parked around the corner from *Lucille's*. The look on her face was a look that said, "It's payback time." Collette was beginning to see all red. As red as the red nylon lights that hang on top of the restaurant. As Collette turned the corner, guess who was outside of the main entrance having himself a stogie? Her husband, Martin, calmly smoking his cigar as if he did not just *brutally* beat his son. Collette, however, wouldn't have cared if Martin was in the middle of Times Square, in broad daylight. She was going to make him pay. Collette walked her way down the street towards Martin. The closer she got to him, the redder her eyes began to see. The more rage she felt, and the closer to the devil she got.

Collette then pulled out the Balisong knife from her purse. She twirled it in her hand like a pro, grabbed it by the handle, and gave Martin a quick and bloody slash to the back of his left arm. The same arm he was using to hold his cigar. Martin did not even see it coming. The knife cut right through his $1,200 jacket.

Martin screamed as he turned around. And when he saw who it was that cut him, his eyes popped out of his head in shock.

"*COLLETTE*! JESUS FUCKING CHRIST!" Martin screamed.

"YOU SON OF BITCH! HOW DARE YOU HURT MY SON, YOU FUCKING COÑO!" Collette shouted, with a now bloody knife in her hand.

But it was not long before the two security guards in the restaurant disarmed Collette of the knife and tackled her to the ground. Collette started kicking, screaming, and crying herself into a frenzy. But the two guards overpowered her to the point where she could not move an inch. Now on the ground, Collette sees Martin get into a car with one of the guards and drove off.

As the police arrived, the other security guard informed the two officers of the situation. Standbys and onlookers came from the sidewalk. Guests, who still had food in their mouths and napkins tucked in their shirts, came running out of *Lucille's* to see what all the commotion was about. Some even took pictures and recorded Collette as she was tackled to the ground. The officers then handcuffed Collette, picked her up from the ground, read her Miranda rights, and placed her in the back of their squad car.

As Collette sat in the backseat, tightly cuffed, she was able to calm herself down and breathe. Suddenly, everything became a hazy blur to her. She did not even remember cutting Martin. It was a feeling inside, as if she blacked out.

The two police officers made their way into the squad car, ready to take Collette to the Midtown South Precinct. The officer in the passenger seat made a sarcastic comment saying, "*So*, we got ourselves the *female* O.J. Simpson with *us* tonight. She came with a knife and buck-fifty her *HUSBAND*, and she didn't even bother to wear no *gloves*." The other officer laughed as he said, "*Oh yea*, I remember that time. But *this* time, *we got the knife*. Oh, we *got* the knife, and you *know* what that means, right, lady? *That* means your ass is *booked,* and your ass is *cooked*."

News vans began to pull up to *Lucille's* to do their *breaking news* coverage. But then a very, *very* familiar face came out of one of those news vans. It was Zarin, as she was pulling a late-night shift at her news station. And since it was at *Lucille's*, the restaurant Zarin goes to every Friday with her gal pals, Zarin wanted to know what was going on. It was at that moment that Zarin spotted Collette in the backseat of the police car. Zarin's face dropped as if she saw a ghost. Seeing Collette in the back of a police car was the *last* thing she would have imagined. As Zarin ran over to Collette, the police car pulled off. Zarin asked one of the other officers on the scene where they were taking Collette. He told her which precinct, and then Zarin made a few phone calls.

As the squad car heads to the Midtown South Precinct, Collette has remained silent for the entire ride. Being that Monica is an attorney, she thoroughly taught Collette well about her rights. Monica also told Collette that if she was ever in trouble, to *not* talk to the police without her being present. Monica would always say this to Collette, "*Anything* you say *will* be used against you. And when you're in that interrogation room, only say these four words, "*I want my lawyer.*"

This was going to be a long night indeed. But it was a good thing that Zarin spotted Collette in the squad car. Zarin immediately called Monica and Tomi and notified them of Collette's situation. They both came straight to Collette's aide. Monica was coming to take care of the legal part, and Tomi was coming to take care of the financial part.

Chapter 26

It is now 2:05 am; Collette was placed in a cold and dirty jail cell. Sitting across from her are two women. One of them was asleep on the far end of the bench, leaned up against the wall. And the other woman was this very young yet charismatic prostitute. The prostitute wore a platinum blonde wig that fell to her backside, a bright-orange fur coat, a white cut-up shirt that showed much cleavage, a mini-skirt, and black knee-high boots. But what stood out the most to Collette was this woman's eyes. The prostitute had these fake eyelashes that looked like Thika palm trees and had iris that was the color of azure, beautiful features indeed.

"Hey momma, what you in for?" Said the prostitute.

"It's a long story, baby. I don't even want to get into it," Collette responded.

But the young prostitute was hungry for a conversation or simply for someone to listen to her. The prostitute has been in the cell for over ten hours, and no one has bothered to bail her out. So, the prostitute began to talk while Collette just listened. She said to Collette, "I wasn't always like this, you know? Out on the streets, selling my body for money. I had dreams, but don't we all, right? I wanted to get into selling other things, be an entrepreneur. Until one day, my mother sold *me* to a trick when I was thirteen. She even told the guy that he didn't have to wear a condom *if* he was willing to pay extra. And *that* became a traumatizing habit. Then man after man came for me. I've laid on my back so many times. I've had so many nightmares of men raping me. Some mother, huh? You look like you're judging me. Are you judging me?"

Collette quickly responded, "Oh, no, baby, please, I wouldn't judge you. I'm just a little shocked that a mother would *do* that to her own daughter." The prostitute then carried on, saying, "Yea, that was my momma. But you know what? After *all* that she put me through, *all* the men, all the *beatings*, I still somehow found it in my heart to forgive her. She's dead now, but I told her before she died that I loved her and that I forgave her. Maybe it was just my beliefs, my spirit within me that said,

"*Forgive your mother, love your mother.*" Miss, do you think I did the right thing by forgiving her?"

At that moment, Collette's faith in God grew enormously. Here's a young woman who's been through hell. Her mother pimped her out, sold her to many men. Abused her even, yet this young woman still found it in her heart to forgive her mother. It made Collette reflect on what happened tonight. Her husband, Martin, crucified their son because of his sexuality. But can Collette forgive him? Also, can she convince Emilio to forgive his father as well? Perhaps forgiveness will take time.

As Collette began to talk to this young prostitute, she responded, saying, "Mamí, I think by you forgiving your mother, you did a *beautiful* kindness. Not just for her, but for yourself. You gave her peace in her heart before she passed away. You'll never know why she chose to abuse you in that way. But for you to forgive her, that says so much about your character as a young woman. You said you wanted to be an entrepreneur, right? Well, I'm a realtor, a broker, to be exact. I think I could help you break into this business."

Collette then gave the prostitute her information to look her up when she gets out. Then, out of nowhere, Collette heard a familiar voice. "Get her out of there, *now!*" Monica said as she was walking behind the officer. The officer quickly put the key in the jail cell and unlocked the gate.

"Nica," said Collette. "How? What? How did you kno—"

"Coco, say no words; let's just get out of here," Monica said.

Collette got up, hugged the young prostitute, and said to her, "Please look me up, baby. And I'll see what I can do for you." The young woman thanked Collette for her generosity. As Collette walked out of the jail cell, she hugged Monica and thanked her for coming to her rescue. But Collette then realized that she didn't even know the young woman's name. "Oh, wait a minute, Nica, I'll be right back," said Collette.

"Sweetie, what is your name?" Collette asked.

"Oh, my name is Angel, Angel Lopez. You can find me on Facebook too."

"Okay, I will, baby. Thank you."

Collette then blew Angel a kiss and waved goodbye as she and Monica walked out in front of the precinct lobby. Tomi was in the lobby, waiting for Collette to be released. As they saw each other, Tomi stood up from the bench and hugged Collette.

"Girl, you scared me to *death*," Tomi said. "Are you alright?"

"I'm okay," Collette said softly. "It's been a crazy night; I can't go home. I can't see Martin's face right now. But I *have* to see my kids."

"The kids are okay," said Monica. "I talked with Mia, and she said that she went to the hospital with Emilio.

"How's Emilio doing?" Collette asked.

"He's doing fine, but they're going to keep him overnight for observation," said Monica.

"Okay…Wait a minute, *how* did you guys know I was here?"

"Zarin told us," Monica said.

"And how did *she* know I was here?"

"She was at the scene with her news crew. She saw you in the police car."

"Oh my *God*. But wait, how did you get me out so quick?"

"Tomi and I have our connections."

"Yes, we made some urgent phone calls, and it's all taken care of," said Tomi.

"Ladies, this is just all too much for me right now."

"Look, can we just finish this outside? I *hate* it in here. Smells like ball sacks," said Tomi.

As they walked out of the precinct, Collette grew concerned about Emilio and asked if one of them could drop her off at the hospital. But it was already a quarter to three in the morning, and the hospital visiting hours were done. So, Tomi insisted that Collette goes home with her for the night, and they will visit Emilio in the morning. "What about Mia?" Collette said. Monica told her that Mia is staying over at her friend Sara's house.

Collette's mind was still all over the place. She did not know what to do at that moment. Finally, not knowing what else to say, Collette blurted out to Tomi, "How much was the bail? I *have* to pay you back." Tomi looked at her as if she was insane. "Coco, fuck the *money*, fuck paying me back. I just wanted to make sure you were okay. We weren't going to have you staying in that jail cell," Tomi said. Collette then calmed herself down and agreed to go with Tomi and crash at her home. As the three of them left the precinct, Monica hugged Collette and Tomi and told Collette that she would be in touch later. Collette thanked Monica and said goodbye. Tomi and Collette then got into her limo. "Benjamin, take us to my townhouse over on east 72nd street," Tomi said.

It was a quiet drive. No music playing, no drinks, no fun. Collette was sitting on one side, looking out the window with teary eyes. The streetlights were streaming through the windows, shining on her face. Tomi was sitting on the other side, going back and forth from looking out the window and looking at Collette; Tomi felt for her friend.

Collette then pulled out her phone and sent a text to Mia. In the text, she said, "Hey baby, I'm so, *so* sorry for leaving you like that. I know this was really hard on you tonight. But don't worry. I'm going to do everything in my power to fix our family. Family is everything. I'm going to stay with your tía, Tomi, for the night. Just to clear my head. And I will see you and Emilio first thing tomorrow morning. Mamí loves you very much, baby."

As it was already early Wednesday morning, Collette realized that later Wednesday evening, Tomi has her charity fashion show. Collette mentions the fashion show to Tomi, but Tomi quickly said, "Coco, my love, your mind is worried about all the wrong things right now. The bail, the fashion show. I don't care about any of that shit right now. You girls are my life. Nothing is more important to me than you ladies. Capisce? Of course, there's my husband and my mom. But it doesn't matter *what* I have going on. If *any* one of you were ever in trouble, I would drop what I'm doing, and I would be there for you. You *know* that, yes?"

Collette slid closer to Tomi and placed her head on Tomi's right shoulder. Her tears began to fall on Tomi's arm. Collette said, "You know I appreciate you and the other ladies so much. You girls are my sisters. And yes, I know you would do *anything* for *any* of us." Tomi then kissed Collette on the top of her head and then leaned her head on top of Collette's. "And besides, I postponed the grand opening of *Orell Llero*, *and* the fashion show to next week, on my birthday. It wouldn't be right if I didn't have all of you girls there with me," said Tomi.

They finally made it to Tomi's townhouse. As they got out, Tomi thanked Benjamin and gave him $5,000 and something extra through his cash app. The townhouse was so sophisticated that it has its very own security guard at the main entrance.

"Hello, my love, how has your night been?"

"Oh, very well, Mrs. Belacone," said the security guard. "Thank you for asking. And yours?"

"It was *interesting*."

In they go, but this was *not* your ordinary townhouse. Tomi owned the entire townhouse, all seven levels of it. Tomi had the townhouse renovated and decked out with the Crème de la Crème. Tomi had pictures of models wearing her clothes on the main floor, hanging all over her walls, and some of Thomas's sculptures were in the living room. The third level was Tomi's master bedroom, and the other floors were the movie theater and guest rooms. Oh, not to mention, there was even a private swimming pool at the bottom level. Before, Tomi put the townhouse on the market, asking for $40 million. But she then decided to hold on to it, only because she likes to swim.

It was now 3:16 in the morning, and Collette was a little restless. So, she and Tomi made their way into the kitchen, and Tomi brewed some coffee.

"Oh, do you have decaf?" Collette asked.

"I *do*, actually," said Tomi. "Oh shit, I forgot I don't have sugar here. But I have Stevia sweetener? Is that okay?" Tomi said to Collette.

"Yea, I like sweetener," said Collette. "By the way, Stevia is your middle name, right? How did you get a middle name like that?"

Tomi broke out in laughter as she began to think about the story of how she was given the middle name of Stevia. As Tomi was making the coffee, she said, "*So*, I didn't get my middle name from the actual sweetener. Let me just say that first. When my mother was a couple of weeks pregnant with me, she was out partying at *Studio 54*. Back when Quaaludes were being passed around like candy. And drugs and alcohol were a way of life. My mom was *real* good friends with one of the owners of *Studio 54*, Steve Rubel? I don't know if you've ever heard of him. Anyway, she was talking with Steve that night. She told him that she was pregnant, with *me*, of course. So, *he* said, in his high-pitched voice, "Oh, Arianna, Arianna! If you have a daughter, name her *Stevia*, name her after me, okay?" So, *Steve*? *Stevia*? You get the picture, right? But my mom said she was *not* naming me "*Stevia Llero*." However, she *loved* Steve Rubel. So, she ended up making my middle name Stevia. But after I was born, Steve and the other owner, Ian, began to get into legal trouble with *Studio 54*. A couple of years after *that*, the party was over. And after my momma had me, she never saw Steve again. But my mother told me this; *she* said that it was the *best* time of her life. And that there will *never* be another time like that again."

After hearing the story of how Tomi got her middle name, Collette could not help but smile. "Uh, see, *that's* what I want. Right there, a smile. That's what I want to see, Coco," Tomi said as she pointed to Collette with joy. Tomi was happy to put a smile on Collette's face; she needed that after the night she had.

But what also crossed Collette's mind was the fact that Tomi *never* mentioned her father. Collette then asked, "You know; you've never talked about your father to any of us before." Tomi responded, "That's because I never met my father. My mom was a *wild*, hipster type of woman. *Totally* out there, living her best life, fucking *whoever* she wanted, and the results of that were her three kids. So, for all *I* know, *my* father could be Donald fucking Trump," said Tomi. Collette rolled her eyes as she said, "Oh God, *please* don't mention his name. After that 2016 presidential crisis, I can't stomach it."

As the coffee was about ready, Collette still wanted to know how they bailed her out of jail. Collette could not help herself. She wanted the truth. "Tomi, about tonight, with bailing me out. How were you and Monica able to bail me out? Usually, I would have to wait until a court hearing, right?" Collette said. "Oh, Coco, I guess you won't rest until you know, huh?" Tomi said as she poured the coffee. "You know I can't," said Collette.

As Tomi took a sip of her coffee, she said, "I know a couple of judges' wives. I dressed them in some of my outfits for some political events. When Zarin called me and told me you were arrested, I immediately made some phone calls to some very powerful people, and that was that."

"Just like *that*?" Collette asked.

"*Just* like that," Tomi responded.

"But what about the knife?"

"*Knife*? What knife?"

"Oh, *right, what knife?*"

"It's politics, my love. I have my connections, and Nica will take care of the legal part."

It was then that Collette realized that Tomi was *much* more than glitz and glamour to the world. Tomi had *power*, lots of it. Collette was so grateful for Tomi and Monica bailing her out. She learned that who you know goes a *long* way.

"You know what? I'm just going to shut the hell up now, and let it be, and say *thank you*. Because I did *not* want to be in that jail cell," Collette said. Tomi laughed hysterically and hugged Collette. "Oh, my Coco, you're a mess. Come on, let's go up to the theater level," Tomi said. As they exit out of the kitchen, Collette began to go up the stairs.

"Uh, *bitch*, where are you going?" said Tomi.

"Oh, is this the wrong way?" Collette responded.

"*No*, but the elevator is quicker."

"What the *fuck*, there's an *elevator* in here?"

"*Uh-huh*. It goes to all the levels."

"Well shit, where's your helicopter?"

"Oh, it's on the roof."

"*WHAT?*"

"Coco, *I am kidding*. I do *have* a helicopter. But not around here."

"Oh my *God*, Tomi. *It must be nice.*"

As they come out of the elevator, Tomi and Collette made their way into the theater room. The theater seated about twelve people, with the popcorn machine right outside the theater room. Tomi was in the mood for an old black and white picture. So, she found the *perfect* movie, one of her favorites, *Gilda,* starring Rita Hayworth and Glenn Ford. As they were watching the movie, they found themselves relating to the character of Gilda in so many ways. "You know, one of Tommy's favorite actors is George Macready. But that's *only* because they both have a scar on their face," said Tomi.

The movie was playing, and eyes were closing. Collette was beginning to fall asleep as Tomi was still watching the movie.

"Coco, babe, go sleep in the guest room. The bed is so comfortable," Tomi said to Collette.

"Oh, but these theater chairs are so comfortable. I can't move from here," Collette said humorously.

It wasn't much later before Tomi joined Collette in counting sheep. Suddenly, Collette's phone began to ring. She slowly woke up from hearing the ring tone. As she reached over to grab it from the other chair, she saw that it was her husband, Martin. A spark within her ignited the flames of anger and anxiety. Collette was *not* ready to talk to him.

As the phone stopped ringing, Collette began to look around. The movie screen was back on the main menu, casting a plethora of movie selections. Collette looked over to Tomi, who was fast asleep. *Then*, a message came up on Collette's phone. It was a voice message from Martin. Even though she did not want to speak with Martin directly, she was open to hearing what he had to say. Collette slowly got up from the theater chair, as she did not want to wake up Tomi. As she headed out of the theater room, Collette went up to the fourth level, the guest room. The guest room looked like something out of a dream. It had a king-size bed with the softest furry comforter Collette ever felt. Twelve-foot ceilings and a bathroom to die for. On the wall across from the bed was a massive picture of Tomi as a kid and her mother, Arianna, walking on the beach in Santa Cruz, California.

As Collette sat on that bed, she almost fell asleep again; it was so comfortable, as Tomi said it was. Collette then pressed play and heard Martin's long voice mail. In the voice mail, he said, "Collette, it's me, baby, your husband. Listen, all that has happened within the last ten hours. I don't know what came over me. I just lost it. I love that boy more than he'll ever know. But I just, the way it all happened, me hearing your voice message and putting two and two together. My son, Emilio, is a gay man. I couldn't handle it, Coco. I can't understand it. And what I don't understand, I tend to hate it. But I was dead wrong. I did a terrible thing. That's our son, and I've beaten him *so* badly."

As Collette continued listening to Martin's voice message, his voice becomes emotional, "I kept hitting him and hitting him, and I couldn't stop. But then I realized this was *my son*. How could I hate my own *son* just for being gay? I stopped, I looked him in his eyes, and I told him I'm sorry. I am so, so, sorry, baby. I know that forgiveness from him is out of the question. I don't know if you can forgive me, and you probably shouldn't. But please, please forgive me. Find it in your heart to forgive me. I'll turn myself in to the police if I have to. I just beg of you, forgive me. I'm sorry, and I love you so much," Martin said. The voicemail then ended.

The whole time, Collette had her hand over her mouth with a slow flow of tears falling. At that moment, she thought of the young prostitute, Angel Lopez, who she met in the jail cell. Collette thought about how Angel forgave her mother for what *she* did to her as a child. Then, Collette began to wonder if she has it within *herself* to forgive Martin.

Collette then grew more curious towards Angel Lopez. So, she looked her up on Facebook to see who this young woman is. As Collette typed her name, Angel's picture was the third profile that popped up. In her profile picture, Angel had the same platinum blonde wig as in the jail cell. In addition, Angel's page was public, so Collette was able to see all her pictures.

About ten minutes into browsing through Angel's Facebook post and looking at her photos, Collette came across something that was somewhat mind-boggling. First, Collette realized how young Angel is. Angel just turned nineteen a little over a week ago. At only nineteen years old, Collette could not believe that a baby like her is on the streets, soliciting herself just to survive. And then, it became even scarier as Collette came across a post that took her breath away. It was unbelievably unexpected—a post that confirmed Collette's faith in the universe and how things really *do* happen for a reason. Collette found a post on Angel's Facebook page that was a memorial post of Angel's late mother. Can you guess who her mother was?

Angel's mother was Martin's *ex*-wife, *Lily* Lopez. The young woman that Collette was sitting across in the jail cell is the daughter of Martin's late ex-wife. If you remembered from the beginning, Martin was already *engaged* to Lily Lopez when he first met Collette. And then he *married* Lily while he and Collette were still involved with each other. What a small, *small* world we live in, right? And getting smaller day by day.

Collette gaged, she could not believe it, but it was very true. Collette then began to have an epiphany about it. As she sat on the bed, she began to think about who Angel's father could be. Until it hit her, *hard* to the core of her stomach. Collette believes that Angel could be Martin's daughter. As if Collette needed any more drama on her plate. She had to get to the bottom of this. So, she then sent Angel a friend request on Facebook. But Collette thought to herself and said, "Damn, she's in jail right now. She may not get back to me right away." As that bed was getting more comfortable, Collette could not help but fall back to sleep.

As the sunrise began to create the morning sky, Collette received another phone call. Waking up again by her ringtone, Collette looked at her screen. *This* time, the call was from Mia. Collette quickly answered and had a heart-to-heart with Mia. They exchanged words, emotions, and forgiveness. Collette told Mia that she has to see Emilio in the hospital and then she'll come to see her right after.

Collette went back into the theater room, where Tomi was still sleeping. She grabbed her Chelsea boots and gently woke Tomi up.

"Tomi, Tomi," Collette softly spoke. "Hey babe, sorry to wake you. I'm going to head out now. I have to see Emilio and take care of some other things. Thank you for everything. You're my angel, and I love you."

"Oh, okay, Coco. I love you more. I'll walk you out," said Tomi.

"Oh no, you go back to sleep."

"No, it's okay; I have to get up myself and take care of some business."

After Collette put on her boots and coat, she headed to the door. She then hugged Tomi and said, "Thanks again, babe. Since you've postponed the fashion show to next week, I'll probably see you all then. I don't think I can do a Friday night at *Lucille's* right now." Tomi responded, "That is ridiculous; we shouldn't have to break our tradition. Oh, I have an idea. How about we all rendezvous at my home in Southampton? Oh, no, eighty-six that. I keep forgetting you guys have kids. So, I guess I'll just go there with Tommy. Yea, I'll see you all next Friday at the Fashion show. Which is also my *birthday*! And we are going to have a *great* fucking time."

Collette smiled and laughed as she gave Tomi another hug and kiss before leaving. She then headed out the door and made her way out onto the street. A cold gust of wind woke Collette right up. She thought about how she would get home. And that is when it hit her that she left her Mercedes Benz around the corner from *Lucille's*. So, Collette had to make a new plan. She now must take a cab to where her car is parked, see Emilio, then Mia, and *then* try to contact Angel Lopez. A busy Wednesday for Collette indeed, as she has some running around to do in the city. On a mission to recover and rekindle her broken family.

Chapter 27

About 6,755 miles away from all of the drama back in the city. Thirteen hours ahead of New York's time, Wendy is enjoying some fine dining at The Ritz-Carlton in Tokyo. Wendy and her mother, Suzi, are having their own "mother and daughter" time. As for EJ, he is with his grandpa Pat, listening to old traditional Japanese bedtime stories. As Wendy and Suzi sit near the window, they have one of the most beautiful views of the Tokyo Tower. The whole skyline is simply breathtaking.

Wendy grew excited as her delicious chocolate cake, and ice cream arrived at their table. Blown away by the eloquent decoration of the dessert, Wendy just had to take a picture of it and upload it to her Instagram. Suzi, however, has been having trouble keeping her sugar down, so she passed on having dessert and just ordered some tea.

As Wendy takes a fork full of the chocolate cake, she dips it in the raspberry filling. The look on her face as it melted in her mouth was *beyond* priceless. She was on cloud nine. As Wendy enjoys her dessert, her mother, Suzi, tells her about what has been on her mind. As Suzi takes a sip of her tea, she said this to Wendy, "Wendy-san, there's a real specific reason why we invited you and EJ with us on this vacation. Your father and I have been giving this some thought for years. And I do mean *years*. The city is excellent; we love New York. But we love Japan better. So, we have decided that we are moving here to Tokyo, for good."

Right in the middle of a bite of her cake, Wendy gave her mother a jarring look. She was utterly shocked and thrown off by what her mother just said to her. Wendy began to look down at the table as she placed her fork back down, with the piece of cake still attached, and remained silent. Suzi knew that Wendy would not take it well. But that was not all Suzi had to say. Suzi continued by saying, "We also would like for you, EJ, and Edward to move here with us. I think it would be a *great* thing, don't you?"

Wendy then looked up at her mother, shook her head, and said, "No!" That's *not* a great thing! Mother, are you serious? My whole *life*, I've been living in the United States. We've lived in the city for *decades*, and now you want to move to Tokyo? And you want *my* family to move here with you and dad? Mother, that is *not* going to happen."

Suzi looked at Wendy as she took another sip of her tea and then looked away, out at the window. Wendy, still a little shocked by her mother's proposal. But Wendy had even more to say. "Mother, you and dad leaving the city; what about me? What about *EJ*? I don't want him growing up not having a relationship with his grandparents. I went through that with *my* grandparents; you know that. Them living here in Japan, I missed out on *so* much quality time with them. I don't want that for EJ. And I don't want that for you and papa either," Wendy said.

Suzi remained silent as she kept sipping on her tea. Trying to ease the tension, she then asked Wendy, "So, how's the cake?" Wendy was only three bites into her dessert. But she was so upset that she lost her appetite. The ice cream was melting with the cherry still on top.

Suddenly, Wendy felt a little nauseous. She excused herself from the table and made her way into the restroom. She felt this pull within her stomach and started to breathe heavily. Next thing you know, everything she ate was coming back up.

Wendy went into one of the stalls and began to vomit. She was in there for a good minute, spitting and gagging.

As Wendy lifted her head from the toilet, a sudden sense of emotion began to come over her. She cried at the fact that her parents have decided to move to Tokyo and leave her. Wendy has very few family members in the states. She has an older sister, but *she* lives in Los Angeles with *her* family. But as far as the city, Wendy's parents are the *only* immediate family she has, and for her mother to drop the bomb on her like this, Wendy had to let it all out. And with all the issues she has at her job, the timing could not have been any worse.

Back at the table, Wendy calmed herself down and asked the waiter for the bill. Unfortunately, Wendy could not eat the rest of her scrumptious chocolate cake. She did not even look at the rest of her dessert. The ice cream wholly melted, and the cherry sank to the bottom of the bowl, leaving only the stem visible.

Suzi wanted to make peace with Wendy. She said to her, "Wendy-san, you *must* understand. *My* obaasan, your *great-*grandmother, is buried here. *Your* obaasan, *my* mother, is buried here. I don't want to be buried in the states. Your father and I only stayed in America to give you and your sister other opportunities. Otherwise, we would have moved *ages* ago. I already asked your sister if she would move as well, and *she* said that was out of the question. Regardless of if you say no, your father and I *are* moving to Tokyo to live out the rest of our lives. And that is final."

Wendy heard enough for the evening. After her regurgitating moment in the restroom, Wendy decided to go out and get some fresh air. She wanted to take a walk around Roppongi square. So, Wendy asked her mother if she could take care of EJ while she walks around. "Of course, I will," Suzi responded.

Wendy then went down to her hotel room. She went into her room to grab her purse and her coat. It was indeed a chilly night in Tokyo. Wendy then made her way to her parent's hotel room to check on EJ. Their room was only several doors down the hall. As Wendy knocked on the door, her father, Pat, answered. Suzi had already come down but was in the bathroom changing into her nightclothes. EJ was fast asleep on the couch. Knowing about his little "bedtime problem," Wendy went over to check his pajamas. A sigh of relief as his pajama pants was dry. She then kissed him on the back of his head and gave it a gentle rub.

"I'll be back in a little bit, okay?" Wendy said to her father.

"Okay, Wendy-san. Don't get lost," Pat responded.

Now riding in a cab, Wendy could not help but be fascinated by the lights and the nightlife of Tokyo. Of course, in her mind, *nothing* beats New York City. But Tokyo gives the city a run for its money. Wendy saw all the storefronts, the electronic billboards, and the highly advanced technology. This experience suddenly began to increase Wendy's pride in her Japanese culture and appreciation of her roots.

People were all around, some still wearing a facemask in this now post-*Covid-19* world. Wendy herself still wore a facemask while she rode in the taxi. As she came to a stop in front of the Roppongi Hills, she got out of the cab. "Arigatō sayōnara," Wendy said to the cab driver. Wendy is grateful to her parents for teaching her the Japanese language ever since she was a child. It is coming in handy for Wendy as she understands signs, maps, and menus in Japanese.

As the cab driver pulled off, Wendy began to stare up at the buildings. She loved it so much. It was like déjà vu. Seeing high-rise buildings, just like in New York City, it almost felt like she never left. But then Wendy looked down on the street and saw *thousands* of Japanese people. She knew *then* that she was not in "*Kansas*" anymore.

It was a whole different culture, *her* roots: a different pace, a different atmosphere. But the one thing she noticed that was very similar to the United States were people walking around with their heads down, gazing down on their phones. So many people were walking by with that blue-lit screen glowing up their faces. Wendy realized how social media and these smartphones changed the entire *world*, and not just America.

Since Wendy was on vacation, she wasted no time on her phone. Although, she did put in her new Apple AirPods to listen to music, which had this innovative, revolutionary, multi-language translation feature. For example, if someone speaks in a different language, the microphone installed in the AirPods could *translate* that foreign language into the language *you* speak. It is like having a translator hearing aide. Apple is still on top.

Wendy walked and walked the night away. Listening to one of her favorite songs called *"Life's What you Make It"* from the eighties rock band *"Talk Talk."* Even though her feet were a bit cold, Wendy was glad she wore her flats instead of her heels. She would not have been able to walk for too long. As Wendy came to a stop at the traffic light, she saw a tiny little shop on the corner of the Roppongi intersection. The shop was so small that if you blinked, you'd walked right past it. But for some reason, Wendy spotted it dead on.

The closer Wendy came to the shop, the clearer she was aware of what the shop is. It was a fortune teller shop. Wendy, standing in front of the shop, looking up at the Nylon light that said, "Yumi's Fōchun." Since Wendy was listening to the same song by *Talk Talk* for the last fifteen minutes, she decided to see what exactly *her* life would be made of. Wendy then entered the fortune teller shop. It had a rather interesting smell. The smell of hot tea and pine. The kind of pine you smell from kitchen cleaning products. Then, behind the beaded curtains came a short, older lady with the most *beautiful* burgundy Kimono with a cream wrap. The patterns on her Kimono were incredibly fascinating. It had dragons, Sakura, trees, and other beautiful flowers. Wendy fell deeply in love with it.

"Kon'nichiwa, oh my God, I *love* your Kimono. Oh, I'm sorry, do you speak English or no?" Wendy said to the older lady.

"Of course, I do," said the lady. "I have many American tourists who come to have their fortune told. Please, have seat."

Wendy then sat down at the older lady's table. On the table, there was a large crystal ball. It was the typical look of a fortune-telling setting. "So, are you going to turn on the crystal ball and *twirl* your hands around it like a *Harry Potter* movie?" Wendy humorously said to the older lady. The older lady laughed as she said, "No, my dear, I just like it for decoration. *I* go by cards and written words in my *secret* book."

As Wendy waited for the older lady to prepare, she began to look around the small shop. There were pictures of flowers, more dragons, and even jade bracelets hanging by a thread. Somewhat identical to the green jade bracelet given to Wendy by her great-grandmother.

"Is your name Yumi, ma'am?" Wendy asked the older lady.

"Yumi is my *family's* name," said the older lady. "Fortune-telling has been in my family for *centuries*. You call me Woomi."

Wendy could not help but smile as she put the older lady's name together. "Woomi Yumi?" Wendy said in her mind. The fortune-teller, Woomi, then came to the table with a deck of these large golden cards.

"Now, *your* fortune, *your* shuffle," Woomi spoke.

"Oh, okay," said Wendy. "There; is that enough shuffling?"

"No, keep going. I tell you when you stop."

"*Okay*... Um, should I keep shuf—"

"Keep going!"

"Oh, alright. *And I'm shuffling.*"

"*Yes*, now give it *one* more shuffle."

"Alright... One more *shuffle*. There; that's a lot of shuffling."

"*Yes, very* good. Ready for your fortune, Wendy-san?"

"Uh, yes... I guess I am."

Wendy became nervous around this fortune teller, Woomi Yumi. The reason being is the fact that *Wendy* never told Woomi her name. And for Woomi to already know what her name is, it startled Wendy. But it also let Wendy know that perhaps *Woomi* is the real deal.

The first card Woomi flipped over from the top of the deck was the "*Labor*" card. It had a picture of an ancient Japanese sickle and pieces of gold. Woomi then goes into explaining this card. "Ah, *labor*, this card represents a job, a career. There's some kind of change happening with your profession." Wendy looked at the card and then looked at Woomi. The first card was indeed accurate. Woomi then revealed the second card. It was a picture of two people with a sack, and it had the word "*Nomad*." Woomi then explained to Wendy what *this* card meant. She said, "This card Wendy-san, this card means that someone in your life is going to make a move, someone very special to you indeed. But you don't want them to go."

Again, Woomi's accuracy was spot on, and it was beginning to frighten Wendy. Wendy felt *that* card is talking about her parents moving to Tokyo, and she does not want them to leave. Wendy's palms grew sweaty, and her legs began to shake. Then came the third and final card. It was like slow motion when Woomi turned the card over and placed it on the table. On the last card, it was a picture of five hands. The hands formed in the shape of a circle. The word for *this* card was "*Unity*."

Woomi elaborated about this card and said, "This card is quite essential. It speaks of a bond, a sisterhood in your life. This unity you have with four other people is substantial. And you would do *anything* for each other." Wendy was so dumbfounded. She was not expecting this woman to be so accurate about what is currently happening in her life. But the fortune reading did not reach its' conclusion just yet. Woomi then opened her *secret* book.

As Woomi began to turn the pages, she asked Wendy what her complete birthday is. "My birthday is January 1st, 1990," said Wendy. Woomi then turned to a specific page, took her index finger, and ran it down the page. she then lifted her head from the book, looked at Wendy, and said, "I'll let *you* read this, my dear."

Woomi then turned the book around, slid it towards Wendy, and pointed at the written fortune. As Wendy read the fortune out loud, she said, "*A new life is soon to come into yours. But in the moment of good fortune and blessings, forgiveness will be in great need.*" Wendy looked up from the book and asked Woomi what this means. But Woomi explained to Wendy that she would have to live and experience *this* fortune. And that it cannot be explained verbally.

"Well, Wendy-san, that concludes your fortune-telling," Woomi said.

"Wait, aren't you going to read my palm?" Wendy said as she opened her hand out to Woomi.

"Oh, of course," Woomi said and then slapped Wendy a five. "There's your *palm reading*."

In a humorous moment, Wendy felt that she fell victim to too many Hollywood movies. But the last message stuck with her. What new life was soon to come into hers? And what did the fortune mean when it said, "*Forgiveness will be in great need.*" It swirled all over in Wendy's mind for the rest of the night. She then said goodbye to Woomi.

As Wendy exited out of Yumi's Fōchun, she turned around to look at it one last time. The cold wind was beginning to blow her hair into her face. Wendy had a moment. She thought about her high school sweetheart, Mark, and how *he* may be the new life that comes into *her* life. But *his* life isn't exactly new to her life. Then, out of nowhere, Wendy hears her name being called from behind her.

"Wendy-san! Hello, Wendy-san!" Woomi shouted.

"Oh, Woomi," Wendy said as she turned around. "Is there something wrong? Did I forget something?"

Woomi then opened *her* hand out to Wendy. Wendy looked down at Woomi's hand and said, "Oh my God, I forgot to pay you. I am *so* sorry. Oh, I'm embarrassed." But that was not what Woomi was thinking of. She said to Wendy, "No, no. Open your *hand,* Wendy-san. Like *this*." Wendy then opened her hand, and Woomi placed something extraordinary on top of it. It was a pink Origami butterfly. Woomi then said to her, "When the *right* time permits, you open this Origami. There is one more special fortune, written inside just for you."

"When will I know the right time to open this?" Wendy asked.

"Deep inside you, you will know. You will *feel* the right time," Woomi responded.

Just as Wendy was about to walk away, Woomi snatched the money out of Wendy's hand and said, "Arigatō." Wendy looked at her hand, then looked at Woomi, and smiled at that hilarious moment.

As Wendy hailed down a cab, she could not help but acknowledge her admiration for Tokyo's much friendlier cab services compared to the city. As Wendy was riding, she looked at the Origami. She wanted to open it now, but she trusted Woomi enough and decided to wait until the right time permits. Wendy just sat back and enjoyed a smooth ride back to the Ritz-Carlton on this cold chilly night.

As Wendy finally arrived, she paid the cab fare and was nicely greeted by the concierge outside of the Ritz-Carlton. It was late; she knew her parents and EJ were asleep by this time. So, Wendy went straight to her hotel room and plopped on the bed. For a good minute, her face was buried in the pillows. She did not want to be bothered by anyone or anything. She then turned around and began to stare at the ceiling. After that, her mind went completely blank, as if she did not just have a fortune-telling experience.

Then suddenly, Wendy began to feel that same nauseating feeling from earlier. She then got up from the bed and made her way to the bathroom. Another regurgitating moment had occurred. On her knees, leaning her head into the toilet. As her upset stomach began to calm down, Wendy began to wonder what exactly she ate that was making her sick. She *did* have an excessive amount of sushi since she's been in Tokyo.

Wendy then looked over at the clock on the nightstand. It was 12:19 a.m. Thursday morning. Which meant it was still *Wednesday* morning in Manhattan. So, Wendy gave Edward a call. But there was no answer. She knew his show was in the tech week and assumed he could not answer his phone. So, Wendy left a voice message instead. "Hey Eddie, it's me. I was hoping I could've caught you before you went to rehearsal. But I know it's tech week, and you're busy. But listen, I've been kind of sick today. I was vomiting and feeling a little light-headed. I *knew* I shouldn't have eaten all that sushi. I'm guessing that's what it is. But I just wanted to call. It's wonderful here in Tokyo. I love this place. I wish you were here with me and EJ. My parents also dropped a bomb on me. They say they're moving here for good. And *I'm* not happy about that, but I guess we'll see. Oh, and I went to this fortune teller lady not too long ago. She was *actually* dead-on, as far as my life. And she gave me this cute, pink Origami Butterfly. She said not to open it until the *right* time permits, whatever that means. Anyway, I'm going to try to get some sleep. I love you, babe. Bye," Wendy said.

As Wendy hung up her phone, she went back to the bathroom to brush her teeth and remove her makeup. She then took a good look in the mirror. She did not say anything. Instead, she just stared at herself. In her mind, she was thinking about her life and thinking about her future as a wedding planner. Does she stay and wait it out with her boss, Mrs. Shultz? And hopefully, *someday*, gets that partnership? *Or* does she go her *own* way and be her own boss? Only time shall tell. Wendy then shut off the bathroom light as well as the hotel room light. She then undressed out of her clothes and put on her nightgown as she retired for the night.

Chapter 28

B ack in the states, it is still Wednesday morning. Collette had plans to go straight to the hospital to see Emilio. But those plans were put on hold as she had to go to the NYPD tow pound to retrieve her Mercedes Benz. That Tuesday night, when Collette went after her husband, Martin, she parked right next to a fire hydrant. The car sat there throughout the night until the NYPD had it towed.

After paying a considerable fine, Collette retrieved her car, and instead of going to Emilio first, she headed straight home to see Mia. Mia text Collette to tell her that she came back home after staying at her friend Sara's house. Even though Collette wanted to check on Emilio first, she was more concerned about Mia at that time. Mia is only fourteen, and she was left alone in that situation with her brother. And Collette wanted to make sure that she's okay.

As Collette arrived home, she went straight into the elevator and pushed the button to the ninth floor. As she arrived on the ninth floor, she headed to their apartment and pulled out her keys to open the door. Surprisingly, not only was Mia there, but Emilio was there as well. Both Emilio and Mia were sitting there on the living room couch. Collette moved swiftly over to them and hugged both of them so tight. She just cried in their arms, pouring out her apologies for leaving them. Both Mia and Emilio rubbed their hands on Collette's back. Collette did not have any words for them as her guilt overpowered her.

"Mamí, it's okay," said Mia. "Emilio's safe now. He's home."

"I'm just so sorry, babies," Collette cried.

"Don't cry, Ma," Emilio spoke.

"And Mamí, there's something we must confess," said Mia.

"What?" Collette said to both of them.

"I lied to the police about Papí. I told them that Emilio was jumped and mugged by some thugs in the subway."

"Why would you do that, Mia?"

"I'm sorry, Mamí. I panicked. I didn't know what to do after you left."

"Did they buy it?"

"Yes, I think so. The cop said they would keep an open investigation. We're sorry, Mamí. We just didn't want Papí in trouble with the police."

Collette then asked Mia and Emilio if they have seen their father since last night. But they haven't seen him. As Collette gathered her words together, she said this to them. "You guys, I am *so sorry* for leaving you here the way I did last night. You guys needed me, and I just lost it. I promise I will *never* do that to the both of you again. And Emilio, baby, I know it will take a long time for you to forgive your father for what he did to you. But I pray that you will find it in your heart to one day find that forgiveness."

Emilio remained in silence, looking down at the floor as he shook his head in a gesture of saying "no." But Collette does not want him to carry hatred in his heart for his father. So, she carried on, saying, "Baby, please, *don't* hold this hatred inside of you. Because what it will do is prevent you from ever loving anyone else again. You will close your heart and end your trust with people. People that you love and who love *you*, and you will suffer in misery, alone. I don't want that. For *either* of you."

Emilio and Mia looked at each other. They knew Collette made sense, and they agreed with her. "It *will* take a long time for me to forgive him. But for *you*, Mamí, I'll try," said Emilio. But Collette quickly corrected Emilio as she said, "*No* Papí, don't forgive him for *me*. You must forgive him for *yourself*. Just like

I have to forgive him for my *own* reasons." Emilio *then* understood what Collette meant.

At that moment, Collette thought about the young woman she met in jail, Angel Lopez. But being that Collette was *just* released from jail last night, she does not want to be anywhere near that precinct. As Collette walked into the kitchen, she opened the home screen to her phone and looked at her Facebook profile. Surprisingly, Angel accepted her friend request. In Collette's mind, she assumed that Angel was released from jail. She then sent a direct message to Angel saying,

"Hey love, thank you for accepting my friend request. But listen, this is very important. Can you meet me at *Bob and Patty's Diner*? It's over on 30th street, between 8th and 9th. Meet me there by 3:00 p.m. I have to talk to you."

Collette made her way back into the living room and told Emilio and Mia to meet her at the Presbyterian Church at 5:15 p.m. She told them not to be late. Collette then grabbed her keys and bag and headed out the door. She had to hurry, as it was already a quarter to 3 p.m., Collette headed down to the lobby and made her way to her car. As she got in her car, she received a response from Angel.

"Hey, what's up, momma? I'm glad you found me. And yes, I know where that place is. I've met some of my tricks there. I'll see you soon."

Twenty minutes later, Collette arrived at *Bob and Patty's Diner.*
It took her *another* ten minutes of driving around to find parking.
Finally, she found a ticket-safe parking space two and a half
blocks away. She then made her way to the diner. As Collette got
inside, there was no sign of Angel. So, Collette got a table by the
window to spot Angel once she walks by the diner.

About five minutes later, Collette spotted Angel walking
on the other side of the street. Angel then crossed the street,
making her way towards the diner. As she came close to the
window, Collette knocked on the window to get Angel's
attention. Angel then saw Collette and waved at her as she was
heading into the diner. Angel looked nothing like the way she did
last night, as she was not wearing makeup or that platinum blonde
wig. Angel wore a jacket with a thick sweater, black leggings,
and some Timberland boots. She looked rather beautiful outside
of her "work clothes." Angel also had these *beautiful* thick curls
of hair down to her shoulders. That moment, Collette noticed how
much Angel resembles Martin and wanted to get to the bottom of
things with her. Angel then took a seat at the table with Collette.

"Hey, sorry I'm late. I took a Lyft over here," Angel said.

"Oh, no worries, babe," said Collette. "I just got here myself.
Are you hungry?"

"I'm always hungry."

At first, there was a lingering moment of silence. The two
begin to stare at each other until the drinks had arrived. Then

finally, Angel broke the ice. "*So*, what did you want to talk to me about?" Angel said. As Collette took a sip of her decaf coffee, she put the cup down and began to talk. She said to Angel, "I wanted to know a little bit about you, Angel. Can you tell me some things about your life? Only if you're okay with it. I'm not trying to be nosey; I know we don't know each other. But I have my reasons why."

Their meals had arrived. Collette was in the mood for breakfast, so she ordered pancakes. Angel, however, had a taste for a cheeseburger and fries. As Angel picked up a French fry from her plate and ate it, she became an open book. She said to Collette, "Well, I just turned nineteen about a week ago. I live with some of the other girls who work out on the streets with me. They're older, so they look after me. I stay with my pimp sometimes too. As far as my *past*, I never met my dad. My mom told me that he left her for another woman he already had a baby with. She caught them walking down the street one day while my dad was carrying his son. It was so crazy because *that* day, she found out that she was pregnant with me. Then she would always tell me that my father is dead. But what she *really* meant was that he was dead to *her*. My mom never really recovered; I don't think, from my father leaving her like that. I have *no idea* where he is or who that woman is. There's a piece of me that believes he *is* dead. So, I guess it doesn't matter. I just have to do what I have to do to survive."

As Angel took a bite out of her cheeseburger, Collette briefly stared at her. Guilt never felt so heavy for Collette's consciousness. Collette knew right then and there that Angel was telling the truth and that she was for sure Martin's daughter. But before Collette came to that solid conclusion, she had to ask Angel one last question.

"Did your mother ever tell you what your father's name was?" Collette asked Angel.

"Of course, she did. His name was Martin... *Fernandez?* Yep, Martin Fernandez was his name." Angel responded.

Angel is entirely clueless about what is going on; Collette, on the inside, is all over the place emotionally. She is looking at Martin's long-lost daughter. Afterward, Collette asked Angel if she had time to go with her somewhere. At first, Angel was hesitant. Even though she is beginning to like Collette, she is still somewhat of a stranger. "Have you been to church lately, Angel?" Collette asked. Angel shook her head as she replied no, but she told Collette that she prays every day. Angel prays for a better life—a life with a family. Collette then reached for Angel's hand on the table and said, "Today, your prayers *will* be answered. Please, come with me, Angel."

After they finished up at the diner, Collette and Angel headed across town to the Presbyterian Church, as they will soon meet up with Emilio and Mia. From the beginning, Collette had this all planned out. She had a great feeling that Angel was, in fact, Martin's daughter. And she thought it would be special for Angel to meet her family. As they arrived at the church, Collette and Angel went inside and took a seat. It was relatively empty, and Emilio and Mia had not arrived just yet.

Angel, growing rather curious, asked Collette why she brought her here. Collette looked at her and said, "I brought you here because it was meant to be. I brought you here because I *am* a believer. Many things happen for a reason, sweetie. *Reasons* that we can't explain. Me getting arrested last night was for a reason. We were placed inside the *same* jail cell for a *reason*. I brought you here to not only *tell* you but to show you." Angel began to look around the church. "Show me what?" Angel asked. Collette finally told her the truth. She held Angel's hand and said to her, "Baby, *I* was that woman who was with your father. I was the woman your father had an affair with while he was married to your mother. We have two kids together. And I brought you here because I want you to meet your brother and sister. I'm, I'm *sorry*, baby. My God, you look so much like him."

Angel's face looked as if she saw a ghost. The unbelievable news took her breath away. Angel then stood up from the bench and began to distance herself from Collette.

"No, this can't be true," Angel said with her teary eyes.

"Yes, I'm sorry, baby, but it's true. You have every right to be upset right now, but please don't," Collette responded.

But Angel did not want to hear anymore. She stepped away from Collette and was heading out of the church. As she was walking out, she stopped in her tracks. She saw Emilio and Mia making their way into the church. She had a feeling that it was them because they all looked so much alike. Collette then made her way towards Angel. She touched Angel on her shoulder and told her, "This is Emilio and Mia, your brother and sister. You don't have to be afraid of us. *We* are your family. And we'll figure this whole thing out together, okay?"

As Collette introduced Angel to Emilio and Mia, the three of them slowly went in for an embrace. Collette just stood there, tears running down her face as she covers her mouth with her hands. Then, out of nowhere, incomes Martin. Mia turns and looks as she sees her father. Martin stood there with his left arm in a sling from the cutting incident done by Collette last night.

"Papì, how did you know we were here?" Mia said to Martin.

"I have your iPhone on my tracking, baby," said Martin. "I saw that you were here. So, I came."

Emilio slowly backpedaled as he maintained his distance from his father. Collette stood right next to Angel, as Martin is entirely oblivious that she is his daughter. As Martin stood there, he said, "Who is she?" They all looked at Angel as Collette told

Martin the truth. "This is our newest member of the family. Meet Angel, your daughter."

Martin stood still, didn't say a word as he looked at Angel. He then began to walk towards her. As he got close, he took a good look at her. For Martin, it was like staring into a mirror. They both became in sync with each other as both Angel and Martin shed tears together. Martin placed his hand on her cheek, and then he hugged her. He held on to her very tightly as he began to bawl his eyes out.

"I thought you were dead," said Angel. "My mother told me you were dead."

"Oh God no, baby. Oh my God, oh my God," Martin cried.

After Martin let Angel go, he then sat down on the bench. As he looked up, he said something that Collette never knew before. "I *knew*, I knew you existed, Angel. But I pretended that you didn't; I, I pretended that you weren't even born and that your mother was just lying about being pregnant with you. But I knew, and I am *so* sorry. I have asked God for forgiveness. But now, I ask for *your* forgiveness—all four of you. Emilio, I know you probably can't right now, but I *beg* you, son. I beg you to please; please forgive your Papì. Coco, I need your forgiveness, Mia; I *need* your forgiveness. And Angel, baby, I *need* your forgiveness more than anyone. I beg all of you," Martin cried.

A moment of silence as they all looked at Martin. Seeing Martin, a grown man, crying and pleading with his family. Angel then made her way towards her father. She rubbed her hand on his backside. And as softly as Angel could, she said to him, "I forgive you, Papi." Mia then joined in with her forgiveness. A trio of tears came forward from the group. Collette looked at Emilio as he kept his distance from them. Collette then walked towards Emilio, looked at him as she said, "Remember what I told you back home in the living room? Emilio responded, "Yes, I remember." Collette took Emilio's hand as they both walked towards Martin, and they hugged him.

It was a beautiful, heart-warming, Kodak moment for the family. It was a moment that gave birth to forgiveness. And what better place to have that than a church? Collette got what she prayed for that day, as did Angel. To bring her family back together and rekindle their love for each other.

Chapter 29

The next day, a Thursday afternoon. Monica is on her lunch break, and the case she is working on is kicking her ass. She wants to take her mind off work for the entire hour of her lunch break. As she walks down the sophisticated Fifth Avenue, she began to window shop. There was one store in particular where she saw a lovely turtleneck sweater. It stopped Monica in her tracks. She just loved the way it draped over the mannequin. As Monica walked into the store, she looked over to the employee at the register and said, "Good afternoon." But the employee did not return any greetings. She just looked at Monica and gave her a half-ass grin. It was one of those grins that people give when they don't want to be bothered with you, but they do not want to come off like an asshole.

But in this case, this employee was a bitch to Monica. Monica thought in her mind, *"Well, she's rude as hell."* But Monica paid her no attention. She was not going to be in this store for long, as she knew what she wanted. She then walked over to the mannequin that was sporting the turtleneck sweater. It was a thick-knitted, German-chocolate brown turtleneck. And Monica knew it would look great on her.

"Excuse me, sir," Monica said to the other employee. "But do you have this sweater in size 8 or 10?"

"No, we do not," the employee responded very bluntly.

Monica stood there as he walked away to tend to other customers. As she stood there, she began to have an epiphany. Monica noticed that she was the *only* African American customer in the store. Hell, she was the only African American *person* in the store. She was beginning to be under the impression that her business is not welcomed in the store. But Monica refused to be intimidated. She continued to look around. But then, Monica noticed something else was happening. There were two male security guards in the store. One was posted in the front, and the other would make his daily rounds at each section. As Monica looked around, she realized that she was being followed all around the store. Every time Monica looked at the security guard, he would play it off as if he was not following her. He would turn his head and pretend that he was not keeping his eye *solely* on her.

Monica grew so angry that she began to whip the hanging clothes across the racks. She tried to keep her composure. Then Monica walked over to the shoe section, *just* to see if that security guard would follow. And sure enough, that same security guard was right on her tail. It was not long before Monica realized that this security guard is racially profiling her. But Monica was no one to be reckoned with. With her background as an attorney, not only did she know her rights, but she knew how many *civil* rights violations this store was committing, right at that moment.

"Is there a problem, sir?" Monica projected to the security guard. "You've been following me around this whole damn store. Is there a *problem*?"

"Ma'am, there's no need to raise your voice," said the security guard. "I'm just doing my job."

"Oh, your job is to follow around black people in the store and racially profile them? *That's* your job?"

The other customers, who just so happened to be all Caucasian, began to look and speculate. One of them even pulled out their phone and began to record the situation. And without surprise, the female employee at the register did not waste any time calling the police.

Meanwhile, Monica was going back and forth, having a heated altercation with the security guard. Then the security guard said to Monica, "Look, take it easy. We've been having some shoplifting incidents at our store, and we just *have* to take our necessary precautions, ma'am, that's it." But Monica was not buying that at all. She demanded that she speak with the manager.

While Monica waited for the manager, she said to the security guard, "This is *completely* unacceptable, and I am *mortified.* And the fact that *you,* sir, said that the store's been having shoplifting issues, you're using *piss-poor* judgment in *assuming* that *I* would be a shoplifter simply because of my skin color. You, that woman at the register, and the other employee ought to be *ashamed* of yourselves for treating me with such disrespect. For God's sake, it's *2023.*" Monica was in full form. She tried her absolute best to keep her emotions in tack. Then, finally, the manager came out of his office.

"Yes, I was told you wanted to see the manager?" said the manager.

"Are you the manager?" Monica responded.

"I *am*; how can I help you?"

Monica then spoke her mind to the manager as she said, "The moment I walked into this store, I was racially profiled. Two of your employees, as well as *this* security guard right here, were *very* disrespectful to me. He has been following me around all over this store. I am completely offended and *utterly* insulted at his accusations that I am a shoplifter."

"I never said she was a shoplifter, sir," said the security guard.

"Have you been following her around the store?" The manager asked.

"She's under the impression that she's being followed, but I'm just doing my daily rounds."

As Monica carried on, the manager simply stood there, nodding his head up and down to her. Monica was not sure if he was even listening to a word she said to him. Then in his response, the manager said, "Well, okay, first, my *sincerest* apologies that you felt you were being mistreated. Um, but we have had some burglary incidents here at our store. So, we just like to keep our eyes on the merchandise. But if you felt that *you, specifically,* were being watched and followed around the store. My apologies again."

This moment became so awkward and humiliating for Monica. But then it grew worse as two police officers showed up. As mentioned, the female employee called the cops as soon as she felt things were escalating.

"Hello, who's the manager?" The police officer asked.

"Hi officer, I'm the manager," The manager responded.

"And what seems to be the problem?"

"Oh, no problem, officer, we have it under contr—"

"*Oh,* I believe there is a problem," Monica projected.

"Uh, ma'am, can we continue this outside? So that we don't disturb the other customers?" said the officer.

"We *sure can,*" Monica responded.

Monica then made her way towards the exit with the two police officers. As she was walking out, she looked over to the female employee at the register, the one who called the police. The employee did nothing. She looked up at Monica, adjusted her glasses, and then looked away. In her mind, Monica said, "Racist ass *bitch*."

As they were outside, the two police officers began to talk with Monica. And again, Monica is an attorney. She pretty much had her way with the two officers and told them that she would be filing a complaint and possible lawsuit against the company for discrimination and racial profiling. The police officers then took down her information and filed a report.

As Monica and the officers went their separate ways, she turned around and looked inside the same store that she was not welcomed. The other customers were inside, shopping as if nothing happened. The female employee who called the cops was just smiling and oh so chipper with the "white" customers. Monica just could not believe it. She was *so* enraged on the inside. She wanted to go back in there and give that woman a piece of her mind. But Monica took a deep breath, exhaled, and quickly walked away from that store.

As Monica looked at her Apple watch, she realized that she had ten minutes left of her lunch break. And she did not even *eat* lunch. But after that situation, Monica lost her appetite completely.

As Monica headed back to her office at the law firm, she stormed into her office and threw her bag on the floor. Some of her colleagues caught notice of her behavior. One of them came into her office and said, "Hey, Monica, is everything alright?" As Monica sat down in her chair, she had her hand covering her forehead and eyes as she shook her head. "No, no, I am *not* okay right now. I just need a minute," said Monica.

As Monica sat there in her office, she received a text from Zarin. In the text, Zarin said, *"Hey Nica, I'm at work in the news station right now. I wanted to ask you about one of your clients. Was one of your clients' name Amir Jamestown?"* As Monica read the text, she replied to Zarin and confirmed that Amir Jamestown is one of her *former* clients. Zarin then replied saying, "Oh, Nica, I'm so sorry to be the one to tell you this, but he was found shot to death last night in Red Hook, Brooklyn. I'll send you the link to the article. I'm so sorry, babe."

Just when Monica thought her day could not get *any* worse, she was hit with another bomb. She opened the link that Zarin sent her. As she opened it, there was the headline in bold font. "**BLACK MAN SHOT TO DEATH IN RED HOOK**." Monica's hand was shaking as she held the phone. Her thumb was even shaking as she scrolled up her screen, reading the article. As Monica read the article, she saw that it was, in fact, her former client, Amir Jamestown. He was shot twenty times, all over his body.

Monica told him to stay out of trouble. She did not know if this was done by someone who was retaliating or by someone at random. But all she knew was that she had to get out of there and go home. The real world gave her enough bad news for one day.

As Monica got home, she took off her coat and shoes and placed her bag down on the floor. Then her husband Sammy came down the stairs. He said, "Oh, hey babe; why do you have the front door open? It's freezing out." Monica was so drained that she forgot to close the front door. "I was just about to head out to pick up the kids. Hey, what's the matter?" Sammy said as he looked at Monica's face of absolute melancholy.

Monica could not hold it in anymore. She collapsed in Sammy's arms and cried herself a river. Sammy kept asking her gently, "What's wrong, baby? Talk to me." As Monica got herself together, she then said to Sammy in her broken voice, "I just had a horrible day. I just found out that one of my former clients, Amir Jamestown, was shot and killed last night. And I was racially profiled in a store today. I'm just *so* upset and infuriated at the same time. It's just too much right now."

Sammy then comforted her as Monica continued to let it all out. It was not the first time Monica ever felt the pressures and humiliation of racism and prejudice people. She was constantly teased growing up for her dark complexion, hair, and even for being smart. Other girls would tease her and call her a "know it all." It was all building up inside of her for *years*. But for some reason, today, Monica could not take it anymore.

"Listen, just stay here," Sammy said. "I'm going to get the kids. I'll be right back."

"Okay," Monica responded.

About a half-hour later, Sammy came back with Miles and Briana. Monica was now calm after her hysterical meltdown. As the kids came in, Monica said to them, "Hey, where's my sugar?" They went over to Monica as she gave them warm hugs and kisses to their cold cheeks. Monica then had them sit down with her. She felt that *now* was the time for Miles and Briana to understand the *real* world they live in as African Americans.

As Briana and Miles sat on the living room couch with Monica, she told them what they needed to know. Monica said, "So, my babies, something happened to mommy today. Something cruel and very ignorant. Today, I walked into a clothing store, and I was racially profiled. Do you know what that means?" They both shook their head and said no.

Monica then continued by saying, "So, racial profiling is something that occurs when an *ignorant* person approaches you and tells you that you are not welcomed. Or do not belong in the place you're at, just because you are black, Latino, or any person of color. As you get older, the both of you will come across some ignorant, racist people in your lives. People who believe they are better than you. People will believe they are superior and have some kind of authority over you because of your skin color. We live in a racist country, my babies. And Miles, when you get older, there may be times when you get harassed. There may be times when you get pulled over by police, and they will mistreat you simply because you're a black man in America. If or *when* that ever happens, I want you, *always* to keep your composure. *Always* keep your hands where they can see them. Because… Because if you ever move the wrong way, they…."

Monica had to stop herself as she was beginning to get emotional. Both Miles and Briana began to comfort her as she started to cry. Briana held her mother, and with her sweet, innocent voice, she said, "Mommy, don't cry. Daddy will protect us." Monica then looked up to Sammy with a teary smile. That was the sweetest thing she could have heard from her child. "You're absolutely right, baby. Daddy *will* protect us," Monica said as she gave Sammy a wink of her eye.

It took Monica's six-year-old daughter, Briana, to say *that* for Monica to realize that Sammy was *indeed* the man of the house. And for the *very* first time, Monica was okay with that, one hundred percent. Even though Monica is the *woman* of the house, she was okay with Sammy being the head of the family. Monica felt that Miles would learn how to be a *good* man from his father by doing so. And from that point on, Monica promised herself that she would treat Sammy like a man who can lead.

Later that night, Monica was restless while Sammy and the kids were fast asleep. She thought about the challenging day she endured and how she could use some help from the outside. She then began to take another look at Dr. Melissa McAdams' website. Dr. McAdams is the therapist Monica saw the ad for in the cab. As Monica looked at more testimonials from Dr. McAdams' patients, she took one deep breath and exhaled as she made her decision final. Monica decided that first thing in the morning, she will make an appointment with Dr. McAdams.

Afterward, Monica then went into the kitchen and fixed herself some yogurt with fresh fruit. As she took a fruity scoop of her yogurt, she then turned off all the lights downstairs and made her way up to her bedroom. Before heading to *her* bedroom, Monica opened Miles' bedroom door to look at him. She noticed that he left on his flashlight. Monica smiled as she walked over to turn it off. Miles has a slight fear of the dark. As Monica stood there, she thought, "*I have to get him a night light.*"

Monica then kissed and brushed her hand on the back of Miles' head. On her way out, she took another brief look at him. Monica was thinking about what she said to Miles earlier, about him being a black boy in America. *Fear* lurks inside her, a fear that she will not always be around to protect her son in such a crazy, racist world. But in her mind and soul, Monica has faith that he will do very well for himself. "Good night, king," Monica softly said as she walked out of Miles' room.

Monica then walked into Briana's room as the door was half-opened. Surprisingly, Briana was still awake. Monica looked and said, "Bri, what are you still doing up?" Briana looked at Monica and said, "Mommy, does the color of my skin make me ugly?" That question swiftly took Monica's breath away. She could not believe that her daughter would even *think* of something like that at six years old. Monica then sat down on Briana's bed and had Briana sit on her lap. All Monica could do was shake her head at that moment.

"Baby, *why* would you even think something like that?" Monica said.

"I see how boys in my classes treat girls that are lighter than me. They treat them better than they treat me," said Briana

It was like Monica heard the same story that *she* went through growing up. Kids treated Monica differently because *her* complexion was darker. But this time, Monica was too tired to shed any tears. She held Briana tightly and said to her, "You are one of the most *beautiful* little girls to ever come into this world. As I told you and your brother earlier, there will be ignorant people in this world who will believe they are better than you. Or that you are not enough because of the color of your skin. But baby, let me tell you something. The color of your skin is *not* a punishment. It is *not* ugly, nor is it a choice. I want you to promise me something, baby. *Promise* mommy that you will *never* sell yourself short in this world. And that you will always love who you see in the mirror *every* day. Because I love you more than *anything* in this world, and you are *so* beautiful. You are a beautiful brown skin little angel."

Monica then gave Briana multiple kisses on her face. "You're beautiful! You got it? You *got it*?" Monica humorously said, still kissing Briana. Briana, giggling as she said, "Okay, *okay*, I got it. I'm beautiful." Monica smiled at her, and Briana smiled right back. She then tucked Briana back into bed, kissed her one more time, and said, "I love you, Bri. And don't worry about those *boys*. In time, the right *man* will come into your life." Briana responded, "Okay, mommy, and I love you too. You're my hero." And with her tiny hand, Briana blew Monica a kiss.

Monica was so touched by what Briana just said to her. It brought tears to her eyes. As Monica headed towards her bedroom, she realized that she left her yogurt in Miles' room. So, she quietly went back into his room and grabbed it. She then made her way into her bedroom; Sammy was comatose. Monica then went into the bathroom to put on her bonnet and nightgown. After scooping up her last spoonful of yogurt, Monica brushed her teeth, washed her face, and looked at herself in the mirror. She took a good look, reminiscing about her childhood as a dark-skin little girl.

It was that moment when Monica remembered asking *her* mother the same question that Briana asked her. And Monica's mother said this, "Nica, baby, the color of our skin can *never* define beauty *or* ugliness. What defines our beauty is *who* we are from *within*. And for people to see *true* beauty, they must first learn how to love. For *love* is the perception of beauty."

Monica never forgot that. She then began to laugh as she headed out of the bathroom. Monica laughed because she realized how different it is now that *she* is raising children of her own. Now that the shoe is on the other foot, Monica has her *own* way of explaining things to *her* children.

As Monica got into bed, she reached over to Sammy and laid her head on top of his chest. Dead silence in the bedroom, minus the NYPD sirens, echoing throughout the streets. Even though Monica had a very rough day, she was grateful to have a family to come home to. A family who loves her and who *she* loves in return.

Chapter 30

O n the road, on a Friday afternoon. Tomi and her hubby, Thomas, are sitting in the back seat of her limo. Tomi enjoys her wine and fruit, while Thomas gives her one of the best foot massages she ever had in her life. As the ride runs smoothly, they began to listen to their favorite, Ole' Blue Eyes himself, Francis Albert Sinatra. But of course, the world knows him as Frank Sinatra. The song *Angel Eyes* was playing, one of Tomi's favorites.

They are driving to their mega-mansion in Southampton, New York. Tomi just purchased the mansion last December as a Christmas present for her and Thomas. It was on the market for $45 million. But Tomi, being the *great* negotiator that she is, was able to haggle the sellers down to $41 million. Since Tomi has no children of her own, she wanted to have a special place to celebrate Christmas. Not just for her and Thomas but also her friends and their families. Tomi always desired to have laughing, happy children opening their presents on Christmas morning.

As they continued to ride on route 27, Tomi began to conversate with Thomas. They talked about the trip she took to L.A. a couple of weeks ago. Thomas said, "So, we never had time to talk about your trip to Los Angeles. How did it all go?" As Tomi took a bite out of her pineapple slice, she told Thomas, "It was *fabulous*, babe. It all went *very* well. Closed deals with some buyers. I had a consultation with Dr. Ginger. She says hi, by the way. And what else… *Oh*, I didn't find any houses that *I* fell in love with. At least not at *those* prices. So, I called up Coco, and she gave me the *best* advice. She recommended that I buy *land* instead—*that* way, we can do anything we want with it. *So*, I bought 37,834 square feet of land. Now *you* can build our dream home, baby. Where we can make our dreams come to life."

That put an instant smile on Thomas's face. As he continued to rub Tomi's right foot, he said, "Oh God, I'm so lucky to be married to a filthy fucking rich wife." Tomi laughed as she responded, "I bet you are, baby. Now, kiss mommy's foot." But Thomas did more than a kiss as he put her foot in his mouth. At first, Tomi gaged and said, "*Ew*, you sick fuck." But five seconds later, Tomi felt this *hidden* sensation she never felt before. Her face began to change as Thomas continued. "Oh, my good lord. Tommy, I think I need you to do this more often," Tomi said as she enjoyed Thomas worshipping her feet. It was a very sticky rest of the trip.

About thirty minutes go by, and they finally arrived at their palace. Talk about a *mansion*; their three-story property is sitting on 17,597 square feet. Eleven bedrooms, thirteen bathrooms, and a heated interior swimming pool with a guest house. A tennis court, a twenty-two seated movie theater, a ten-car garage, and very close access to the beach. In fact, the beach is right in the back of the house. Tomi is really living the *good life*. And Thomas is right along with her on the journey.

As they pulled up in the long driveway, they stopped in the oval-shaped parking area in front of the house—a white exterior with thirty-foot pillars in the front entrance. The mansion looked like something that came out of Rome. Benjamin, Tomi's limo driver, made his way to the back of the limo to open the door. As Thomas stepped out, he just looked at the house and began to sigh.

"Ah, just *look* at this place," Thomas said proudly. "Babe, we should just live out here permanently. What do you say?"

"I say *NO*," Tomi said sarcastically. "Manhattan is like an hour and a half away from here. *Not* including traffic. I need to be close to my city."

As Benjamin grabbed their luggage and placed it in front of the main door, Tomi asked him for a favor. "Benjamin, my love, could you do me a solid and do some grocery shopping for me? I have my chef arriving soon, and I just want to have everything prepared for him," said Tomi. Benjamin was more than happy to do that for her. Tomi already made a list of what her chef needs to prepare the meals for the evening. Tomi and Benjamin then made their way over to the garage.

"Take the Bentley. The keys are on the wall," said Tomi.

"Um… Can I take the Maybach instead?" Benjamin asked.

"Oh, I forgot I bought this. *Actually*, it was a gift from Tom—"

"Oh, *SHIT*! Ms. Belacone, I didn't know you had the *Lambo* up in here *too*. Oh, can I take it out for a spin?"

"Whichever one you want, babe. Be my guest."

"*BET*! Uh… Can I *keep* this car?"

"*Fuck* no."

"Yea, I figured you'd say no. It doesn't hurt to *ask*."

"Benjamin, can you just get the groceries, *please*?"

"Will do, Ms. Belacone."

As Tomi walked back to the front entrance, Thomas already made his way inside. The front entrance has two sets of doors. The second set of doors requires a unique code that only

Tomi and Thomas know. Thomas thought it was best to have that extra security. Simply because of the expensive artwork and luxurious cars that they keep at their home.

Inside the main entrance, you are greeted by one of Thomas's masterpieces. A seven-foot-tall Greek goddess, half-naked, with Thomas' signature scar marking on her face. Thomas calls this piece *"The Birth of Beauty, The Death of Pain."* He showed this piece during some of his galleries. Of course, people were willing to pay top dollar for it, but Thomas said it was priceless.

As far as the rest of the house, there were twin staircases parallel to each other, going up at a curvaceous angle. It was a sight for the sorest of eyes—the deluxe craftsmanship of the chandelier. Over 50,000 crystals were sparkling from above. From Basquiat to Warhol and a couple of Picasso paintings, Tomi had multi-million-dollar artwork throughout the house. Of course, she had another large picture of Andrey Hepburn. But there is one picture that Tomi has on the wall in her office room. It is a picture of the late Amy Winehouse. For *years*, Tomi was obsessed with Amy Winehouse. She loved to listen to Amy's song *"Love is a Losing Game,"* the live version. She would listen to that song over and over. But when Amy Winehouse passed away, a piece of Tomi never fully recovered.

But every time Tomi walks into her office room, she blows a kiss at the picture of Amy and says, "Hi Amy, I've missed you." And that is just what Tomi did as she walked into her office. She then placed her handbag on her desk and turned on her iMac. Even though Tomi likes to keep her work in Manhattan *only*, she had to respond to a group of emails to prepare for the grand opening and the charity fashion show next Friday, which is also her birthday.

As Tomi sat down at her desk, she received a text message. As she read the text message on her phone, she lifted her head and began to stare straight ahead at the wall. She had the same exact reaction as she did when she received that text message at *Lucille's*. Tomi said not one word. She then snapped out of it and began to open up her emails. One by one, Tomi responded to each email. One of the emails was from her sales and marketing team supervisor. The email said:

Good afternoon Tomi,

I just wanted to give you an update on our sales chart. Since you pulled that *brilliant* stunt with modeling the new winter coat, in the *nude*, our sales have catapulted to 300%. You are a mastermind.

Best regards,

Katie

Tomi was happy to know the great news. She was even more excited to learn that after the deals she made out in Los Angeles a few weeks ago, her net worth has increased from $11.7 billion to $14.3 billion. When it came to business and making that almighty dollar, Tomi was in a league of her own. But then the excitement was short-lived when she opened her email from her accountant, as it is tax season. In *that* email, it said:

Good afternoon Tomi,

I *hate* to be the bearer of bad news, but it is time for Uncle Sam to get *his* cut. And this year, he wants a big slice of the pie. So, can we meet up sometime next week?

P.S. Don't kill the messenger... ☹

Sincerely,

Susan.

"Where's Ronald Reagan when you *fucking* need him?" Tomi said to herself sarcastically as she read the email from her accountant, Susan. Tomi already knew that she was going to owe tens of millions of dollars. But for a woman as wealthy as Tomi, it would not affect her in the slightest. She always played the game moderately and played by the rules. Tomi *never* wanted to be audited by the IRS. She worked her ass off for two decades to earn her spot at the top. And even though Tomi made a fortune in the last twenty years, she was never obsessed with money. She *loves* money but has never been obsessed with it. And she has always been financially responsible and a financial *genius* when it comes to investments.

As Tomi finished responding to her emails, she received a text message from her assistant, Carmelo. In the text, Carmelo said, "Hey Ms. Bellas, I just wanted to remind you about Tuesday night. You said you wanted to come with me to the club to do some scouting for male models, yes?"

Even though Carmelo is going to the club to scout for a new *man*, Tomi needed a few more male models for her charity fashion show. So, Tomi replied to Carmelo's text, saying, "Hey Melo, my love. Yes, we are still on for Tuesday night. Remind me of the name of the club again?" Carmelo quickly responded with the name. As Tomi read the club's name, she could not help but roll her eyes and laugh hysterically. Tomi then sent Carmelo a voice note saying, "Who the hell would name their nightclub, *"Test-Tick-Cools?"* Carmelo responded with *his* voice note, saying, *"Well,* Ms. Bellas, it *is* a nightclub predominately owned by *gay* men. *I* find it to be quite ingenious."

As Tomi finished with emails and talked to Carmelo, she reached out to her ladies as she wanted to see them. She sent a group text to the four of them saying, "Hey ladies, I wish you were all here with me. But I understand; we all have our shit to do. But I don't want us to break our seven-year-long tradition and not see each other this Friday evening. *So,* how about we have ourselves a Facetime date tonight? Since you're still in Tokyo, Wendy, can the rest of you girls chime in at midnight? Get back to me ASAP."

Three out of the four replied to Tomi and confirmed they would be present. Wendy had yet to respond. That is when it hit Tomi, and she realized it was very early in the following day in Tokyo. And that Wendy was probably sleeping. Tomi sent another text saying, "Wendy, my love, hopefully, you'll see this in time." So, the Facetime meeting was set for midnight. Tomi and the rest of the ladies were looking forward to it.

As Tomi looked at her watch, she saw that the time was already 6:30 p.m., and she was beginning to grow an appetite. Benjamin did not come back yet from grocery shopping. Tomi was hoping that she at least kept some snacks in the pantries in the kitchen. Walking down the long hallway to the kitchen, she began to look at the pictures on the wall. Tomi was reminiscing about all the great memories she had from her fashion shows. Meeting other celebrities and all the places she has traveled to, all over the world. It made Tomi reflect on herself, understanding how blessed she is to have such an incredible, fascinating life. But still, in her mind, Tomi would give it all up just to have been a mother, biologically.

As Tomi made her way into the kitchen, she opened her fridge, only to see water and champagne. The last time Tomi and Thomas came to this house was in January. Back when Thomas hosted an art gallery in their home. Then, Tomi looked inside the pantry. Her eyes were screaming, "YES," as she saw boxes of her favorite snack in the whole world, *Rice Krispies Treats.* But there was one problem; the Rice Krispies Treats were at the very top of the twelve-foot-high pantry. So, Tomi had to find a small ladder, which she did, grabbed the whole box, and began to munch away. As Tomi finished her second Rice Krispy bar, she looked out into the far end of the kitchen. She saw Thomas outside, walking on the beach. Normally, he would not walk out on the beach by himself. Tomi assumed that he had something on his mind. So, she grabbed her coat and made her way out there.

As Tomi went out, the sky had a mixture of blue and gray as the night was beginning to emerge. It was cold out but not freezing. As Tomi walked toward Thomas, she said, "Tommy, what are you doing out here all by yourself?" Thomas just looked at her; he did not say a word as he leaned in for a kiss. "Kiss me twice, so I know you mean it," Tomi said. So, he kissed her again. He never heard Tomi say that, so he asked her, "Where did *that* come from? I never heard you say that to me." Subconsciously, Tomi was thinking about her mother at that moment. For Tomi's entire life, every time she kissed her mother, her mother would say, "Kiss me twice, so I know you mean it."

So, Tomi then told Thomas that her mother is not doing so well. And that her health is rolling on a decline. It came as a surprise to Thomas, as he knew nothing of his mother-in-law's health issues.

"When exactly were you planning on telling me?" Thomas said. "I had *no idea*. How sick is she, Tomi?"

"Well, let's just say that she's comfortable," Tomi responded.

The two text messages: the first text message that Tomi received was at *Lucille's*. And the second text message that she received was recent, in her office room. Those two text messages were from Tomi's older brother, Frankie. He was the one who was giving Tomi an update on their mother's condition. She's been sick for quite some time now.

Thomas grew upset by the news of his mother-in-law's illness. Tomi had to explain to Thomas that her mother did not want *anyone* besides her children to know about her health problems. Tomi's mother, Arianna, has always been an upbeat kind of woman.

Still standing on the beach, Thomas began to walk away from the house and away from Tomi. Tomi, following behind him, said, "I'm sorry for not telling you, Tommy. But what do you want me to say? My mother didn't want me sharing her business and getting people all worked up and worried about her. I *had* to respect my mother's wishes." But Thomas could not accept that. He responded, saying, "Tomi, I'm not just some dear friend of yours that you share special moments with. I'm your *husband*; *that's* my mother-in-law. She means a lot to me. We've had a *great* relationship throughout these years. And now you're telling me that she's *dying*?"

Tomi, standing there on the beach, felt like she was sinking into the sand. Thomas looked at her with disgust. As he moved closer towards Tomi, he said, "When my mother was sick, you were the *first* to know. And when she died, what you did for her, taking care of all the medical expenses, paying for her funeral service, *and* the fifteen-foot mausoleum. She was *so* grateful, Tomi. *I* was grateful… Look, I'm sorry for yelling. I, I just wish you would have told me sooner." Thomas then made his way back to the house while Tomi just stood there out on the beach. Tears of sorrow and heartbreak began to fall down Tomi's face. She now has to cope with the fact that her mother is in the final chapter of her life. And now, more than ever, she misses and needs her girls.

Chapter 31

It is five past midnight. Tomi had a very lonesome rest of the evening as Thomas decided to skip dinner and stayed on the other side of the house. But Tomi is not going to let that ruined her quality time with her girls. Tomi Facetimed the others and waited for them to join in. Collette was the first to join, and Tomi gives off her best smile.

"Hi, my Coco," Tomi said enthusiastically. "I've missed you."

"Bitch, we were *just* together like two days ago; *relax*," Collette said humorously.

"I know, don't mind me," Tomi laughed. "That's just the phony white bitch coming out of me."

Both of them broke out into heavy laughter. Monica and Zarin then chimed in, wondering what humor they missed out on. As the four of them were on Facetime, they waited for Wendy to join in on the meeting. It was 12:15 a.m. in New York, which made it 1:15 p.m. in Tokyo.

"She should be up by now. It's the afternoon over there," said Zarin.

"Just give her a few more minutes. Nica, are you wearing one of those hair bonnet caps," Tomi spoke.

"Yea, it keeps my hair nice and neat when I sleep," Monica said.

"You know, I was *going* to have my models wear them down the runway at one of my shows. But one of my African American employees told me that would *not* be appropriate. Thank *God* I listened to her because she was *right*," Tomi responded.

"*Ooh*, girl, I'm glad you listened to her too," Monica laughed.

"I *third* that," said Collette.

As Tomi was using Facetime on her iMac, she received a text from Wendy. In the text, Wendy said, "Hey, I'm sorry for missing your text. I just got out of the shower. I will join in, just give me five minutes. I have to get dressed." Tomi was excited as she spread the news to the others. So, they waited, *longer* than five minutes.

Finally, Wendy joined in. Her hair was still a little damped from the shower. The four of them began to welcome Wendy with positive energy and open arms. All five of them now seeing each other from their screens at home. Well, except for Wendy, of course, who was calling from her hotel room in Tokyo. As they were all now together, Tomi was the first to speak. She said to the others, "First of all, I am so glad that we were all able to come together and make this happen. I know it's late, and you gals are probably *so* tired. But I didn't want our tradition of meeting up on Fridays to fall flat. *Plus*, we've all been through some stuff this past week. And Tommy is quite upset with me. He's upset because I didn't tell him that my mother is ill. And she's not doing well at all. And I know, I should have mentioned it to you all as well. But my mother wanted to keep this between her children *only*. So, I didn't know what else to do."

As Tomi finished her piece, the rest of them felt a growing sense of sorrow for her. But Tomi, however, was not looking for sympathy or pity. Instead, she told them that she is doing okay. Tomi continued by saying, "*Okay*, that's what's been going on in *my* neck of the woods. How about you guys?"

Collette decided to go next, as she had a lot on her plate. Collette said to them, "So, first, I want to say thank you for you ladies bailing me out of jail the other night. But you have *no idea* of the miracle I've encountered."

"*Wait*, Coco, you were in *jail*?" Wendy asked.

"Oh my God, Wendy, I forgot you didn't know. It's a *long* story, babe," said Collette.

"Yea, my love, you've missed the craziness. But Coco, you were saying something about a *miracle?*" Tomi spoke.

As Collette continued her story, she said, "Yes, a miracle. Nica, remember that young girl who was in the jail cell with me? Well, she told me to add her on Facebook. So, I did; I sent her a friend request, and she accepted it. I began to look around at her pictures, being nosey, of course. Then I came across a photo of her late mother. Her mother was Lily Lopez, *Martin's* ex-wife, who *he* left to be with me. I told you ladies that story years ago. Anyway, the young woman is Martin's daughter. We all came together at church and welcomed Angel into our family. That's her name, Angel. *Now* we're beginning our process of forgiveness. And *my* mother and father are pieces of shit. They won't accept Lisa for who *she* is. My mother is worse, I told her about Emilio, and she flipped. So, I don't think we'll be seeing much of each other anymore. That was *my* week, though."

This was beginning to be a night of truth-living and vulnerable confessions for all five of them. Zarin then gave her story. As she cleared her throat, she said, "Well, first let me say this, ladies. I am so sorry for putting you on that crazy, wild goose chase. Meli, Neal's twin sister? She is a *lovely* woman. The girls love her already. She'll make a great mother. But earlier this week, Neal and I had to go to the girl's school. Something happened to Darsha, and she's traumatized by it. One of her classmates sent a pornographic video to her phone, and she was so upset about it. She kept throwing her phone in the garbage. Neal and I were *furious*. So, we went to the school and let those people have it. We told them that if this happens again, we'll slap them with a lawsuit."

"That is absolutely unacceptable," said Tomi. "I would make a lawsuit right now. What do you think, Nica?"

"That's not my specialty, but I could look into it," Monica said.

"Well, Neal and I have been talking about it, and we think that it's best to transfer the girls to another school."

"Oh, I see, okay. Wendy, my love, you want to go next?" Tomi said. "Tell us what's going on in Japan. I hadn't been to Japan since the grand opening of my store back in 2019. Right before that damn pandemic."

Wendy then made her speech. She said, "So, let me just start from the very beginning. When we landed and got off the plane, my dad couldn't find his luggage. So, we had to stay at the airport for an hour before they finally found it. *Then*, as soon as we got to the Ritz-Carlton Hotel, my mother wanted to go to the cemetery to see my grandmother and great-grandmother's gravesite. I was like, "*Mom, do we really have to go there right now? Can't we wait a few days?*" But she insisted that we get that out of the way first. So, we all went and paid our respect. EJ didn't really understand where we were. But anyway, I've also been feeling a little sick these past couple of days. I think I had *way* too much sushi or something. I've been vomiting a few times.

Oh, and my parents are planning on moving to Japan. And they want *me*, Eddie, *and* EJ to move with them. And *that* was their plan all along. To get me to come to Japan with them and talk me into moving here. Go figure, huh?"

"You better *not* leave us, *and* you have my godson," said Zarin.

"Oh, I am not going *anywhere*," said Wendy. "I have too much going on in the city. It's my *life*, and your girls are a huge part of my life. As you already know."

"Of course, you're one of us, babe," Tomi said. "And you *can't* be replaced. Alright, Nica, you're up."

Monica took a few seconds before she spoke. She then took a deep breath and said, "Well, I didn't have a good day *yesterday*. I was on my lunch break, walking down Fifth Avenue. I just needed to clear my head. This new case that I'm working on has been kicking my ass, and I just wanted to take my mind off of work. So, I saw this turtleneck in the window of this store. *Loved* it! I absolutely loved it. So, I walked in, and the woman at the register was a snotty, *racist* ass bitch. She gave me this bullshit-ass smile, just like this… " Monica then imitated the woman by demonstrating the smile. The ladies all began to laugh at Monica's facial expressions.

Then, Monica continued, "So *then*, I asked the other employee if they have the turtleneck in *my* size. But he was even worse. Both of them were so fucking rude. But that's not the *worst* thing. One of the security guards was *following* me around the fucking store. Yes, you heard me correctly. He was *following* me around the store. And when I confronted him about it, he said that some shoplifting incidents took place, and they need to take precautions. So, *I* said to him, "So, you're only taking necessary precautions on people that look like *me*? Because I don't see you following anyone else around."

Tomi and the others started shaking their heads on their screens as they were disgusted by what they just heard. But Monica was not finished with her story. She carried on saying, "So then I demanded that I speak with the manager of the store. I waited for the manager, and when he finally came out, I told him exactly what had happened. I told him that I was racially profiled. I told him that his employees *and* security guard were disrespectful and that I didn't appreciate it. He was somewhat of a nice person. He apologized to me for the mistreatment. But then he gave me the same bullshit excuse about there being shoplifting incidents. But that's not all. That same bitch at the register called the fucking cops on me. Because I was arguing with the security guard. She got frightened, I *guess*, so she called the cops. But it's all good. I just filed a complaint to the company and planning on making a lawsuit. I got time for those racist bastards."

Tomi was *dying* to know which store exactly that Monica went into to shop. When Monica told her the name of the store, Tomi said, "I knew it! I *fucking* knew it! I know that store. I even know the manager that you talked to. And no, *he's* a piece of shit too. He knows how to *hide* his bigotry very well. Nica, don't even stress it, babe. My new storefront will be opening up right across the street from them. And I *will* be putting those sorry pricks out of business."

Monica felt a little better about that. But something else was still bothering her. Especially the fact that she was racially profiled. She decided just to get it off her chest. Monica then said, "I talked with Miles and Briana. I was telling them about racism in this country. I feel terrible, as a *mother*, that I have to teach my kids about racism. And late last night, when I was tucking Briana in, she asked me if her skin color makes her ugly. I was *so* heartbroken. My baby girl doesn't feel that she's beautiful enough because of the *color* of her skin."

The news brought a few tears out of Tomi's eyes, as well as the others. Monica also mentioned that her former client, Amir Jamestown, was murdered. And it *was* a retaliation attack. Then, Monica asked a question to the other four ladies. A *burning* question that opened up a solid conversation. Monica said, "You know what, ladies, since we're here, just talking, have any of you ever *dealt* with racism? Or have been racially profiled?" All of a sudden, Zarin, Wendy, and Collette were all shouting at the same time. They were very vocal in confirming that they were mistreated before. Tomi had to calm them down by saying, "Ladies, *ladies*, okay, alright, one at a *time*."

Zarin began to tell them about *her* experience with racism and prejudice. She said, "Listen, back when the tragic events of the September 11th terrorist attacks happened, I was a senior in high school at that time. After the terrorist attacks, I was bullied, harassed, and assaulted. Sometimes my brother and I were chased down the street by other kids after school. They would even call me Osama bin Laden's daughter. People thought that because we look similar to Muslims or people from the Middle East, they assumed we were terrorists. Or that we represented them. And you guys see *me*; I *do* look like I could be from Pakistan or Afghanistan. But as you all know, my family's from India. And *our* religious belief is *Hinduism*, not Islam. But you know, here in *America*, people don't care. They think what they *want* to think and believe what they want to believe."

The other ladies looked at Zarin with a bit of sympathy for her, as they did not know that she went through such a traumatizing experience as that. "Damn, Zarin, I didn't know you went through *that*," said Monica.

Zarin continued, saying, "Yea, Nica, it was a living nightmare. And you know what, to be honest with you girls, when it comes to racism. I feel somewhat partly responsible for how black men are perceived to be criminals. Every time I get on the news panel, I report on the news and media about black men either getting shot or them *doing* the shooting. Black man this, black woman that. The news media creates narratives for our society to keep the masses living in fear. But *I'm* just a journalist and a TV news anchor. I have to follow that protocol. And you know what's so sad about that? I don't even like to *use* the term "Black" to identify African Americans. I like to say *African Americans*. But that doesn't follow *their* agenda. The powers that be want us *only* to use "black" to identify African Americans."

Zarin said a handful for sure. Her comments gave Monica some personal thoughts about identifying herself as "black." But then Wendy had a lot to say about *her* experience with racism as well.

Wendy said, "So, *my* experience actually happened from *Eddie's* side of the family. Well, first off, let me just get *this* out of the way. When Eddie and I first started dating, my parents disapproved of him. They really wanted me to stay within my Japanese culture. But you know I love Eddie so much. I told my mother, you *can't* help who you love, you know? And I know the whole thing already. I know the stereotypes and stigmas of Asian women dating Caucasian men. As if Asian women *only* date White guys for security. But let me be clear, *I* was the family's breadwinner at the beginning of *our* marriage. Business comes and goes in Eddie's line of work. But those bills kept coming. There were *many* times when I had to take care of the bills on my own. So, *yea*, I love my husband for *who* he is. Not for money."

Wendy had to get that off of her chest. But she had more to say as well. Wendy then talked about the night she met Eddie's family. Wendy then said, "Oh, I remember when I first met Eddie's family. We went to Eddie's parent's house; I met his brothers, sisters-in-law, and parents. And all of his nieces and nephews were there too. But his *mother* was by far the worse. When I came into the house, the *first* thing Eddie's mother said to me was, "Oh, *hi*, so good to finally meet you. Oh, not to worry, I made fried rice for dinner. But I'm sorry, we ran out of soy sauce." I'm standing there thinking, "are you fucking *kidding* me right now?" But what pissed me *off* was that Eddie didn't say *shit* to them the whole night. But *then*, oh my God, as we all were sitting at the dining room table having dinner, oh God. Eddie's older brother actually had the *audacity* to ask me, "So, Wendy, is it true that the *Chinese* invented the fireworks?" So, *I* said to him, "I believe they did, but I'm not exactly sure because I'm *Japanese*, not Chinese." And *then*, Eddie's little nephew said something that made me want to *throw* his little ass out of the *fucking* window. He was ten at the time. Eddie's nephew said, "Well *hey*, Vietnamese, Chinese, Japanese, get-on-your-*knees* and massage my back. Isn't that what you always say, dad?"

The ladies did nothing but gaged after hearing that. "Girl, I would've whipped his little ass," said Collette. "I was *livid*. I couldn't believe it. And Eddie's brother gave me this awkward smile as if he was utterly embarrassed and exposed as being a racist," Wendy said.

They were all letting it out in the wee small hours of the morning. Wendy also talked about how the "Anti-Asian Bill Act" made it somewhat *worse* for Asian people. She believed that it put more of a *target* on the backs of Asians than it prevented hate crimes.

Collette then began to speak *her* mind as she said, "You know, there was one time when I was a guest staying at the Plaza hotel. Martin and I wanted to do something special because it was our anniversary. I was on my way down to the Guerlain Spa on the fourth floor. As I was walking in the hallway, this *"Karen"* bitch *literally* said to me, "Excuse me, but can you tidy up my room? I also need fresh towels and a bathrobe. Oh, Uh, *Por favor*?" So, not only did this bitch insult me by *assuming* that I worked there as a maid. But she also assumed that I didn't speak English. So, I had to regulate that bitch. I said to her, "First of all, I *do* speak English. *Secondly*, I don't work here. I am a guest here, just like you." *Then*, I was about ready to *kill* that bitch when she asked me, "Oh, well, what escort company do you work for?"

"Oh, my fucking *GOD!*" Tomi shouted. "Coco, you are *LYING!* *Please* tell me you're lying?"

"I wish I were, babe. But I *can't* make this up. I'm just not that good. But that's how much of a racist, ignorant ass bitch she was," Collette responded.

After hearing the other four, Tomi had to look deep into her past to see if something happened that was derogatory towards her. But *fortunately*, there was nothing. And that is when it hit Tomi. She realized then how fortunate she is. She became fully aware of her privilege. The only thing that she could say to the four of them was the truth.

Tomi then said to them, "Ladies, I'm going to be honest with you. After hearing what the four of you went through, as far as racism. I have to admit that I can't fully relate to it. And yes, I am a wealthy white woman with *all* the privileges. I mean, I'm an Italian, and *Italians*, once upon a *time*, were *not* accepted as "white" people. I remember my momma telling me that she was *often* called a guinea, a grease ball, and many other offensive words when she was growing up. And anyone whose last name ended with a vowel was mistreated. My momma also told me about *Sacco and Vanzetti*. But, again, I know that I am a privileged white woman in America. It's *no* secret, and I'm fully aware of the racism in this country, *especially* after seeing the whole George Floyd murder. That was *so* inhumane, and I cried when I saw that son of a bitch cop place his knee on George Floyd's neck for damn near ten minutes. I was mortified and embarrassed as an American." All four of them agreed with Tomi's comment, as they had nothing to add.

"But you ladies know I have a good heart," said Tomi. "And I would give the shirt off my back to *any* of you."

"Aww, Tomi, we know that," Collette said. "And we love you."

"Hey ladies, I'll be right back," Wendy said as she walked away from the camera.

As the other four were still on the line, they began to hear something a little disturbing. Wendy forgot to put her phone on mute, and they heard the echo of her vomiting in the bathroom. Tomi said, "Oh my God, Wendy, are you okay?" The noises continued for a good solid minute. They then heard a toilet flushing in the background. As Wendy came back to the camera, she was wiping her mouth with a napkin.

Collette then said to her, "Wendy, you have to see a doctor, Mamí. Make sure you're not suffering from food poisoning. How much of that sushi did you eat?" As Wendy got herself together, she responded saying, "I had one too many, that's for sure. But I will go to the doctor as soon as I get home. I'm fine now, it's like it comes and it goes. But we leave here on Tuesday morning. So, I'll make an appointment for Wednesday. But actually, I have to get EJ; he's with my parents. So, I'll talk to you girls when I get back. I love you so much. I can't wait to see you all back home. It's been real."

They all said their goodbyes to Wendy, blowing little kisses at their cameras. But before Wendy got off, Tomi said to her, "Oh Wendy, my love, before you go. We're going to have the grand opening to my storefront *and* the charity fashion show on the same day, on Friday, which is also *this* bitch's birthday (Tomi said as she points to herself), and I am treating you girls to a spa date on Thursday. If you can make it, babe." They all loved that plan. Wendy then said goodbye and got off the line. Then, one by one, each of them said goodbye to each other, leaving Tomi there with an empty screen. She was happy to see everyone. It was a *great* conversation for all of them, getting things off their chest and having each other show love and support. But now, it was time for Tomi to call it quits and head to bed.

Before making her way to the master bedroom, Tomi makes rounds throughout the house. No matter what, Tomi makes sure she checks all the windows and doors to ensure they are locked and secured. All were closed and locked, except for one. It was the same door that Thomas walked out of when he was on the beach. *This* time, he was sitting outside in the lounge area with the fire pit burning.

Tomi saw him and then made her way outside. Thomas had this massive blanket over him as he sipped on his cup of coffee. As Tomi stepped to him, she asked, "You got room for one more under that cover?" Thomas gave her his handsome smile and said, "For you, always." Tomi then slid under the cover with Thomas, lying in his arms as he kisses her frontal lobe.

"I'm sorry for being an asshole today," Thomas said. "I know your chef probably worked hard on that meal."

"It's okay, babe," said Tomi. "Don't worry about it. Let's just enjoy the moment we have right now."

So, that is what they did. They enjoyed that moment between the two of them. Even though the weather was cold, it was perfect for the setting. They both sat in front of the fire pit, listening to the natural sounds of waves hitting the beach. No phones, no distractions. Then Tomi said something to Thomas that was needed. She said, "I love you, Tommy." He then looked at her as he said, "I love you more, baby." Then he quickly kissed Tomi two times.

"Why did you kiss me like that?" Tomi said as she giggled.

"So you know I meant it," said Thomas.

"Aww, Tommy… You *were* listening."

That touched and melted Tomi's heart so much. Not just for him kissing her twice, but simply because he listened to her. As these two lovers sat under the moonlight, Thomas begins to sing to Tomi. And he thought of the *perfect* song that they both love. "*Let's swim to the moon uh-huh, let's climb through the tide*," Thomas sung. It was the lyrics from the song "*Moonlight Drive*" by The Doors. It then became a duet as Tomi joined him.

As they finished their duet, Tomi felt that this was the perfect time to talk with Thomas about regrets. As her 44th birthday is approaching, Tomi realizes that she is not getting any younger, and not having any children has taken its toll on her life. But she needed to tell Thomas that. She needed to know how he feels.

"Babe, I need to know something," Tomi said as she sat up. "Do you regret *not* having any children?"

"Well, we didn't have much choice, you know?" said Thomas.

"Well, no... I mean, there were other alternatives like surrogate mothers."

"But you said you didn't want to do any of that. No adoptions, no surrogate mothers."

"I know, I said I didn't want any of those optio—"

"Why the sudden change of heart? Do you want to have kids now?"

"I mean, *maybe*, while we're still young enough to chase after them without having a stroke or heart attack... Oh, I don't, Tommy. So much time has gone by, and my eggs are *useless*."

As Thomas continued to listen, Tomi said, "I'm just accepting the reality that we are getting older, and eventually, we will not have any children to inherit our empire. I guess we *should* have adopted children a long time ago. But you *know* that wasn't my thing, Tommy."

Dead silence, minus the ocean waves and chilly breeze. Thomas then took Tomi's hand and told her something that she *needed* to hear. "Tomi, we have been living a life that very, *very* few people have a chance to experience. We have traveled *all over* the world and met some incredible people. I have absolutely *no* regrets about anything, and neither should you. It wasn't God's plan for us to have children. But it *was* his plan for you and me to share a life together. And you've done *so* well for yourself, baby. You are my absolute *best* friend in this entire world. And you are the love of my life. In this life, and the life beyond. Now, is all of that something to be regretful about?"

Tomi, a little emotional, gently ran her hand through Thomas's hair as she shook her head. She responded, saying, "No, I guess it's not. Thank you for saying that. I guess *not* having kids of our own was one of the unfair *imperfections* that come with life. But you're right, baby. We have lived a *remarkable* life so far. And I look forward to spending the rest of our lives together as we *continue* to enjoy this life. And you are the love of my life too."

They both shared the most passionate kiss and then retired for the night. Tomi's regrets in life were beginning to fade. She realized and accepted that not having children was out of her hands. But what was *in* her hands was helping parent-less children all over the world. It was that moment when it hit her that she could lend a helping hand to children in different countries. The idea was so grand, so *rich* that it changed her perception of motherhood. Tomi now understood that to be a mother is not always about giving birth. Being a mother is not entirely about just bringing them into the world. Tomi understands now that it is about *how* a mother raises her children in this world.

This night, Tomi dismissed her selfish requirements of what it takes to be a mother. She decided to create a new purpose with her fortune and help the parentless children of the world who suffer from poverty and lack of love. Perhaps *this* is part of the rebirth of Tomi.

Chapter 32

Monday morning has arrived. Monica is now sitting in the lobby as she waits for her appointment with the therapist, Dr. Melissa McAdams. A little nervous as Monica twiddles her thumbs together. All she hears is the sound of Dr. McAdams' secretary tapping away on her keyboard. As Monica looks at the secretary, the secretary looks back at her with a smile. Not the kind of phony smile the employee gave her in the clothing store last week, but a *genuine* smile. About seven minutes go by, the door opens. Dr. McAdams finally stepped out of her office with her patient and wished that patient a great day.

"*Hello*, you must be Monica Taylor," said Dr. McAdams

"Hi, yes I am," Monica responded as they shook hands.

"I'm Dr. Melissa McAdams. Why don't you come in."

Dr. McAdams was an attractive woman. Five-foot-seven inches tall. A dirty blonde hairstyle, Gucci glasses, dressed in a dark green suit. Monica, still a bit nervous about all of this. Simply because of what her mother once said to her about therapist when she was younger. Her mother said, "If you ever seek therapy, make sure you find a black woman. What does a white woman know about a *black* woman's problems?" But Monica is nothing like her mother. Her mother has a somewhat "old school" approach to handling things. So, Monica then decided to leave all of her fear in that lobby.

As Monica walked into Dr. McAdams' office, she looked around at the furniture. Dr. McAdams' office had the perfect view, overlooking the entire lower Manhattan area; you could see straight ahead at One World Trade Center. There was also a bookshelf; books from authors Monica never even heard of before. Dr. McAdams' desk was right next to the window, with two chairs placed across from the desk. Monica then sat in one of the chairs as she continued to look around. She saw that Dr. McAdams *surprisingly* had a sculpture created by Tomi's husband, Thomas. As mentioned, Thomas' work is very well known in the art world. As Dr. McAdams sat down in her chair, the session began.

"So, Monica, how are you doing today?" Dr. McAdams spoke.

"I'm doing okay," Monica said softly. "It's a brand-new day. Can't complain."

"It *is* a brand-new day, yes," said Dr. McAdams. "And *great*, that's great to hear."

As they both sat there, Monica noticed something on Dr. McAdams' desk. She saw a picture of Dr. McAdams with what appears to be her husband, an African American man, and their two children. As Monica continued to look, she said, "You have a *beautiful* family. How old are your kids?" Dr. McAdams looked at the picture and smiled as she said, "Oh, thank you so much. Yea, my babies; so, *Kacey* is eleven, and Kenny Jr. is seven, going on *seventeen*. He's a handful, let me tell you, *always* pushing my buttons, just like his father. But they're both *terrific* kids. As for my *husband*, well, we're actually separated right now. We're now seeking marriage counseling. Uh, there I go again. Speaking about *my* life, when I should be concerned about my *patients'* life. I'm *so* sorry, how's *your* family?"

Monica then told Dr. McAdams about her family, her career, and life in general. Monica told her just about everything she needed to know that has been on her mind. Monica even brought up her minor altercation from the luxury store and being racially profiled. Dr. McAdams just sat there and listened. She was not the kind of therapist that makes little footnotes in a book, documenting her patient's thoughts. As Monica concluded her part of the dialogue, Dr. McAdams began to speak.

As Dr. McAdams slowly shook her head up and down, she said to Monica, "So, after hearing all that you told me, I don't believe that you are overworked or even overwhelmed. You seem to be exaggerating the issues you've dealt with in life. You mentioned that your parents were always in your life. And they took care of you and your siblings, yes?" Monica confirmed Dr. McAdams' analysis is accurate.

Dr. McAdams then continued, "So, you never *suffered* in your life. But because you are an African American woman, you feel that the *suffering* of African American *people* is also *your* suffering. And with all of the clients that you had to defend in your career. The majority of them were African American. In some way, you believe that if you ever lost a case, that you would *not only* be failing your client, but you'd be failing African American people, as well as yourself. You also mentioned that your *uncle* went to prison for something he *didn't* do, and then he passed away shortly after being released from prison, right? Well, I feel that you hold on to this heavy guilt. Your job gives you the responsibility to keep African American people out of prison, *especially* if they are innocent. But it always traces back to what happened to your uncle. And the fact that one of your *former* clients was recently killed. That guilt is now eating you alive right now."

Monica was mind-boggled by how knowledgeable Dr. McAdams is and her attention to detail. She could tell that Dr. McAdams has been doing this for years. But then Dr. McAdams wanted to speak on something else. She said, "Monica, you talked about your husband, Sammy. Was there ever any sense of jealousy between you? As far as success?" "*Jealousy?*... I don't know. Why do you ask?" Monica said.

412

Dr. McAdams responded, "The reason I asked is, well, *my* husband, Kenny Sr. He's always had this jealousy towards me because I made *triple* the yearly salary as *he* did. He never liked the idea of a woman being the breadwinner of the family. And you mentioned that Sammy was flat broke for *years* before he became a successful musician. So, I'm sure that *now* there is no jealousy. But if I may, woman to woman. Us being married to a man who makes less money begins to create guilt for *our* success within our subconscious. You follow me?"

"I *hear* you, but could you elaborate a little bit more, please?" Monica said to Dr. McAdams. "Oh, of course; so, as I said, *guilt*. Making more money than our husbands create guilt, to the point where we dumb down *our* opinions, we dumb down our appearances and our pride, and our *voice* as women, so that we could make our man *feel* like a man. But what we as women sacrifice, we *lose* our individuality as women. We lose our *identity* as a woman as we try *so hard* to please our man. And *that* is what has affected *my* marriage with my husband. I wanted to *please* him by falling to *his* level, and I began to lose myself," said Dr. McAdams.

"Dr. McAdams, I can relate with you so much right now," said Monica. "Oh, I'm sure you *do*. But Monica, woman to woman, *don't* lose yourself because of the burden of guilt. Love your husband, *yes*. *Always* love him, but you *must* love yourself more. You don't know your worth just yet. And *that* is why you have been feeling worth*less*. You are a successful African American woman. You make a *great* living. You are intelligent, and you had a *wonderful* childhood with loving parents. And you have a loving husband with two great children. *And* you have friends. Overall, you have a *great* life, Monica. You now have to realize that and acknowledge your blessings. There is no reason to feel guilt. Never feel guilty for being blessed," said Dr. McAdams.

Monica never in her life had someone break it down for her in such a way before. Not her mother, not Tomi, Zarin, Wendy, or Collette. Dr. McAdams was the real deal after all.

"*Okay*, we have about five minutes left," Dr. McAdams said. "Is there anything else you want to touch on before we wrap things up?"

"Yes, there is," Monica responded. "As a white woman. Did you ever feel guilt or regret for being married to a black man?"

Dr. McAdams looked at Monica with a bit of side-eye as she was unsure where Monica was going with such a loaded question. But Dr. McAdams had no problem with responding. Dr. McAdams then said, "I *think* I know why you asked me that question. You asked me that question because you feel that *I*, being a *Caucasian* woman, who married an *African American* man, *stole* him away from potentially being with an *African American* woman. I think I'm pretty accurate, yea?" With a guilty look on her face, Monica responded, "I'm sorry, Dr. McAdams, I didn't mean to pry. It's none of my business." But Dr. McAdams did not take it to heart.

Dr. McAdams continued as she said, "That's okay, Monica. So, *about* my husband, Kenny had an affair *with* an African American woman, who just so happened to be my very best friend. I'm doing everything in my power to keep our family together. But I guess society saying that *"we are not supposed to be together"* got the best of him. Or maybe he just felt tired of disappointing his family. And *now*, I am a mother taking care of my two children, *our* two children. But I'm okay with that. Because as I said, *I know* my worth now, as a woman. No matter how much I can love a man. As a *woman, I know my worth*. But to answer your question of if I ever felt *guilty* of marrying a black man? No, absolutely not; I love Kenny. But if things don't work out between Kenny and me, the very best thing that came out of *this* marriage was my beautiful kids. And that's *all* I have to say about that."

As the therapy session came to its conclusion, Monica was at a loss for words. Dr. McAdams thanked Monica for coming in and told her that she is welcomed back anytime. As Monica walked out of Dr. McAdams' office, she saw another one of Dr. McAdams' patients sitting in the lobby. Dr. McAdams told her other patient that she has to use the restroom and she will return shortly. Monica then stood there with a look of clarity on her face. As she looked over, Monica saw the other patient looking at her with a smile on her face.

"What?" Monica asked the woman.

"Dr. McAdams is a *Baaaadddd bitch,* isn't she?" The other patient humorously said to Monica.

"Oh, *yea*, I wasn't ready for her. But I'm glad I came here."

"So am I. I've been coming to her for years now."

"Really? And she's helped you?"

"Yes, I just take it one day at a time."

"Yea… Well, have a good day."

Monica then headed to the elevator and pushed the down button. She had her head held high for the rest of the day. Dr. McAdams gave Monica more than she was expecting to gain from the therapy session. What stuck out to Monica the most was Dr. McAdams saying to her, *"No matter how much you can love a man, know your worth as a woman."*

Monica's pride was lifted. Her guilt for success has diminished. And her love for herself, as a woman, grew more prominent than ever before. Even though that was her very first therapy session, Monica felt a sense of instant relief as she headed back out into the real world. It was safe to say that this would not be the last time Monica meets with Dr. Melissa McAdams.

Chapter 33

A lovely Tuesday afternoon. Collette has just left her office. As she was heading to her car in the parking lot, she ran into her new buddy, Jimmy Ferguson. Jimmy is the homeless man that she gave some money to the other day.

"Hello, Ms. Fernandez, good afternoon. How are you?" Said Jimmy.

"Hi, Jimmy, please, call me Coco," Collette responded.

"Oh, sure, of course."

"And I'm doing great; how about yourself?"

"I'm hanging in there. Taking it day by day."

"That's good to hear, Jimmy. Listen, I'm glad I ran into you. Because I have something lined up for you."

As Jimmy listened to Collette, she pulled out some paperwork for Jimmy to have. "I made a few calls. Okay, I've made *a lot* of calls, and I have some good news. I found a job for you," Collette said as she smiled. Jimmy's eyebrows raised so high as Collette told him about the job offer. She said to him that there was an opening as a janitor in her office building, and she found him an apartment at an affordable price. Collette also told Jimmy that she would take care of the first three months of rent while he settles into this new reality. Jimmy could not say a word through all his tears. He was just so grateful to Collette that she would go through all this trouble for him.

"Ms. Fernandez, I... I don't know how to thank you," Jimmy said with a broken voice.

"It's *Coco,* and you don't have to thank me," Collette said. "Thank our Lord and Savior, Jesus Christ."

Collette hugged Jimmy and gave him some more money. At first, he would *not* accept it, but she insisted. She then handed Jimmy the paperwork with all the information about the job, apartment, location, and the landlord that Jimmy must meet. His gratitude for Collette was difficult to express. He just could not believe that someone would care so much. Before going their separate ways, Jimmy said to her, "I've been praying for some help for so long. And now those prayers have been answered. God bless you, Coco."

Collette brought both of her hands together as she blew Jimmy a kiss. It warmed her heart to have the chance to help Jimmy and that he was willing to *accept* the help. As Collette turned around and walked to her car, she heard a woman's voice saying, "Coco, Coco!" She turned around to see who was calling her name. It was her mother,

Gloria. Collette was surprised to see her mother in Manhattan. Gloria rarely comes into the city.

"What are you doing here, Mamí?" Said Collette.

"I was hoping I could talk with you," Gloria responded.

"About?"

"About what happened to Emilio and about Liam."

"*Lisa* Mamí, *Lisa*."

"I want to talk to all three of you if that's okay?"

Collette had to think about it. The last time she tried to have a conversation with her mother about Lisa and Emilio, Collette was ignored. But Collette agreed to set up a meeting with her mother. She said, "Alright, Mamí, I'll reach out to Emilio and *Lisa,* and we can all meet at *Lucille's.* Is Papí going to come or just you?" "It'll be just me, Collette," said Gloria.

Collette then got in her car and made a few phone calls. She reached out to Lisa first. Fortunately, Lisa was off from work today. But Lisa was hesitant to see her mother for the first time in two years. After Collette talked with Lisa, she agreed to meet as long as their mother would be respectful. Collette then called Emilio, and he was also available as he just finished his morning class. So, Collette set the meeting up. But she has no idea of what will come of this.

Collette sent a text to her mother, giving her the time to come to *Lucille's.* Gloria responded that she would be there. Collette then went straight to *Lucille's* from the parking lot in front of her office. The closer she got to the restaurant, the more nervous she became. But if this meeting was going to remove the tainted wedge between her mother and Lisa, Collette was ready.

An hour later, Collette is sitting at her reserved booth. Business is going very well as customers are coming in during their lunch break. As Collette sits there, she sips on some freshly brewed decaf coffee, waiting for Emilio, Lisa, and her mother to arrive. Coming down the stairs from his office, Martin was on the phone. He then turned around and saw Collette sitting down at the booth. Martin walked over to Collette, surprised to see her sitting there during lunch hour.

"Hey, you're here early," Martin said as he got off his phone. "Are you meeting up with your girls?"

"Hey, no, I'm not," said Collette. "My mom wanted to see Emilio and Lisa. So, I told them to come here."

"Oh, okay. Well, I just got off the phone with Angel. We're going to do some running around. So, maybe we'll see you later? Tell them all I said hello."

"Will do, babe."

"I'm glad you found her, Coco."

"She found us, Martin… She found us."

"God's plan, right?"

"Always. I'll see you later. Love you."

"I love you too, baby. Good luck with your mom."

"Thanks."

After Martin left *Lucille's*, Collette looked at her watch to see the time. She called everyone over an hour ago, and her patience was beginning to fade. It was not much longer until Lisa showed up. Collette saw Lisa at the main entrance and began to wave her hand to get Lisa's attention. Lisa saw Collette and told the host that she knows where she's going. As Lisa made her way toward the booth, Collette got up and hugged her firmly. Collette has not seen Lisa since she was in the hospital recovering from her surgery. Lisa looked better than ever as she had the biggest smile on her face. And Collette *saw* the happiness on Lisa's face as well.

"Sis, you are so *gorgeous*," Collette said as Lisa turned around. "Ay Dios mío. Los hombres babearán."

"I feel like a whole new woman, Coco," Lisa said. "And I'm going to *be* the woman that I've always dreamed of being."

Collette was so happy for Lisa. Living her truth in a false world is difficult for anyone. But Lisa had the courage to live as her authentic self. Collette admired that the most about Lisa. No matter how much their father tried to beat it out of Lisa, no matter how many times, kids in the neighborhood would chase Lisa down the block, bullying and teasing her for being a trans kid. Lisa stayed true to herself on the *inside*. And as Collette sees her now, blossoming into the beautiful woman that she is. It was like a miracle that Lisa survived.

Lisa then took a seat in the booth. She had a craving for a milkshake. Funnily enough, milkshakes were recently added to *Lucille's* menu. So, Lisa ordered a strawberry shortcake milkshake.

Collette ordered one as well. While they waited, in came Emilio. Lisa was glad to see him after so long. She gave him the biggest hug. But as Lisa saw the bruising that Emilio suffered at the hands of his father, Lisa said, "The bruises all look too familiar." But since that drama was all put to the side, it did not create any conflict.

Then the milkshakes came to the table. God, did they look so delicious. They came in these giant glasses. There was strawberry syrup at the bottom, twirling up to the top of the glass. Whipped cream on the top, covered with cake crumbs and more syrup, and *then* a whole strawberry pierced on the rim of the glass. Emilio was so mesmerized by it that he had to order one himself.

Another half-hour goes by. Collette, Lisa, and Emilio have all finished their Strawberry shortcake milkshake. But still, there was no sign of Gloria. So, Collette decided to call her mother to see where exactly she is. As Collette moved away from the booth, the phone began to ring. Gloria then picked up.

"Mamí, you have us all waiting here," Collette said irritatingly. "Where are you?"

"I… I can't do this, Coco. I'm sorry," said Gloria.

"Oh my God, Mamí, now is your chance to redeem yourself for all your wrongdoings with Lisa. If you back out now, you… You may never hear from us again."

"Alright, fine, I'm on my way."

As Collette hung up the phone, she took a deep breath and exhaled. She then went back to the booth and told Emilio and Lisa that she is on her way. Ten minutes later, Collette sees her mother, Gloria, coming into the restaurant. She sees her mother asking the host where she is, and the host pointed over to the booth where everyone was sitting. Collette kept her eyes on her mother like a hawk as she made her way to the booth. Finally, as Gloria made her way to the booth, she stood there in silence. Gloria was standing there, staring at Lisa. She has not seen Lisa in over two years, before all the procedures. For Gloria, it is *a lot* to take in.

"Mamí, you always told me it's impolite to stare at people. Have a seat," said Collette.

"Actually, Coco, I said it's impolite to stare at *strangers*."

Collette let that one slide, as she already knows her mother just *had* to have the last word. Gloria finally sat down. The booth is shaped like half an oval. Lisa was sitting on the far end of one side, Emilio sat next to her, then Collette sat beside *him*, with Gloria on the other end.

As Gloria settled in, she said to them, "I'm sorry for keeping you all waiting. I wasn't sure if I was going to go through with this. And Collette, I'm sure you're wondering why I have the sudden change of heart. Well, that night when you sent me the pictures of Emilio beaten up. I... I was in shock. I didn't believe you when you said Martin did that to him. But then I realized that your father did the same thing to Liam."

Collette stopped her mother from talking as she keeps disrespecting Lisa. "Mamí, for the *final* time, *her* name is LISA. *Lisa* Mamí, *enough* with you deadnaming her." Gloria just sat there in brief silence. Some of the guests sitting at other tables began to turn their heads as the commotion was picking up. Gloria then took a few seconds before she gathered her thoughts together.

"Can we do this *right*, Mamí?" Collette projected. "Can you speak to her with the proper pronouns and her *real* name?"

"Just let me speak, without *any* interruptions. *Please?*" Gloria responded.

Gloria then began to drink some water to clear her throat and continued what she had to say. "This was not easy for me. I was raising a child that I *didn't* understand. To have a *son*, *telling* you that he is a *girl*, TRAPPED inside of a boy's body. That is something that *no* mother can prepare herself for. When I told your grandmother that her grandchild was a trans kid, she no longer wanted *anything* to do with me. She didn't even want to see her own grandchildren. *Why* did you *think* you two haven't seen her for *years*? She wanted *nothing* to do with it. I lost *my* mother because of *Lisa*," said Gloria.

Collette and Lisa just stared at their mother as she continued speaking and became emotional. Gloria then said, "The last time I saw my mother was at her *funeral*. She didn't even want to see me on her *death* bed. And *then*, not even five months later, your uncle Carlos, my one and only brother, calls me crying, *telling* me that he has *AIDS*. And *then*, two months after that, *he* dies. Do you understand what I am *saying* to you? This *gay shit*, this *trans shit*, has *ruined* my *family*. It has ruined my *life*. I was just so scared, Coco. I was scared of losing

Lisa to that AIDS virus, and I'm scared of losing Emilio. I've lost *so much*. I just couldn't handle it anymore. *No mas perder*."

Not a dry eye was sitting in that booth. All four of them sat there with teary eyes. But Lisa had to give her mother a piece of her mind. Lisa said, "You think this was easy for *me*, Mamí? Do you think it's easy for me to walk down the streets, being judged and stared at? I had to go through *hell*. Who I am, it's *not* a *choice*, Mamí. No matter *how* much you or Papí tried to beat it from out of me, no matter how many times you sent me to church and tried to pray it out of me, *this* is who I am. I'm a woman, *Una Mujer*, a *human being*. And for what it's worth, this is no one's fault. I know who I am now, Mamí. And that's never going to change."

Collette had to chime in now as she said to her mother, "I understand, Mamí. I understand that you went through *so* much suffering. But so has Lisa, and it's not fair that you *continue* to make her suffer. Or even Emilio, it's not fair. All they need from you is *love*. And *respect*. I've been trying to make peace with Lisa ever since Papí beat her in the middle of the street. That was my fault; *I* was the one who told you and Papí that Lisa was wearing your shoes in the bathroom. And I cannot change or erase the past. But Lisa has forgiven me. If you can find it in your heart, to accept Lisa as she is *today*, a *woman*, hopefully, she can forgive you as well."

Gloria looked at Lisa and then at Emilio. As Gloria sat there, tears rolling down her face, she began to shake her head as she slid her way out of the booth. Gloria then grabbed her belongings and walked away from her family. Collette tried to stop her from leaving.

"Mamí, MAMÍ!" Collette shouted.

"*No*, Coco, no," Lisa said. "Let her go; it's over. We tried."

"Mamí, not everyone is going to accept who we are," said Emilio. "It's the world we live in. All *we* can do is simply *live*."

Collette then put her hands up against her forehead as she began sobbing her eyes out. Through her tears, she said to Lisa and Emilio, "I'm so sorry; I just wanted our family to stick together." Both Emilio and Lisa began to hold and comfort Collette in the booth. Even though Collette felt that she had failed her sister and her son, in a way, she has helped them. She has shown them that even in the family, you will not have that love and support. However, the most important thing they will ever need in this life is *self-love*. Collette taught them that *self*-love is the key to surviving in this world. It will give both Lisa and Emilio the courage and pride from within to make something of themselves and lead a very fulfilling and meaningful life.

Chapter 34

Later that evening, Tomi met up with Carmelo at the nightclub "*Test-Tick-Cools*" to scout for potential hot male models for the charity fashion show on Friday. Because Tomi did not want to make a scene, she snuck in from the back door and met Carmelo in the V.I.P section. The club looked like something out of a dream. The club was *filled* with New York City's finest of men. More than half of the men in the club were shirtless and in tip-top shape. Tomi had a plethora of men to choose from. As Tomi and Carmelo stood on the upper level in the V.I.P. section, looking around the dance floor, they began to discuss who they see that has potential.

"Uh, Ms. Bellas," Carmelo spoke. "Can we talk about your sexy ass going *viral*?"

"Oh my God, stop it!" Tomi blushed. "Well, I don't mean to *brag*, but yea, I pulled a clever stunt with posing naked in my winter coat."

"O… M… *Mother Fucking* G…" Carmelo shouted. "Ms. Bellas, you are a gen*Yasss*, not a *genius*, but a gen*Yasss*!"

"Oh, *stop* it, silly boy," Tomi laughed. "Gen-*Yasss*… *Silly*."

The night carried on, Tomi and Carmelo looked all over the club for the right group of men who could deliver on the runway. Carmelo was the *perfect* wingman. From the balcony, Carmelo would point at some of the guys on the dance floor. As soon as a guy looks up and sees Carmelo pointing in his direction, the guy would then point at *himself* and say, "*me?*" And Carmelo would say "yes, you" and make a gesture for them to come up. Of course, since Carmelo and Tomi were in the V.I.P. section, the guys were more than happy to come up.

Ten men were invited up to the V.I.P. section. Tomi began to examine each of them as she would in a fashion show. She looked up and down at their physique. As mentioned, most of the men were already shirtless. So, Tomi did not have to worry about asking them to undress. As Tomi finished her little *go-see*, she said, "Gentlemen, I must say that not only are you *gorgeous*, but you are sexy, *physically* fit, women would just *throw* their panties at you. *However*, I am not Judy Garland. This is *not* the wonderful land of Oz. And I am *not* looking for a bunch of *munchkins* to be walking down my runway. I mean, what the *hell* are you guys, *5'5*? I'm sorry, but good Christ, you *all* should have eaten your goddamn vegetables growing up. Gentlemen, thank you anyway, you can go now." "TO THE *LEFT*, TO THE *LEFT*, bitches," Carmelo shouted.

Tomi was not pleased with all the men being "Height challenged." As she finished her glass of champagne, Tomi had to use the restroom. But since she was new to the club, she did not know where it was. Tomi asked Carmelo, "Melo, my love, where's the ladies' room?" Carmelo responded, "Uh, It's not in *this* club, Ms. Bellas. This is a *gay* club. Not too many bitches be up in *here*." Tomi then rolled her eyes and began to look for the restroom. As she walked around, holding her bladder, she spotted someone standing near the bar. It was difficult for Tomi to see his face amongst all the men waving their arms around, voguing like *Studio 54* and the ballroom scene. But it was something about this guy that made Tomi not take her eyes off of him.

He then left the bar and started to walk away, farther from where Tomi was standing. So, she then pursued him. Coincidently, he walked into the restroom. Now, Tomi was able to kill two birds with one stone. As Tomi walked into the restroom, she saw two guys tonguing each other down. They saw Tomi and stopped. "Oh please, don't mind me, fellas. Just *using* the bathroom." The two men looked at Tomi with disgust on their faces and walked out of the bathroom. Under her breath, Tomi sarcastically said, "Y'all bitches were kissing like two teenage virgins on prom night *anyway*."

Even though Tomi *did* have to use the bathroom, she did not want to go into one of the sitting stalls and potentially lose that guy. There were three different closed stalls in that bathroom. She did not know which one that mysterious guy went into. So, Tomi being *Tomi*, she used one of the *standing* stalls. Tomi simply lifted her skirt, then lifted her *leg*, and began to urinate, standing up. The next thing you know, that mysterious guy came out of one of the stalls and caught Tomi in the act.

"Holy fuc… BITCH!" Said the mysterious guy.

"Oh, no, it's, it's *not* what you think," Tomi said as she flushed the stall. "Listen, I'm Tomi Belacone. I'm a fashion designer. I saw you standing out there, and I wanted to introduce myself."

"Oh, *yes*, I know who you are," he said. "I'm Brad, Brad Versace."

"Ah, Brad *Versace,* huh? Any relations to the late great *Gianni Versace?*"

"Ha, I wish."

"Hey, you *never* know… *So, Mr. Versace*, let's talk."

Tomi then sat on top of the sink counter and began to have a conversation with *"Brad with the good hair,"* as she now called him. Brad was undeniably a beautiful soul—great facial features, smooth skin, with that sex-appealing stubble beard that women would *drool* over. And not to mention, he was well over six feet tall. Tomi wanted him *badly*. She then asked him, "So, I'm doing a fashion show this Friday. It's a charity event to help stop the world's pollution problem that has created climate change. I want you to be a part of that and walk the runway. So what do you say? You interested?" As soon as Brad was about to open his mouth, in came Carmelo.

"Oh my *God*, Ms. Bellas," said Carmelo, "I've been looking *all* over for you. You've been *here* this whole time?"

"Yes, Melo, baby, I think I found the *perfect* candidate."

"Uh, *no,* Ms. Bellas, you *didn't*," Carmelo said with disgust. "What you found was a *lying* piece… of… SHIT!"

"Wait, *what?*" Tomi said. "What are you talking about? You know each other?"

"Ms. Belacone, Carmelo is my ex-boyfriend," Brad said. "We dated for about two years, and things *didn't* work out between us."

"Uh, maybe that's because you were a fucking *PIG*, who couldn't keep his *dick* in his fucking pants! Did you ever think of *that?*"

Both Carmelo and Brad began to have a heated exchange of words. Tomi then had to break it up and *cook* this diva beef. She said to them, "Gentlemen, let's not bring up old shit from the past. What's done is done. Now, Carmelo, whatever problems you have with Brad, I need you to be a *professional* and put that shit to bed. Brad, my offer still stands. *If* you're interested in walking in my fashion show, you can call *my assistant*, Carmelo." Carmelo looked at Tomi in shock, as if his jaw was scrapping the bathroom floor. Then Tomi and Carmelo came out of the bathroom.

"Ms. Bellas, *please* don't make me do this," Carmelo vulnerably said. "It took me *so long* to get over him."

"Listen, Melo, if he calls, all you have to do is *book* him. I'm not asking *you two* to have a "kiss and makeup date." *Hell*, you don't even have to say goodbye to him when you hang up the phone," said Tomi.

Carmelo was not happy with Tomi's decision. But she *is* the boss, and the *boss* got what she wanted that night. As it was getting late, Tomi had to leave the club to head home and get some rest as she had someplace very important to be the following morning. And she did *not* want to be late.

It is now Wednesday morning, and Tomi is up with the birds. She already called her limo driver, Benjamin, to make sure he was on his way to her Soho penthouse. She also asked him if he could pick up two dozen roses from a florist shop nearby. As Tomi gathered her things together, she called Thomas and told him that she is going to visit her mother at the nursing home on Staten Island. He was not able to join her as he is working on a house in upstate New York. Tomi understood and thought *perhaps* she should spend some quality time with her mother alone.

Tomi then made her way down to the lobby of her apartment. Benjamin was already there, waiting for Tomi to come outside. As he opened the limo door, he said, "Good morning, Ms. Belacone. I placed the flowers in the back for you. Also, I took the liberty of getting you your favorite from Starbucks. Your peppermint hot chocolate and two chocolate chip cookies." She thanked Benjamin for his thoughtfulness and hopped in the back of the limo as he drove her to Staten Island.

As Tomi was riding, she was beginning to reminisce about her relationship with her mother. She began to look back at all the extraordinary times they had together. Tomi's brothers, Pauly and Frankie, were always doing their own thing. But Tomi and her mother

432

were like Thelma and Louise. They would go on their journeys, take road trips around America, listen to artists such as *John Denver, America, The Doors, The Beatles, Perry Como, Dusty Springfield, Lee Hazlewood, and The Mamas, and The Papas.* You name them, and they listened to those artists on the road. So much of what Tomi is comes from her mother.

As Tomi was riding, she put in her Apple AirPods and played one of her mother's favorite songs, *"My Autumn's Done Come"* by Lee Hazlewood. Tomi remembers listening to this song as a little girl while her mother would take her for late-night drives. That is how Tomi came up with her "Midnight Runs" in the city. From all those years of driving around with her mother at night. At that time, her mother was driving a 1979 baby blue Volkswagen Beetle convertible, rooftop down.

One night, Tomi and her mother, Arianna, were on their way to California. Tomi was half asleep with the wind blowing through her and Arianna's hair. Tomi would hear her mother's beautiful voice singing the Lee Hazlewood song as she looked over to her. Tomi remembers it like it was yesterday. But now, *that* yesterday is long gone. And Tomi is about to face the reality of today.

Tomi finally arrives at the nursing home where her mother is now residing. As she got out of the limo with the flowers, Benjamin said, "Take as long as you need, Ms. Belacone; I'll be waiting right here."

Tomi then kissed Benjamin and said, "You're the best. Thank you." Tomi took a huge breath and exhaled. She then walked into the nursing home and headed to the front desk to check-in. Her mother was located on the third floor. Tomi got into the elevator and pushed number 3. As she reached the third floor and headed to her mother's room, she saw her older brothers, Pauly and Frankie, in the hallway.

"Hey, guys," Tomi said. "How's momma doing?"

"She's sleep," said Pauly. "I was just about to head out. So um, good to see you."

Tomi and Pauly never really got along as much. But she was always close with Frankie. Pauly was always the brother with his hand out, asking for money. But rarely did he say thank you. Until one day, Tomi said to him, "no more money." After that, Pauly cut all ties with her. But Frankie was the total opposite. Tomi put down the flowers and hugged Frankie so tight.

"How have you been, sis?" Frankie said. "I've missed you."

"I miss you more, Frankie," said Tomi. "I've been good."

"Listen, we've done all we could. The *doctors* have done all they could. It's out of all our hands, you know?"

"Yea, Frankie, I know. *C'est La Vie.* That's what momma would always say. But I'll see you later, okay?"

"Okay."

Frankie then grabbed his coat from inside their mother's room and took his leave. As Tomi picked up the flowers, she then made her way into the room. As she stood there, she looked at her mother. Her mother was lying there in bed, with her eyes closed and a nasal breathing tube in her nose. There was silence in the room, minus the beeping of the heart rate monitor and the crinkling of the plastic wrapping from the roses. Tomi then walked over to her mother and kissed her on her cheek. As Tomi sat down, she heard a soft, sweet voice began to speak.

"Kiss me twice, so I know you mean it," Her mother said.

"Hi, momma," Tomi said as she kissed her mother again. "I thought you were asleep."

"No, I was *pretending* to be asleep. So I wouldn't have to hear Pauly *bitching* about who's going to get my trust fund."

"Oh, momma," Tomi said as she broke out in laughter. "I know, Pauly is… *Pauly*. There's no changing him."

"You and Frankie are my jewels, my muse. Pauly, I don't know where he came from. Probably because you all had different fathers."

Tomi then asked her mother about that. She was *inquisitive* to know who exactly her father was. Tomi said, "So, momma, I think now is the right time, more than *ever*, for you to tell me who my father is. Or *was*, for that matter." Arianna looked up to the ceiling and shrugged her shoulders, as she did not have a clue. Arianna said to Tomi, "Baby, I wish I had the answer to who your father is. But I was a *messy* bitch. I was just living the free, nomadic, hipster life. If I saw a man, and I liked him, I *fucked* him." Tomi was not prepared for her mother's cussing and told her to take it easy.

Arianna then continued as she said, "Tomi, the bottom line is, I'm sorry. I know that I didn't give you kids the proper upbringing. You know, with having a mother *and* father taking care of you. But as you know, I never met your grandfather. I lost my father in WWII when I was a baby. Your grandmother never fully recovered from that. I guess I just felt that knowing who your father is, wasn't that important. But that was *my* ignorance. Having a father is *very* important in *every* child's life. But I didn't give that to you, baby girl. And I'm *so* sorry."

"I'm not going to *cry*. I'm *not*," Tomi said as she was getting emotional. "Momma, you don't have to apologize."

"Oh, but I *do*, Tomi. Especially now that my time is almost up."

"Momma, don't say that right now."

"It is Tomi; it's almost tim— almost time."

"Are you okay? You need some water?"

"Yes, please."

Tomi walked over to Arianna's dresser to grab some water and a straw for her mother. "Thank you, baby," Arianna said as she began to sip on the water. As Tomi was looking at her mother, she thought about death and wondered if her mother had any fear of it. Tomi said to her mother, "Momma, are you afraid? Of dying? Do you believe it? In an afterlife?" Arianna looked at Tomi and began to roll her eyes in disgust. Arianna responded, "Aww honey, you know I don't believe in all that stuff. I just *enjoyed life*. For what it is. And that's all I wanted for you kids. To *enjoy* your lives. For whatever time you're offered in this life. I was never afraid of *dying*, baby. I was just *terrified* of *not living*. *Not* living this precious gift that we call life. Death is the easy part. You just *die*, and that's it. No more pain and suffering. No more money, no more taxes. You just *fade away* into the unknown. If there is an unknown."

As Tomi put her head down and began to shed her tears, Arianna reached for Tomi's hand and said, "Listen, baby, I don't want you *ever* to be afraid of anything. Not even of losing me. Don't worry about death or an afterlife. Because if you live your life right in *this* lifetime, you won't *need* another life after this. Live your life with love and grace." It was tough for Tomi to hear her mother speak like this. It was almost as if her mother was ready to say her goodbyes. But Tomi is *not* ready for that. She is not ready to say goodbye.

"*Momma*, I'm just not ready for you to go," Tomi said emotionally. "I need you here with me."

"I will *always* be with you, Tomi," Arianna spoke. "I'll be right there, within your heart and your farts."

Tomi then belched out with laughter. That is one thing about Arianna. She *always* has such an unapologetic sense of humor. And she could always make Tomi laugh. "Momma, stop trying to make me laugh right now," said Tomi. Arianna responded, "But that's the whole *point*, baby. When I leave, I don't *ever* want you to give up on laughter. Whenever you have a great laugh, and then I pop up in your mind at that exact moment, don't let my demise be the dead-end to your laughter. Because when I come to your mind, that just means that I'm laughing right along with you."

After Arianna said that, Tomi just could not hold it in anymore. She laid her head on her mother's shoulders and just cried a storm. Arianna gently ran her hand through Tomi's hair. All Arianna could say at that moment was, "I love you, Tomi. *Always* know that I love you." As Tomi could not get any more words out through the traffic of her tears and emotions, she just nodded in understanding. Even through death, this mother and daughter bond will *never* be broken.

Chapter 35

Later on, it's late Wednesday morning. Wendy, whose jet-lagged, has made her way to her doctor's office. They arrived back in America last night. Wendy was so tired from the flight; she decided for her and EJ to stay over at her parents' house in Queens. But since Wendy had a doctor's appointment, she asked her mother, Suzi, if EJ could stay with them while she goes. Suzi said that was not a problem.

As Wendy waits for her doctor, she sent a text to Edward, telling him that she was at the doctor's office and that she'll be home soon. After a few minutes go by, there was no response from Edward. Finally, her doctor was ready for her, and Wendy went into the holding room. They did their usual, checked her blood pressure and breathing.

Then the assistant told Wendy that her doctor would be with her shortly.

Wendy was feeling great today. Maybe *too* great, as she was very alert, and her senses were crystal clear. And then, finally, her doctor knocked and opened the door.

"Hey Wendy, good to see you," said the doctor. "How are you doing?"

"Hi Dr. Greenberg, I'm doing fine, and you?" Wendy responded.

"Oh, can't complain. Patients have coming in with the flu lately. But that's common around this time."

Dr. Greenberg, a short Jewish woman, has been Wendy's doctor for the last seven years. Dr. Greenberg is also the doctor who delivered EJ five years ago. So, after their brief greetings, Dr. Greenberg said to Wendy, "So, what brings you here today?" Wendy then broke down the story and said, "*So*, I just came back from vacation. I was in Japan with my family. Now, I *love* sushi, but I think I had *too* much of it the first few days I was there. So, I began to feel nauseous and began vomiting, usually during the morning time. I felt so sluggish for the whole trip. I also threw up on the airplane. Thank *God* I made it to the bathroom on time. But as of right now, I feel *great*. I can smell damn near anything; my hormones are a little high. Is this what happens during food poisoning?" Dr. Greenberg looked at Wendy with a straight face and shook her head as she said, "*Noooo*."

Dr. Greenberg then put on a pair of latex gloves and began to examine Wendy closely. First, she ran a few tests on Wendy and examined Wendy's breast. As Dr. Greenberg touched on Wendy's chest area, Wendy began to fidget.

"Ouch, I'm sorry, Dr. Greenberg," said Wendy. "My breast is a little sensitive. It's been like that for a few days now."

"Wendy, my dear," Dr. Greenberg said with a smile. "I think I have to give you *one more test*. I'll be right back."

As Wendy sat there, she did not know *what* to feel. She did not know whether it was something good, bad, or ugly. As Wendy waited, her nerves began to turn up in volume. Finally, as Dr. Greenberg came back in, Wendy looked at the box that Dr. Greenberg was holding, and she was utterly dumbfounded.

"Oh my God," Wendy said in shock. "Could this *be*?"

"I believe so, my dear," said Dr. Greenberg. "Why don't you go into the bathroom and see what it says."

Wendy then took the box, went to the bathroom, and shut the door. As she took care of her business, she had to wait for a good minute. Then, as Wendy looked at the test, she covered her mouth with her hand, shocked with tears of happiness as the results emerged. That's right; Wendy is pregnant! She is having another baby. Wendy then went back to the holding room where Dr. Greenberg was waiting for her. As Wendy had the pregnancy kit in her hand, she showed it to Dr. Greenberg with a teary smile on her face.

"Congratulations, mommy!" Dr. Greenberg said as she hugged Wendy. "You're having baby number *two*. This is *so* exciting."

"I'm just *so* dumbfounded," said Wendy. "Like, I should have *known* the symptoms since I already had EJ."

"Oh Wendy, my dear, lightning never strikes the same way twice. The symptoms *always* come randomly, and they catch you off guard. Wait, is it the same *way* or the same *place*?"

"I don't know Dr. Greenberg. But I now must tell Eddie, I have to tell my friends, and I have to tell my parents. They're going to be *so* excited."

Wendy thanked Dr. Greenberg, got herself situated, and got dressed. She sent Edward a text saying, "Hey Eddie, I'm on my way home right now. I have some exciting news." Wendy wanted Eddie to be the *first* to know about her pregnancy. So, for now, she reserved sharing the news with the other four ladies. Wendy was not too far from home, so she decided to speed walk the four blocks to her apartment.

As Wendy walked into the apartment lobby and saw the security guard at the front, she said hello to him. The security guard gave Wendy a look as if he knew something that she doesn't. But she was too excited to pay it any mind. She went to the elevator and gave the "up-arrow button" a good push. As she then waited a few seconds, the elevator finally came down. When Wendy got in the elevator, she saw the security guard looking at her with an awkward stare. Wendy thought to herself, "*What the hell is his problem?*" But again, she was too excited to let anything interfere with her great news. As she got off of the elevator, Wendy made her way to her apartment.

As Wendy took out her keys to unlock the door, she realized that the door was already unlocked. She then turned the doorknob and opened the door. What Wendy saw was the beginning of her *worst* nightmare. Wendy saw the disturbing decorations of another woman's clothes spread throughout the floor. The woman and Eddie's clothes left a trail to the master bedroom. Wendy's heart was racing at full speed as she heard them. She heard sounds of passionate moans coming from her bedroom. She walked towards her bedroom as slow as a turtle. It was as if the hallway was stretching. The more she walked, the farther it stretched. The closer Wendy came to the bedroom, the louder the moans projected. Wendy, walking in fear, seeing another woman's pants, shoes, bra, *and* panties lying on the floor. As she made her way to the crack of her bedroom door, like tunnel vision, she saw *her* husband, Edward, in *her* bed, having sex with another woman.

The look on Wendy's face was like a crying *Mona Lisa.* The love of her life was having an affair. All she can hear was the woman's voice, moaning and saying, "Oh Eddie, oh, it feels so good." Wendy did not know what to do at that moment. So, she slowly back-peddled away from the bedroom door. She covered her mouth to prevent herself from being heard. She then turned her back to the cracked door of her bedroom as she was heading out of the apartment. But then, Wendy stopped herself. She stood there in the hallway; her broken heart began to leak her pain as the sponge of anger soaked in *every* drop. Wendy then turned back around, now facing the cracked door of her bedroom. With heavy footsteps down the hallway, Wendy stampedes through the door. Edward and his mistress were immediately startled. As Edward turned around and saw his wife, standing there with her teary face, he knew he made an irreversible mistake.

"Wendy, baby," Edward said. "I, I, I'm *so* sor—"

"IN OUR *FUCKING HOUSE*? IN OUR *BED*?" Wendy screamed.

"Babe, please, just *calm down*."

But Wendy was a million miles away from calmness. She began to throw whatever she could get her hands on in the bedroom. A remote, a hairbrush, a shoe, *anything* that could cause physical pain once it landed. Edward and his mistress were standing there in the bedroom, naked and helpless, as Wendy continued to throw things at a fast speed as if she was Steve "Dalko" Dalkowski. Edward finally was able to grab Wendy and hold her down to detain her.

"GET OFF OF ME!" Wendy shouted. "GET THE *FUCK* OFF!"

"Please, Wendy, *please*! Let me explain!" Edward cried.

The mistress then hopped out of the bedroom and skedaddled as she wanted *no* parts of that. As Edward still had Wendy pinned to the ground with his hands, he pleaded with her. He said, "Baby, *please*, don't fight me. I'm going to let you go. But please just stay there, okay?" As Wendy calmed herself, Edward then released her. He then grabbed his underwear and quickly put them on.

Wendy was in another world. A world where she did not know anybody. If only you could see the look on her face as she looked at Edward. She could not believe it. After *all* those years, she could not believe that the love of her life would betray her.

"In *our house*? In *our bed*?" Wendy cried.

"Wendy, baby, I am so, *very* sorry you saw this."

"Don't call me baby anymore. I'm not your baby. I'm no one's baby," Wendy softly said.

Wendy then walked out of the bedroom, grabbed her bag, and left the apartment. Tears began to pour down her face as she got into the elevator. Wendy uncontrollably cried all the way down to the lobby. As the elevator doors opened, people were waiting. As she saw them, they looked at her with an alert, wondering what was wrong. But Wendy just wanted to get out of there. As she headed for the exit, she saw that same security guard with the same look on his face. It was then that Wendy realized that he *knew* all along.

As Wendy went outside, it suddenly began to pour down rain. As if her day could not get any worse. But what is ironically sad about this day is that Wendy had some of the best news to tell Edward. She is pregnant with their second child. But unfortunately, that good news was crushed by Edwards' unfaithful infidelities. Nevertheless, with all her strength, Wendy was able to wave down a taxi. As she got in the cab, the cab driver was waiting to receive her destination. But Wendy had absolutely no clue of where to go. She could not be at her home, and she was too embarrassed to go to her mother. So, where does she go? To Tomi? Zarin? Monica? Or Collette?

"Ma'am, where to?" said the cab driver.

"Head to Queens, 11th street and 47th avenue."

The one place where Wendy could go that was somewhat a place to clear her head was her office. Yet, the tears continued to flow down Wendy's face as she leaned her head up against the window. It was as if the raindrops on the backseat window were racing her teardrops to the ground. She was devastated and heartbroken. In her mind, Wendy thought, *"How could this happen? I had the greatest news to tell him. And he was sleeping in my bed with another woman."* The cab driver noticed in his rearview mirror how upset Wendy is.

"Ma'am, it's not my business, but are you okay?" said the cab driver.

"No," Wendy said as she shook her head. "No, I'm not okay right now. Just get me where I need to go, please."

"Yes, ma'am."

About a half-hour later, the cab driver pulled up in front of Wendy's work building. Wendy then paid the cab driver and got out of the cab. As she walked into the building, she was drenched in the rain but drained of energy. Wendy did not even say hello to any of the security guards at the front desk. She then went straight to the staircase as she did not want to get on the elevator. As Wendy reached her floor, several of her co-workers said hello to her. But Wendy just walked right past them. A stone-cold face as she walked to her office. As she got into her office, she closed the door behind her, sat down at her desk, and began to cry, more than a baby ever could.

But the thing is, her office had glass walls. So, people could see her crying, as did her boss, Mrs. Shultz. Mrs. Shultz then came into her office and said to Wendy, "Come with me to my office right now." As Wendy looked up from her desk, she saw that it was Mrs. Shultz. Mrs. Shultz gave Wendy a look that said, "*Come on now.*" So, Wendy then wiped her face, got up, and followed Mrs. Shultz to her office. As Wendy followed Mrs. Shultz to her office, her co-workers continued to stare.

When she got into Mrs. Shultz's office, Wendy took a seat and began to weep some more. But Mrs. Shultz heard enough as she said, "Wendy, get yourself together. I can't have you crying like this in my office." She then handed Wendy some tissue to wipe her face. As Mrs. Shultz took a seat at her desk, she began to have a conversation with Wendy.

"So, tell me what happened, Wendy?" said Mrs. Shultz.

"I don't want to talk about it right now," Wendy spoke. "I just want to be alone."

"Wendy, my dear, I don't think you should be alone. You're very upset."

"Mrs. Shultz, *please*, I just need a moment to myself in my office."

"Okay, let me guess. Something happened with your husband?"

Wendy grew silent once Mrs. Shultz made that *accurate* assumption. As Wendy took a look at her, she responded, "How did you know this is about my husband?" Mrs. Shultz could not help but smile and laugh at Wendy. "May I remind you, *Mrs.* Date-Collins, that I have been doing this business for *years, decades. I know* when a man has broken a woman's heart. And from the looks of it, the hurt is irreversible. Am I still right?" said Mrs. Shultz. Wendy then gave Mrs. Shultz a gentle head nod and responded, "yes."

"But that's not all," Wendy said. "I went to the doctor today, and I found out I'm pregnant."

"Really? Oh my God, Wendy!" said Mrs. Shultz. "Well, that's *great* news! Congratulations!"

"But I walked in on *my* husband, having sex with another fucking woman. In *our* bed."

"Oh God, Wendy, I'm sorry, honey," Mrs. Shultz sympathized. "Listen, take some time to yourself. I'm going to grab some coffee. You want?"

"No, Mrs. Shultz, I'll just head back to my office."

After Wendy went back to her office, her heartbreak and the melancholy mood turned into something much darker. She began to become angry and felt the need to do something to get back at Edward. But Wendy did not know what to do just yet *until* she looked in her handbag and pulled out a business card.

Let's go back to when Wendy shared a cab with her high school sweetheart, Mark. That night, she rejected the idea of coming up to Mark's hotel room. When he gave her his card and then made a move, Wendy threw his card right out of the cab when he got out. And *then,* Mark threw it right back into the cab with her. But when *Wendy* got out, she did not leave his card in the back seat. Instead, she took it with her and kept it all this time.

For Wendy, this is the *perfect* time to give Mark the call that he was expecting. So, she dialed his number and let it ring. But there was no answer. So, as it went to voicemail, Wendy left a message saying, "*Hey, Mark? Hi, um, it's Wendy. I was just calling to see if you were, I don't know, still hanging around the city? I know you said that you were only here for several weeks. So, um, if you're available to talk or have a drink or something, call me back. Okay, bye-bye.*"

Wendy's integrity was beginning to fail her. As much as she loves and adores Edward, her blood-thirsty *hunger* for revenge was too intense for her faithfulness. A few minutes went by as Wendy sat down at her desk. Then she received a text. Thinking it was Mark, she quickly opened her phone to check the message. But it was not Mark. It was Edward. In the text, Edward said,

"Wendy, please, come back to me. I know I completely mess things up. I know I have betrayed our family. But please, come back and just give me a chance to apologize and beg you for forgiveness."

But Wendy was not ready or *willing* to see Edward at that time. Wendy still wanted to give Edward a taste of his own adulterous medicine. Her phone then began to ring. It was Mark finally returning her call. As Wendy answered, she held the phone to her ear, listening as if she's receiving top-secret information. Mark told her to meet him at his hotel room, the same hotel that he stayed in, the night they ran into each other. Wendy said to him, "I'll be there later tonight." But Mark did not want to wait that long as he responded, "No, I want you here *right* now, baby."

Wendy had nothing else to do. EJ was still with his grandparents. So, to *her* knowledge, Wendy had nothing to lose. Wendy then grabbed her things and headed out of the building. She hailed down another cab and gave the cab driver the address to the Dominick hotel. As Wendy rides, she kept receiving messages from her husband, Edward. *This* time, she did not even bother looking at her screen. Wendy was on a mission to break her vows, just like Edward.

A few quick knocks on Mark's hotel door as Wendy finally arrived. Mark opens the door, looks at Wendy, and says, "I knew you would call sooner or later." As Mark leaned in for a kiss, Wendy hesitated and leaned away from Mark's attempt. Mark's eyebrows raised with the "*Okay, whatever*" facial expression, and then he closed the door.

"Can I have a drink," Wendy asked.

"Uh, *sure*, what would you like?" Mark spoke. "I have some vodka, Jack Daniels, and *of course*, white wine."

"White wine will do, thanks."

"Are you okay?" Mark expressed as he hands Wendy the wine. "You seem a little *jittery*."

"I'm just not having the best day today."

"Would you like to talk about it?"

"No."

"You sure? Because I think you wan—"

"NO! I don't want to talk about it, Eddie."

"Who the hell is *Eddie*?"

Wendy knew she made a mistake by calling *Mark* her husband's name. She then put down the white wine and poured herself half a glass of vodka. As Wendy was about to chug it back, she stopped herself quickly as she almost forgot the *fantastic* news of her pregnancy. So, no more alcohol for her. Wendy then immediately put down the drink and gathered her things together. She realized that she made another mistake in coming to Mark's hotel room.

"Wait a minute, where are you *going*?" Said Mark.

"I'm sorry, Mark. But I have to leave," Wendy responded.

"What the hell, Wendy, wait!"

Mark quickly ran over to the door to keep Wendy from leaving. As awkward as this moment was, he *demanded* an explanation from Wendy as he said, "Wendy, *this* is fucking insane. *First*, you call me, you ask me if we can see each other, then you come here, you *don't* want to talk, and now you're *leaving*? What the fuck is the matter with you?" Wendy gave Mark a look of defeat on her face. She then buried her head into his chest and began to sob. He comforted her as best as he could with the lack of knowledge as to *why* she is feeling this way.

"Okay, okay. Let's sit down and talk. Tell me what's going on," said Mark.

"My husband is having an affair. I caught him red-handed this morning, in our bed with another woman," Wendy responded.

"Oh, *I* see. And you decided to come *here* in hopes of returning the favor?"

Wendy went silent as she was at a loss for words. She no longer knew *what* she wanted. But not Mark; he knew *exactly* what he wanted. Mark then made a move, a *seductive* move, to help Wendy decide which way she would go. As Wendy sat down on the couch, Mark tried again as he leaned in for a kiss. And *this* time, there was *no* rejection from Wendy. It was a kiss that cut the cloth of betrayal. It was a *kiss* from her past, a *kiss* that was *bitter* but *better*. It has been over *ten years* since Wendy kissed another man. And Mark indeed gave Edward a run for his money.

Mark then planted another kiss, and another, and another. Wendy was entirely out of her comfort zone, *out* of her element. Yet, there was no denying of her enjoyment. She wanted this, and she needed this. As Wendy continued to engage with Mark, their fornication went from the couch to the floor, knocking over Wendy's handbag. As her handbag tumbled over, something fell out of it. It was the crinkled-up, pink origami Butterfly she received from the fortune-teller, Woomi Yumi, back in Tokyo.

Then, Mark turned Wendy over. Now, Wendy lying flat on her stomach, Mark began kissing on her shoulders, all the way down her backside. Wendy then looked over to her right to see that her handbag had taken a fall and saw the pink origami Butterfly on the floor as well. Then suddenly, there was a knock at the door. It was the maid saying, "Housekeeping, Hello?" Frustrated, Mark said, "Oh, *Christ*! What does it take to get some *fucking* privacy around here?"

As Mark answered the door, Wendy felt the strongest urge to grab that origami from the floor. The fortune-teller, Woomi Yumi, told Wendy that when the right time permits, that she should open it. So, Wendy crawled over to grab the origami. As she opened it, there was a special message *hidden* inside, written in Japanese. As Wendy reads, it said, "*Revenge is never the way to recovery. To seek revenge is to recycle the pain.*" Wendy then looked up from the origami and thought to herself, "*I lost my entire fucking mind. I have to get out of here, now.*" Wendy quickly got herself situation, put her shirt back on, and her shoes and coat.

As Mark came back, he was carrying fresh towels and washcloths given to him by the maid. He was hoping to finish what they started, but he clearly realized that was *not* about to happen. Wendy saw the instant disappointment in Mark's eyes. As she picked up her bag from the floor, she said to him, "Mark, I'm *terribly* sorry for all of this. I admit, there's a part of me that wants this *so* badly. But I can't let that part of me, get the *best* of me. I am a married woman. I took vows with my husband, and I can't break them. I have to go. Goodbye."

As soon as Wendy walked out of that hotel room, she walked a little taller that day. She faced temptation and dismissed it. There was something about that message in the origami that told her, "This is not the way." She listened to her inner spirit and spared any potential regrets. Wendy was proud of herself.

Wendy then made her way down the street as she was looking for another cab. As she waved one down, she received a call from her mother, Suzi. Suzi was asking her when she was coming to pick up EJ. But with all that has happened, Wendy had no idea of what she was going to do. She did not want to see Edward *nor* be in the apartment. So, Wendy asked her mother for a favor and asked if EJ could spend the night. Suzi said that was okay, but her concern for Wendy began to grow. But Wendy wanted to assure her mother that everything was fine. Even though *clearly*, everything was not.

While Wendy was riding in the cab, the only thing left for her to do is be with her ladies. She needed them now more than ever. Wendy sent them a group text. It was not a group text she wanted to send, but she had to tell them the truth. The text said,

"Hey ladies, I've missed you all. I arrived late last night. And now I'm in the city. But I'm afraid I have some bad news. And some rather good news too. The bad news is, I, too, have an "oink situation." But this time, it's not a false alarm. I caught Edward having sex with another woman in my bed. Can I see you all right now, please?"

Wendy's phone began to vibrate uncontrollably. Every three seconds, a text was coming in from the other four. "OMG, What? Wendy, baby, yes, I'll come to see you wherever," Zarin replied. "I am so sick of these fucking pig bastards. And yes, I'll come to see you, baby," Collette replied. "Un-fucking-believable! Name the place, babe," Monica responded. "Okay, hold on, ladies. Let's all meet at Silvianna's Spa and Treatment. She owes me a favor. Be there in an hour," Tomi replied.

Wendy then gave the cab driver a change of directions as she is now heading to the spa. As Wendy continues to ride, she began to think about the fortune-teller, Woomi Yumi. Then suddenly, Wendy had the most significant epiphany. She remembered clearly what her fortune was in Yumi's *secret* book of fortunes. It said, *"A new life is soon to come into yours. But in the moment of good fortune and blessings, forgiveness will be in great need."*

As Wendy thought about it, she could not believe how spot on the fortune was to her life. The *"new life"* that is soon to come into Wendy's is related to her pregnancy. And little did Wendy know that the new life was *literally* coming *into* her. But now, she also understands why the fortune said, *"forgiveness will be in great need."* The fortune was telling Wendy that eventually, her husband, Edward, *will* be in great need of her forgiveness.

Chapter 36

The truth has been delivered, the whole truth, and nothing but the truth. Wendy told it all to the other four as they sat there in *Silvianna's* Spa. She told them every detail about what happened in her apartment, how she went to her office and cried like a baby, and *then* how she went to meet with her high school sweetheart at his hotel and came *close* to sleeping with him. And Wendy *also* told them that she is pregnant.

"Okay, fuck *both* of them," said Collette. "Fuck Edward, fuck Mark. Our focus right now is the baby. So, *fuck* Mark."

"Well, no, I'm glad that she *didn't* fuck Mark," said Zarin.

"Wendy, Collette is right. The baby is the priority now. And I'm so proud of you for not giving in and sleeping with him," said Monica.

"So, *that* was the reason why you kept throwing up, huh?" Tomi spoke. "It wasn't the sushi after all."

"This is so nuts," said Zarin. "I mean, the same day you find out you're pregnant is the *same* day you catch your husband with his dick in another woman."

"Life is such a trip, ladies, *literally*," Tomi said as she sipped her champagne.

"I don't know what to do, ladies," Wendy spoke. "I haven't even told Eddie that I'm pregnant. I haven't even told my parents."

They all were in agreeance that Wendy was stuck between a rock and a hard place. Unfortunately, in this situation, they did not have much advice to share with Wendy. Wendy decided that she needed to clear her mind of all that was happening for at least an hour. Wendy then changed the subject and asked about Tomi's charity fashion show coming up on Friday.

Tomi made sure that the whole spa was closed for the five of them. She wanted to make sure that her girls were well taken care of and pampered. They were in their pearly white bathrobes and the fluffiest of slippers. Their faces were covered with aloe-green facemasks with slices of cucumbers covering their eyes. An hour of relaxation as they received one of the best massages a woman could ask for. Afterward, all five of them were sitting in these golden pedicure chairs, getting their toenails painted.

"Wendy, my love," said Tomi. "I hope this is giving you some type of serenity right now."

"Thank you, Tomi," Wendy responded. "It is, actually. And I truly appreciate all of you coming together at the drop of a hat for me."

"Of course," Collette spoke. "We'll always have your back, sis."

"That's right, *always,*" said Zarin.

"Yes, this is what we *do*. We love you, babe," Monica added.

"And I love you all too. I wouldn't have been able to go through this without you girls," Wendy said as she smiled.

About an hour goes by at *Silvianna's* Spa, and Wendy was ready to call it a day. All four of the ladies offered Wendy their home to stay for the night. Wendy thanked them for their offers, but she decided to head to Queens and be with EJ at her parents' house. So, they all said their goodbyes, gave each other hugs and kisses, and went their separate ways. As it was just Wendy and Tomi left, Wendy received yet *another* text from Edward that said,

"I promise I'll stop texting you, if only you just come and see me. *Please*?"

As they stood outside, Wendy showed Tomi the text message and asked her what she should do. Since Tomi was the oldest out of the five of them, she did have some advice for Wendy. "Wendy, my love, it's not like Edward is this guy you had a crush on, and it didn't work out. He's your *husband*, and yes, he broke your heart. He made a *terrible* decision in bringing another bitch under *your* roof, in *your* bed. But now, the stakes are high. You both have a child together, with another on the way, that he doesn't know about yet. So right now, you have to do what's best for your family. I know this will be hard for you but *talk* to him. I don't know what the fuck he's going to *say*, to earn your *forgiveness*. But there cannot be any healing without the truth," Tomi said.

At that moment, Wendy decided that she was willing to talk with Edward. "You're right, Tomi; he's still my husband. And even though I'm so heartbroken, I still love him. But you're right. I'm going to go see him," said Wendy. Tomi then responded with quickness, "Oh no, *fuck* that! You don't go to see *him*; he has to come to *you*. *You* decide the time and the place. He needs to earn *your* forgiveness. Not the other way around."

Wendy smiled and said to Tomi, "I guess I still have a lot to learn about life and this love and marriage shit." Tomi then kissed Wendy on both cheeks and headed into her limo. As Wendy gave it some thought, she knew of the perfect place to meet up with Edward. She then quickly walked up to the back seat of Tomi's limo and knocked on the window. As the window slid down, Tomi told Benjamin not to take off just yet.

"What's wrong?" said Tomi.

"Nothing; I was wondering if your limo driver could drop me off somewhere?" Wendy asked.

"Oh, of course, get in. Where to?"

"The place where Eddie and I had our first date and our first kiss."

"Oh, well, *where is that?*"

"It's a place that every New York City couple goes to, a place where love is bor—"

"*BITCH*, tell me where we're *going* so Benjamin can *take* you there!" Tomi hilariously shouted.

"Oh, God, I'm sorry. The Brooklyn Bridge. I have to go to the Brooklyn Bridge."

As Wendy hopped in the limo, Tomi told Benjamin that they are making a pit stop before heading home. As they ride to the Brooklyn Bridge, Wendy finally responded to Edward. She told him to meet her on the Manhattan end of the Brooklyn Bridge as soon as possible. He quickly responded and told her he would be there.

Fifteen minutes later, Wendy had arrived near the Brooklyn bridge. As she got out of the limo, Tomi said to her, "Good luck, my love. I hope everything works out between you guys." Tomi then kissed Wendy on her forehead and drove off. As Wendy began walking, she closed up her coat as the temperature dropped about a couple of degrees. But still, it was a fabulous, clear night to walk the bridge.

As Wendy made it to the tower on the Manhattan side, she sat down on the bench and waited for Edward to show up. For what it was worth, the scenery was rather beautiful. Very romantic indeed. Perhaps that is why it was the perfect place for their first date and their first kiss. Even looking at it through the bridge's steel cables, the

Manhattan skyline never looked so stunning from that angle. One World Trade Center was just *glowing* in the night sky. The city lights, the cars, one by one, driving through the Brooklyn Bridge. This was New York City at its best.

Ten minutes later, Wendy sees someone coming her way. The closer he came, the better she saw his face. It was a very familiar face; it was Edward. "Hey… Thank you for meeting with me," Edward said. As Wendy looked at Edward, she stood up from the bench, keeping a decent distance from him. "Yea, so, before you start pouring your heart out, I have something to tell you. Before I caught you *fucking* another woman in *my* bed, in *my* home. I went to the doctor. I'm pregnant, Eddie; we're having another child. And you picked the *"perfect"* time to try to impregnate another woman," Wendy spoke.

"You're, wait… You're *pregnant?*"

"Yes, Eddie, I'm pregnant. So where do we go from here?"

Edward was stunned by such loaded news. He had no way to prepare himself, nor did he have a response for what Wendy just told him. Knowing now that his family will grow into four, Edward had to make things right with Wendy. His thoughts and his words were not entirely in sync. But he gave it his all.

Edward took a deep breath and said to her, "Wendy, remember when we exchanged our vows? The part where it says, *"For better or for worse?"* What you saw today, that was the worst of me. I made the worst mistake of my life by betraying you. I betrayed your trust and your love for me. And if I could apologize to you a million times in one lifetime, I would do that. And I know it would still not be enough. But I am truly, *very* sorry. I know I don't deserve any forgiveness right now. But if you ever find it in your heart, to forgive me; just please, *please* forgive me."

Wendy just stood there with tears falling from her eyes. Edward even fell to his knees as he begged her for forgiveness. Strangers were walking by, but it did not matter. It was like a scene right out of a movie. But Wendy knew that *this* was reality. And she was more of a realist.

Wendy then looked up to the sky. Up there, she saw the moon, fuller and brighter than she has seen it in a long time. As she looked, she thought about the fortune, she thought about the baby, she thought about everything that could go wrong *if* she accepts Edward's apology and forgives him. Wendy asked herself, "What if he cheats on me again? What if I have this child, he then has *another* affair and leaves me with two kids? What if he's no longer *in* love with me anymore?"

"Wendy, *please*, say something to me," said Edward.

"Oh Eddie, stand up," Wendy said.

Wendy then took one deep breath, exhaled, and said to Edward, "Do you remember our first date? We both were low on money, so we didn't even plan something fancy. We just had a slice of pizza, some ice cream and then walked here, on the Brooklyn Bridge. You told me something that I never forgot. *You said, "If we were ever to be married, and I cheat on you. That is the day that you'd know I've fallen out of love with you. But that would never happen."* Is that what happened, Eddie? Did you fall *out* of love with me?"

Edward just looked at her, stuck in the purgatory of love and *being in love.* Wendy then continued by saying, "Just look down the *road*, Eddie. The two of us, raising our two children, yet we're not in love with each other. We're just co-parenting. Is that going to be us in ten years? Am I going to be another single mom raising her kids?" Edward then held her as she began to lose control emotionally.

"No, baby, *no*," said Edward. "I did *not* fall out of love with you."

"Eddie, how could I ever *trust* you again?" Wendy cried.

"Don't ask that; just believe me. Believe that you have seen the worst of me in this marriage. And I promise you, I *promise* you that I will *never* betray you again."

Edward then pulled Wendy to him as she collapsed in his arms while his chest became the firm pillow for her tears. Edward himself cried a storm as tears fell on top of her head. The love was still there. But it has taken a tormented turn for them. Wendy, however, did not mention a word to Edward about her encounter with Mark. But then again, why would she?

Wendy got her emotions together as she wanted to show Edward something on the bridge, which has been there since their first date. It was a rusted-up lock, with the initials of their first names and their first date marked on it. Wendy remembered the exact spot where she left it, ten years ago. And it was still there.

"Oh my God, Wendy," Edward spoke. "I can't believe it's still *here*."

"June 8, 2013, to be exact," said Wendy. "We were so young."

"Remember on our wedding day? When your father made the "*Just Married*" sign on the back of the car?"

"Oh my God, yes," Wendy chuckled. "He spelled it "*Just Marryed.*" He was terrible at spelling."

"Yea, people kept laughing at us as we drove down the street."

"Hey… Look!" Wendy said. "Look at the lock. I never realized that the initials of our *first* names spell "WE.""

"Wow, it does. Maybe that's a sign."

"A sign for what, Eddie?"

"A sign that says "WE" belong together."

"More like a sign that says "WE" have a dilemma, and *we* have to fix this."

Forgiveness, love, and betrayal. Three things that Wendy must juggle now. As Edward and Wendy walked back into Manhattan, she told Edward that it would take time for her to accept his apology and fully forgive him. Wendy also mentioned that she would *not* be returning to their apartment until he gets rid of that bed. Wendy did not care how much it would cost; she refused to sleep in the same bed that Edward has now contaminated with another woman. Wendy then told Edward that the only way their marriage can be saved is by sitting down with a marriage counselor to discuss their dilemma. But how does one forgive who they love once that person has betrayed them? Of course, it is possible. But the *question* is, is it worth it?

Chapter 37

Today is an extravagant day. Not only is it Friday and its payday, but it is the day of the grand opening of *Orell Llero* on Fifth Avenue. It is *also* the day of the charity fashion show, *and* it is the "*Queen of New York*," Tomi's birthday. Tomi is now a forty-four-year-old, self-made billionaire. This is now Tomi's 316th store, as she has stores scattered all around the world. She would have had a storefront in Manhattan years ago. But she wanted Thomas to design it. So, Tomi waited for the perfect space to be available, and Thomas created a state-of-the-art store. And from the looks of the store, it was well worth the wait.

Right now, Tomi is standing in front of the grand opening of her new *Orell Llero* storefront. She made sure she scheduled the event at noon. That way, the other four ladies could attend the event during their lunch hour. Thomas was there, as well as Carmelo and others who were in attendance. Some were fans of Tomi, paparazzi, the press, onlookers recording with their phones, as well as security and store employees. Right before Tomi was about to make her brief speech, Monica walked up to the store. Tomi was so excited and happy to see Monica there.

"Oh, *there's* my girl," said Tomi. "Thank you for coming, my love."

"Of *course*," Monica spoke. "I wouldn't have missed this; where's Coco and them?"

"I talked to Coco, and she's on her way. Zarin and Wendy are coming together."

Tomi was holding off on her speech for as long as she could. She wanted to wait for all four of them to be there. But she had to proceed. As Tomi held the microphone, she said, "First, can you just give yourselves a round of applause for being here on this wonderful day?" A brief pause as the crowd begins to applaud.

"WE LOVE YOU, TOMI!" projected by an entourage of women. "I love you more, thank you! Thank you, and welcome to the grand opening of my 316th *Orell Llero* storefront, *right here*, on Fifth Avenue. I know it's cold out here, but hey, it's winter season, yes? But not to worry, because we have the *hottest* selling winter coats in the *world*. Our sales have skyrocketed to over *three hundred* percent. Now, one may say that *I* could take all the credit for that, *especially* since my little exotic *one-woman show* a couple of weeks ago… Oh, that rhymed." The crowd then gave off a round of laughter.

Tomi then continued with her speech and said, *"However,* I *can't* take all of the credit. I have the most *outstanding* sales and marketing team. They are *brilliant* masterminds. They know how to get my brand out there in the world. As of today, our social media platforms have accumulated over 150 *million* followers. Not that any of you probably *care* about that."

The crowd began to laugh at Tomi's last comment. Tomi became even more charged when she saw Zarin, Wendy, and Coco show up next to Monica. The look on Tomi's face was of pure gratitude. She almost looked as if tears were about to fall down her eyes.

As Tomi looked at them, she had this to say, "Ladies and gentlemen, before I cut this ribbon, let me just say this one last thing. I think it's already known that I am a *multi*-billionaire, yes? Well, excuse my language, but all the money in the *world* doesn't mean a *Goddamn* thing if you don't have *real friends* by your side. Friends who love you and have your back, no matter what. Without friends, without family, this money, this success, none of this would put happiness in my heart. And I'm just very fortunate to have those real friends, and I love them dearly."

Tomi's words of sincere gratitude were felt by the other four. Collette was the one who sparked another round of applause. Now, it was time for Tomi to cut that ribbon. As Tomi grabbed the golden scissors, she said this, in honor of her late grandfather, *Orell Llero,*

"*Nonno, this one's for you.*" Tomi then gave one quick snip of the scissors, and the store was officially opened.

But before Tomi let anyone in, she wanted to take group pictures with her ladies. They all came together and had their Kodak moment. As the cameras were flashing, Monica looked out in the crowd and saw some *very* familiar faces. It was the faces of the two employees and the manager that she had the altercation with at the luxury store. Monica then tapped Tomi on her shoulder and whispered in her ear, saying, "Remember the employees and manager from the store? They're right over there." Tomi looked over to where they were standing and responded, saying, "Oh *yes*, I see them. Let's go over there and have a *chat*."

Tomi and Monica then made their way towards the two employees and Edgar, the luxury store manager. As Tomi approached Edgar, they exchanged a few words.

"Well, *well*, Edgar, *it's been* a while," said Tomi.

"Hi, Mrs. Belacone, *wow*, congratulations!" Edgar responded.

"You're too kind. So, listen, I would like to *reintroduce* you to *my friend,* Monica. It seems that you gave her some problems in your store the other day: you and your two *rude* employees.

As Edgar looked at Monica, he *instantly* knew who she was and remembered the altercation. The two employees had a look on their faces that said, "Boy, did we fuck up." Edgar, the manager, did not know what to say at that moment. So, to finish them off, Tomi said, "I *would* say next time, but since *this* bitch right *here* has just opened her new store, right across from *your* establishment, there won't *be* a next time for you. But I *will* say this. If *you* or your shitty-ass employees *ever* disrespect one of my friends again, I will personally see to it that your business *ceases* to fucking exist. Have I made myself *exclusively* clear?"

Edgar, the manager, just shook his head in fear and said, "Yes, ma'am. That, that won't ever happen again. And I'm sorry again, miss, for the trouble we caused you in our store the other day." Standing there with a smile of victory on her face, Monica said to Edgar, "You just never know *who* knows who, don't you?" As Tomi and Monica walked away from Edgar and the two employees, they gave each other a fist pound.

"Mission accomplished, my sister," Tomi smiled.

"*Hell yea, damn,* that felt good. Did you see their faces?" Monica responded.

"Oh, I *live* for that, Nica. Fear in this business is *always* stronger than love.

"So, should I still file that lawsuit on them?"

"Oh, *fuck* yeah! I just *love* wiping out the competition."

"Oh, you really are *Cruella*."

"*Yes* bitch, *Cruella* and *proud*."

Later on that evening, the ladies were all in attendance at Tomi's charity fashion show. Movie stars, rock stars, fashion elite, they were all around. They were some of the very generous donors who helped raised $29 million to help with the conflicting issues of climate change. Tomi herself donated an additional $11 million.

As guests gathered around the runway, the V.I.P. section had seats already reserved. Tomi and the other four were sitting right in the front. The interior of the runway was all white, and the design was shaped like the lowercase letter "i." The runway stretched about thirty feet long, and at the very end, there was a glass bridge connecting the circular platform that represented the *dot* for the lowercase "i."

When it comes to fashion shows, Tomi is an avid minimalist. She wants the audience to focus *solely* on the merchandise the models are presenting. There was a total of thirty-five models in the back, waiting to hit the runway. Twenty-five were female, five were male (including Brad Versace, a.k.a. Brad with the good hair), and the remaining five were non-binary. Tomi has always been an innovator who did things *her* way. She loves to break the rules in this industry. And she always wanted to give people fair opportunities. It did not matter if you were black, white, blue, orange, or red. Regardless of people's sexual orientation or gender identity, Tomi *never* discriminated. Unless if you were short. Perhaps that is why Tomi stays on top.

Before the show started, Tomi's assistant, Carmelo, came upon the runway to introduce Tomi. As Tomi came out from backstage, she received a standing ovation. Then, Carmelo surprised her when he made the entire audience sing *"Happy Birthday"* to her. That touched

Tomi so much. She then hugged and kissed Carmelo, and he handed her the microphone. As Carmelo took his seat, Tomi began to make her speech.

"Good evening to all of you. And thank you for that *sweet* "*Happy Birthday*" song. Melo, I'm going to *get* you later. But no, tonight is a *very s*pecial night. It is a night of "challenge." A challenge that goes *beyond* our social issues, beyond black and white, beyond religion, and beyond the challenges of our relationships with people. *This* is a *global* challenge. A challenge that requires *all* people, the entire *human* race to come together to help stabilize our environment and *prevent* further damage to our *only planet*. As far as the only planet *we* can breathe and live on. Tonight, in this space, you all have shown up and showed *OUT*! Since October of last year, we have raised over 29 *million dollars*. Yes! Give yourselves a round of applause." Tomi waited for everyone to settle down before she continued.

After the cheery applause, Tomi continued, "You have all done so well. I thank you for caring. And to let you know, *all* the money that we've raised will be going directly to my business partners who run their non-for-profit company "*Green and Blue Loves You.*" They've traveled worldwide to find *many* resources to help create a better future for our world and the generations to come. Okay, So, I've talked enough. Let's bring out these gorgeous, sexy, and handsome models to show off my *new* and *exclusive* collection. I leave you all with this quote that my mother once said, "If the *climate* can change, so can we." Thank you so much, and enjoy the show."

Another round of applause as the show was about to begin. As Tomi made her way down the stairs to her front-row seat, she and Monica began to have a little chit-chat.

"Nice batch of words, my sistah," said Monica.

"Oh, thanks, babe, I only had to rewrite it about fifty *fucking* times," Tomi responded humorously.

"It was *perfect*. I couldn't have done a better job."

"You're too kind. I'm just glad that so many people showed up. And I'm *so* happy that things are back to *some* social norm. That COVID-19 shit kicked our *asses*."

"Oh God, yes. And I'm glad we don't have to wear those damn facemask anymore."

"*That* was a pain in the ass. My makeup was *always* smudged. And *then,* people would catch an attitude if you took it off in public. I'm like, "What the *fuck*," people acted like I took off my *fucking bra*."

"Right; oh, *girl*, you are *crazy*," Monica laughed. "By the way, thank you so much for this afternoon. I feel so much better."

"You know what Nica, thank *you*. You showed me how I could *use* my privilege *against* racist pricks like those at that store. We still have such a long way to go, my love. Not just in *this* country, but in this *world*."

"You got that right. But you're one of the good ones, whose making that change. And I'm just very blessed to have you as my friend. As my sister. I love you, Tomi."

"*Aww*, I love you more, Nica," Tomi said as she hugged Monica.

The lights over the audience have dimmed, and the show has begun. They are using tracks from the iconic album, "*808s and Heartbreak*," from the genius mind of Kanye West as theme music. The sound of heavy drums began to play, as the first song is "*Love Lockdown.*"

The first model came out. It was a female model wearing a single-shoulder cream dress. The dress was covering her left shoulder, showing lots of skin all the way down. It was a piece that Tomi's grandfather, Orell Llero, sketched. People were very attentive, flashing cameras from every direction. The second model to come out was a shirtless male model. It was Tomi's new protégé, Brad Versace, a.k.a. Brad with the good hair. He was sporting the new mauve jeans with mauve color sneakers from the exclusive *Orell Llero* collection. As Brad went down the runway, Carmelo couldn't bear to look at him. He rolled his eyes in disgust and looked away.

"Melo, *seriously*?" said Tomi. "You're *really* going to be shady like that?"

"*Yes*, Ms. Bellas," said Carmelo. "He's a male ho and a bastard."

"A very *fine* male ho bastard," Tomi laughed.

"Is he off of the runway yet?"

"Yes, Melo, relax."

Tomi, Monica, Collette, Zarin, and Wendy were all wearing pieces from the new *Orell Llero* collection. This night, you couldn't tell them anything. They were styling and profiling, dressed to impressed, showing off the best of them, and hiding the rest of them.

And even though Wendy is going through what she is going through, she could not help but smile as she was flabbergasted by the different outfits displayed on the runway. Wendy was making visual notes of which pieces she wanted for herself.

As the show was going on, Tomi's phone was vibrating. It was a phone call from her mother's nursing home. At first, Tomi was startled and terrified to answer it. She thought it was going to be *that* call. She then got up from her seat and headed backstage. Before answering, Tomi took a deep breath, exhaled, and then answered.

"He— Hello?" Tomi said.

"Tomi, hi my daughter, it's momma," said Arianna.

"Oh, my God, *Momma*," Tomi sighed. "Hi momma, I thought I was getting a *different* phone call."

"Oh, no, I'm not dead yet, darling," Her mother said humorously. "I called to wish my baby girl a happy birthday. I'm *so* proud of you and the successful woman that you have become. Your grandfather would be over the moon proud of you as well."

"Oh, momma," Tomi cried. "Thank you so much. This birthday is by far my favorite."

"You know, Tommy came to visit me earlier today."

"I did not *know* that. He didn't say anything to me."

"Yea, well, I gave him something to give to you. I hope you hold on to it forever."

"Oh… What is it?"

"It's my goodbye letter, baby."

"Okay, Momma, *now* you're talking crazy. I will see you first thing Monday morning, on *your* birthday, okay? I love you so, very much."

"Okay, my dear, and I love you more, Tomi. I love you; I love you."

As Tomi hung up her phone, she began to shake her head in disbelief and denial of what her mother was saying. She then shook it off and headed back to her seat. As Tomi hit the corner, she encountered two men in a secluded area backstage, making out. As the two men realized Tomi spotted them, they separated, acting as if they were not doing anything. And once Tomi saw *exactly* who they were, she laughed hysterically as it was Carmelo and Brad, tonguing each other down.

"MELO! WOW, *SERIOUSLY?*" Tomi shouted. "You were *just* calling Brad a ho, and *now* you're locking lips with him?"

"No, no, no; Ms. Bellas, see, what *happened* was—"

"Save it, Melo! Melo, baby, I'm not judging. Brad is *fine as fuck*. *Rekindle* that love, baby, but *after* the show, okay? Let's go!"

The rest of the show was a huge extravaganza. Exotic and exquisite pieces, one right after the other. It was a success, and Tomi was proud of the results. As people came to congratulate her on a job well done, all of the moving around made Tomi grow fatigued and drained. She was ready to head home. As Tomi got the rest of the ladies together, she said to them, "Girls, I can't thank you enough for all your love and support today. Besides my momma and Tommy, I wouldn't want to spend my birthday with anyone else besides you ladies. I love you all *so* much." As all of them gaged and sighed, they went in for a group hug. It was a *true* Kodak moment. One of the photographers caught noticed of their interaction and made his way towards them. "Ladies, look this way!" said the photographer. And they did, as they were glammed up from head to toe.

"You ladies look *great*," said the photographer. "Are any of you single?"

"No, my love," said Tomi. "Look at the ring on our fingers. We're *all* married women."

"Oh, excuse *me*," the photographer spoke. "Well, hey, all of you pose *just* like that. Hold your wedding rings up *just like that*."

As the five of them posed with their hands up, showing off their wedding rings, the photographer did a countdown. "Okay, on the count of 3, I want you ladies to say, *"Ring Pack*!" One, two, *three*, *"RING PACK!"* An ensemble of *"Ring Pack"* was said by the five of them as the picture was taken.

"Um, *Ring Pack*?" Zarin said to the photographer.

"Yea, you know, the *Rat Pack*, the *Brat Pack*, the *Ring Pack*? Get it?

"Oh… *Sure*," Zarin responded confusingly.

The five of them then said their goodnights and began to part ways as they wine down for the weekend. Another week down for these women. Now it's time for them to head home and be with their husbands and children, except for Wendy, as she heads back to her parents' house in Queens. Tomi had to stay behind a little longer and finish her rounds of greetings and praises. A night she will never forget—a birthday for the history books.

Chapter 38

Tomi's phone is ringing at the break of dawn. It is Sunday morning; she and Thomas are fast asleep at their home in Southampton. It is only a quarter to six in the morning, and the sun has barely risen. But her phone is ringing. Tomi begins to move around, waking herself up. As she heard her phone ringing, she reached for it on the nightstand. A hazy vision in her eyes as she was ripped from her sleep and cannot see the caller ID as clearly. So, Tomi just answers and says, "Hello?" As Tomi listened, her mood became cold and blue, just like their bedroom. Thomas began to wake up himself as he felt Tomi moving around. He looked and saw Tomi sitting on the side of the bed with the phone to her ear. He heard Tomi's broken voice as she said, "Okay, okay, I will. Thank you so much. Bye-bye." Thomas crawled closer to Tomi on the edge of the bed and asked her, "What's wrong?" As Tomi lifted her head to the ceiling with falling tears down the side of her face, she quietly said these two words, "She's gone."

"*Who's* gone?" said Thomas. "*Arianna*? Your *mother*?"

"Yes, she's… She's *gone*, Tommy," Tomi cried. "She's gone."

"Oh, dear God," Thomas said, holding her. "Oh baby, I'm *so* sorry, I'm sorry, I'm sorry, I'm sorry."

"I was *just* going to see her tomorrow for her 81st birthday. I *knew* I should have gone to see her yesterday."

"Oh baby, I'm *so* sorry," Thomas cried. "Listen, I'm going to take care of *everything*, okay? Don't move; I'll be right back."

Tomi just sat there with a thousand thoughts running through her mind. A part of Tomi was happy that her mother stuck around long enough for *her* birthday. But another part of Tomi was heartbroken, as her mother didn't stick around for her own. *All* the memories she shared with her mother were flashing in her mind, one by one. Tomi's *best* friend, the love of her life, has left her now. Tomi couldn't hold it in anymore. Her tears began to overpower her face, and she broke down. She cried and cried and *cried*. She was then able to collect herself for one minute. But all Tomi could say in that one moment was, "*fuck* cancer."

The following Saturday, Tomi held a memorial service for her mother. It was Arianna's lifelong wish that she did *not* have a funeral service.

She agreed to a memorial service as long as everyone wears *nothing* but white. Arianna also told Tomi that she wanted to be cremated and have her ashes scattered on any beach of Tomi's choice.

The memorial service was held at Tomi's new storefront, *Orell Llero,* on Fifth Avenue. It was spacious enough to fit at least 450 people, and there were three different tiers. Tomi was pleased with the way the store was decorated for the memorial service. Wendy used her creativity as a wedding planner and helped with the decorative vision. There were pictures of Tomi's mother around the entire store; photos of when Arianna was very young, pictures of her and Tomi together, and pictures of Arianna with all three of her kids. Tomi hired the photographer who took the pictures at the fashion show. He blew up the images of Tomi's mother to life-size and had them placed on easels.

Tomi was hanging in there as best as she could until she saw her girls come in. Wendy, Zarin, Monica, and Collette were *all* dressed in white. As Tomi saw them, it was like she saw her four angels. She walked to them with falling tears on her face. They all gathered around her for the longest group hug Tomi ever received. Sobbing and sorrow were all that came from them.

"We're so sorry, baby," said Collette.

"I just wasn't ready," Tomi cried. "I wasn't ready to say goodbye."

"Sammy is on his way now," said Monica. "He has his trumpet with him."

"Okay, thank you guys so much for being here," said Tomi.

As more people came to pay their respects, the ladies' husbands had arrived. Thomas was already in attendance, as was Carmelo. Then Neal arrived to pay his respects to Tomi. A little after Neal arrived, Sammy came through with his trumpet, ready to play a song in tribute to Tomi's mother. Martin then arrived with some flowers for Tomi. He walked to her and gave her a kiss and hug as he also paid his respects. And lastly, Edward, Wendy's husband, had arrived.

"Hi Tomi," said Edward. "I'm so sorry for your loss."

"Thank you, Edward," Tomi responded.

"Is uh, is Wendy already here?"

"She is, and Edward, please, don't ever hurt my girl again."

"I promise you; I won't ever betray her again."

"Make that promise to *her*, Edward. Make that promise to your kids."

"You're right… I will, Tomi."

As the memorial service reached its conclusion, an open microphone was available for anyone who had a story to share about Tomi's mother, Arianna. Tomi's older brother, Frankie, was the first to speak about his mother. He talked about his childhood and how his mother was *full* of life and adventure. Frankie told everyone that his mother saw life as the *ultimate* gift, and she never wasted a minute of it. As Frankie finished *his* piece, Tomi's *oldest* brother, Pauly, went up to make a speech. As Pauly got up and spoke, he literally said *only* this, "My mother was a hell of a woman. She had a great life with a great family. Uh… This isn't really my thing, this *speaking* stuff. But uh, she will be missed. Thanks." At that moment, all Tomi could think of in her mind about Pauly was, "*Oh, go to hell, you fucking prick.*"

A few more went up to speak. Afterward, Tomi went up to say her part. As Tomi got up on the platform, she cleared her throat and said, "We meet again, this time under different circumstances. My mother and I were very close. Not only was I her baby, but I was her one and only daughter. We kept no secrets from each other. She told me that after she had Frankie, that she didn't want any more children. But then *I* came along. She planned to have an abortion. But she told me that something inside her told her to *keep this* baby. So, she did; she decided to have me, and I ended up being her baby girl. She once said to me that perhaps it was my *grandfather's* spirit telling her to keep me. I'm *so* glad she listened to him because we ended up having the *greatest* mother-daughter relationship any two women could *ever* have. We even smoked pot together. I didn't *like* it. But she would just say, "*Welp, more trees for ME!*"

Everyone shared a good laugh on that one. Then Tomi continued and said, "We had the greatest bond. We *truly* did." As Tomi looked up, she saw one of the pictures hanging up on the second level. It was a picture of Tomi at eleven years old, hugging her mother at Venice Beach. As Tomi kept looking at that picture, she paused, and her eyes became watery. She then wiped her eyes and finished up her speech. "Sorry… Um, as we all know, we truly only have *one* mother in our lives. And I'm just glad that I not only *had* a mother, but *we* had a *great* relationship. And I'm *so* happy that the last thing we said to each other was, "*I Love You.*" And momma, wherever you are, if you're listening, I'm going to miss you *so much*. And I love you *forever.*"

As Tomi stepped down from the platform, she went over to hug Wendy. Collette then walked over to rub Tomi's back and comfort her while Zarin and Monica stood close by. Thomas then introduced Monica's husband, Sammy, as he plays a song called "*I waited for you,*" which was one of Arianna's favorite songs by Chet baker. And my God, Sammy played that piece *so* beautifully. Sammy even brought two of his band members to collaborate with: one playing the flute and the other on the keyboard. All five of the ladies stood there, holding each other as they listened to Sammy play an incredible version of the song. Sammy and his bandmates put a lot of love into that space.

As Tomi stood there, she closed her eyes, letting the music fill her body up with serenity and peace. *Peace* in knowing that her mother is no longer in pain, no longer fighting a battle. And that she's resting peacefully now. Tomi then opened her eyes, looking at more of the pictures that surrounded her. The more pictures Tomi saw, the bigger the smile she made on her face. At that moment, Tomi realized that *all* the memories she shared with her mother were special ones, memories that are instilled in her mind forever. As Tomi reminisced about her mother, she thought about every time her mother would say, "*Kiss me twice, so I know you mean it.*" That made Tomi chuckle, and then it made her a little emotional. But in that split second, Tomi remembered what her mother said to her. *"When I leave, I don't ever want you to give up on laughter. Whenever you have a great laugh, and then I pop up in your mind at that exact moment, don't let my demise be the dead-end to your laughter. Because when I come to your mind, that just means that I'm laughing right along with you."*

As Sammy and his bandmates finished that beautiful song, a massive round of applause came from all three levels. Tomi then looked at Sammy, blew him a kiss, and pantomimed, saying, "Thank you!" And Sammy blew a kiss right back at her.

Later that night, Tomi and her husband Thomas went back to their home in Southampton. Tomi walked out to the beach with a burgundy marble urn, carrying half of her mother's ashes. As Tomi got close to the ocean water, she opened the urn and began to spread her mother's ashes onto the wet sand. She did that over and over until the urn was empty. Tomi then took a minute as she looked down at the sand, watching the ocean water cover her feet. She then looked straight ahead at the dark ocean with a sprinkle of stars in the sky. As Tomi was rubbing the urn, she began to think about her mother.

A few moments later, Tomi turned around to find Thomas walking towards her. As she looks at him, with the wind blowing her brown hair in front of her face, Thomas said to her, "Never have I seen *anyone* more beautiful." Thomas then kissed her, *twice* and hugged her from behind as they stared out at the dark ocean.

"How are you, baby?" Thomas said.

"I'm okay, Tommy," said Tomi. "I'm okay right now."

"You're thinking about her?"

"Of *course*, I am."

"And what is she saying to you?"

"Keep breathing. Keep smiling. Keep living."

"Yea, that's her talking to you for sure."

As Thomas let Tomi go, he then pulled something out of his pocket. It was an envelope with Tomi's name on it. Thomas said, "Your mother wanted you to have this letter. I went to visit her the other day. She made me swear not to look at it, so I didn't."

"Can you hold the urn, baby?" Tomi asked.

"Of course," said Thomas.

As Tomi took the envelope, it said on the front, "*For my baby girl, Tomi.*" Tomi then opened it. Inside was a folded piece of paper. As Tomi slowly unfolded it, it was the sweetest, most innocent, elementary letter she had ever received. Teardrops began to fall straight down on the letter as Tomi let it all out. Tomi knew that her mother was too weak to write a full letter. But when she opened this letter and saw this, she saw her mother. Minimalistic, straight to the point, and with conviction. This was a letter that Tomi would cherish for the rest of her life.

For My Baby girl
To my Tom!

Dear Tomi,

I ♡ U

Forever Love.
xoxo momma

Chapter 39

A week has gone by since the memorial service for Tomi's mother. Wendy and Edward have made different living arrangements ever since his affair. Wendy and EJ stay in Queens with her parents, while Edward stays in their apartment in Manhattan. It has been somewhat convenient for Wendy because her office is in Queens, literally a fifteen-minute drive from her parents' house. And Wendy's parents have been such a great help with EJ and with taking him to school.

Wendy and Edward are now waiting in the lobby of a marriage counselor, Dr. Bernadette Curry, Ph.D. in Psychology, and sociology, recommended by Wendy's boss, Mrs. Shultz. This session is their first appointment. Unfortunately, Wendy and Edward are sitting with an empty seat in between each other. As they wait, Edward begins to speak to try and break the ice between them.

"Are you a little nervous?" Edward asked.

"Yes, I am," said Wendy. "I've never had to do something like this before."

"Yea, I know. I screwed things up in our family."

"*I'd* say so," Wendy confirmed. "Hopefully, you'll tell me why once we go in."

Another six minutes go by, Dr. Bernadette Curry finally comes out of her office. Dr. Curry, a Caucasian woman in her mid-fifties. She had a short, blonde edgy haircut with very stylish black glasses. And she had one of the deepest cleft chins you would ever see. As Dr. Curry saw Wendy and Edward, she walked to them and introduced herself.

"Hi, I'm Dr. Bernadette Curry," said Dr. Curry. "You must be Wendy and Edward, yes?"

"Yes, hi, it's nice to meet you," Wendy spoke.

"Nice to meet you too. Why don't we step inside my office."

As Wendy walked in, she saw Dr. Curry's twelve-foot-tall bookshelf that stretched across the wall. She grew curious to Dr.

Curry's knowledge and wondered how many of these books she read and was not hesitant to ask.

"Dr. Curry," said Wendy. "Exactly how many of these books have you read?"

"Would you believe me if I said, "all of them?" Dr. Curry responded.

"I surely would *not*. But I would guess you read some."

"Well, *truthfully*, I read about eighty percent of those books. A dozen of them I wrote myself."

"I'm so sorry," said Edward. "But can we get started? I'm kind of under the gun today."

"Oh, um, yes, we sure can," Dr. Curry responded.

"There's no need to be rude, Eddie," said Wendy.

"No, no; that's fine. Please, take a seat on the couch."

As Edward went to sit on the right end of the three-seated couch, Wendy sat on the left end, leaving space between themselves, just as they did in the waiting room. Dr. Curry noticed the tension between them instantly. She sensed that whatever they were currently going through could not be a slap on the wrist solution. Dr. Curry knew that this was a potential marriage-ending situation. As Wendy and Edward sat there on the couch, Dr. Curry sat in a single chair, facing them. She took a good look at the two of them before she spoke. As Dr. Curry adjusted her glasses, she said, "So, I'm not even going to waste your time. I will just cut right to the chase and asked, "Who is the one having an affair?" Wendy, like a tattle-telling child, immediately pointed her finger at Edward.

Edward looked at Wendy, and then he looked at Dr. Curry. As he did not have any comeback for that, he simply confessed to Dr. Curry, "It was me; *I* stepped out and slept with another woman. As Dr. Curry listened to Edward's story, she began to make more eye contact with Wendy. She observed Wendy's body language. Dr. Curry has been doing this for so long that she knows when a spouse is *hiding* something from the other spouse. She knew that Wendy was withholding information.

"Hold that thought, Edward. Let's go to you now, Wendy," said Dr. Curry.

"*Me?*" Wendy responded.

"Yes, Wendy. You seemed to have been very uncomfortable while Edward was speaking."

"Well, *yea*, hearing him talk about sleeping with another woman is *very* uncomfortable for me, Dr. Curry."

"I understand that. But that's not what I'm referring to. Is there something that *you* would like to share with Edward?"

"Like what?"

"*Like*, has there ever been a time where *you* stepped out on Edward?"

"Excuse me?"

"Have you ever *cheated* on Edward?"

"I can't believe you're even asking me that question."

As Dr. Curry adjusted her glasses once again, she realized that she had to explain to Wendy her approach as a marriage counselor. Dr. Curry said, "So, perhaps I wasn't *clear* in the beginning. I do *not* approach my work as a side chooser. I look at marriages from *both* sides. I want to know the husband's side of the story, and I want to know the wife's side of the story. I am *not* someone who plays the "gang up on the husband" game. I need to know the truth from both parties. If there is something that you need to say to Edward, now is the *perfect* time and *place* to share it with him. So, I will ask you *again*, Wendy, have *you* ever cheated on Edward?"

Wendy sat there on that couch in dead silence. She looked at Dr. Curry with a blossoming mask of guilt on her face. Wendy then looked at Edward, who was already grilling her. Her silence alone was slowly confirming her infidelity. As Wendy looked down, Dr. Curry said to her, "Wendy, I need you to look up and tell the truth. Look at your husband and tell the truth." As Wendy then looked at Edward, her eyes began to water up, as did his because he already knew her answer would break his heart.

As Wendy opened her mouth to speak, she said, "A few weeks ago, on a late night, I ran into my high school sweetheart, Mark. We haven't seen each other since we left for college. We shared a cab ride that night. As we arrived at his hotel, he invited me up to his room. I told him that I'm married. But that didn't stop him from giving me that invitation. He then gave me his card, and I kept it."

Edward did not like what he was hearing, *nor* did he like where this story was going. Dr. Curry then told Wendy to continue with her story. As Wendy continued, her mood was getting darker. She continued saying, "The day I caught Eddie in bed with that woman, I was *so* fucking angry. I threw *anything* I could get my hands on at the both of them. I just couldn't believe that he would bring some bitch to *my* home, where I am raising *our* son. I'm like, "Why, *why* would he do that to me?" So, I wasn't going to be that wife who just sits there and cry a river. I wanted some payback; *I* wanted *revenge.* So, I called Mark, and I told him that I wanted to see him that day." As Wendy continued talking, Edward got up from the couch as Wendy's story began to put him on edge.

"Edward, please; I need you to stay seated and listen to your wife," said Dr. Curry.

"I don't think I want to *hear* any more of this doc," Edward retorted.

"I understand. But Wendy listened to *you.* Now *please*, show her the same respect."

"I'll listen, but I'd rather stand."

"Okay, have it your way. Wendy, please, continue."

Wendy then took a deep breath and exhaled as she told the rest of her story. "I called Mark and asked him if we can meet up. He said to come to his hotel room. So, I went straight there. And when I got there, he started to kiss me. He kissed me all over, and I *liked* it. I liked it a lot. I'd say we came close to third base before the maid came knocking on the door. And when Mark went to the door, I took that as a sign that this wasn't for me. At that moment, I realized *how much* I still love my husband. Even after I caught him in *my* bed with another woman, I still love him. So, I got myself dressed and told Mark I had to leave, and that's exactly what I did. I took vows, Dr. Curry. I always said that I will *always* remain faithful to my husband if I ever got married, no matter what. And I'm still in love with you, Eddie. Nothing's changed about that. But why? *Why* did you betray me?"

Wendy's emotions began to fill the room as she told her story. Edward's face grew melancholy and shameful as he realized how much pain he has caused Wendy. He then walked over to the window as he looked straight across the Hudson River, over to New Jersey. Dr. Curry then began to speak.

"Edward," said Dr. Curry. "Was there a specific reason why you slept with another woman?"

"No, no, there wasn't," Edward responded.

"How often did you sleep with this woman?"

"I don't know… It was off and on for about a couple of weeks."

"A couple of *weeks*?" Wendy shouted. "She was in *my* bed multiple times?"

"NO, no! That was just that one time. I didn't think you would be back home so soon. I'm sorry."

"*Now* I know why you weren't answering my text all those times *or* phone calls. It makes perfect sense now. How do you find the time?"

"Okay, *time out*," said Dr. Curry. "Edward, just have a seat, *please*, *for me*."

As Edward sat back down, he took a minute to cool off. Dr. Curry took off her glasses and held them in her hand, biting the temples as she began to think about what was going on between them.

As Dr. Curry looked at Edward, she then asked him some more questions.

"Edward, you said that you're a director, correct?" Dr. Curry asked.

"Yes, I'm a director of ballet performances."

"Okay, was that *always* your dream? To be a director?"

"Yes, and it's been a dream come true."

"Okay, *now*, let me ask you *this* question."

"Go ahead, doc."

"Who is your wife to you, Edward?"

"Excuse me?"

"*Who is* your wife to *you*? Do you see her as a woman, as a human being, with dreams of her own?"

"*Of course*, I do. And I've *always* paid attention to her dreams."

"Well, I think Wendy and I *both* find that hard to believe, considering the fact that you've committed adultery."

"OH, so this *is* a "gang up on the husband" game."

"No, I want to get to the bottom of this, Edward. To help you both save your marriage."

"Well, how can you do that, doc? I've cheated; she messed around with her "high school sweetheart." So, *how* can you help us, huh?"

Dr. Curry took a few seconds before she spoke. She then got up from her single chair and sat down in the middle cushion between Wendy and Edward. She then took Edward and Wendy's hands and joined their hands together. As they held onto each other, Dr. Curry said to them, "You know, I believe that the love is still there, *deep* inside the both of you. But Edward, I feel that you've lost sight of something with Wendy. You've lost sight of the *importance* of your family. I asked you about your career as a director. And *then* I asked, "Who is your wife to you?" Is Wendy just another brain to you? A different brain to store in *your* ideas and dreams? Or perhaps, you've never truly acknowledged *her* ideas and *her* dreams. *Maybe* you fell in love with her silence. I feel that Wendy has lost some importance to your life, Edward. And you've *lost* some respect for your wife in the process. And *that's* why you brought another woman into the home of *your* family. But I don't believe this marriage is over, not one bit. The love is still there, you two. However, the respect is missing."

Edward and Wendy were not ready for that analysis from Dr. Curry; she broke things down in a way they never heard before. Then, as Dr. Curry got up from the couch, she told them that forgiveness is a marathon and not a race. And that this is going to take more than one session.

"Wendy," Dr. Curry spoke. "What is it that you want from Edward right now?"

"I don't know," said Wendy. "I don't know. But with our second child on the way, I *do* need him."

"And Edward, what do you want from Wendy?"

"I want her to know that I love her. And what I did, I betrayed my whole family. I was a selfish pig, and I'm so sorry, Wendy."

"Okay, well, that's all the time we have for today. I would like to see you two again. Hopefully, there will be some progression next time?"

"I hope so, Dr. Curry," Wendy responded. "Thank you."

As Wendy and Edward left their marriage counseling session, they began to walk in a small park area. Wendy saw a park bench and took a seat. Edward was tired of sitting, so he began to slowly pace back and forth as he and Wendy had their *own* one-on-one *private* session.

"Your *high school sweetheart*, huh?" Edward projected.

"Well, at least I was strong enough to stop anything from happening," Wendy responded.

"From the *sound* of it, the only thing you stopped was him sticking his *dick* in you."

"Well, what do you want me to say, Eddie? Huh? What the *fuck* do you want me to say?"

"Nothing, *say* nothing. But, you know, back on the Brooklyn Bridge, I *thought* we were on the right track. What happened?"

"I don't *know*, Eddie. Shit, I go on vacation, and I come back to find you in *our* bed with some *dizzy* bitch. Who is she anyway?"

"Look, it doesn't *matter* who she is."

"Well, I want to know."

"You *really* want to know who she is?"

"Yes, right here, right *now*!"

"*She is nobody*, nothing. Just a piss poor actress who was willing to *fuck anybody* to be cast in a show. And *I* simply said, "*What the fuck?*" There was no love involved, not even lust."

"*Wow*, okay. I think I've heard enough from you. I'm leaving now, and I hope that bitch "*Me Too*" your fucking ass."

Wendy then got up from the park bench as she could no longer stand the sight of Edward. Edward stood there near the park bench as Wendy walked away with watery eyes. He then went after her and said, "Wendy, Wendy, wait, stop!" As Edward caught up to her, he said this last thing to her before she left. "Wendy, I don't want us to have to keep doing this for the rest of our lives. That woman means *nothing* to me. I didn't even give her a damn part in my show." Wendy then sighed in disgust as she rolled her eyes and walked away from Edward. But Edward stopped her again and continued.

"Wait, wait, wait, I'm sorry. Look, you're pregnant with our second child. What I *truly* want from you is to be healthy while you're carrying our baby—no more of this arguing. I will do *whatever* it takes to keep our marriage *and* our family *together*. But that's not going to be possible if you're not on board with me, Wendy."

As Wendy stood there, looking at Edward, she gave it much thought at that very moment. She then began to cover her ears, her face all twisted as the NYFD fire trucks flew past with their loud sirens.

"Did you get rid of that goddamn bed, as I said?" Wendy asked.

"I did," said Edward. "I've had the mattress replaced, as well as the base and the headboard."

"That's a start then," Wendy grinned. "EJ misses you. I guess it's time that we come back home and give our family some time to heal."

"Thank you, baby," Edward smiled. "I *promise* you won't regret this."

"Um… I'll let you know when you can call me baby again," Wendy said as she winked at Edward.

Wendy then told Edward that she is going back to Queens to pack her things and get EJ. He was happy that she is going to come back home with EJ and work on their problems. As Wendy walked away, Edward called her name. As Wendy turned around, he said to her, "life is a stage, and we all play a part. I just thank God that you play the brilliant role of my wife." Wendy put her hand over her heart after Edward said that to her. She then walked back towards him and gave him a kiss and hug. As she held him, Edward whispered in her ear, "We're going to be *fine*. I *promise* you; we're going to be *just* fine. And I'm sorry."

Back in Queens, Wendy had to make a pit stop at her office. She received an email from her boss, Mrs. Shultz, saying that she wants to meet with Wendy in her office. Now, *usually*, whenever Mrs. Shultz sends her employees an email saying that she wants to have a meeting, that says one or two things: either you are receiving a promotion, *or* you are getting that pink slip. And *Wendy* is the best Mrs. Shultz has when it comes to wedding planning. So, Wendy knew for sure that she was *not* getting fired.

Wendy made her way to the floor of her office. She then walked into her office and put her coat over her chair. On her desk, there was a note. The note said,

Meet me in my office ASAP!

Sincerely,

Mrs. Shultz

As Wendy placed her bag in her chair, she made her way over to Mrs. Shultz's office. In her mind, Wendy believes that Mrs. Shultz has finally come to her senses in *why* she should make her a partner. As Wendy came to Mrs. Shultz's front door, she gave it a good knock. "Come in!" Mrs. Shultz said. As Wendy opened the door, she saw that Mrs. Shultz was not alone. There was a man in there with her.

"Ah, *Wendy, just* in time," Mrs. Shultz spoke. "I want you to meet Roger Ping."

"Hi Roger, it's nice to meet you," Wendy responded.

"Oh no, Wendy, that's *Mr. Ping* to you, my dear."

"I beg your pardon?"

"Mr. Ping is now your new boss. I've made *him* my new partner."

"Your *partner?*"

"*Yes*, and I have told him how *great* you are as *my* wedding planner. I think you two will work *perfectly* together."

As if Wendy needed any more issues or stress for the day, her boss has just finalized her chances of *not* becoming a partner. So, at that moment, Wendy gave it some thought, and she made a decision that *she* felt was best for her.

"Mrs. Shultz," said Wendy. "I've learned a lot since I've been here."

"You sure have, Wendy," Mrs. Shultz responded. "I've taught you well."

"You did, and I appreciate it. But I think you've taught me *very* well. *Too* well."

"And your point is?"

"I think it's time that I move on from here."

"Wait, you mean you're *quitting*?"

"I'm resigning my position as your wedding planner."

"*Wait*, now, *Wendy*; Now, you know I'm one of the best in *town*. Where else would you *possibly* go?"

"You'll see. Mr. Ping, it's been real."

"May I remind you, Wendy, that you're under contract?"

"So, *sue* me bitch."

Mrs. Shultz's face dropped after Wendy told her off. Wendy then walked out of Mrs. Shultz's office and gathered *all* her things together from *her* office. She grabbed two boxes from the storage area and then asked one of her co-workers to help her bring everything down to the lobby. Afterward, Wendy then waited for her cab with the biggest smile on her face. At that moment, Wendy could not help but think about that fortune-teller, Woomi Yumi. That first card that was dealt, "*Labor*," that card was telling Wendy what she needed to do. She needed to *leave* her job behind and begin a *new* journey. And that is exactly what Wendy did.

About twenty minutes later, Wendy shows up at her parents' house with the two boxes filled with her office belongings. Her mother, Suzi, not yet aware of Wendy's resignation from her job, began to question Wendy.

"Wendy-san," said Suzi. "What are you doing here so early? And *why* do you have these boxes?"

"Because mama, I made one of the best decisions of my life today?"

"*Ah*, you're divorcing Edward?"

"No, I quit my job today?"

"You WHAT?"

"I resigned from that company. I'm not working for them anymore."

"Are you already having a mid-life crisis?"

"*No*, mama, it's more like a rebirth. I'm a phoenix who rose from her ashes."

"More like you rose from *insanity*."

"Mama, don't say that."

"I hope you know what you're doing, Wendy-san. And I *told* you *not* to marry that man. But you no listen to me."

"Mama now's not the time for your, "I told you so" lectures."

"You have one child, Wendy-san, with another on the way. *What* are you going to do?"

"I'm going to keep my faith, mama. Keep faith in my marriage, in my career, and my life."

"You're an adult. It's your life. And I *do* have faith in you that you will be okay."

As Wendy was ready to leave, Suzi sat her down to tell her something. As they sat down, Suzi held Wendy's hand and said, "Back before your sister and you were born, your father had an affair. He was with her, off and on, for about three months. Then, one day, she called the house. She couldn't handle the reality that *I* was your father's one true love. She couldn't handle being the piece of meat. So, she called, and I answered the phone. She told me *everything*. Where they dated, where they had sex, and how many *times* they had sex. I was heartbroken, Wendy-san. So, I *confronted* your father about it, and he asked me, "Are you going to leave me now?" And then *I* asked, "Do you want me to?" I thought he *loved* her and that *I* was going to be replaced. But he said he didn't love her and that he only loved me and how sorry he was that I had to find out about her."

Wendy sat there with her mother, listening to her mother's experience of being cheated on by her father. Wendy then asked her mother how she was able to forgive her father. And what Suzi said, changed Wendy's life forever. Suzi said, "I was able to forgive your father because we only have *one* life to live on this earth. That's it. And once it's gone, it's gone forever. There's no coming back. Life is too precious, Wendy-san. I love your father so much, and I know he loves me too. To find *true love* in this little, tiny planet that we live on. *That,* my daughter, is a true blessing. And you must do *everything* in your power to protect that. *Forgiveness* is the greatest armor you can have for protecting your marriage *and* your family." Wendy then hugged and kissed her mother as she appreciated her mother's knowledge and wisdom of life, love, and marriage.

"I love you, mama," said Wendy.

"I love you too, Wendy-san."

Later that evening, Wendy met up with the other four ladies at *Lucille's.* Wendy told them about her marriage counseling session with Edward and how they *will* work things out. They were happy for Wendy and supported her decision. Collette asked Wendy if her decision had anything to do with her being pregnant with their second child. Wendy told Collette, "I would still be with Eddie, regardless. I know it may take some time to forgive him fully. But I'm willing to make that effort while still being with him."

Wendy also told them about her resignation from her job. In addition, she told them about her plans to start her own wedding and events company. And as always, her friends were right there to support her in any way they could.

"Well, you already know I can help you find the right real estate in this city for your company," Collette confirmed.

"Wendy, my love, I already have a blank check ready for you. So, whatever you need, just name the price, and it's done," said Tomi.

"Oh my God," said Wendy. "You girls are the freaking *best*. You have *no* idea how much I appreciate you all."

"That's what we're all about, babe," said Zarin. "We look out for each other."

"Absolutely; we're sisters for life, and that's never going to change," said Monica.

As they all sat there, they joked and laughed the night away in their favorite reserved booth. No matter what they went through, whether it was drama with their husbands, troubles with their children, or even the loss of a loved one. They still managed to keep a tighter reign and protect their sisterhood. And, of course, life continued to go on.

Chapter 40

Nine months later, on November 27th, 2023, a new life has come into this world. After seven and a half hours of labor, Wendy and Edward welcomed their baby girl, "Bella Marie Date-Collins." She had Wendy's face and Edward's big ears. She was as precious and as beautiful as she could be.

As Wendy was lying there in the hospital bed, surrounded by family, she held Bella in her arms. Wendy, looking down at her perfect face as she sleeps. A few minutes go by, and there is a knock on the door.

"Hiiii," said Tomi. "Hi mommy, *Congratulations*!"

"Hi, Oh my God, you're all here." Wendy softly spoke.

The other four ladies had shown up with balloons, teddy bears, and flowers. They each came over and kissed Wendy on her cheek, as well as hugged Edward. Wendy was so overwhelmed with joy that all her friends were there to see the baby. And being that Edward was on camera duty, he had them all stand next to Wendy as he took a few snapshots of the five of them with baby Bella. It was a beautiful day to bring life into the world. As Tomi stood next to Wendy, Wendy asked her something.

"Would you like to hold her, Tomi?" Wendy asked.

"Oh, *of course*, I'd love to," said Tomi. "Oh my God, she's so *tiny*."

"So, Tomi… Edward and I gave it some thought. And we would be more than honored to bless you as her Godmother."

"*Me?*" Tomi said with emotion.

"Yes," said Edward. "We think you're the *perfect* candidate."

"Oh my God. It would be my *honor* to be this little one's Godmother. This means *so much* to me; you have *no* idea. Thank you," Tomi cried.

A room now filled with tears from everyone. This right here was a special moment—a room filled with family, friends, and love. Nothing could have gone wrong that day.

Several weeks later, it is the most wonderful time of the year. Christmas lights are now decorated up and down the city streets. The

Christmas tree is up and lit over at Rockefeller Center, and the Radio City Christmas Spectacular is showing.

Monica, Sammy, Miles, and Briana are doing very well. Monica has beat another case that she was working on for several months. And Sammy has just come back from a two-week Christmas tour. Monica has made her therapy sessions with Dr. Melissa McAdams a weekly necessity.

Zarin and her family are doing well. She and Neal's marriage has been better than ever before. Darsha and Joshna transferred to a private school. After Darsha's incident, Zarin and Neal felt that was best for both of the girls. Zarin's sister-in-law, Meli, is doing great now. She was reunited with the father of her child and married him several months later. Zarin and the family remain in touch with her to make sure she is not a stranger.

As for Collette, she has found it in her heart to forgive Martin for his actions. So have Emilio and Mia. Angel has grown quite close to the family now. She has earned her G.E.D. and is currently attending college. Collette was also freed from those charges the night she had the altercation with Martin in front of *Lucille's*. Thanks to Tomi and Monica's connections, of course. As for Lisa, Collette checks in on her as much as she can as Lisa is doing her own thing. As for their mother, Gloria, Collette has barely talked to her since Gloria walked out on them at *Lucille's*.

Wendy and Edward are doing just fine. Through all the married counseling sessions with Dr. Curry, their marriage has become much healthier and meaningful. Edward has kept his word and has remained a faithful husband. EJ has recently had his sixth birthday on December 11[th,] and he has outgrown his bedwetting problem. As for baby Bella, she is the *cutest* little one-month-old you'd ever lay eyes on. And her *Godmother*, Tomi, cannot get enough of her. Tomi has already set up a college trust fund for baby Bella. Wendy's parents also decided to hold off on their move to Japan and help take care of their new granddaughter. Wendy could not be happier with their decision. Wendy has *also* founded her very own wedding planning company, *"Future of the Brides Weddings and Events."* Tomi and Collette pulled through for her on the real estate and financial support. Wendy could not be happier with how everything turned out. And as for her *former* boss, Mrs. Shultz, she is no match for Wendy's ingenious planning and innovative creations.

And as for Tomi, her new winter line collection has had record-breaking sales. She continues to keep her grandfather's legacy alive by designing pieces related to his sketches. And After a few more deals and some more investments, Tomi's new net worth jumped to $20 billion. She has also opened two more storefronts of *Orell Llero*: one in Sydney, Australia, and Toronto, Canada. Tomi also created a global foundation for homeless and parentless children all over the world. The foundation is called *"The Hearts of the Future."* The foundation helps children find their families, if possible, and creates better lives for them. As for Tomi's husband, Thomas, he just came back from Los Angeles, as his construction and design team are 90% completed with his and Tomi's mega-mansion on the land she purchased back in February.

It is now Christmas eve, and the ladies have brought their families together to celebrate the holidays at Tomi's home in Southampton. Tomi's dream of having all her friends' families together at her home for Christmas came true. Tomi even invited Carmelo, Angel, and Lisa.

In the living room, there was a sixteen-foot tree with the most beautiful lights and exquisite decorations. Behind the tree, upon the wall, was a massive picture of Arianna, Tomi's mother. And underneath the tree was a mountain of gifts for everyone. *Everyone* was in the Christmas spirit, gathered around in the living room, wearing their own ugly Christmas sweaters.

Tomi felt the urge to say something to everyone. As she cleared her throat and got everyone's attention, she said, "First, I would like to thank every one of you for coming out here to celebrate Christmas with Tommy and me. This has been my absolute *dream* come true, to share such a special holiday with *my* ladies and your families. You know, *family* was something that I never had much of growing up. And I'll admit, it was never fun growing up and not having much family to visit and spend time with. But my mother made it work. She made the best of it. And as of today, *I've* made the best of my life. I've achieved so much in the last two decades. I'm wealthy, successful, and I've made history. But this is the God's honest truth;

all of that wouldn't mean *anything* if I didn't have the people in this room, here with me right now. It's about family, friends, having people who love you for who you are. I've learned that a long time ago, and *that's* where my true wealth lies, with *my* sisters. I love you girls to the moon and back. So, let us raise our glasses of *eggnog* and toast to our families."

As they all raised their glasses, there was such mystic and magic, and love in the room—an unforgettable Christmas eve, not just for Tomi, but for all of them.

About ten minutes after Tomi's heartfelt speech, the five of them came together outside near the fire pit. *This* time, they all had a mug filled with hot chocolate. Lisa, Carmelo, and Angel are taking care of baby Bella while the other kids play video and board games. And all their husbands went into the pool room and did the manly bond. So, the ladies had some alone time.

"Girls," said Collette. "It has been one *hell* of a year."

"Oh, Coco, you are *not* lying," Wendy responded.

"Oh, I *third* that," said Zarin.

"It has indeed," Monica added. "But we made it through all of that. And we've *grown* as women."

"Damn straight," said Tomi. "Even though we have hot cocoa, let's make a toast anyway."

"Okay," said Wendy. "What are we toasting to?"

"Um... To *us*. To the Ring Pack," Tomi laughed.

"The *Ring Pack?*" Zarin laughed. "Oh my God, isn't that what the photographer guy called us at the fashion show?"

"Yea, *yea*, I like that," said Collette. "Yea, let's go with that. To the *Ring Pack*."

"To the *Ring Pack!*" Monica spoke.

"Ah, *FUCK!*" Tomi shouted.

"What happened?" said Wendy.

"I burnt my damn tongue. *Fucking* hot chocolate is *too hot. Shit!*"

"*Only* Tomi," Collette laughed.

"Uh-huh," Monica laughs.

"Oh, will you *bitches* shut up?" Tomi laughed. "Let's try this again; Merry Christmas, to the *Ring Pack…* Cheers."

"TO THE RING PACK!"

And so, the ladies toast their hot chocolate to themselves, to "*The Ring Pack*." As they took on whatever challenges the Big Apple threw at them, their wounds healed, for the most part, and their bond grew more potent than ever before. The unbreakable sisterhood they share is the blessing of a lifetime. These five women make it work in such a divided, judgmental world. Yet, their relationship is proof enough to *show* the world that it is about the *human race*. And the only way we can ever *heal* our world is with these four letters: L.O.V.E.

Acknowledgements

I would like to take the time to say thank you to all of you who took this journey and read the entirety of this book. I cannot thank you enough for your commitment to such a lengthy book. I hope you found it entertaining, enjoyable, heartfelt, and true to life. Even though it may not be relatable to your personal life, hopefully, it was well worth the trip.

I would like to also thank my mother and father for all their love and support. I want to thank my family and the *few* friends that I have for their support as well. You all know who you are. I wish to acknowledge and thank some people I had the pleasure of doing business with and supported me in promoting my books. I want to thank Star from *The Star Report*, *Mr. Skinny*, and *Hip-Hop News Uncensored*. I want to thank my high school teacher, Shea Richardson, and my college English professor, Henry "Hank" Stewart.

Last but not least, I would like to thank the entity from above who blessed me with this story. Now, I know some people may not believe this. And you have your right not to believe in anything spiritual. But *I* believe that I was blessed from above with delivering this story to you, the reader. When I tell you that this book wrote itself, I mean *just that*. I was merely a vessel, and this story was in my mind like a movie. Everything you have read, I saw it in my mind before I wrote it down. This story was given to me from above. I genuinely believe that. With that said, I thank you again for going on this journey with me. And hopefully, I will be able to get you on the next journey to come. Take care, stay safe, and God Bless.

About the Author

Jordan Wells was born in Orange, New Jersey, but was raised in East Orange, New Jersey. He graduated from Centenary University, earning a bachelor's degree in business, with concentrations in finance and marketing. He is also a professional actor, a member of the Screen Actors Guild- American Federation of Television and Radio Artists. His fifth book, *"The Ring Pack,"* is his debut novel. His fourth book, *"A Lonely Rose,"* is an addition to Wells' poetic collection. *"The Healing,"* is Wells' third book. *"Mirrors and Reflections"* is Wells' sophomore book. And his debut book, *"Logged Off: My Journey of Escaping the Social Media World,"* was a monumental achievement in Wells' life, and will continue with his creative writing ventures.

The Ring Pack 2

Coming in 2022

The ladies will be back!

#THERINGPACK

The Ring Pack 2

A Novel

The ladies are back!
And this time, there's more drama,
More dilemmas, and more wine.
But what's stronger is the bond between them.
And they're going to need it.

Jordan Wells

Jordan Wells

Made in the USA
Middletown, DE
20 April 2022

64354594R00326